DIVIDED KINGDOM

RUPERT THOMSON is the author of eight highly acclaimed novels, of which *Air and Fire* and *The Insult* were shortlisted for the Writer's Guild Fiction Prize and the Guardian Fiction Prize respectively. His most recent novel, *Death of a Murderer*, was shortlisted for the 2008 Costa Novel Award. His memoir *This Party's Got to Stop* was published in 2010.

BY THE AUTHOR

Fiction

Dreams of Leaving
Air and Fire
The Insult
Soft
The Book of Revelation
Death of a Murderer

Non-fiction

This Party's Got to Stop

Praise for *Divided Kingdom*

'Wonderful and full of wonders ... a uniquely disturbing tale for our time' *Literary Review*

'The ideas behind Thomson's novel buzz with originality, sparking contemporary connections and recalling *Brave New World* and even *Gulliver's Travels*' *Observer*

'Relentlessly compelling and enormously impressive ... With the sheer silkiness of Thomson's prose and his delicate and subtle understanding of our emotional lives – and what happens when they are ruptured or blocked – the commonplace is rendered strange, evocative and sensuous' *Daily Telegraph*

'A masterclass in the art of narrative' Boyd Tonkin, *Independent* Books of the Year

'Thomson is probably the best writer of my generation' Amanda Craig

'Thomson creates a portrait of Britain that is seductively detailed, disorientating, sometimes funny and often horrifying ... he is a master at creating an atmosphere of alienation and suspicion' *Sunday Telegraph*

'With *Divided Kingdom* Thomson extends the reach of his matchlessly strange imagination to create a tightly-knit, deftly-designed political fable and a richly ingenious satire on the arbitrary classifications that often fix our identity' *Independent*

'Arresting ... compelling ... Thomson's most striking talents as a writer are his extraordinarily vivid descriptions and his often hallucinatory imagination ... He is one of the supplest and most imaginative of British novelists' *LA Weekly*

'It would be cruel to deprive anyone of the imaginative pleasures, surprise and suspense that [...] *Divided Kingdom* offers. Thomson's new world is utterly menacing and intensely satisfying' *Newsday*

'*Divided Kingdom* is Thomson's best yet; it might be, in fact, his *Brave New World*' *Salon*

DIVIDED
KINGDOM

RUPERT THOMSON

B L O O M S B U R Y

LONDON · NEW DELHI · NEW YORK · SYDNEY

First published 2003
This paperback edition published 2012

Copyright © 2005 by Rupert Thomson

The moral right of the author has been asserted

A CIP catalogue record for this book
is available from the British Library

Bloomsbury Publishing Plc, London, New Delhi, New York and Sydney
50 Bedford Square, London WC1B 3DP

ISBN 978 1 4088 3312 4

10 9 8 7 6 5 4 3 2 1

Printed in Great Britain by CPI Group (UK) Ltd, Croydon CR0 4YY

www.bloomsbury.com/rupertthomson

To darling Eva, with a love that knows no boundaries

It was as if a curtain had fallen,
hiding everything I had ever known.
— Jean Rhys

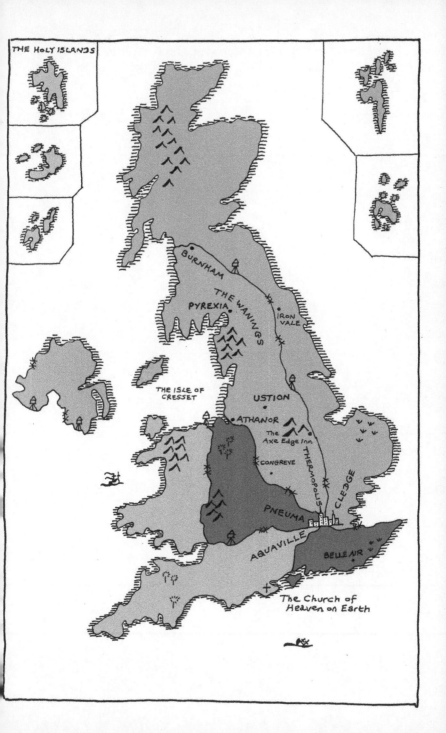

There were men in my room, and it was bright, too bright, and I was being lifted out of bed. I didn't struggle or cry out; I didn't make a sound. The uniforms they wore felt cold, as if they had just been taken from the fridge.

I was told to wait on the road outside our house. Rain drifted past the street lamp, rain so fine that I could hardly feel it. I watched as a soldier fastened a strip of cloth around my upper arm. My shadow bent where it fell across the kerbstone, like a piece of cardboard folded in two places.

They put me in the back of a lorry, along with people of every age, all of whom wore armbands, none of whom I recognised. No one spoke, or even moved. I remember no violence, only the silence and the constant, weightless rain.

From where I was standing, by the tailgate, I could see my parents. They hadn't had time to dress properly. My father wore pyjamas, a suit jacket and a pair of slippers, and his face had lines and creases on it, as though sleep had crushed him in its fist. My mother's feet were bare.

My mother's feet . . .

And her blonde hair flattened slightly on one side where it had rested against the pillow. She was calling my name in a high, strained voice, and reaching out to me, her fingers clutching at the air. Embarrassed, I turned away, pretending I didn't know her. I smiled apologetically at the people all around me.

'I'm sorry,' I said.

3

That's how my memory begins.

No, not my memory. My life.

When dawn came, I was standing on a railway platform. The sky had clouded over, a swirl of white and grey above the rooftops, and there were puddles everywhere. A goods train rumbled through the station without stopping, its trucks heaped with coils of barbed wire. I was handed tea in a plastic cup and a slice of bread that was thinly spread with margarine. Now it had got light, I could see that the cloth band round my upper arm was red. I didn't feel homesick, only cold and tired, and I seemed to understand that I shouldn't think too deeply, as someone who swims in a river might stay close to the bank for fear of treacherous currents.

That same day, after a journey of many hours, we arrived at a large, dilapidated house in the country. There were only eight of us left by then, all boys. Thorpe Hall crouched in a depression in the land, a kind of shallow, marshy bowl, and the property was surrounded by woods, the massed oaks and chestnuts flecked with silver birches, like a head of hair beginning to turn grey. A moat encircled the house on three sides, the surface of the water cloaked in slime, the banks fenced off by reeds. Ancient, stately fish glided through the stagnant depths, the gold of their scales spotted and stained, as if with ink. The lack of elevation and the narrow lead-paned windows gave the house a prying yet short-sighted look. I had the feeling it was aware of me. If I ever ran away, it would somehow know that I had gone.

By the end of my first week our numbers had swollen to more than seventy, the oldest boy being fourteen, the youngest five. In charge of us were two grown-ups, Mr Reek and Miss Groves, and they issued us with grey blazers, each of which had a scarlet peacock stitched on to the breast pocket. I counted eighteen bedrooms altogether, but conditions were cramped and primitive, and some boys, myself included, had to sleep on horsehair pallets in the upstairs corridors.

Winter had set in, and none of the radiators seemed to work. In certain rooms the chill stood so thick and solid that I couldn't believe it wasn't visible; if I walked through a room like that, my hair would feel cold for minutes afterwards. I scratched my initials in the ice that formed on the inside of the windows, not knowing that my name would soon be taken from me. There was no laughter in the house during those first few days, no grief either, just a curious vacant calm – a sort of vacuum.

In the small hours vixens tore the air with their shrill cries.

One boy hung himself in an upstairs lavatory. His body was removed the same evening in an ambulance. I saw no blue lights flashing on the drive. I heard no siren. Nothing disturbed the darkness and silence that surrounded us. Two days later, a service of remembrance was held in the chapel. In his sermon the vicar described the boy's death as a tragic accident, though everybody knew the truth lay elsewhere. Another boy was found striking his head repeatedly against a wall. He, too, was removed from the house, and no one ever saw him again. These were the early casualties of the Rearrangement, as it was called, and they were seldom spoken about, and then only in hushed tones in some distant corner of the garden, or in bed at night once all the lights had been switched off.

We no longer had to wear the strips of red cloth on our arms, but I would sometimes feel a slight constriction, a tightness around the muscle, and I would find myself glancing down to make sure it wasn't still there.

Christmas came.

On Christmas Eve we watched a carol concert on TV. Mr Reek tried to encourage us to join in with the singing, but we had no hymn books and very few of us knew all the words. In the middle of a carol I saw my parents at the far end of the room. They were smartly dressed, my father in an overcoat, my mother in a knitted shawl and knee-length boots. They would be on their way to midnight mass, I thought, and I rose to go with them. By the time I reached the door, though, they had gone. I called for my mother and felt someone take my hand, but when I looked up it was just Miss Groves. I managed not to cry until I was upstairs, in my bed.

The next morning I stood by the tree with all the other boys. We got one present each. Mine was a pair of socks, powder-blue, with a pattern of brown puppies up the side. I remember thinking that there must have been some kind of mix-up. I remember, also, that there was nobody to thank.

It didn't snow.

Early in the new year an official from the government paid us a visit. At breakfast that day we were told that he was a highly distinguished man and that we should all be on our best behaviour. I watched from a window on the first-floor landing as the limousine slid down the drive on wide, fat tyres, its black roof gleaming in the winter sun. I would have given anything to have had a ride in it. Later, we assembled in the main hall. With his sparse, chaotic hair and his drab raincoat, the government official came as something of a disappointment to us – I suppose we had been expecting him to be glamorous, like his car – but then he began to speak.

'Children of the Red Quarter,' he said, and a thrill went through every one of us. We didn't know what the man meant exactly, but clearly he was referring to us. Children of the Red Quarter was what we were. What we had become.

In his speech he told us we should be proud of ourselves. 'You're to be admired,' he said, 'because you're rare. Although there are only a few of you, your significance cannot be over-estimated. The future depends on the example you set to others. One might even say that the fate of the entire nation rests in your hands.'

Afterwards we ran down the corridors and out on to the drive, all holding imaginary steering-wheels and making engine sounds. We had, each one of us, become the chauffeur of that shiny night-black limousine. *Children of the Red Quarter*, we were shouting. *Children of the Red Quarter*. We still had no idea what it meant. We were excited without knowing why. It was the effect of flattery – instantaneous and powerful, but strangely hollow too.

That night we ate pork that had been roasted on a spit, and we drank juice made from crushed apples, and we were allowed to go to bed an hour later than usual, on account of it being such an important occasion.

On the following Monday classes began in the old ballroom. Along one edge of the room four windows stretched from floor to ceiling. Through their watery, distorting glass I could see the formal garden with its lawn, its box hedges and its gravel paths. The other side of the ballroom had been panelled in wood and painted a delicate shade of green. Set into the panels, and echoing the windows in their dimensions, were four mirrors in which the light that flowed in from outside seemed to deepen and shimmer. At the far end of the room stood a low stage where string quartets or dance bands would once have played. Sometimes I would catch a glimpse of a trombone in the shadows, or the curve of a French horn, the brass perfectly smooth and glowing, like honey poured over the back of a spoon, and sometimes the air would rustle at my elbow, a flurry of movement that only lasted a second, as if a girl in an evening gown had just whirled by. I never felt the room was haunted. I simply thought it had seen happier days, livelier days, and that traces of that time remained, as the smell of toast or bacon will linger in a kitchen long after breakfast is over.

Desks had been arranged in rows on the parquet floor, and we were seated alphabetically. My name being Micklewright, I found myself between Maclean and Abdul Nazir. Nazir was always crying, or on the point of crying, the dark sweep of his eyelashes permanently clogged with tears. I hadn't cried at all except for once, on Christmas Eve, after the carols, but I'd had no sightings of my parents since that night. There was something in me, perhaps, that couldn't stand it. Couldn't stand to be reminded. I often had the feeling, looking at Nazir, that he had taken on the burden of my sadness, and that he was crying not just for himself but for me too. As for Maclean, he didn't seem remotely upset. If I caught his eye, he would flick paper pellets at me. He had long bony wrists, and both his ears stuck out like the handles on a sporting trophy. Our teacher was the stout but enthusiastic Miss Groves. Sitting beneath crystal chandeliers, frowned down upon by several gilt-framed portraits of men in armour, we were to learn about the new political system that had come into being, and why the government official thought we were so special.

On our first morning Miss Groves taught us about our country's recent history. It had become a troubled place, she said, obsessed with acquisition and celebrity, a place defined by envy, misery and greed. Crime was rampant: the courts were swamped, the prisons overflowing. Divorce followed marriage as quickly and predictably as teenage pregnancies followed puberty. Homeless people slept in every doorway, ditch and underpass. Racism was more widespread and more firmly rooted than ever before. Violence lurked round every corner. It wasn't just a matter of grown-ups killing grown-ups. Children were killing children. With the police force woefully under-manned, people had started taking the law into their own hands. If you didn't like the way somebody drove, you smashed his headlights with a jack. If you had a suspected child molester living in your neighbourhood, you lynched him. If a burglar broke into your house, you shot him dead. For decades, if not for centuries, the country had employed a complicated web of manners and convention to draw a veil over its true nature, but now, finally, it had thrown off all pretence to be anything other than it was – northern, inward-looking, fundamentally barbaric.

It had been a time for extreme measures, Miss Groves went on, two smudges of pink colouring her cheeks, and the government had not flinched from its responsibility. The Prime Minister and the members of his cabinet had met in secret chambers, far from the eyes and ears of the electorate. Down there – for the chambers were underground, relics of a war that had been fought roughly half a century before – they talked, they argued, they even wept, and in the end they reached a decision: they were going to do something bold, something extraordinary . . . In our makeshift classroom, we were breath-less with anticipation. Miss Groves told the story so well, with such a gripping command of atmosphere and detail, that we could hardly wait to find out what happened next. At this point, however, she stepped back.

'See you here at nine o'clock tomorrow,' she said.

We were there, of course. We were even early. We were going to school, we were being taught history, of all things, but at the same time we were learning about ourselves, what had happened in the recent past and what would happen in the near future. Our lives had become books that we couldn't put down.

What the government had decided to do, Miss Groves told us on that second morning, was to reorganise the country's population – the entire population, from the royal family down. She paused. It was a lot to take in. We had probably heard the word 'rearrangement', she went on. Well, that was the name they had given their initiative. They divided the population into four distinct groups, not according to economic status or social position, not according to colour, race or creed, but according to *psychology*, according to *type*. How had they defined types of people? Miss Groves turned to the blackboard and wrote THE HUMOURS in block capitals. She asked whether any of us knew what the words meant. No one did.

For almost two millennia, she said, from Hippocrates onwards, medicine had been based on the idea that there were four bodily fluids or humours – black bile, yellow bile, blood and phlegm. I glanced at Maclean. We both wrinkled our noses. But Miss Groves had already faced the blackboard again, and she was drawing a large circle, which she proceeded to divide into four equal sections. She wrote BLACK BILE in one section, YELLOW BILE in another, and so on, until each section contained a humour. It was then that a boy called Cody interrupted her.

'What about piss, Miss Groves?'

Laughter skittered through the ballroom, a brittle, breathy sound, like leaves being blown across a floor. Leaves that were dead, though. Miss Groves swung round. Her face was stiff, and all the colour had drained from her lips and cheeks.

'Who was that?'

Cody put his hand up. 'It was me, Miss. I wanted to ask about urine. Isn't urine a bodily fluid?'

He had something of the fox about him, I'd always thought, his brown hair tinged with red, the cast of his features alert, sardonic, sly.

'Leave the room, Cody. I'll deal with you later.'

All eyes followed Cody as he stood up and walked to the door.

'Any other questions?' Miss Groves said.

I stared at the scarred lid of my desk, my heart beating hard, my throat dry. I felt Miss Groves's gaze pass over my head like a searchlight's penetrating beam.

'I want you to imagine,' she said carefully, her voice still drawn tight, 'that the circle is your body. Imagine your good health depends on the correct, the *judicious*, balance of all the humours. Once you've imagined that, then let the idea expand. Imagine the circle is the whole country – the body politic, as it's sometimes called.

'You see' – and she stepped towards us, enthusiasm rising in her once again – 'the theory of the humours is built on notions of harmony and equilibrium, and these were the very qualities that were lacking in the country prior to the Rearrangement. In the deep and distant past doctors used humoral theory to address all kinds of human ailments, everything from physical infirmity to moral imperfection. All of a sudden, though, it was the body politic that needed treatment.'

The wind lifted and hurled itself against the tall windows. Above our heads the chandeliers shuddered and shook like glass birds ruffling their feathers. I thought of Cody waiting in the draughty corridor outside and wondered whether he was beginning to wish that he had held his tongue.

There were four humours, Miss Groves explained, and each humour could be matched to a different personality or character. She drifted towards the blackboard again. Under YELLOW BILE she wrote CHOLERIC, under BLACK BILE she wrote MELANCHOLIC, under PHLEGM, PHLEGMATIC, and under BLOOD, SANGUINE. Difficult words, she said, turning back to us, but not so difficult to understand. Choleric people were known for their aggressive qualities. They led lives packed with action and excess. Melancholic people, by contrast, were morbid and introspective. What interested them was the life of the mind. Phlegmatic people were swayed by feeling. Empathy came naturally to them, as did a certain spirituality, but they tended to be passive, a little sluggish. As for sanguine people, they were optimistic, good-humoured and well-meaning. They were often held up as an inspiration to others. Miss Groves's eyes swept over our faces. 'Do you see where this is going?' she said. 'No, not yet, perhaps. But you will – you will.' And she smiled knowingly.

That night, in the bathroom, Cody showed us the backs of his thighs. The skin was striped with livid weals where Miss Grove's cane had landed, but he had no regrets. Rather, he seemed to view the punishment as the price he had paid for some valuable information, which he was now in a position to pass on.

'When she beats you she sort of grunts,' he said, 'just like a sow.'

During the next few days Miss Groves gave us the rest of the story. Everyone in the country had been secretly examined, assessed and classified, all in strict accordance with the humours. As categories, they were only approximate at best, and there had been injustices, of course there had, but that could not be helped. At this point she had stepped forwards again, her eyes seemingly lit from the inside, like lamps. In times of crisis, she said, the good of the many always outweighed the misfortunes of a few, especially when the health of an entire nation was at stake.

Once the population had been split into four groups, the land was divided to accommodate them. What had been until then a united kingdom was broken down into four separate and autonomous republics. New borders were created. New infrastructures too. New loyalties.

'All this is going on,' Miss Groves said, 'even as we speak,' and turning to the nearest window, her face took on a kind of radiance.

In her opinion, symbolism would play a crucial role during this transitional phase. People's lives, both public and private, had been disrupted. They had to be given something fresh, something clear and powerful, with which they could identify. It had been decided that the countries would be colour-coded. The territory assigned to those with a choleric personality would be known as the Yellow Quarter, choler being associated both with yellow bile and with fire. Since phlegm was allied to water, the home of the phlegmatics was to be the Blue Quarter. Although melancholia originated in black bile, the authorities rejected black as a defining colour. It had too many negative connotations. They drew on the earth instead, which was the melancholy element, and which was generally personified in ancient iconography as a woman in green garments; it was to the Green Quarter, therefore, that melancholic people would belong. As for sanguinity, it derived from blood. The region set aside for those of a sanguine disposition became the Red Quarter.

To strengthen the identity of the four new countries, each had been provided with its own flag. In one of her lighter, more creative moments, Miss Groves invited us to come up with our own versions, based on what we had already learned. A fair-haired boy called Jones won first prize. His design – a flag for the Red Quarter – made use of a magnified photograph of blood, which he'd found in a magazine. The pattern of red and white corpuscles looked industrious and poetic, and it was wonderfully clever too: all sanguine people would carry their national flag inside themselves, whether they liked it or not (so would everybody else, of course, but as Jones quietly pointed out, for them it would be something to aspire to, a goal, a dream).

After the prize-giving, Miss Groves produced examples of the real thing. The choleric flag had a yellow background on which there stood a salamander. According to Aristotle and several other early naturalists, the salamander was believed to live in fire. On the phlegmatics' flag a sea horse floated on a cobalt ground, the sea horse suggestive of the diffident, the indeterminate, while the melancholic flag showed a rabbit crouching on a field of green, the rabbit being one of the animals used in iconological representations of the earth. The flag that would fly in sanguine territory was a peacock resplendent on a scarlet ground. Those of sanguine temperament were held to be ruled by the air, and Juno, its goddess, was often portrayed in a chariot drawn by peacocks. Though the use of animals appealed to me, especially the mythical salamander, I still thought Jones's effort outshone everything I'd seen, and I told him so, which made him blush and look away.

In Miss Groves's final lesson, she returned to her point of departure. A chill wind blew that morning, and the chandeliers shivered and chattered overhead. Untidy scraps of grey cloud flew past the windows. The desk to my immediate right stood empty. Poor Abdul Nazir had been removed from the house some days before.

'The reason why you are special,' she said, 'as I'm sure you will have realised by now, is because you have all been classified as sanguine.' She raised her voice a little, to combat the moaning of the wind. 'If you will bear with me, I would just like to read you a short passage from a work that was written more than four hundred years ago.' Producing a small thick book with a cover of worn brown leather, she cleared her throat and began:

> If there were a monarch or prince to be constituted over all temperatures, this sanguine complection should, no doubts, aspire to that hie preheminence of bearing rule; for this is the ornament of the body, the pride of humours, the paragon of complections, the prince of all temperatures. For blood is the oile of the lampe of our life.

Even when she had fallen silent, Miss Groves continued to stare at the page from which she'd read, then she slowly closed the book and let her eyes pass solemnly across our faces. 'You have been wonderful pupils,' she said, her voice trembling now, 'and I have nothing left to teach you. Go out into the world and do your best. I wish you all every success.' With that, she turned and hurried from the room.

Maclean nudged me, and I looked round. The light shone through his big, translucent ears. 'A little too much phlegm this morning,' he said, 'don't you think?'

He had learned his lessons well.

Among other things, Miss Groves had taught us that the family had been in serious decline for years, decades even, and it was a measure of people's conservatism, their fear of change, that the idea had lasted as long as it had. How could people with little or nothing in common be expected to live together? How could they achieve stability, let alone happiness? Anyone with an ounce of common sense could see that it was a recipe for disaster. In short, the family could be held responsible for society's disintegration, and the politicians who masterminded the Rearrangement had felt compelled to acknowledge the fact. But how to act on it? They soon realised that the answer was already lying on the table in front of them. If they rearranged the population according to the humours, then they would automatically be dismantling one concept of family and establishing another in its place. The new family would be a group of people who shared a psychological affinity – people who got on, in other words. Blood ties would be set aside in favour of simple compatibility, and if that wasn't a propitious unit on which to base an efficient and harmonious society, Miss Groves had argued, then she would like to know what was.

As the weeks went by, I noticed that the number of boys being billeted at Thorpe Hall was gradually decreasing. By the end of February only thirty-six of us remained. Slowly but surely the authorities were finding us new families, new places to live. You never knew who was going to be taken next, though, or whether you would ever see each other again. In this uncertain climate, our friendships deepened and became invested with an air of desperation and romance. We started making rash promises, secret pacts. *We'll remain in contact, no matter what. We'll seek each other out. We'll never forget.* Some boys cut the palms of their hands or the tips of their fingers and then mixed their blood together, swearing that they would be brothers for fifty years, a century – for all eternity. Others went further.

In early March Cody and Maclean got married. The wedding was held in a bathroom on the top floor after lights-out. Cody improvised a bridal veil out of a pair of net curtains which he had pilfered from a little-used passageway behind the kitchen. Maclean wore a crocus in the top buttonhole of his pyjama jacket. Their rings were identical – chunky, dull-silver, hexagonal in shape (Maclean had crept out of the house one evening and unscrewed two nuts from the back wheel of Mr Reek's car). I can still see Cody's eyes glittering behind his veil as he walked along the moonlit landing, the rest of us singing 'Here Comes the Bride' in a harsh whisper, and I can see Maclean too, waiting patiently beside the bath with his hands clasped in front of him and his chin almost touching his collarbone. After the ceremony the happy couple slept in the same bed, arms wrapped around each other, rings wedged firmly on to the middle fingers of their left hands. A few days later Mr Reek had a crash. I imagined one of his wheels bowling away along the road, merry, almost carefree, like a race-horse that has unseated its rider, while the car slewed sideways, the exposed hub and axle spitting sparks.

It was during this time that I became friends with Jones, the boy who had won first prize in the flag-drawing competition. He was one of those who felt threatened by the idea of being moved, of being placed once again among people he didn't know, and there came a point in our friendship when he would talk of nothing else.

'But what if I don't like them?' he would say. 'What if they're cruel to me?'

'You'll be all right,' I would tell him.

'I don't know. I can't sleep.'

'Stop worrying so much,' I would say. 'You'll be fine.'

He would shake his head and stare at the ground, his eyes watery and anxious.

One day I found him in a shabby, cheerless corridor towards

the rear of the house. He was standing on one leg, like a stork. Thinking he was playing a trick on me, I laughed and pushed him on the shoulder. He hopped sideways, but managed to steady himself by putting a hand against the wall, and once he had regained his balance he continued to stand on one leg, as before. He didn't speak at all. Behind him, at the far end of the passage, the door had been left half-open, revealing an upright section of the garden – sun falling across a gravel path, a canopy of leaves. I walked round and stood in front of him.

'Jones?' I said. 'What are you doing?'

The look in his eyes was so blank that I couldn't think of anything else to say. I had never seen such an absence of expression, such utter emptiness. My first impression was that he was staring at an object or a surface only inches from his face but there was nothing there, of course. Later, I thought it was more as if some vital component had gone missing, the part of him that made him who he was. The thin strip of illuminated gravel at the end of the corridor had the brightness of another world, a world that lay beyond this one – a world Jones might already have entered. I think I shivered as I stood in front of him that morning. He didn't seem to see me, though. He didn't even appear to be aware of me.

At first nobody noticed, but Jones carried on, day after day. He would stand on one leg for hours at a time, and always in that same gloomy passageway. Other boys jeered at him and called him names, but he never once reacted. If they pushed him over, he simply picked himself up again and went on standing as before. His expression never altered. After a while the boys lost interest and more or less ignored him. 'There's Pegleg,' they would say. Or, 'Hello, Stork.'

In the end, someone must have alerted the authorities, I suppose, because Jones was removed. I had been sent out to the vegetable patch that day to plant onions with Maclean and several others, and I didn't realise Jones had left until we sat down to supper in the evening. I assumed a home had been found for him, and I hoped his new parents would treat him well. I was sorry not to have been able to say goodbye.

Curiously enough, the corridor he had occupied didn't seem empty after he had gone. It was as though he had left something of himself behind, a kind of imprint on the air, as though, by standing there like that, he had changed that part of the house for ever. Perhaps that's what is meant by the word 'haunted'. In any case, I never felt comfortable in that corridor again and avoided it whenever I could.

It must have been spring when I was summoned to Mr Reek's office because I remember looking through the window and seeing daffodils beside the moat, their yellow trumpets nodding and dipping in the wind.

Reek stood in front of me, a sheet of paper in his hand. 'From now on,' he said, 'your name will be Thomas Parry.' He laid down the sheet of paper, then took off his spectacles and stared intently at the far wall. 'Thomas Parry,' he said. 'A good solid name. You could be anything with a name like that. Anything at all.' He brought his eyes back into focus and peered down at me. 'Do you realise what an opportunity this is?' His voice shook ever so slightly, as if he suspected I didn't appreciate what was being done for me. 'Just think of it. A completely fresh start. A new beginning.'

He must have made dozens of such speeches.

'There's something I want you to bear in mind.' He had walked to the bright window, and was gazing out in the direction of the woods. I had found a bird's skull in there, bleached white, light as air. 'If you should see any behaviour,' he said, 'which doesn't fit in with your notion of the sanguine disposition, it's your duty – your *duty* – to report it to the authorities.' He looked at me over his shoulder, a shaft of sun picking out a tuft of ginger hair in his right ear. 'Do I make myself clear?'

'Yes, sir.'

He studied me for a long moment. 'All right, my boy. You may go.' He stood there in the sunlight, waiting for me to leave the room.

'I've been worried about Jones,' I said.

'Jones?' The skin on the bridge of Reek's nose knotted momentarily. 'Ah yes. Jones. He's been' – and he paused – 'well, he's been transferred.'

'Where to?'

'I'm afraid that's confidential,' Reek said. 'I can't tell you that.' He came and squinted down at me, his mouth crumpling in an attempt at a kindly smile. 'There's nothing else, is there?'

A few days later I was put on a train. A woman travelled with me, I've forgotten her name. She had been given the task of introducing me to my new family, overseeing what must, in many cases, have been an extremely awkward transition. During the journey I got my first glimpse of how the country had been divided up. Towards lunchtime, in the middle of nowhere, the train slowed down and stopped. I could see no sign of a station, only an embankment bristling with spear-shaped purple flowers.

'The border,' my companion murmured.

I opened the window and looked out. A poorly made wall of concrete blocks had been erected at right angles to the track. Starting on level ground, it sloped up the embankment and then vanished from sight. Two parallel lengths of barbed wire straggled along the top, making the wall higher and more difficult to scale. Soldiers with guns stood in the spring sunlight. Their shadows pooled around their feet, blackening the stones. Half closing my eyes, I pretended that everyone was melting. A man walked an Alsatian down the outside of the train, the dog tugging on its lead so forcefully that the lead and the man's arm formed a continuous straight line. I crossed to the window on the other side. Here, too, the wall stopped just short of the rails, but the gap was filled by a sliding wire-mesh gate. Soldiers began to pass through our carriage, some with green braid on their uniforms, some with scarlet, and each time they appeared the woman travelling with me had to produce a sheaf of official documents, which the soldiers scrutinised, their eyes shifting between the lines of writing and my face. At last, after a delay of perhaps an hour, the train lurched forwards again and the border was behind us.

'I hate being checked like that,' the woman said. 'I always feel guilty.'

I nodded, as if I understood. 'Me too,' I said, which made her laugh.

The train gathered speed. We had entered the Red Quarter, which was to be my new home, and I felt my heart beat harder. Our destination was Belle Air, the woman said. A pretty place, apparently. She'd never been before. As the train swayed through a landscape of open fields and narrow lanes, she told me a little about the family to which I was going to belong. My father's name was Victor Parry. He was fifty-two years old and worked for the railways, as coincidence would have it. He was an electrical engineer. My sister, Marie Parry, had just turned seventeen. She wanted to go to university, to study environmental law.

'And my mother?' I said. 'Who's going to be my mother?'

The woman's face clouded over for a moment. I was to have no mother, she told me, but she was sure that Marie, my sister, would be more than capable of looking after me.

'No mother,' I said quietly.

Gripping the point of my chin between finger and thumb, the woman tilted my face upwards until I was staring into her eyes, which were round and solemn. 'You must take things slowly,' she said. 'Give everyone time to adjust, yourself included.'

We changed trains in the capital, then travelled south, passing red-brick houses with grey slate roofs, street after street of them, all parallel, as if that part of the city had been combed. One row of terraced housing swept up towards the railway line, and I was able to look through windows into people's homes. I saw a young woman pulling a sweater over a child's head. Then another woman, older, standing at a sink. Something about these glimpses made the breath catch in my throat, and I had to look away, but before too long the houses were gone and we were out in the countryside again.

By the time we approached Belle Air, the sky had taken on a pale, almost supernatural colour, neither green nor blue, and a shoal of tapering clouds swam close to the horizon, their bellies tinted amber by the setting sun. In the foreground a river coiled lazily through flat meadows. A man sat huddled on the far bank, fishing. Two swans paddled near by, a disdainful arch to their long necks. The town itself stood on a hill, the houses clustered round a medieval castle that appeared to have been carefully restored. While at the holding station, I hadn't tried to imagine what the next stage of my life was going to be like. I hadn't dreaded it, as Jones had done, nor had I looked forward to it particularly. I suppose I simply assumed that everything would somehow fall into place. But now, for the first time, I could see the future taking shape around me, and I felt that my faith in things was about to be tested.

The train stuttered and slowed. Through the windows of a brewery I saw beer bottles jostling on a conveyor belt. It occurred to me that similar bottles would pass along the belt tomorrow, and the next day, and in six months' time. Where would I be by then? Who would I be with? On the bottles went – impervious, determined, slightly unsteady. Next door, at the bowling club, the floodlights had been switched on. A solitary man in a white shirt and grey trousers stood on a lawn that was so smooth that it might have been shaved rather than mown. As I watched, the man leaned down. His right arm swung forwards, and a big dark ball came curving across the perfect grass towards me. No sooner had the man released the ball than he began to follow it with nimble, urgent steps, as though he regretted having let go of it, as though he no longer trusted it, as though he feared what it might do. The ball kept rolling, growing larger and larger, until it seemed that its voluptuous, hypnotic revolutions might swallow me completely, but then the train slid into a tunnel, its brakes wincing and grinding, and when we emerged again into the fading light, the brick walls and hanging baskets of a station rose up before me, and the train shuddered to a halt. My companion touched me on the arm. We were there.

I had been hoping for a long walk, which would have given me the chance to prepare myself, but the woman stopped outside a green door no more than a few hundred yards from the station. My nerve had held all day. Now, though, I found my stomach tightening, and the palms of my hands were wet. She heaved a sigh – almost, I felt, on my behalf – and pressed the bell once, firmly. A window on the first floor scraped open, and an elderly man with a huge bald head peered down.

'Ah,' he said.

The man's head withdrew, and the window crashed shut. The woman smiled at me, dimples showing in her cheeks. She was trying to convince me that what was happening was normal.

When the front door opened, the man's eyes jumped from the woman's face to mine and his lips drew back and his teeth appeared, grey-white, like ancient cubes of ice. Was he smiling or gloating? I couldn't tell. It was even possible that he had suffered an involuntary spasm of some kind. Clearly we had come to the wrong address. I'd been led to believe that people who lived in the Red Quarter were special and rare, like black pearls or white whales, like four-leafed clover, but so far as I could see there was nothing remotely special or rare about the man standing in the doorway. He was just plain odd. I turned and gazed at the woman who had brought me there, endeavouring to compress all my doubts and fears into a single look, but she merely nodded at me and those smooth dents showed in her cheeks again.

'You must be Thomas,' the man said finally. Reaching down, he took my right hand in his and shook it vigorously. 'Very pleased to meet you. Very pleased indeed.' He tried to step back, so as to let the woman pass, but the doorway was too narrow. 'Do come in,' he said. 'Both of you. Follow me.'

There had been no mistake. This was Victor Parry, my new father.

My first glimpse of my new sister, Marie, came half an hour later, and with her appearance I felt the anxieties that had taken hold of me begin to loosen their grip. I was sitting in the living-room with Victor Parry and my travelling companion, about to reach for a cup of tea, when I heard light footsteps on the stairs – or, rather, I heard a series of subtle creaks, as though someone was walking on tiptoe, trying their utmost not to make a sound. Glancing beyond Victor Parry's shoulder, I saw a girl framed in the open doorway. She was dressed in a black ribbed sweater, a short, slightly flared red skirt and a pair of black tights. As I caught her eye, she winked at me and put a finger to her lips, then she disappeared from view.

'Marie? Is that you?' Victor's head half turned, but only in time to hear the door to the street click shut. He let out a heavy, almost vaudevillian sigh. 'You'll have to forgive her,' he said. 'She's always off out somewhere, doing God knows what.'

I had already forgiven her, of course. That dark hair curving in beneath her chin like the blade of a sultan's dagger, those lips that slanted a little, as if one side of her mouth weighed more than the other. That conspirator's wink, which the grown-ups hadn't noticed. During the weeks that followed, Victor would often refer, half in jest, to the fact that Marie had abandoned him in his hour of need – and what's more, as a result of her leaving the house like that and staying out for half the night, poor Thomas had been forced to wait until the next day before he even so much as *set eyes* on his new sister, whereupon Marie and I would exchange a look of barely suppressed amusement. We knew better. It was our secret, though. I loved Marie from the beginning – but not as a sister exactly, and not as a mother either.

I quickly realised how lucky I was to have been placed with the Parrys. Marie led her own life, the exuberant, dishevelled life of a seventeen year old, but she never made me feel excluded or unwanted. As for my father, Victor, it simply wasn't in him to treat me badly, though he did tend to veer between mild hysteria and complete absent-mindedness, a pattern of behaviour which, like so much else, I would only fully under-stand in years to come. This much I knew: his wife, Jean Parry, had been taken on the same night as I had, another victim of the Rearrangement, and he was still mourning the loss of her, still adjusting to her absence. Marie seemed to care less – on the surface, at least. Maybe, like me, she kept all those feelings hidden. I sometimes wonder if there wasn't a sense in which they looked on me as some sort of substitute for Jean, a kind of reimbursement. But perhaps that's overstating it. Distraction might be a better word. I was something that would take their minds off the violence that had been done to them, something that would alter the shape of their sorrow. Marie took it upon herself to try and occupy the maternal role, just as my travelling companion had implied she might, while Victor assumed responsibility for the running of the household. Seen from the outside, then, my arrival had a beneficial effect, since it forced them to pull together and begin to function as a unit again.

As for my other parents, my real parents, I never heard what became of them, and I could never quite bring myself to ask. There was the loss itself, of course, which was hard enough, but I was also battling a sense of shame. I had turned my back on them, you might even say that I'd betrayed them, and I didn't know how to come to terms with that. It was easier to pretend they didn't exist. What's more, in the circumstances, asking such a question would have seemed ungrateful, if not callous – and besides, I doubt whether Victor or Marie would have been able to tell me anything. The rift between past and present was absolute, for all of us. The image I was left with, of two people standing on a road in the middle of the night, people who hadn't even had the time to dress properly, was one that I consigned to the very darkest corner of my memory, and there it remained, like a discarded childhood toy – the ukulele with its broken strings, the moulting, one-eyed teddy bear.

We were living in momentous times, historic times – the country had been dismembered, families had been torn apart, whole sections of the population were suffering from what became known as 'border sickness' – and yet I seemed to take it all in my stride. I remember Victor sitting at the kitchen table with a newspaper on one of my first mornings in the house.

'That Song fellow's going to be Prime Minister,' he said.

I remembered Miss Groves mentioning the name. To her, Michael Song had been something of a hero. He had attended the underground meetings that altered the nation's destiny for ever, and later, when he had been classified as sanguine, he had founded a new political party, installing himself as leader.

'I saw a poster yesterday,' Victor said. 'Michael Song. Voice of the People.' He snorted. 'Talk about putting the cart before the horse.'

He picked up his newspaper, but put it down again almost immediately.

'There was rioting in the Yellow Quarter last night,' he said. 'The police used tear-gas and rubber bullets.' He mentioned a place I'd never heard of. 'I used to live round there, when I was in my twenties.'

He wasn't talking to anybody in particular. He was just talking. As I watched him, it struck me that he might be addressing the space that had formerly been occupied by Jean, his wife.

'There are tanks on the streets,' he said. 'There are *curfews*.' This last word came out high-pitched, a measure of his disbelief.

Marie was slouched over the table, face propped on one hand, eyes lowered. Her other hand rested loosely against a mug of tea, which she had yet to touch. I had heard her come in late the night before, swearing under her breath as she collided with the linen chest outside her room.

'What's a curfew?' I asked eventually.

In truth, I wasn't all that curious. I was just trying to fit in. The events that had upset Victor seemed academic to me, remote, even foreign. Perhaps I lacked the proper context – after all, I had spent five months in the middle of nowhere, shielded from the worst of what was going on – or perhaps it was the eerie matter-of-factness of a child who, having experienced a trauma of his own, decides simply to get on with the business of living, which in my case meant acquainting myself with my new environment. And there was so much to get used to, so much to explore.

The house itself was more than a hundred years old. Appropriately enough, an antiques dealer occupied the ground floor, though the over-elaborate and gloomy furniture didn't sell, and a health-food shop soon took its place. We lived in the maisonette above. The staircase that led up from the pavement was dark and uneven, with creaking wooden steps, and the walls bulged, as if, like bodies, they contained a variety of soft yet vital organs. There was a sitting-room on the first floor at the front and three smaller rooms – kitchen, store-room and toilet – at the back. From the sitting-room I could look down into Hope Street, a narrow, bustling parade of shops, and if I leaned out far enough I could see the pub on the corner, the Peacock, where Victor sometimes stopped for a pint on his way home from work. Climb another flight of stairs, which felt still more rickety, and you would find three bedrooms and a bathroom. Victor spent most evenings up there with his door ajar and his radio tuned to the concerts of classical music that were broadcast live from the capital. He had become involved in redesigning a section of the Red Quarter's railway network, a task which he appeared to relish. When going to bed, I would often glance into his room, and there he would be, poised over a sheet of tracing-paper with a pencil. His detailed maps of electrical systems covered every available surface, the long, slim cardboard cylinders in which his finished drawings travelled to and from the office leaning against the wall in the corner like so many snooker cues.

One night, though, just a few weeks after my arrival, I stopped in his doorway and saw a high-heeled silver sandal on the table, illuminated by a lamp. Victor was sitting in front of it, hunched over, a pair of kitchen scissors in one hand. When he sensed my presence, he almost jumped out of his chair, trying at the same time to hide the sandal under a newspaper. 'Off – off to bed, Thomas?' he stammered. 'Well, goodnight. Sleep well.' I looked at him for a moment longer, then I, too, said goodnight. I couldn't expect to understand everything about these people, I thought to myself, not all at once, and there were probably questions I would never be able to ask.

Moving away across the landing and down a short corridor, I passed Marie's room. I would often pause to gaze in wonder at her clothes, which would be lying in a tangle on the floor, her dresses drooping across the foot of the bed like people who had fainted, her underwear foaming and frothing out of her chest of drawers in little frozen waterfalls of cotton, silk and lace. The room I had been given was one of the smallest in the house, no more than eight feet square, and its single window gave on to a row of scrubby back yards and gardens, a car-park half buried in weeds, and the blank side-wall of a working-men's club, but after the noise and overcrowding of the holding station I loved the feeling it had, of being an eyrie, a refuge, my own private domain.

Sometimes, when Marie came home after an evening out, she would look in on me. Light would open in a triangle across my bed and she would lean down, placing her lips on my forehead or my cheek, and a scent would float off her, not just the perfume she wore, but alcohol, cigarette smoke, and cold, clean sweat from all the dancing she had done, it was the sweet smell of the night, a world I didn't know as yet, and I would lie there with my eyes closed and my heart leaping, and I would breathe her in, right to the bottom of my lungs. When she straightened up again, her clothes would seem to whisper to me, then the fan of light would fold itself away, the door would shut and I would hear her stumble back into her room and kick off her shoes, two quick tumbling sounds across the floor, like dwarves turning somersaults, and a new silence would descend, thicker than before and deeper, more inhabited somehow, the silence of my breath mingling with my sister's and my father's, the silence of our dreams.

Despite the promises I had made to other boys – *I'll look for you, I won't forget* – and despite the enduring clarity of my memories of those days, I thought I had left Thorpe Hall behind for ever, but this turned out not to be the case. I had only been living on Hope Street for a few months when I discovered that Maclean had been placed with a well-to-do family at the top of the town, and that he would be attending the same school as I was. The first time I saw him again, that autumn in the playground, I had no trouble recognising him, his wrists protruding from the arms of his blazer, his ears the size of dustbin lids.

'What's your new name?' he asked.

'Parry,' I said. 'Thomas Parry.'

He nodded.

'What about you?' I said.

'Simon Bracewell.' He shrugged. 'It's all right. Now listen,' he said, and he threw a furtive glance round the asphalt yard, then drew me close. 'About Cody,' he said. 'We're divorced now, but we're still good friends. He's living with a family in the northwest. His new name's De Vere, by the way.'

'De Vere?'

'I know.' Bracewell shook his head.

I glanced at his left hand. 'What happened to your ring?'

Bracewell grinned. 'On our last night we took them off and tied them together with a piece of wire and threw them in the moat.' He looked down at the ground, and his face became serious. 'I don't think I'll ever marry again.'

Though we used to sit next to each other for lessons, we hadn't been particularly close, but this now changed. In term-time he came round to my house at least twice a week, and during the holidays we spent whole days together. I was both intrigued and delighted by the way his mind worked. If it hadn't been for Bracewell, for instance, I'm not sure I would ever have noticed Mr Page. There was a dry-cleaner's on Hope Street, almost directly opposite our house. If you walked past the open doorway you could smell the fluid they used, which was called perchloroethylene and which would become – not inappropriately, I thought much later – the defining smell of my childhood. Mr Page ran the place. He had narrow eyes that curled up at the edges, and his mouth was the same – a wide, thin curve, like a slice of melon after you've finished eating it, like the rind seen sideways-on.

'He looks as if he's smiling all the time,' Bracewell said.

He told me that it put him in a good mood, just to look at Mr Page. If everybody had a Mr Page living somewhere near by, the world would be a much happier place, he thought. One question did bother him, however, and he returned to it again and again. What if Mr Page lost his temper? Would he still appear to be smiling?

I persuaded Bracewell to push the prospect of Mr Page not smiling to the back of his mind, otherwise it would never happen. Bracewell agreed. Instead, we sat on my doorstep and were content simply to soak up a sense of well-being from the man on the other side of the road. Later, I realised that what we saw in Mr Page was something the authorities called 'eucrasia', a state of balance where all your humours are in harmony with one another. In that respect, at least, we were proving ourselves to be true disciples of the new regime.

By the following spring the work of rearranging the population had largely been accomplished. Throughout the divided kingdom the walls of concrete blocks had been reinforced with watch-towers, axial crosses and even, in some areas, with minefields, which rendered contact between the citizens of different countries a physical impossibility. If you had been classified as sanguine, then you remained in the Red Quarter for the term of your natural life. Attempts to cross the border illegally were punishable by prison sentences, and if you defied the guards they had the right to open fire on you. All this to prevent what was now being referred to as 'psychological contamination'. In the hush between Christmas and New Year, a hush intensified by a heavy fall of snow, an Internal Security Act was simultaneously passed in all four countries. Anybody suspected of 'undermining the fabric of society' could now be arrested on unspecified charges and held without trial for up to two years. Some time afterwards, when I was in my twenties, I heard it rumoured that the government had introduced tranquillisers into the water supply in order to guarantee a peaceful transition. This seemed a little far-fetched. But even if the rumours had some truth to them, there were obviously quite a few who never drank from the tap. In the Yellow Quarter, for instance, where resistance to the new regime was at its strongest, not a day passed without somebody being shot dead for trying to escape. In the Green Quarter, on the other hand, a number of people killed themselves, leaving notes and letters which claimed the government had deprived them of the will to live; special cemeteries were set aside for those who had died by their own hand, and several bridges and tall buildings had to be pulled down since they were believed to encourage suicidal thoughts. Only in the Blue Quarter was the protest non-violent, but even there the authorities witnessed a spontaneous outpouring of grief and despair. Every morning border guards had to remove the bouquets, photographs and hand-written elegies that had been deposited at the base of the wall during the hours of darkness, and it was said that their barracks were so full of cut flowers that they resembled maternity wards.

We paid very little attention to any of this during those early years, Bracewell and I. One could make a case for the fact that we were behaving in character, I suppose. We were sanguine, after all. We liked to look on the bright side, make the best of things. But also – and more importantly, perhaps – our energies were entirely taken up with the man who ran the dry-cleaner's. Though we spent many tranquil hours basking in Mr Page's aura of well-being, there was always a part of us that remained on tenterhooks, waiting for the miraculous, the almost unimaginable moment when he no longer appeared to be smiling.

I had been a member of the Parry household for about twelve months when a brown envelope arrived in the post. Victor took one look at the scarlet peacock stamped in the top left-hand corner and passed the letter to Marie, then he went and stood by the kitchen window. I watched Marie's dark eyes skim the half a dozen lines of type. I was being summoned to the Ministry of Health and Social Security, she told me. She didn't think it was anything to fret about, just a routine interview, but the air in the room had stretched tight, which told me there was probably more to it than that.

When the day came, Marie walked me down to the Ministry, an imposing edifice of glass, flint and pale stone that backed directly on to the river. It was April or May, a chill wind blowing. The Red Quarter's flag snapped and shuddered on its pole. As we climbed the wide, shallow steps to the entrance I tilted my head back and looked up at the roof, and the rapid flight of clouds past the eaves gave me the impression that the building was falling on top of me. My hand in Marie's, I hurried onwards, through the double-doors. The hallway in which we found ourselves had the atmosphere and dimensions of an atrium, the space filled with the whisper of voices, the slither of shoes and also with an inexplicable ghostly laughter, and all these sounds seemed to swarm and mingle in the air above us. We reported to reception and were told to take a seat. A man in a dark-grey suit appeared in front of us just moments later.

'Thomas Parry?'

Smiling at Marie, he asked her to wait where she was. He led me through a roped-off area guarded by a man in a maroon uniform, then past a bank of lifts and on into a maze of open-plan offices. As we walked, he asked me all about myself – how old I was, where I went to school, what I was going to do in the holidays. Though there was nothing original about his line of questioning, he seemed relaxed and jovial, which put me at my ease. At last we reached a door. He knocked twice with a crooked forefinger, then drew the door open and ushered me inside. Installed behind a desk was a stout woman with pink cheeks.

'Sit down, Thomas,' she said.

My stomach slowly turned over. 'Miss Groves. What are you doing here?'

She smiled. 'I work for the Ministry.'

'But I thought –'

'You thought I belonged at Thorpe Hall,' she said. 'I was just there temporarily, the same as you. How are you settling in?'

'Fine, thanks.'

'And your father? How's he?'

I watched Miss Groves across the desk. The transformation she had undergone since I last saw her reminded me of the fairy tale where the grandmother is actually a wolf. I thought about Victor with his pair of scissors and his silver shoe, and somehow I trusted him more, even though he had been trying to hide things from me. I felt that his lie was visible whereas hers was not and I decided that while it would be politic to appear to be cooperating I would say as little as possible.

'It's difficult,' I said.

Miss Groves leaned forwards hungrily, as I had suspected she might. 'Really? And why's that?'

'I don't see very much of him. He's working so hard, for the railways.'

'The railways. That's right. Is he enjoying it?'

'Oh yes. Sometimes, on my way to bed, I stop outside his door. There's always music on, some kind of singing usually, and he'll be studying his plans.' I looked down into my lap and wrinkled my forehead, as if I were thinking. Abruptly my forehead cleared and I looked up again. 'Sometimes he even chuckles to himself.'

I'm not sure why I said that. It wasn't true. But somehow I felt that Victor was under threat, and needed protecting.

Without taking her eyes off me, Miss Groves straightened in her chair. 'And your sister Marie? What about Marie?'

'We get on really well.'

'No sign of melancholy?' Miss Groves said casually.

I shook my head.

'No hints of phlegm or choler?'

'No.'

Her short pale fingers began to peck viciously at the keys on her computer like a flock of blind hens eating grain. From time to time she glanced up at me suspiciously, as though she expected to catch me in the middle of an indiscretion.

At last she closed the file and sat back. 'Do you remember our final lesson together,' she said, 'when I read to you about the sanguine temperament?'

'"The paragon of complections,"' I said. '"The prince of all temperatures."'

'Very good.' Miss Groves's eyes glowed, just as they had glowed in the ballroom at Thorpe Hall, with the chandeliers trembling above our heads and the men in armour watching us sidelong, across their cheeks. 'And to the best of your knowledge, Thomas,' she said, 'is that what you see around you?'

For some reason I thought of Mr Page just then, conjuring him up so vividly that I even caught a whiff of perchloroethylene.

'Yes, Miss Groves,' I said. 'That's exactly what I see.'

I would have been roughly eleven when Victor took me on my first field trip. As we climbed into his clapped-out four-door saloon that morning I thought once again what an unconventional car it was – unconventional for the Red Quarter, that is, sanguine people having little or no attachment to decay – though, knowing Victor, he would probably have argued that the old banger was proof of his optimistic nature, since he firmly believed that it was going to last for ever. I remember asking him if he was taking me to the office. The office? he said. No, not today. He grinned at me across one shoulder. Knowing better than to press him on the subject, I settled back and watched as we reversed past a wall smothered in convolvulus, the limp white bells brushing against the side of the car. In the end, I was happy just to be going somewhere with him.

We didn't talk much during the journey. We never had talked much. I often felt the pressure of his curiosity, though, especially since I received my first summons to the Ministry. There had been other interviews, of course – like visits to the dentist, they occurred at regular intervals and filled me with a sense of trepidation – and I had stuck to my theme, embroidering a little when I thought it appropriate – how grateful I was to have been placed with such a wonderfully sanguine family, how lucky I had been, and so on – but I had never mentioned the content of these interviews to Victor, nor had he asked. His was a silent insistence. It was as though he was trying to get me to own up to something, but without compromising himself, without committing himself in any way. At the same time there was the feeling that if nothing was said then everything must be all right and we could go on as we were.

After driving for an hour, we turned along a one-lane road that led to a modest red-brick railway station.

'It's derelict,' Victor said, 'but not for much longer, I hope.'

We stepped out of the car into hazy sunlight.

The line used to serve an area of the country that was now the Blue Quarter, Victor told me, but as a result of the Rearrangement it had been suspended and the station had become irrelevant. In his opinion, though, it could be resurrected. With a bit of imagination and some capital investment, it could be turned into a junction station for the Red Quarter's new south-western network.

Ignoring the danger signs with their jagged lightning bolts and hollow skulls, we struck out across the tracks, the silver of the rails concealed by rust. We climbed down into a urine-stained underpass, our feet crunching on broken glass. We stood thoughtfully on silent platforms. Weeds flowered among the sleepers. The smell of buddleia and cow parsley was everywhere. But Victor's eyes were darting about, and I knew that his vision had come alive. He was imagining the trains that would pass through the station, some pausing, others rushing on towards the coast. He could already hear the power humming in the insulators that hung like grubby concertinas above our heads.

I left him standing in the shade and wandered off along the rails. Two or three hundred yards from the station, where the track curved to the west, I came across a row of carriages that had been abandoned in a siding. A window in the top half of one of the doors had been left open. Glancing round, I made sure nobody was looking, then I hoisted myself through the gap and half fell, half dropped to the floor inside. It was quiet in the carriage, the way someone who's been gagged is quiet. A feeling of suppression and restraint.

Entering one of the compartments, I slid the door shut behind me. Two bench-seats faced each other, both covered in a faded turquoise velour. I sat by the window for a few moments. The sun draped itself across my lap. Twisting quickly, I pulled my trousers and pants down, then I lay full-length on the seat and began to rub myself against the rough, almost prickly upholstery. I was thinking of the time I came home to find Marie sunbathing on the small tar-papered roof below my bedroom window. It was one of those warm, still afternoons when the sky forfeits all its colour. The smell of dandelion sap floats in the air, and the tarmac softens at the edge of the road, and if you put your weight on one foot you can leave a print that lasts for ages. Marie had been lying on her back in a blue-and-white-striped bikini with a pile of unopened text-books beside her, one hand beneath her head, the other resting lazily across her belly, and I had to step away from the window, into the shadow of my room, so as to hide my erection. Closing my eyes, I thought of Marie in her bikini, then I thought of how she often bent down to kiss me late at night and how, once, by accident, our lips had touched, and before too long a cloudy juice came springing out of me.

I was just pulling my trousers up when I heard Victor calling.

'Thomas? Where are you?'

I dropped to the floor between the seats, then slowly lifted my head until my eyes were on a level with the window. Victor stood fifty yards away, next to something that looked like a giant cotton-reel. He was staring southwards, the fingertips of his right hand pressed upright against his mouth. Still crouching low, I crawled out of the compartment and into the corridor.

'Thomas?'

I could tell he was worried, and somehow that made me feel good. I took it as proof of something. I didn't want it to end, not yet.

Leaving by the same half-open window, I lowered myself on to the loose chippings and edged cautiously along the row of carriages, back in the direction of the station. Once, I kneeled down and peered past the great brown disc of a wheel. I watched Victor take a few paces and then stop. He called my name again. Bending double now, I hurried on. Only when I was clear of the last carriage did I straighten up and walk out into the bright white sunshine.

'I'm over here,' I shouted.

Victor moved towards me, shading his eyes. 'I've been looking for you everywhere.'

'Sorry. I was just exploring.'

Victor nodded approvingly. 'Just think what we could do with this place . . .'

Driving home, we wound all the windows down. The warm air that rushed through the inside of the car smelled of creosote and new-mown grass. Victor put on one of his opera tapes and we both sang along as loudly as we could, even though it was in a foreign language and we hardly knew any of the words.

That summer Bracewell and I would often cycle out into the lush countryside that surrounded Belle Air. One cool grey

morning we found ourselves in a thickly wooded area somewhere to the north-west of the town. To record our presence, we
decided to carve our names on a tree. Bracewell used the
penknife first. I watched him work, a knob of bone protruding
on his wrist, as if he had a marble sewn beneath the skin. When
my turn came, I used one of the letters in his name to make my
own. Apart from anything else, I thought it would save time.

```
              B
      P A R R Y
              A
              C
              E
              W
              E
              L
              L
```

Afterwards, I stood back, pleased to have found a connection
between our names. In demonstrating that they could be inter-
wined, I had harked back to the secret ceremonies that had taken
place at Thorpe Hall, the mingling of who one was with
someone else, the sense of a shared destiny.

But Bracewell just frowned. 'Like something in a cemetery,'
he said.

Which, in the light of what happened moments later, I came
to perceive not as a rebuke so much as a presentiment.

As the road left the wood, it dipped downwards, curving right
then left, with grass banks on either side. By the time it
straightened and levelled out, we were pedalling frantically,
racing each other. I saw the danger first and shouted out. We
both braked hard, Bracewell's back wheel sliding sideways and
spilling him on to the tarmac. No more than fifty yards ahead of
us, the road broke off in mid-air.

Leaving our bicycles on the ground, we crept towards the
drop and then looked over. Thirty or forty feet below lay a heap
of shattered concrete and macadam. On either side of it a

motorway reached into the distance, its six lanes silent, utterly deserted. Nothing moved down there except the weeds and grasses shifting in the central reservation – a kind of narrow wild garden. All thoughts of the grim fate that might have been ours were obliterated by the mystery of what now awaited us.

Though the citizens of the Red Quarter still drove cars – no one could deny the pleasures of the open road, especially in a country where the population was relatively small, just over five million – they had launched a series of impassioned campaigns against the motorway. To sanguine people, motorways signified aggression, rage, fatigue, monotony and death. Motorways were choleric, in other words, and had no place in the Red Quarter. Some had been converted into venues for music festivals or sporting events, and others had been fortified, then turned into borders, their tall grey lights illuminating dogs and guards instead of traffic, but for the most part they had simply been allowed to decay, their signs leaning at strange angles, their service stations inhabited by mice and birds, their bridges choked with weeds and brambles or, as in this case, collapsing altogether. In time, motorways would become so overgrown that they would only be visible from the air, half-hidden monuments to an earlier civilisation, like pyramids buried in a jungle.

We only had to look at each other to know what should happen next. We hauled our bicycles over a fence, then wheeled them down the embankment and out on to the motorway's hard shoulder. We began to ride north – in the fast lane, naturally. There was the most peculiar sense of risk attached to this. We were like people who believed the earth was flat, and who, despite our belief, had decided to travel at high speed towards the edge. I suspected Bracewell felt it too because I saw a flicker of apprehension in the grin he gave me as we set out. There was also a feeling of suspended danger, as if the silence and emptiness were only temporary and the real life of the motor-way might commence again at any moment. More than once, I turned and looked over my shoulder, just to make sure that nothing was coming.

But nothing came, not ever, not in all the many hours we

spent out there. I sometimes wonder whether we hadn't entered a parallel world which the two of us had somehow jointly imagined, a place where the anxieties of our daily lives could find no purchase, a place where we could finally throw off the wariness that informed so many of our thoughts and actions, and be ourselves.

I sometimes wonder if we weren't bound together after all.

One evening, while I was sitting at the kitchen table doing my homework, Victor appeared in the doorway. He needed to have a word with me, he said. I put down my pen and followed him upstairs. The sky was already dark, and Marie had gone out with friends. A cushioned silence filled the house.

In Victor's bedroom I took a seat next to his workstation, its surface hidden beneath the usual clutter of drawings, letters, documents and maps. The TV was on, with the sound turned down. Michael Song was addressing the nation. I was always struck by how polished he looked, almost literally *polished*, and how convivial too, like some worldly uncle you wished you saw more often. I watched as Victor switched the TV off, then lowered himself pensively on to the edge of his divan. We sat in silence for a moment or two. A slightly blurred circle of lamplight trembled on the carpet, but the rest of the room lay in deep shadow, mysterious yet open to conjecture, like the prairie beyond a camp-fire. The muted lighting seemed to invite confidences, confessions even, an effect that may well have been intentional.

'They're saying he's going to be re-elected,' Victor said, 'which is no great surprise really, is it?' He looked steadily into my face, gauging my reaction, then his gaze dropped to his hands. 'I've heard rumours, Thomas. Children being taken into families and then reporting to the authorities. Members of those families being imprisoned as a result.' There was another long pause. 'I suppose what I want to ask you is this,' he said eventually. 'Did the authorities tell you to spy on us?'

The question didn't surprise me particularly or make me nervous. At some deep level, perhaps, I had known that it would come.

'Not exactly,' I said.

Victor's pale eyes seemed to blacken. 'What do you mean, "not exactly"?'

I repeated what Mr Reek had said in his study on that bright spring afternoon, and then told Victor about my visit to the Ministry and the unexpected reappearance of Miss Groves. It came as a relief to be able to rid myself of all this information. Until that moment I hadn't realised quite how burdened I was.

'I thought so,' Victor said. 'My God.' His left hand closed into a fist, and he wrapped his other hand around it and held it tightly. His great bald forehead gleamed. 'So have you said anything? Have you reported us?'

'No.'

'And would you?'

I hesitated. 'No, I don't think so.'

'Why not?'

This time I paused for longer. I wanted to express what it was that I had felt within a day or two of arriving at the house – what I still felt, in fact – but it was difficult. I had never thought to put the feeling into words before, not even in my head. Then, suddenly, I had it – or something that seemed close enough.

'Because I want you to be happy,' I said.

Victor rose to his feet and walked over to his wall of books. He stood with his back to me, touching the spines of certain volumes with fingers that seemed unsure of themselves. Finally he turned to face me again. His eyes had a silvery quality that hadn't been there before. 'You're a good boy, Thomas, and we're glad to have you here. You know that, don't you?'

I nodded.

'We haven't talked a great deal,' he went on. 'That's my fault entirely. I've had other things on my mind, I'm afraid. Also, to be honest, I didn't trust you. I was sorry for you, of course, being taken from your family like that, and I felt responsible for you in some strange way, but I didn't trust you.' He looked at me. 'That sounds dreadful, I know.'

I shook my head. 'I understand.'

'Do you?' He squatted down in front of me, gripping my shoulders. 'Do you really?'

'Yes.'

'Is there anything you want to ask?'

I was about to shake my head again, then checked myself. 'There is one thing.'

'What?' Victor leaned forwards, his eyes intent on mine.

'It's Mr Page,' I said.

Victor's head tilted a little, and an upright line showed in the gap between his eyebrows.

'What happens when he gets angry?' I went on. 'I mean, does he still look as if he's smiling?'

For a moment Victor remained quite motionless, then his mouth opened wide and several odd inhaled sounds came out of him.

It was the first time I had ever heard him laugh.

Although I had asked about Mr Page and then reported my findings to Bracewell, his influence on us both had waned considerably. Once in a while, out of a quaint sense of loyalty, we would sit opposite the dry-cleaner's, but we were no longer expecting any miracles and we never stayed for very long. After all, we had a new passion now – the motorway.

We had only ridden out to the broken bridge a handful of times when we chanced upon an abandoned service station about a mile to the north. We immediately adopted it as our headquarters. There were curving roads with pompous white arrows painted on them, which we delighted in disobeying. There were meaningless grass-covered mounds. Inside the building was an arcade that was lined with video games, their screens all smashed, and a restaurant with wicker light-shades that hung from the ceiling like upside-down waste-paper baskets. Sometimes we would sit in the entrance, under the glass roof, and try to imagine what it was like before. Cars would park in front of us and people with weird old-fashioned hair-styles would get out. They would walk right past us, relishing the opportunity to stretch their legs, and we'd be sitting there, in the future, invisible.

We must have absorbed something of the atmosphere of the times, I suppose, since we invented a whole series of what we referred to privately as 'border games'. One morning we cycled further north than usual and found a section of the motorway that was in the process of being dug up. In our minds, the area instantly became a no man's land, with construction workers standing in for guards. We would pretend to be people from the Blue Quarter – unstable, indecisive types – or, better still, violent criminals from the Yellow Quarter, and it would be our mission to cross into sanguine territory, which was on the far side of the road. Camouflaged by pieces of shredded tyre, we would hide in the long grass at the edge of the building site and study the guards' movements through binoculars made from chopped-up bits of one of Victor's cardboard tubes. The game required audacity, cunning and, above all, patience. Each escape attempt was carefully orchestrated and timed to perfection, and it could take an entire morning to carry it out successfully. Once, we were spotted by a man in a yellow hard hat. He lifted an arm and took aim at us, two fingers extended like the barrel of a gun, thumb upright like a trigger. Ducking down, we imagined the thrilling zip of bullets in the air above our heads. On weekends one of us would have to assume the role of guard. I would prowl among the cement-mixers and scaffolding poles, clutching a second-hand air rifle I had bought in a junk shop on Hope Street. On my head I would be wearing an old motorbike helmet that was the shape of half a grapefruit. If it was Bracewell's turn to patrol the border, he would often bring his mother's spaniel along and pretend it was an attack dog.

We spent whole days out at the motorway, fortifying our headquarters against intruders or thinking up variations on the border game or just lying on our stomachs observing the guards, and every now and then we would talk about the old days, that peculiar, almost dreamlike time when Thorpe Hall had been a kind of home to us. On one such afternoon we decided to fit the service station with an alarm system. We used a length of fishing-twine as a trip-wire, fastening one end to a pile of dinner plates which we'd found in the kitchens at the back. As Bracewell unwound the twine across the main entrance, he surprised me by saying, 'Do you remember Jones?'

My heart speeded up. I had never married Jones, I hadn't even mixed my blood with his, but I had listened as he voiced his worries and I had done my best to reassure and comfort him. When he began to act strangely, I believed it was at least partly my fault. I had failed him, somehow, and that was a source of private shame to me. Then, when he was taken away, my shame redoubled, because secretly, somewhere deep down, I was relieved that our awkward friendship was over. Even now, more than three years later, I blushed at the mention of his name, but fortunately Bracewell was busy stacking plates and didn't notice.

'Jones,' he said. 'You know. Stork.'

'What about him?'

'I know what happened.'

'He was transferred,' I said. 'Reek told me.'

Bracewell sat back on his heels and steered a crafty look in my direction. 'Reek was lying.'

'So what happened then?'

'They sent him to a mental home.'

My throat hurt now, as though I had been shouting.

'He was round the twist,' Bracewell said. 'Don't you remember?'

He told me that he had been waiting in Reek's office one day when he noticed a letter lying on the desk. The letter had the name and address of an asylum in the top right-hand corner, and it confirmed Jones's recent arrival.

'Where did they send him?' I asked.

Bracewell shrugged. He hadn't bothered with the details.

'The way he used to stand there on one leg like that – for hours. I could never work out how he did it.' Bracewell stared into space for a few moments, then shook his head and, getting to his feet, walked out into the car-park. Once there, he turned and studied the place where the twine stretched across the entrance. 'I don't think they'll see that,' he said, 'do you?'

It seems to me that part of the true function of a mystery is precisely that it remains unsolved. The world would be far too neat a place if the things that puzzled us were always, eventually, explained. We need unanswered questions at the edges of our lives. In fact, I'd go further. It's important *not* to think we can understand everything. *Not to understand.* The humility that can come from that. The wonder. Every now and then, though, one of the less pressing mysteries is revealed to us, as if a god had decided to satisfy, in some small way, our natural craving for symmetry and resolution.

I had forgotten all about the silver sandal until Victor took me upstairs one evening to show me a book that he'd been working on. We sat facing each other in the lamplight, our knees almost touching. The book rested on his lap. Two feet high, some six or seven inches thick, it had the formidable dimensions of a family bible. He had bound it himself, he told me.

'You know what it's made of?' His eyes had grown paler and brighter, as light bulbs do before they blow.

I scrutinised the book. 'I can see leather –'

'Yes,' he interrupted, 'but what *kind* of leather?'

I bent closer and ran my fingertips across the cover. There were pieces of leather, but there were pieces of suede too, and rubber and canvas and raffia, all ingeniously and meticulously stitched together into a sort of patchwork.

'It's *shoes*,' Victor said, unable to wait any longer.

'Shoes?'

When they came for his wife, he said, they hadn't given her the chance to pack. She had taken almost nothing with her – none of her shoes, for instance, and she had always loved shoes. He had bought many of the pairs himself, of course. After she had gone he couldn't bear to look at them, and yet, at the same time, he couldn't bring himself to throw them away. Whenever a pair of shoes caught his eye, he remembered something that had happened – a dinner party, a walk in the mountains, a game of tennis. He remembered their life together, and how happy, how very happy, they had been. There were some shoes that she hadn't worn at all, that she'd been saving for a special occasion, perhaps, and it saddened him still more to think that she would never even put them on. Then, as he lay in bed one night, unable to sleep, the idea came to him: he would turn the shoes into a book.

'What do you think, Tom?' he said. 'Am I mad?'

Just then I saw my mother's bare feet on the road, and they were wet, and the pink polish on her toenails was chipped. I had to push the image swiftly to one side. Instead, I concentrated on the book in front of me. I concentrated hard. I could make out eyeholes now, and buckles too, and half a strap. And there, round the middle of the book's wide spine, was a section of the famous silver sandal. On the back, a hiking boot revealed itself. Then a plimsoll, an espadrille – a flip-flop. I began to get an almost visual sense of who Jean Parry had been.

'It's like a photograph album,' I said.

'Yes,' Victor said in a strange loud whisper. 'Yes, that's right. Clever boy.'

I asked him what was inside.

The story of his wife's first life, he said, the one she had lived before she was taken. Each chapter was narrated by a different pair of shoes. He had given the shoes voices. He had let them speak. It was heretical, of course, in that it celebrated the world that had existed prior to the Rearrangement. On the evidence of this book alone he could probably be imprisoned – or, worse still, transferred to the Green Quarter, where almost everyone wrote books, apparently. 'So don't say anything.' His eyes darted into the gloomiest corners of the room, as if government officials might already be lurking there. 'Not a word.'

For the first time I realised the extent to which Victor had been on guard against me ever since I had appeared on his doorstep. The absent-minded, ghostly quality that had char-acterised so much of his behaviour may well have been rooted in the grief he felt over the loss of his wife, but he had also been intent on concealing the outer, more complex edges of his own identity. He had seen me as an intruder and also, potentially at least, as an enemy. It must have been exhausting, I thought, to have had to keep himself so hidden, while at the same time being compelled to work, to live, to function normally, but then I suspected that he, like so many others, had become used to leading a double life. The Rearrangement had created a climate of suspicion and denial – even here, in this most open and cheerful of countries. People had buried the parts of their personalities that didn't fit. Their secrets had flourished in the warm damp earth, and it was by those secrets that they could be judged and then condemned. In showing me the book of shoes, Victor had placed his life in my hands. He had decided to have faith in me, and I determined, from that moment on, that I would never disappoint him or let him down.

By the time I turned fifteen I was two inches taller than Marie, and every now and then people would mistake us for lovers. Since my experience in the railway carriage, I had imagined all kinds of closeness with Marie, but never that. I had so many pictures of her stored inside my head, some real, some invented. They weren't wrong, just private. When we were seen as a couple, though, I felt as if someone had found out, and all the guilt came down on me, and all the shame, and anger too, a bright, crooked flash of anger through me, like a shiver. Marie thought it was hilarious, of course.

Gradually, I came to expect the comments, and I prepared myself. One morning, in the supermarket, somebody touched me on the elbow, and I turned to see an old woman smiling up at me. It warmed her heart, she said, to see two young people so much in love. I thanked her. Then, leaning closer, I told her that I had never been happier – and, curiously, I didn't have the feeling I was lying. Marie almost choked. I watched her disappear round a stack of cereals. *You know what you should do?* the woman said. I shook my head. The woman's smile widened. *You should marry her.* I wish I could have found this entertaining, as Marie did. When I got home, though, I sank into a deep despondency. My dreams had come true, but only for a few moments, the moments during which an old woman in a supermarket had believed me, and now, once again, they were just dreams, and always would be.

In time, I succeeded in turning it into a game – I would spend hours thinking up different histories for us, fresh dialogue – but secretly I was flattered to be thought of as Marie's boyfriend. I wanted to be seen in that light, I liked the fact that it looked possible, and it would always come as something of a disappointment to me if we went out together and no one said anything.

Every once in a while, Marie would tell me about a fling she was having. On the one hand I felt privileged that she had chosen to confide in me. On the other, I couldn't stand hearing about a person whom I viewed, almost inevitably, as some kind of rival. It split me right down the middle, just listening to her.

I remember an evening when we walked up to the castle, a clear black sky above our heads. It had been raining earlier. Water rushed in all the gutters, and the air was full of river smells, reeds and mud and roots. When we reached the entrance – a pair of tall gates, padlocked at sunset – Marie asked me to give her a hand. I helped her up on to the wall, then she scrambled down the other side, first on to the roof of a garden shed, then down again, into the castle grounds.

Steep steps led to a stone tower, which was the highest point in town. There was a lawn up there, with a lime tree in the middle. Perched on the wrought-iron seat that circled the trunk, Marie lit a cigarette. A single raindrop promptly fell from somewhere and extinguished it.

She grinned. 'You think someone's trying to tell me something?'

We climbed a spiral staircase to the top of the tower, then leaned on the battlements looking east. In the distance a pale glow showed here and there where the downs had been quarried for chalk. Marie began to tell me about Bradley Freeman, her current boyfriend. They had been going out for six months, and she had just discovered that he'd been seeing someone else all along. It took me a second or two to realise that she was talking about the man who had taken me to see Miss Groves on the day of my first interview at the Ministry. He'd been pursuing Marie on and off ever since. I went back in my mind, but I could remember nothing about Bradley Freeman, nothing except his amiable manner and his endless mundane questions.

'Why him?' I asked.

'You wouldn't understand.'

'Why not?'

'Because you're my brother.'

'He doesn't realise how special you are.'

She sent me a sharp dark glance, as if she thought I knew something that I had no right to know, then she looked away again.

'Sometimes he does,' she murmured.

I stared out over the rooftops. They seemed to mill and jostle in the darkness, as though straining at their moorings – more like boats than houses. The ground itself felt uncertain, unreliable. Everything could come apart so easily.

'I wouldn't treat you like that,' I said.

She cupped a cold hand to my cheek, then turned from me and started down the steps. I hesitated, unable for a moment to conceive of any action that was not extraordinary. I would do anything for her, I thought, anything at all.

I caught up with her below the castle, outside a pub called the Silk Purse. She was standing on the pavement, a cigarette alight between her fingers, her eyes fixed on the window. She glanced at me across her shoulder. 'Fancy a drink?'

'I'm not old enough.'

'Of course you are.' She took me by the arm. 'Come on.'

In the lounge bar she ordered two glasses of red wine. And then another two. And then I've no idea how many.

It was the first time I'd ever been drunk. As we stumbled home down streets so narrow that if I ricocheted off one wall I collided with the other, I remember telling her that I loved her, no, I *adored* her, which made her laugh, and her hair fell forwards against her cheek like the tip of a cutlass and her teeth flashed in the black air.

I had to stop and stare at her. 'You're so beautiful,' I said.

She had stopped too, though not because of what I'd said. Something else had just occurred to her. 'What kind of girls do you like, Tom?'

I was staring at her again, but for a different reason now. I couldn't believe she hadn't understood. 'Like you,' I said.

She put a finger to her lips. 'You'll wake everybody in the street.' But she still had laughter in her eyes. They had sharpened at the corners, and the dark parts shone.

I lowered my voice to a whisper. 'Like you.'

She didn't seem to hear what I was telling her – or, if she did, she automatically discounted it.

We came down out of the old town and on to a main road near the station.

'I'm not your brother, Marie,' I said. 'We're not even related – not really.' I felt I was risking everything in saying this, and yet I couldn't hold back. But she didn't take it the way I had expected.

'How much do you remember?' she said. 'You know, from before?'

'Nothing,' I said.

She stopped again and looked at me. 'Nothing at all?'

'Only my name.'

'What was it?'

'Matthew Micklewright.' The words sounded like gobbledegook. I wished I hadn't said them.

'But you were eight years old. Nearly nine. You must remember something.'

I shook my head savagely. 'No. Nothing.' What I was telling her was true, and for the first time ever I was glad it was true. I had an urgent need to deny her something. I was taking a kind of revenge on her.

'That's astonishing,' she said, though she didn't look astonished. She was staring at the ground as if she had just noticed a bird with a broken wing.

As we crossed the river I insisted on walking in the gutter, even though I knew people always drove too fast on that particular stretch of road. Once, I looked up to see a pair of headlights hanging in front of me, and Marie had to pull me back on to the pavement.

'You'll get killed,' she said.

'What do you care? I don't mean anything to you.' It all came out blurred. My tongue seemed to have swollen, filling my mouth.

Back home, I sprawled on the bathroom floor, the black-and-white tiles constantly swerving away from me but never going anywhere. Everything I thought of made me feel sick. I clutched the lavatory seat with both arms, my cheek resting heavily against my sleeve. Cold air rose out of the bowl. I tried to look round, but the ceiling tilted and I fell sideways against the bath.

Hauling me upright, Marie placed a hand on my forehead. I had to reach up and push it away. 'No,' I mumbled. 'Leave me alone.'

The impossible weight of her cool hand.

The impossible beauty of it.

On returning from the public library one evening, I opened the front door and called up the stairs as usual, but there was no response, nothing except the patient tick-tick-tick of the boiler and the creak of the bottom step beneath my foot. Outside, the shops had already shut and the street was quiet. It was the summer before I went to university. I would have been eighteen.

I was standing by the fridge drinking a glass of juice when I became aware of a breathy, repetitive sound coming from behind me. At first I thought a mouse had worked its way into the kitchen wall, but then some instinct sent me hurrying round the corner into the store-room where I found Victor in the shadows by the washing-machine, with his face in his hands. I asked him what was wrong. He shook his head. I reached out and touched his shoulder. His whole body was trembling. I thought of how machinery behaves when it's about to break down – all that pitching and staggering, all that vibration. Head still bowed, he turned towards me. I took him in my arms and held him. Victor. My father. I felt something cold land on the back of my hand and realised he was crying. Then the words came, heaved out of him like sobs. Jean had died, he told me.

He stood in my arms until the light began to go.

His wife had already died once, years before. Now, though, she had died again, and this time she was gone for good. This second death was final, unambiguous, and left no room for hope. Had she suffered? Had somebody cared for her towards the end? Had she wanted to speak to him? He would never know. The gap that had opened up between them would never be closed.

I remember asking how he had found out. After all, it had been a decade since she had been taken from him. Being an adult, she would have kept her name, but her tracks would have been well covered. And even if he had been able to trace her, the law expressly forbade any contact.

'I felt it,' he said.

Waking from a nap, he had somehow known that, at that moment, the woman he had always loved had ceased to breathe. The knowledge reached him with such force that he had jackknifed into an upright position, his heart beating so fast, so loudly, that he imagined he heard footsteps in the street below, a heavy person running.

I asked him if anything like that had ever happened before. He shook his head. 'No.'

He didn't think to question the information, though. For him, it had the incontrovertible power of a divine message or an oracle. It couldn't be verified, neither could it be disproved. Later, I saw that his behaviour had a distinct emotional logic to it. In sensing his wife's death, he had reclaimed her as his own.

Not that it was much comfort to him. He locked himself into his room and refused to come out. I would hear him weeping at all hours of the day and night. He wouldn't eat the meals I prepared for him. He even stopped listening to the radio. And Marie couldn't help. She had troubles of her own.

She had moved back into the house on Hope Street only a few days before. While working for a law firm in the capital, she had fallen in love with one of the senior partners, a married man more than twice her age. She became pregnant by him, but subsequently lost the child. Not long afterwards, he embarked on an affair with his new secretary. Marie resigned. One Sunday morning she appeared on the doorstep with a suitcase, her complexion pale, almost soggy, her hair oddly lacklustre. I remember how frail she felt when I hugged her, as if all the spring and verve, all the resilience, had gone out of her. Less than a week later, Victor woke from his afternoon nap and the period of grieving began.

Marie took a job at the local supermarket – the same shop, ironically, where we had once been mistaken for lovers. She wore a pink-and-white-striped uniform, her name printed on a plastic badge pinned over her left breast, and she dyed her hair a flagrant chestnut-bronze that made her look anaemic. She showed no interest in men – or, if she did, she allowed them to treat her like something off the supermarket shelf: they consumed her, then disposed of her. Once, I walked through the front door after a morning at the library to find a stranger coming down the stairs buttoning his jacket and smiling plumply as though, like a squirrel, he had nuts stored in his cheeks. He muttered a few words as he edged past, his forehead damp all of a sudden. Perhaps he thought I was the husband. Marie appeared above me in the hallway, her dyed hair hiding half her face. She was wearing a bra and pants that didn't match. And Victor in his bedroom the whole time, behind that locked door of his, oblivious . . .

Usually, when I came home, Marie would be sprawled in front of the TV. She wouldn't acknowledge me at all, not even a hello. Every now and then, she would imitate the sound a cash-till makes when it scans a bar-code, that monotonous beep, then she would direct a sickly grin at the sofa or the wall, but that was the most anyone got out of her. Everything about our lives was askew, off kilter. We were all adrift in that small house, with no notion of how to steer a course.

I remember going into her room one evening to tell her that supper was ready. She was lying on her bed, one arm behind her head, a neat round bone showing on the inside of her elbow. Her uniform had ridden up so I could see her bare legs, right up to where her knickers started. I knelt by the bed and put a hand on her thigh, my heart beating so hard that a black mark pulsed in the air between us.

She watched me for a moment across her breasts, her eyes unlit, her breathing audible, almost abrasive, then she sat up fast and pushed me in the chest with the heel of her hand. I fell backwards, hitting my head on her cupboard door. She left the bed and walked past me, out of the room. I heard her footsteps, slow and deliberate, as she made her way downstairs, and then the pinched hiss as she turned the TV on.

In October, I travelled north to take my place at university. There was a part of me that worried about how Victor and Marie would cope in my absence. At the same time, I couldn't deny the feeling of relief that came over me as I walked out of the house. Grief ran down its walls like condensation, and the silence that lay in all the rooms had become so profound, so treacherous, that I feared I might sink into it, as one might sink into a marsh, never to be seen again. During the previous few weeks I had been aware that either Victor or Marie – or even, possibly, both of them – could be removed from the Red Quarter at any moment. In retrospect, it seems astonishing that they were not. We were just lucky, I suppose. Still, I was always waiting for that unfamiliar and yet predictable knock on the front door. As for Victor and Marie, I doubt they would have cared. Though they had followed different paths, they had both reached a state of mind where they didn't believe that things could get any worse.

When I returned to Hope Street for the Christmas holidays, the house seemed poky and ramshackle, but perhaps it suffered by comparison with the university I now attended, a typically sanguine confection of marble, steel and glass. Victor had celebrated his sixty-second birthday in November, and he had decided to take early retirement. Though he no longer locked himself behind his bedroom door, he rarely left the premises, preferring to drift from room to room in his frayed silk dressing-gown, his feet in a pair of leather slippers, the backs of which were trodden flat. The bones showed in his forearms, and his neck had withered to such an extent that I didn't understand how it could support that enormous imposing head of his. His thoughts seemed firmly rooted in the past, as if compensating for the degree to which he had aged. The book of shoes was never far away.

Like Victor, Marie had undergone a physical transformation. She had dyed her hair black again, and it curved beneath her chin in the old way, but she was more restrained than she used to be, almost as though she had been stricken by a fever that had left her permanently depleted. She didn't appear to have any desires or ambitions. Instead, she seemed content simply to stay at home and keep her father company. She was working at the town hall, as a clerk. She was still so young, only twenty-seven. Did she miss that wealthy lawyer? Was she in mourning for the child she had lost? I had no sense of what she might be thinking or feeling. If anything, the months that had elapsed since we had last seen each other had added to our awkwardness, and I found it difficult to know what to say to her. Everything I thought of was either too weighty or too superficial. I knew that we would never again swing hand in hand through the shopping precinct or fall about laughing at the supermarket check-out. The electricity that had crackled in the air between us, the flirtation that had meant so much to me, the love that had lit up my entire life – it was gone, all gone, and it would not return. Night after night, in my small box of a room, I would lie on my back with my arms folded across my chest and I would listen to the wind picking at a loose flap of tar-paper on the roof where she used to sunbathe. Tears would rise to the surface of my eyes and overflow. My cheeks would sting. A spring had welled up inside me, its waters irrepressible, but bitter, acidic.

In April I went home again, but only for a week this time. On the last night, as we ate our supper at the kitchen table, Victor announced that they were thinking of selling the house. The atmosphere in the room seemed to solidify around me. I couldn't even lift my knife and fork.

'You wouldn't mind, would you?' Victor said.

'Mind?' I cleared my throat. 'Why do you want to sell the house?'

Victor looked away across the room. 'Too many memories.'

Though Marie didn't lift her eyes from her plate, something came through the air from her. She was silently agreeing with her father. *Yes, too many memories.*

I pushed my chair back and walked to the window.

My memories too, I thought. My only memories. I remembered how I had stood on the doorstep, eight years old, how I had crouched deep inside myself and peered out, like someone hiding in a hollow tree-trunk. And Jones's words had floated into my head, unwelcome but persistent. *What if I don't like them? What if they're cruel to me?* I remembered my stomach lurching, and the sweat on my palms. The Parrys didn't realise. Or they'd forgotten.

I thought of the life I'd had before, what there was of it. The holding station with its draughty haunted corridors. Rooms possessed of such a chill that your hair turned cold as a corpse's. No sooner had you made a friend than he was taken from you. Then your name was taken from you. And before that? A time that was too painful to contemplate or even remember. A time so precious that it was inaccessible. Yes, they must have forgotten, the Parrys. Or perhaps they'd never bothered to imagine. That what they'd given me was all I had.

A creak came from behind me as someone shifted in a chair.

'Aren't you hungry?' Victor said.

That summer the house was duly sold, and Victor bought a cottage on the south coast with the proceeds. Marie would live there with him. On the day of the move he stalked from one room to another with a claw-hammer, nailing down the lids on tea-chests. Bang-bang-*bang*, bang-bang-*bang*. There seemed to be more space between his features, and flecks of white froth showed at the corners of his mouth. His shoulders and elbows jiggled, as though light electric shocks were being constantly administered to all his joints. He had so many things he wanted to do, he told me, once they were settled by the sea. He would grow broad beans, study astronomy, walk three miles every day, keep bees, collect driftwood ... He wouldn't stop talking. I remember turning to Marie. She was standing beside a packing-case, absent-mindedly fingering the tiny chunks of polystyrene. Her face was slightly lowered, and in shadow.

'And what will you do, Marie?' I asked.

Her lips tilted almost imperceptibly, a strange little quarter-smile. 'Yes,' she said. 'All that.'

That afternoon we drove down to the cottage in Victor's four-door saloon. It was my holiday, and I had offered to help with the unpacking. It would be my first glimpse of the property. As we came within a mile of the coast, Victor pulled on to the grass verge and announced that he wanted to walk the rest of the way. I said I'd join him. Taking his place behind the wheel, Marie drove on.

We set out across a wide, rising flank of downland, Victor and I, the sky towering above us, the air buttery with gorse. Before too long we found ourselves on a path made of chalk and, after walking briskly for about twenty minutes, the property came into view, the white of its walls and the black of its front door standing out against the cliff-top's carpeting of green. The slate roof had the dull sheen of a pigeon's wing, grey with just a hint of rose. To the east, behind the cottage, the cliffs lifted in a steep but languorous curve, while to the west they fell away, affording panoramic vistas both along the coast and out to sea. There were no trees, no bushes, just acres and acres of grass, with the odd patch of white where it had worn away. No one could deny the uniqueness of the location, and yet, at the same time, I had never seen a place that offered itself to the elements with quite such abandon.

'Imagine what the sunsets are going to be like,' Victor said.

But the true precariousness of the situation only struck me when I walked round to the south side of the cottage, where Marie was slumped in a deckchair with her eyes closed, sunning herself. The distance from the back door to the cliff-edge couldn't have been more than fifty yards. Erosion had always presented a serious problem for that particular stretch of coast. The average annual rate was two or three feet, but once or twice in living memory there had been a winter of storms when more than seven feet had been sacrificed. All year round, the sea nudged and prodded at the base of the cliffs, and great slabs of chalk were jarred loose, crashing to the beach below. There was so much chalk in the water, in fact, that the waves close to the shore appeared to be made of onyx. The local authorities had drawn a line on the map to indicate the land they were prepared to defend, but the line never came within half a mile of the coast, not unless a town was involved. From an administrative point of view, then, the cottage had already ceased to exist. Victor didn't care about any of that – and nor, it seemed, did Marie, though it was she who would eventually be left homeless. Victor had lost faith in the whole notion of investment, and as for security he would almost certainly have argued that there was no such thing. *Live in the present* had become his new mantra. *Live for today.*

'You worry too much,' he told me. 'We've got twenty years, and that's looking on the gloomy side.'

'I can see that I'll be visiting less frequently as time goes on,' I said.

He didn't smile, though, or even seem to understand.

During the next few weeks Victor would often ring me up at university to talk about the air quality, the colour of the sky, the peace and quiet.

'Things are better down here,' he said in one of our first phone-calls. 'Things are simpler. I feel as if I've been given a new lease of life.'

'I'm glad,' I said. 'How's the back garden?'

This time he got the joke. 'There's still a few feet left. You should come down.'

I said I had a dissertation to complete, which was only half-true. He told me he understood. He approved of my conscientiousness – he saw himself in me, perhaps – and he was proud of my scholastic achievements. If I put my mind to it, he said, there were no heights to which I could not rise. I remembered him calling my name on that deserted railway line when I was eleven, and I heard, once again, the worry in his voice, the love. How I wished I didn't have to lie to him.

He rang me again towards Christmas of that year and told me they had just experienced the most extraordinary storm. He'd never seen anything like it. Thunder and lightning all night long, ninety-mile-an-hour winds. A sound that was monotonous and deafening, yet curiously strained, he said, like a car being driven too fast in third gear. The rain had fallen horizontally, which made him feel the world had tilted.

'There was a moment when I thought we were going over the edge,' he said, and I detected a kind of glee in his voice.

After I put the phone down, it occurred to me that what he might actually be doing in that cottage on the cliffs – what they both might actually be doing – was committing suicide very slowly, and in the weeks and months that followed I often wondered whether it was respite they were seeking or oblivion.

During my years at university I didn't go down to see them more than three or four times. The ease I had once known in their presence, the feeling that I could share in their troubles and their celebrations, the sense of belonging – all that had fallen away like so much chalk. I didn't think they objected to the comparative rarity of my visits. In fact, after a while, I'm not even sure they noticed.

I would have been in my third year when I heard about Simon Bracewell.

We had lost touch with one another, Bracewell and I. We hadn't argued or fallen out; we'd just drifted apart, as if claimed by different currents. It is often said of the sanguine personality that it tires of things, that it becomes impatient. Well, maybe we reached an age where we simply ceased to interest each other.

I didn't see him for four or five years. Then, one December, I ran into him in the precinct, no more than a hundred yards from where I lived. Though he looked much the same, with the rims of his big ears red with cold, and the sleeves of his coat not long enough to hide his bony wrists, he seemed offhand, distracted, in a hurry. He'd been working in a local garage, he said, as a mechanic. My gaze inadvertently dropped to his ring finger, though the wheel-nut from Mr Reek's car was no longer there, of course. He planned to move to the city, he told me. Start a new life. He appeared to want to laugh at that point, but he couldn't get his mouth to assume the right shape; he ended up frowning instead, as if to indicate the seriousness of his resolve. I was finding it hard to keep the conversation going.

'Do you ever see Cody?' I asked.

He looked at me sidelong, almost suspiciously. 'I haven't seen him for years.'

'What about Jones? Did you ever hear anything about Jones?'

'No. Nothing.'

His eyes kept shifting beyond me, so much so that, in the end, I actually glanced over my shoulder. There was nothing there except a man dressed as Santa Claus, collecting money for charity, and people doing their last-minute Christmas shopping. When I turned to face Bracewell again, he was staring at the ground, and it was then that he said something strange: 'I really enjoyed our time together.'

At first I didn't know what he was referring to. Then, deciding he must be talking about the days we had spent out on the motorway, I simply, and rather lamely, said, 'So did I.'

I should have taken his words for what they were – an epitaph, a valediction.

Shortly afterwards, he disappeared into the crowds of people carrying rolls of wrapping-paper, and Christmas trees, and cones filled with roasted chestnuts.

About eighteen months later, while studying for my finals, I was called to the phone. To my surprise I heard Marie on the other end. I couldn't remember the last time she had rung me, and I knew at once that something must be wrong.

'How's Victor?' I said. 'Is he all right?'

She hesitated. 'It's not Victor. It's Simon Bracewell.'

The details were both sketchy and lurid, she warned me, and none of it had been confirmed by the authorities as yet, but she thought I ought to know. Apparently Bracewell had hidden in the undercarriage of a train bound for the Yellow Quarter. At some point he must have fallen on to the track, though, and he had been run over, either by the train in which he had stowed himself away or by the next train that came along. When the railway police found him, he was almost unrecognisable.

I couldn't think of a single thing to say.

I remembered how little we had said to each other during what Bracewell had called 'our time together'. We had talked about the holding station, and we had talked about school, but we had never mentioned the families we had been placed with, let alone those from which we had been taken. It had the feeling of a tacit agreement – an agreement we both instinctively abided by, but one which I'm not sure either of us really understood. Possibly we had a hunch that if the subject was raised we would have to admit to things that we would rather keep to ourselves. Or perhaps it had been too soon for us to make any sense of what had happened. He would often come over to my house, but I had never been to his, not in all the years we knew each other, not even once. The only member of his family I ever met was Lucky, the spaniel. Somewhere deep down, I suppose I must have suspected that my home life was easier than his, but this was just an intuition, and I made no attempt to look for evidence or proof. Our friendship had found its own level, its own idiom, and it would have been a mistake, I always felt, to try and tinker with any of that.

But I wondered, in the end, at how imperfectly I had known him.

If our border games had been practice, I thought, if they had been some kind of dress rehearsal for the real thing, then they hadn't served him very well. Had he been thinking of escaping even when he was a boy? Should I have seen it coming? Or had the games themselves given him the idea? I went back in my memory, but I could see no difference between his commitment and mine, nor could I remember which one of us had invented the game in the first place. I saw him staring at our names carved on the tree. *Like something in a cemetery.* Then I saw him standing in the precinct, tinny carols being piped through nearby speakers.

The way his mouth had locked. He seemed to have forgotten how to smile. Should I have guessed?

The Yellow Quarter, though. Why the Yellow Quarter, of all places?

'I'm sorry,' Marie said. 'He was your friend.'

'Yes.' I was quiet for a while. Then I said, 'What about you, Marie? How are you doing?'

'Oh, you know . . .'

In the silence that followed, I saw her with such clarity that she could have been standing right in front of me. A self-deprecating smile lifted on to her face, then just as swiftly dropped away. She lowered her head, and her black hair fell forwards against her cheek. Her mouth tilted, as though one side were heavier than the other. Like a pair of scales, I thought. The most beautiful pair of scales in the world. Despite the news I had received, a kind of joy burst through me. I felt that she'd come back to me. We were closer in those few seconds than we had been in years.

Towards the end of my time at university I was contacted by someone called Diana Bilal. She worked for the Ministry of Health and Social Security, she said, and she wanted to know if she could take me out for lunch.

We met in a country pub. Diana was already there when I arrived. I found her in the beer-garden at the back, her face lightly tanned, her brown hair twisted into a fashionable knot. From her voice I had imagined her to be an older woman, but she was young, no more than twenty-eight or -nine.

'We've been watching you.' She smiled at me across the rim of her wine-glass. Her eyes, which were dark, put me in mind of a secret glade in the middle of a forest. Thin gold spokes radiated outwards from the pupils.

She told me they were currently recruiting a new group of trainee assessment officers. When I asked her what the job entailed, she said it was hard to define, falling as it did somewhere between civil servant, psychologist and detective. I should think of it as a stepping-stone, though. Or a springboard, perhaps. I would find myself at the heart of an organisation whose responsibility it was both to guide and to protect society. She spoke briefly of her admiration for Michael Song, who had recently swept to power for the fourth time with a landslide majority. The Ministry worked closely with the government, she told me, which gave employees the opportunity to engage directly with the political process and to play a significant part in the shaping of the future. She named a starting salary that seemed generous. If I was interested, she said, they would be prepared to take me on as soon as I graduated. I would have to move to Pneuma. The capital.

I looked out into the idyllic sunlit garden. All I could see was Victor's book of shoes. I knew full well that Victor blamed the current political system for the destruction of both his family and his happiness. How could I possibly tell him I was thinking of becoming part of that very system?

Diana leaned forwards, her eyes appearing to offer shade and rest. 'Is something wrong?'

'My family,' I began, then faltered.

Her smile returned. 'You're worried about how they might react,' she said, 'which is perfectly understandable. The answer is, they'll never know. We'll arrange a phantom job for you. A front. Something they can be proud of.'

'I would have to lie to them,' I said slowly.

She looked at her right hand, which lay flat, palm down, on the lacy wrought-iron of the table. The fingers lifted, then dropped – one movement, over in a second. I sensed impatience in her for the first time, though she was doing her utmost to suppress it.

'If it's any help to you,' she said, 'we could offer them immunity.'

'Immunity?'

It was Diana's turn to look away into the garden, her fine-boned, agile face in profile. 'They would be exempted from all future testing. They would be granted the right to remain here permanently.' Reaching up, she made a minute adjustment to the wooden comb that held her hair in place. 'Their status would be guaranteed.'

'I didn't know that was possible,' I said.

She sent me a glance that was both ironic and cautionary, but said nothing.

I would be protecting them, I thought. They would be secure. For the rest of their lives. 'Could you give me a few days,' I said, 'to think it over?'

When Diana faced me again, the spokes in her eyes seemed to be revolving, as though some machinery inside her head had just been set in motion.

Shortly after joining the Ministry, I received an envelope in the internal mail marked *Confidential*. Inside, I found a document detailing the imminent transfer of a fifteen-year-old girl from the Red Quarter to the Yellow Quarter. Her name was Chloe Allen. I had been included in the transfer team, my role being described as 'observer'. A covering letter informed me that I would only accompany the relocation officers as far as the border, and I remember feeling relieved about that, the Yellow Quarter being a wild and brutal country by all accounts, where every kind of barbarity was perpetrated in the name of profit or enterprise, or even, sometimes, for no good reason at all. The fact that Bracewell had wanted to escape to such a place still puzzled me.

I met the transfer team in the Ministry car-park one Friday morning, and we drove south in a white minibus. Behind the wheel was Tereak Whittle, strongly built, laconic, in his mid-to-late-twenties. Pat Dunne sat beside him. With her startled eyes, she looked like someone who had become accustomed to witnessing tragedy. I put her age at about fifty. In relocation work it was standard procedure to pair a man with a woman; they brought complementary skills to the job.

We parked outside a two-storey red-brick house. It had a bay window on the ground floor and a small front garden paved in concrete. I stood behind Dunne and Whittle as they rang the bell. The door swung open to reveal a breathless middle-aged man in a green cardigan. He introduced himself as Mr Allen, then showed us into the living-room. While Dunne took out the transfer documents, Mr Allen sat on the edge of his chair and fidgeted. He had the curious habit of rubbing his right thumb against the palm of his left hand, as though trying to remove a stain.

'Should I call her yet?' he said at last.

Dunne glanced up. 'Please do.'

When Mr Allen opened the door, the girl was already on the other side. 'Oh.' He took a step backwards, then turned and smiled foolishly. 'Here she is. Here's Chloe.'

The girl moved past her father, into the middle of the room. Though she was probably no more than average height, she seemed larger than him. She took up all the space in that little house. She devoured the air.

Her eyes descended on Pat Dunne. 'Weren't you due here an hour ago?'

Dunne looked at her, but said nothing.

The girl shrugged. 'Better late than never, I suppose.' She went and stood in the bay window with her back to us, her blonde hair cut level with her shoulderblades and gleaming like gold leaf against the darkness of her jacket.

She didn't seem in the least upset or even disconcerted by the impending transfer. On the contrary, in putting on a black suit for the occasion, she appeared to be mocking the notion that she might be sad to leave. Or she had dressed for the funeral of that part of her life, maybe. Somehow she managed to give the impression that the whole thing had been her idea.

Leaving Dunne and Whittle to fill in the forms with Mr Allen, I went outside to stretch my legs. In the hallway I paused, glancing up the stairs. I could hear someone crying. Chloe's mother, I thought. Or a sister, perhaps. Backing away, I opened the front door and stood on the pavement. All the sunlight had gone. Clouds blundered across the sky, shapeless and clumsy, the colour of saucepans. I'm an observer, I kept telling myself. I'm only here to observe.

Towards midday we boarded the minibus again. The law required that Chloe travel in the back, separated from the rest of us by wire-mesh. Like a dog, she remarked as she climbed in. Pat Dunne corrected her. There was no shame attached to the transfer process, she said. It was simply a matter of doing what was best – for everyone. Chloe nodded but chose not to respond. She was gazing at the house where she had grown up, its curtains drawn against her, its front door closed. Was it relief she felt, or remorse? Or was it resentment?

As we crossed the river, heading north, I began to feel that I was in a draught. All the windows were shut, though. It didn't make sense. After a while the sweet smell of chewing-gum came to me, and I looked round. Chloe was sitting right up against the wire-mesh screen, her face just inches from my own.

'What,' she said.

I turned away from her. She began to blow on my neck again, but much more gently this time. I leaned forwards, my elbows propped on my knees.

'Is she bothering you?' Dunne asked.

'No,' I said. 'It's all right.'

Halfway through the afternoon we stopped for petrol. While Whittle filled the tank, Pat Dunne took Chloe to the toilet. The clouds had broken up, and I walked out across the forecourt, the warmth of the sun pressing itself evenly against my shoulder-blades. A tractor laboured through the field behind the petrol station, gulls fluttering in the air behind it like a handful of torn paper. Time drifted.

After a few minutes I became aware that Chloe was moving towards me, not directly, but in a series of contrived half-circles and hesitations as she feigned an interest in the scenery. She ended up standing beside me, facing the same way. She had unbuttoned her jacket, I noticed, revealing a tight white T-shirt underneath. Once again, her presence seemed to demand something from me. I felt it as a weight, a burden, as if she had fainted and I had caught her in my arms.

'Can you imagine what it's like to be transferred?' she said.

'I don't have to imagine it,' I told her. 'I've already been through it.'

'It was a long time ago, though, wasn't it? You've forgotten.'

I gave her a neutral look.

'You're just like the others.' Half-disappointed, half-provocative, she appeared to be trying to tempt me into some disloyalty or misdemeanour.

'And what are the others like?' I asked, keeping my voice light.

'Look at them.' She glanced across at Dunne and Whittle, who were standing shoulder to shoulder, studying the map. 'They can't think for themselves. They just do as they're told. They're drones.'

She was appealing to my vanity, of course, but I couldn't afford to react. Instead, I had to turn her remarks to my own advantage. *Yes*, my silence said, *I'm just like them. Yes, that's exactly what I am.*

Half an hour later, the road brought us up against the border, and once or twice, when the land fell away to the east, I caught my first ever glimpses of choleric territory. I was both horrified and enthralled by what I saw. There was an industrial complex whose cooling towers and pools of effluent covered an area of several square miles. There was a motorway, each of its eight lanes packed with speeding traffic. There were children on a building site, doing something to a cat.

'You think that's where I belong?' Chloe said.

Her mood had altered during the past few minutes. The reality of her destination had hit her for the first time. I could hear a brittleness in her voice, which I took to be the outer edges of a new and unexpected fear.

'You're wrong.' She let out a short bitter laugh. 'You are so fucking wrong.'

Dunne turned in her seat, speaking to me. 'This isn't bad. Sometimes they scream the whole way.'

I asked her how she dealt with that.

She opened the glove compartment and took out a pair of headphones. 'I got them from a friend of mine who works at the airport.' She grinned. 'Put these on, you can't even hear a plane taking off.'

'What do you think this is,' Chloe said, 'a game?'

The relocation officer spoke past me now, her voice hardening. 'I could give you an injection if you like. Then you'd sleep like a baby.'

By the time we reached the checkpoint it was five o'clock. Knowing how long it could take to cross into choleric territory – hours usually, what with all the harassment and provocation – and aware of the dangers of travelling in that country once darkness had fallen, Pat Dunne decided we should spend the night in the Red Quarter. We wouldn't be the only ones. A tourist settlement called the Border Experience had sprung up in the vicinity, with theme hotels, fast-food restaurants and souvenir shops. Sanguine people came from far and wide to climb the viewing platforms, each hoping for a brief taste of life on the other side. They all had their photos taken with a guard, and they all bought knick-knacks for family and friends back home. It was as if some of the cholerics' notorious materialism had seeped over the wall. On the way to our hotel, I stopped and looked in a shop window. There were ashtrays in the shape of watch-towers, and tiny, realistic attack dogs made of china. There were snowstorms with miniature replicas of no man's land inside. I saw tins of Border Shortbread and Border Fudge, and border guard dolls standing to attention in clear plastic cylinders. I saw mugs with words like 'Furious' or 'Livid' printed on them. My favourite souvenir was a T-shirt. On the front it said *I came I saw I lost my temper.* On the back, simply, *Welcome to the Yellow Quarter.*

At the Frontier Lodge, we took three rooms – one each for Whittle and me, and one for Dunne and Chloe Allen. My room overlooked the car-park – there, below me, was our minibus, dwarfed by tourist coaches – but if I leaned on the window-sill and looked to my left I had a clear view of the border. Two walls ran parallel to one another, about a hundred yards apart. Between them, in no man's land, I could see life-size versions of the souvenirs I had noticed earlier: watch-towers, searchlights, concrete crosses, rolls of barbed wire and a sandy, mined section known as a death strip (in aerial photographs, the border often had the look of a stitched wound). Despite the fact that nothing was happening, I couldn't seem to tear myself away. It was in these eerie halfway places that one was able to appreciate the full power and extent of the Rearrangement, and it inspired an inevitable reverence, a kind of awe.

As I stood by the window, I heard a click behind me and turned in time to see Chloe Allen slip into my room. I watched her lean back against the door until it closed. She was wearing the same outfit as before, only she had removed her black jacket and her shoes. She took a few quick steps towards me, stopping when she reached the bed.

'You're not supposed to leave your room,' I said.

'You don't mind, though,' she said, 'do you.'

Thinking I should fetch one of the relocation officers, I tried to edge past her, but she moved to block my way.

'Let's forget about the other two,' she said. 'Let's run away together.'

Her smile was sly but genuine.

Taking the hem of her T-shirt in both hands, she deftly lifted it over her head and tossed it on to the bed. She was wearing nothing underneath.

'They're pretty, aren't they,' she said.

'Chloe,' I said. 'Put your clothes back on.'

'You used my name.'

I attempted to edge past her again. This time she grabbed the front of my jacket. When I pulled free, she began to flail at me with loosely clenched fists. I caught hold of both her wrists and held her at arm's length. I realised I was laughing. I had no idea why I might be doing that. There was nothing remotely funny about the situation. Chloe was insulting me now, not loudly, but in a malignant, strangled whisper, as though her fury was such that she couldn't find her voice. I pushed her away from me, then turned and hurried out into the corridor.

I tried Pat Dunne's room first. She wasn't there. Whittle had disappeared as well. I stopped a couple who were making for the lift and asked if they happened to have seen a woman of about fifty with curly hair. The man thought he'd seen someone like that. She was further down the corridor, he said. By the drinks machine. She seemed to be having trouble with it, he added, grinning.

When I found Dunne, she was standing in front of the machine, banging the stainless steel with the heel of her hand. 'The fucking thing,' she said. 'It ate my money.'

She must have noticed the look I was giving her.

'I know what you're thinking,' she said, 'but listen. If you go into choleric territory, you have to act like them, or you don't survive.'

'Chloe Allen's in my room,' I said.

Something loosened in her face. 'What? When I left her, she was sleeping.'

'Well, she's awake now.'

When we burst into my room, it was empty. We found Chloe where she belonged, in the room she was sharing with Pat Dunne. She was lying on her side in bed and breathing steadily, the covers pulled up over her face, one strand of dark-gold hair forming an innocent question mark on the pillow. *What, me?*

Dunne looked at me sideways. I held her gaze.

'I didn't imagine it,' I said.

Back in my own room, I locked the door. The air smelled of perfume, its sweetness rendered more intense by the grey walls, the dull blond furniture. I opened the window, then sat down on the edge of the bed.

Let's run away together.

She had noticed me as soon as she walked into the living-room that morning. I had shown up on her adolescent radar. She'd identified me as the one unstable element, a weak point she could probe, exploit.

They're pretty, aren't they.

I decided not to risk another confrontation. I could already picture the sequence of looks that would appear on Chloe's face at the breakfast table as she tried to turn me into her accomplice, her jilted lover, or even, possibly, her rapist. I stayed upstairs until I saw Dunne and Whittle walk her across the car-park. Halfway to the minibus she looked up, scanning the hotel façade, but I stepped back from the window. I don't think she saw me. I waited until the minibus joined the queue of vehicles at the checkpoint, then I went down to the restaurant.

Dunne and Whittle didn't return until mid-afternoon. As we drove back to the capital, they told me about their day. No sooner had they crossed the border than Chloe became totally unmanageable. She had used the foulest language and hurled herself repeatedly against the wire-mesh. In the end they had been forced to sedate her. Whittle thought her behaviour had been triggered by my absence. He found my eyes in the rear-view mirror. 'You know, I think she took a shine to you.'

I laughed softly, then looked out of the window.

Pat Dunne turned to face me. 'What actually happened in your room last night?'

'Nothing,' I said. 'Nothing happened.'

Later, I wondered whether the transfer I had witnessed had been an elaborate test of my moral fibre, with Chloe playing the role of temptress, but then I dismissed the idea as overheated, a paranoid fantasy brought on by the pressures of my new working environment. It was also conceivable that the authorities had been reminding me of the commitment I had made. After all, my family might have been treated much as Chloe had been treated, had immunity not been granted. I couldn't be sure, though, and it wasn't the kind of question you could ask. And even if I had been able to ask, I knew what the answer would be. The authorities would claim that being sent out on the road as an observer was a crucial part of the induction process. I had been given a look at the 'nuts and bolts' of the job, they would tell me, a 'unique insight' into what life was like 'in the field'. I couldn't really have taken issue with any of that.

I had made a pact with the ruling powers, and they were as good as their word: Victor and Marie were left alone. No visits from state officials, no check-ups, no brown envelopes with scarlet peacocks stamped in the top left-hand corner. *They've obviously given up on us*, Victor would tell me over the phone with undisguised glee. *We're hopeless cases*. The way things turned out, though, Victor needed less protection than I had imagined.

I had only been at the Ministry for eighteen months when he succumbed to a massive stroke, his death occurring unexpectedly, and in slightly unusual circumstances.

Marie called me one Tuesday evening, and I caught a train to the coast the following day, but I didn't hear the full story until after the funeral, when everyone had gone home. I sat at the kitchen table, the jagged line of the cliff-edge showing halfway up the window. Marie opened a bottle of gin and poured us both a drink. She told me how she had woken early on the morning of Victor's death, and how the silence had a quality she didn't recognise. When she drew the curtains, she was almost blinded by the whiteness of the world outside. Snow had fallen in the night, three inches of it. To the east, the cliff rose in a glistening curve, smooth as a sugared almond. She went into Victor's room to tell him, but he wasn't there. Though she could just make out the imprint of his body on the counterpane, evidence of a nap the day before, it didn't look as if the bed had been slept in. She searched the cottage from one end to the other, upstairs and down. She couldn't find him anywhere. *Perhaps he's gone into the village*, she thought. And then she thought, *Perhaps he's gone on a journey*. After all, he'd done it before. He was always threatening to up sticks, make tracks. He peppered his conversation with words like 'vamoose' and 'skedaddle'. He was capable of almost anything, she said, in his wild old age.

'What do you mean, he'd done it before?' I asked.

But Marie didn't appear to have heard me.

She found him later that morning, she said, in the back garden. She had come across two shapes lying on the ground, one long and vaguely cylindrical, the other smaller, squarer. She approached the small object first. It seemed safer. She bent down and began to brush the snow away. A piece of pale-green leather showed beneath her fingers. The book of shoes. She knew then what the other shape was. Rising to her feet, she circled him slowly, as though he was asleep and she was trying not to wake him. She couldn't quite believe he was under there. Then, as she stood uncertainly beside him, she heard a quick, stealthy sound and, looking down, she saw that the snow had slipped, revealing the rim of an ear, already bloodless, and some brittle wisps of hair.

'Weren't you frightened?' I asked.

'I screamed.' She grinned at me. 'Have you ever screamed after it's snowed? It's the strangest thing. You feel like you're in a box. The kind of box a ring comes in, or a trumpet. A box lined with velvet.' Something lifted in her just then, and she became Marie again, Marie as she had been when I first saw her, framed in the living-room doorway of the house on Hope Street, mischievous, carefree. Then it dropped again, whatever it was, and she turned back into a woman I didn't really feel I knew. 'I screamed,' she said a second time, her voice without inflection now, 'but there was no one there. A ship on the horizon. A few gulls.'

Later, when we'd finished the bottle, I watched her run her index finger along the table, following the grain in the wood. Outside, the wind swirled against the walls. I was almost sure I could feel the cottage rock on its foundations.

'What will you do?' I asked her.

She shrugged. 'Stay here.'

'Won't you be lonely?'

'I'd be lonely if I moved,' she said.

At least no one would bother her, I thought as I travelled back to the city the next day. My head ached, and my mouth was strangely perfumed from all the gin I'd drunk. It had been a good funeral, though. People had made an effort to be there. At the graveside I had lifted my eyes from the coffin to see Mr Page standing across from me. His black suit looked immaculate – one would have expected nothing less – but something about him seemed out of character, abnormal, just plain wrong. After a while I realised that although his mouth was still doing its best to turn up at the corners it had crumpled in the middle – or to put it another way, *he no longer appeared to be smiling*. How I wish I could have caught Bracewell's eye right then! How I would love to have seen the expression on *his* face! The miraculous, the almost unimaginable moment had arrived, and sadness had brought it about, not anger, but it was too late to have any real impact on me, it was all too late.

If the authorities fulfilled their side of the bargain, so did I. I threw myself wholeheartedly into my new job. As far as Marie was concerned, I was a quality engineer – I looked at companies and came up with ways of improving their performance – but in fact I was employed by a branch of the civil service that was generally considered to be the government's right arm. I worked long hours, arriving home at nine or ten at night. Most weekends, too, I could be found in the office. I had almost no social life. I went out with a girl called Alex, who was a violinist, but she ended it after three months, claiming that we hardly saw each other. Somehow I didn't question the need for such sacrifices – or rather, I always seemed able to justify them to myself. It was up to people like me, I thought, to safeguard the values and integrity of the Red Quarter. Only later did I start to understand why I might have been pushing myself so hard. I *had* to fight for the system, I *had* to believe in it, or my removal from my family would all have been for nothing.

Over the years I rose through the ranks, from a glorified filing clerk to one of a handful of people whose responsibility it was to advise on all transfers, both into and out of the country, but the big promotion came just before my thirtieth birthday. During our lunch together in the beer garden, Diana Bilal had mentioned words like psychologist and detective, hoping to capture my imagination, perhaps, and yet the word that seemed to define my new position most accurately was 'diplomat'. A transfer was, in itself, a highly complex and delicate procedure – no one knew that better than I did – but, viewed in the wider context, it also became a matter of negotiation between two parties who didn't necessarily see eye to eye. I had to deal, on a regular basis, with people who held equivalent positions in other parts of the divided kingdom, and despite all the obvious differences in temperament and perception it was important to try and maintain good working relations. If I disputed one of their initiatives, it could be regarded as an example of Red Quarter impatience or naivety. If they disputed one of mine, I could just as easily see it as Blue Quarter dithering, Green Quarter cynicism or Yellow Quarter recklessness. The job required flexibility and patience as well as sound judgement, and for that reason, perhaps, it was seen by some as a stepping-stone into the world of politics.

Despite all the lies and the deprivation, despite the fact that my original existence seemed buried beneath layers of artifice – not for the first time the image of Russian dolls occurred to me, my lives concealed neatly, one inside the other – despite all that, my work gave me a real sense of fulfilment. If the Red Quarter was a contented and harmonious place in which to live, it was because we, the public servants, had made it so. What's more, I had done everything I could to ensure that my new family was taken care of.

Every now and then, though, especially as I left my twenties behind and moved into my thirties, I thought back to the day when the government official arrived at Thorpe Hall in his chauffeur-driven limousine, and I remembered how he had told us that we were special, and that the fate of the kingdom rested in our hands, and unease would flash through me like a blast of heat. Had I simply become what they had wanted me to become? Was I really so malleable?

Was I the man in the chauffeur-driven limousine?

I was sitting in my office one morning, working my way through a pile of recent case histories, when I heard a knock on the door. I glanced up. The door opened, and Mr Vishram's face appeared in the gap. 'Am I interrupting, Thomas?' Before I could reply, he had installed himself on the only other chair in the room, adjusting his glasses on the bridge of his nose with the tip of a forefinger.

As head of the Department of Transfer and Relocation, Ajit Vishram belonged to the select high-powered group that ran the Ministry. He was also a brilliant scholar, with several works of non-fiction to his name, all of which I had read. People said that he had the ear of the Prime Minister, which wouldn't have surprised me particularly, though I had never raised the subject with him. He openly admitted to a streak of melancholy – all writers are sanguine melancholics, he would declare with a dismissive gesture, as if something so obvious was hardly worth saying – an admission which, given his immediate working environment, was daring to say the least, but also cunningly pre-emptive. Though he must have been approaching sixty, he didn't have a single white hair, and if you chose to overlook the crescents of puckered, purplish skin beneath his eyes, his face was quite unmarked by age. He wore carefully tailored pale-grey suits made from a light, shiny fabric in which silk almost certainly played a part, and he carried himself with a quiet gravity that was often misconstrued as self-importance by those who didn't know him. He seemed to have no sense of the impression he created, however – or, if he did, then it simply failed to engage his interest. He was consistently both stately and impervious. I saw him as the ruler of a small, influential and untroubled country – which, in his rumoured closeness to Michael Song, he very nearly was, perhaps.

'Are you free for lunch tomorrow?' Vishram toyed idly with the power line that led to my computer. 'There's something I need to discuss with you.'

'Yes, I'm free,' I said. 'What's it about?'

He would meet me in the lobby, he said, at half-past twelve, then he rose from the chair and with a humorous glint in his dark eyes and an enigmatic nod he passed out of my office, his progress so smooth that I imagined for a second that he had castors instead of feet. Smiling faintly, I shook my head. The whole episode had been typical of him: he liked nothing better than to tantalise and then withdraw. My concentration broken, I stood up and moved over to the window.

The offices were situated in a part of the city from which the entire kingdom had once been governed. These days, though, everything looked different. The old metropolis had been divided so as to create four new capitals, and my building backed directly on to a section of the border. On the other side of the concrete wall lay the choleric capital, Thermopolis. Sitting at my desk, I could often hear attack dogs barking, and once, when I was working late, I had been startled by the sudden brittle chatter of machine-gun fire. I gazed down into the narrow strip of no man's land. To the left, the border moved in a north-westerly direction, incorporating a square where people used to get drunk on New Year's Eve. The famous admiral now stood in a mined wasteland, peering out, one-eyed, over a tangle of barbed wire. To my right, the border ran across an iron bridge and then turned east along the south bank of the river. The bridge itself had been fortified, with watch-towers at either end and a steel dragnet underneath. Sometimes, in fine weather, I would lean on the window-sill and train my binoculars on the gardens that lay just to the east of the bridge, and I would study the inhabitants of Thermopolis as they gesticulated, insulted one another, and, more often than not, came to blows, and because I couldn't hear anything they said I found it curiously soothing, like watching mime.

As I stared out of the window, my gaze lost its focus and turned inwards. It had been a tricky sort of day from the very beginning. My alarm clock had failed to go off, and I jerked awake at five-past six, which was twenty minutes later than usual. I had been in the middle of a dream, but the dream had faded, leaving nothing except the dimly remembered sensation of a cold wind blowing against my skin, and even then, still half-asleep, I knew that the partial and elusive nature of that memory would frustrate me, and that I would carry that feeling around with me all day. There was something about Vishram's proposal that reminded me of the dream. They shared a sketchy quality, a seemingly deliberate ambiguity, as though they belonged to the same family of experiences. I swung back into the room, trusting that if I plunged into my paperwork once more, if I buried these ambiguities beneath the weight of familiar problems, then I could forget again. I didn't hold out too much hope, though. What was it about these hints and glimpses that disturbed me so?

Seen from above, Pneuma looked a little like an hour-glass, the narrowest point of which measured scarcely a mile across, and it was here, right in the city centre in other words, and a leisurely fifteen-minute stroll from my office, that I had been lucky enough to find a flat.

On leaving work that day, I set off through the park, as usual. Most people moved about on foot, or else rode bicycles. Cars were more or less extinct. As for the underground, it had been deemed both antiquated and unsafe, not to mention bad for the health, and the authorities had shut it down years ago. Our city was a clean, quiet place in which snatches of music could often be heard. Taking off my jacket, I folded it over my arm. It was a warm evening, and groups of students sat in casual circles on the grass. Rows of green-and-white-striped deckchairs faced down the slope, awaiting collection by the park-keeper. To the west, and back-lit by the setting sun, I could see the sheer pale concrete of the Hilton, its rooftop bristling with all manner of aerials and lightning conductors. The Blue Quarter's capital – Aquaville – lay just beyond, with its rheumatic population and its network of canals.

On nearing the north side of the park, I turned down a narrow passageway. It ran between two walled gardens, under a block of flats and out into a cul-de-sac so small and well concealed that hardly anybody knew it existed. Stafford Court stood at the far end, its entrance flanked by two miniature bay trees in square black tubs. As I walked into the lobby, the caretaker's front door opened. Kenneth Loames was an amiable, if slightly cloying man – the human equivalent of glue, I sometimes felt, or chewing-gum; once he made contact, he was almost impossible to dislodge. Normally I slipped by unnoticed, or tried to, but on this occasion, unfortunately, he had spotted me and, still more ominous, he had a subject, he said, that he would like to raise with me. I waited by the lift as Loames searched for the right phrasing.

'I've got flies,' he said at last.

I looked at him. 'I'm sorry?'

'In my living-room. There are flies.' He gestured vaguely towards the half-open door behind him.

'It has been very mild,' I said, pushing the call button on the lift.

Loames stood beside me, gazing benignly at the illuminated numbers. 'You've not noticed any flies, though, Mr Parry? In your flat?'

79

'I can't say I have.'

Loames was nodding to himself. 'So,' he said. 'Busy at the moment?'

'Pretty busy, yes.'

His head angled in my direction, eyes sharpening a little. He asked all the usual questions, but I could often sense others lurking just beneath, like predatory fish. He seemed to suspect that there were things he wasn't being told, and with some justification – in my case, at least.

The lift doors finally slid open.

'Well,' Loames said, 'if you should see anything –'

'I'll let you know.' I stepped into the lift and pressed the button for my floor. 'Have a good evening, Mr Loames.'

When I walked into my flat, the phone was ringing. Thinking it might be the caretaker again, I picked up the receiver and rather wearily said, 'Yes?'

There was a soft pause. 'Thomas? Are you all right?'

The voice belonged to my girlfriend, Sonya Visvikis. She had called to tell me that the people we were supposed to be seeing the following night had cancelled. We could still have dinner, though, just the two of us – or did I think that was a bit dull? Not at all, I said. Actually, I'd prefer it. I could be with her by eight. I paused, thinking she might say something else, but the line fell quiet. In the silence, I heard a faint whine and I glanced round, first one way, then the other, expecting to see one of Loames's flies, but there was nothing there. The noise must have come from outside. A distant ambulance, perhaps. A gust of cold wind from my dream.

'Are you sure you're all right?' Sonya said.

'Yes, I'm fine. Why?'

'I don't know. You sound different.'

'I just ran into Mr Loames,' I said. 'He's got flies, apparently.' Sonya laughed.

'He wanted to know if I'd got any,' I said.

By now Sonya was laughing so hard that she could barely speak.

We had only been seeing each other for about four months,

but I had loved her laughter the moment I heard it. It was voluptuous, somehow, and resonant, so much so that I often imagined she had a musical instrument inside her, something exquisitely crafted, one of a kind.

After the phone-call was over, I cooked myself a light supper, then I moved to the sofa by the window and tried to read. I couldn't concentrate, though. My head buzzed, as if with interference. I had a feeling of incompleteness, of things being just out of reach. Towards nine o'clock I put on my jacket, picked up my keys and left the flat, thinking a walk might help me to relax.

The air that closed around me as I stepped through the glass doors had a dense, humid quality I would never have associated with October. An Indian summer, people were calling it. The first in years. I walked down the street, then along the passageway, and came out into the park, the deckchairs all stacked away now, the students gone. I hesitated for a moment, looking down the path. In the distance, I could see a man standing quite still, his face turned towards me. Afraid it might be Loames again, I struck out across the grass. *Loames* . . . I suddenly realised that the name had a melancholic aspect to it. The way it referred to the earth, even the lugubrious vowels. Extraordinary I hadn't noticed it before. Maybe one day his name would appear on my desk, on a list of people being recommended for a transfer, and Stafford Court would have to find a new caretaker.

A few minutes later, I emerged in front of a building that used to be the palace, its austere façade reminding me, as always, of cold ash, then I walked slowly westwards, through a square of cream-coloured houses with black balconies, before turning south towards the river. By the time I reached the embankment I was sweating lightly under my clothes. I leaned on the stone parapet and looked out over the water. Had I been able to swim across, I would have found myself in the Blue Quarter. There had been a bridge here once, but it had been dismantled during the Rearrangement. Only bridges that complemented the partitioning of the city had survived. In the Red Quarter, for instance, we had several of our own, since we had been granted territory on both sides of the river, but in stretches where the river itself had become the border all the bridges had been destroyed. The roads that had once led to them stopped at the water's edge, and stopped abruptly. They seemed to stare into space, no longer knowing what they were doing there or why they had come. During my early twenties I was gripped by the sense of history that emanated from such places; they were like abandoned gateways, entrances to forgotten worlds. Also, of course, I felt that I had stumbled on a physical embodiment of my own experience. There were bridges down inside me too. There was the same sense of brutal interruption.

I walked on, passing through the muted pools of light that lay beneath each of the street lamps. Like many people of my age, I'd had two names, two lives. Once, I had been someone called Matthew Micklewright, but that person no longer existed, and I wasn't even curious about him now. It was just too long ago, too remote – too *unlikely*. What's the point of clinging to something that has gone? What good does it do? That old name had become as hollow and empty as a husk. A name deprived of breath, of meaning. A name without a face. And then the night when my life began again . . . A strange beginning. Soldiers, bright lights. The cold. And me being lifted, as if by surgeons, into a new world – and crying probably, though I couldn't remember that. But every birth is merciless, perhaps. Then the lorry, the train, and all the hardships and uncertainties of the holding station –

I put a hand on the parapet, my heart seeming to bounce against the inside of my ribs. The dream I had woken with that morning had come back in its entirety. I had been walking in a sunlit garden. A strong wind pushed at the trees and bushes, and the grass rippled on the ground. It was cold in the garden – though like someone who had drunk too much I couldn't feel it. Or if I could, then only as a delicious extra layer to my skin. For a long time that was all I knew – the sunlight on the grass, the wind, the ceaseless rushing sound of leaves . . . And then I saw a boy with light-brown hair standing motionless beneath a tree. He didn't seem to have noticed me, despite the fact that I was walking towards him. He didn't see me. Not even when I stood in front of him. He was naked, I realised. Somehow this hadn't registered until that moment. I looked all around, but couldn't find his clothes. The tree shuddered in the wind. The trunk wasn't visible, nor were the branches. Only a huge murmuring cloud of leaves, which seemed held together by some super-natural force.

Staring out across the water, I trembled, as if the cold wind of the dream had jumped dimensions and was in the world with me. The boy was Jones. Even though he had light-brown hair. Even though he wasn't standing on one leg.

Jones.

Like me, he would be in his thirties by now. Was it true that he'd been sent to an asylum? What had become of him? Had he survived?

The following day I met Vishram in the lobby, as arranged, and we took a tram across town. In fifteen minutes we were standing in a grand but decaying square only a few hundred yards from the border. Though Vishram had stepped out on to the pavement with an air of sublime equanimity, he had brought me, at lunchtime, to the very heart of Fremantle, the red-light district. Here you could find establishments that catered to every taste, no matter how esoteric or degenerate, venery being the one vice to which those of a sanguine disposition were known to be susceptible.

Vishram paused outside a house that looked residential, then climbed the steps and pressed an unmarked bell. The door clicked open. A cool, tiled hallway stretched before us. The staircase curved up towards another door which stood ajar and through which came, in muffled form, the familiar hum and clatter of a crowded restaurant. Once upstairs, we were escorted into a space that skilfully contrived to be both generous and intimate. Lamps with scarlet shades stood on each table, de-flecting attention from the height of the ceiling, while curtains of the same colour framed the three tall windows that overlooked the square. The waitresses wore white blouses and black skirts. They were all young and good-looking, and at least two of them knew Vishram by name.

'I see you're a regular,' I observed once our food had arrived.

He didn't look up from the wood pigeon that he was preparing to dissect. 'They make an exceptional *crème brûlée*,' he said. 'It's a weakness of mine.'

'I didn't know you had any weaknesses.'

He laid down his knife and fork, then pressed his napkin to his mouth. Above the folds of crisp white linen, his eyes were amused, benevolent, and ever so slightly long-suffering.

'There's a conference in three weeks' time,' he said. 'We're thinking of sending you along.'

'It's been a while since I attended a conference. I always seem to be too busy.'

'It's in the Blue Quarter,' Vishram added casually.

I reached for the mineral water and poured myself another glass. I was aware of having to concentrate on every movement I made, no matter how small or insignificant it might seem. My lungs felt oddly shallow.

'The Blue Quarter,' I said.

Vishram smiled faintly. 'You would miss Rearrangement Day,' he went on, 'but they'll probably organise some kind of celebration over there.' Lowering his eyes, he brushed a few breadcrumbs from the tablecloth with the backs of his fingers. 'Though with phlegmatics, of course, one can never be too sure.'

I watched the bubbles rising in my glass. What was being proposed was both a privilege and an affirmation of the Department's faith in me – not many were trusted with a visit to another part of the divided kingdom – and, though I had thought the opportunity might present itself at some point, I certainly hadn't expected it so soon.

The Blue Quarter.

The words glowed inside my head, buzzing sleepily like neon. I was breathing a little easier now. Was I *supposed* to feel like this? What *was* I supposed to feel like? I glanced at Vishram, but his deceptively blank gaze was fixed on one of the more sinuous waitresses as she threaded her way among the tables.

From a political standpoint, the Blue Quarter had always

been a laughing-stock. The past fifteen years had seen thirteen different administrations, each one a coalition, the result being that even decisions taken at the highest levels were constantly reversed and nothing ever got done. As for the citizens themselves, they were reputed to be gentle and unflappable, if a little slow. They had a mystical side as well, by all accounts. In ancient times, the Druid would have been phlegmatic. So would the witch. But in the end I preferred not to generalise, and despite the fact that my job required me to group people together I somehow knew the reality of the Blue Quarter would be more subtle and complex than I'd been led to believe.

'I would need a thorough briefing,' I said at last.

Vishram's eyes reverted to my face, and I thought I saw the shadow of something perverse swimming in their dark-brown depths, but then it was gone and there was only receptivity – the composed, indulgent look of someone who spends his life listening to problems and dispensing advice.

'Of course. But you'd be willing to go?'

I looked at him. Was this a trick question?

'Some people don't trust themselves,' Vishram said. 'They think they'd be tempted in some way – or altered. What's more, there's the old superstition about the border-crossing itself, that one might be mysteriously depleted by the experience, that one might lose a part of oneself – that one might suffer injury or harm.'

Vishram directed his gaze towards the windows. Compared to the room in which we sat, with its intimate lighting and its clandestine atmosphere, the trees in the middle of the square seemed wan, over-exposed.

'It always reminds me of how primitive people were said to feel about being photographed,' he went on. 'They thought their souls were being stolen.'

I leaned back in my chair.

'But you're not worried about any of that,' Vishram said.

It was more of an assertion than an enquiry, and I just held his gaze and smiled.

He nodded. 'Aquaville,' he said. 'It's supposed to be a magical city. The canals, the Turkish baths, the water-taxis . . . Apparently they have an indoor ocean too. You can go surfing half a mile below the surface of the earth.'

I examined Vishram closely for a moment – his manicured fingernails, his elegant yet portly physique. 'You've never been surfing, have you?'

He appeared to place a cough inside his fist.

'No,' I said. 'I thought not.'

That night I cycled over to Sonya's place on the south side of the river. I had met her in a park in June, at the evening performance of an opera. She had walked up to me at the interval, her beauty as classic and unforced as the single string of pearls she was wearing and the slingbacks that she carried carelessly in her left hand. We knew someone in common, she said. A professor at the university. When she put her glass of wine down, the shape of her fingers showed in the condensation. That, oddly, was the decisive moment. Looking at that glass, I could imagine exactly how we might touch each other. I asked if I could see her again, and she wrote her phone number on the back of my programme. Within a few days, we had met twice, and on our third date, after dinner at a jazz club, she took me back to her flat and we made love. Like everybody else I had been close to, she believed I was a quality engineer – *whatever that is*, as she would always add with a crooked smile. I thought at first that she might be a journalist, or even an actress – with her olive skin and dark-brown hair she resembled a famous film star of the previous century – but she worked at the Public Library, in the rare books department. She didn't make much money. I was happy to help her with her everyday expenses, though – buying clothes, paying bills, and so on. Since we both valued our independence, we had kept our own flats, but we tried to see each other at least two or three times a week. She had been married once, when she was in her early-twenties, but she'd had no children. Since she was older than I was, almost thirty-seven, I sometimes wondered what kind of future she imagined for herself, but she had given me no indication that she was dissatisfied with the way things were going. I didn't find it difficult to picture the children we might have together – skinny, dark-eyed, with a laughter as rich and rare as hers.

I waited until we were settled in her living-room with a bottle of chilled white wine, then I told her my news. 'Sonya, they want me to go to a conference next month. It's in the Blue Quarter.'

She reached for her wine and drank. It was another humid night, and all the windows were open. The murmur of voices floated up from the other flats that gave on to the light-well.

'Is that why you sounded so strange when I spoke to you last night?' she said.

'No. I didn't know about it then.'

A shriek of laughter came from somewhere below.

Sonya was staring down into her glass. I had wanted her to be excited for me – after all, to be chosen for such a trip was an honour, whatever your profession – and her muted reaction caught me off guard.

'I've heard stories,' she said. 'About what it's like, I mean.'

'So have I,' I said. 'It's damp. Everyone's ill all the time. I'll probably get flu.'

She didn't even smile.

I reached across the table. Her gaze shifted to my hand, which now covered hers. 'It's a conference,' I said gently. 'It's just work.'

'You don't understand,' she said, and her chin lifted and she looked away from me, into the room.

'Sonya . . .' I rose to my feet and walked round the table. Standing behind her, I wrapped her in my arms and then just held her. Cool air from the window moved across my back.

'I'm sorry,' she murmured. 'I don't know what's wrong with me.'

'It's all right,' I said.

'I'm being stupid.'

'No.'

I had heard stories about the Blue Quarter too – tales of enchantment and possession, of pagan ritual, of bizarre religious cults – but I had heard them from relocation officers, and they had always been notorious for their lurid imaginations. It was partly due to the privilege of their position. They travelled to other quarters on a regular basis. They saw places no one else saw. They could invariably command an audience willing to hang on their every word. But it was also a result of their constant exposure to other people's trauma. The stories they told were defence mechanisms, safety valves, ways of deflecting or releasing pressure. Their humour was gallows humour. The old joke about relocation officers was that they themselves often had to be relocated. They crossed too many borders. They burned out. It was an occupational hazard. I remembered what Vishram had said at lunch. *One might lose a part of oneself. One might suffer injury or harm.*

Sonya carefully detached herself from me and, tilting her head sideways, touched the back of her wrist to her right eye. Then she looked up at me and smiled.

'It'll be amazing,' she said.

I rose out of sleep just after three o'clock, my head cluttered with disturbing images. Not wanting to wake Sonya, I eased out of bed and crept through the darkness to her bathroom. I drank some cold water from the tap, then turned to the window. A full moon hung in an almost cloudless sky. The street below was quiet. I saw three girls stop outside the building opposite. They talked for a while, then I heard the word 'goodnight', and two of them walked away. Alone now, the third girl leaned close to the building's entrance with her head bent, her neck white in the moonlight. She must be having trouble with her keys, I thought. Eventually the door gave, and she disappeared inside. I had been watching with a feeling of nostalgia, even though I had never seen the girl before, and I realised I was thinking of Marie, and how she would have stood outside the house on Hope Street in much the same way, tired certainly, perhaps a little drunk as well, trying to fit her key into the lock. Once through the front door, she would climb the creaky staircase in the dark. As she crossed the landing, she would knock against the linen chest that jutted from the wall, and I would hear her swear under her breath. *Fuck*, I would whisper, imitating her. I'd be grinning. In the morning she would pull her skirt and pants down on one side and show me the mauve-and-yellow rose that had bloomed on her hip like a tattoo. Was it really eighteen months since I had seen her last?

I had been due to attend a seminar on the south coast, and on the spur of the moment I had phoned Marie and asked if I could stay with her. I remembered a cliff-top path, a bright November day. Skylarks were chattering high above, black splinters in the sky's blue skin. The sea sprawled to my left, hundreds of feet down, its waves fluttering like gills. My blood felt fresher for the walk. Then I came over a rise and saw the cottage below, a roof of dark slates, smoke coiling upwards from the chimney and merging with the air. Even at a distance I could see Marie in the front garden, the only figure in a vast panoramic landscape. How solitary her life had become, I thought, now Victor was no longer there.

I drew closer, then stood still and watched her. Bending from the waist, her hair hanging loose on both sides of her face, she was weeding a bed of irises. At last she seemed to sense my presence. She looked round, then straightened slowly, squinting into the light. I raised a hand and waved.

'Oh Tom. It's you.' She walked over in her clumsy wellingtons, touching her right sleeve to her nose. When she embraced me, she laid her head against my shoulder, and I could feel her voice vibrating in my collar-bone. 'I forgot you were coming. I mean, I forgot it was today.'

I stood back. 'You look good, Marie. You look really well.'

'Do I?' She glanced down at her cardigan, which was darned in several places and missing a button, then her eyes lifted again. 'Look at you, though. How much did that coat cost?'

Later that day I sat at the kitchen table with her, drinking tea. She told me she had got a job at the local railway station, in the ticket office. Victor would have approved, I said. She nodded absently, and wrapped both hands around her mug, as if to extract warmth from it. Her bottom lip had split down the middle, and the shine had gone from her hair. She would be forty now. It was hard to believe.

'You can't imagine how anyone can live like this,' she said.

I smiled faintly.

'Things happen here. You'd be surprised.' She had become defiant, as though my presence had ignited some aspect of her that had been lying dormant, just barely smouldering. 'I shouldn't tell you this – he made me promise not to – but I don't suppose it matters now.'

He. Our father.

At breakfast one morning, she told me, Victor had come up with an idea. He had decided to walk round the border. All the way round. He wanted to see exactly where he had been living for the past twenty years. He was curious about 'the dimensions of the cage'. And they had done it, the two of them. They had walked nearly seven hundred miles. It had taken them most of the summer.

'I didn't know,' I said.

'We crossed the border too,' Marie said. 'Illegally.'

She seemed to relish the look that appeared on my face. She had startled me out of my complacency. At the same time, I had a sense of how comprehensively I had deceived her over the years. It had never occurred to her that I might work for the Ministry. She just saw me as someone who obeyed the rules.

'We crossed it in broad daylight,' she said. 'We walked right through. There was no one there.'

'Where was it?'

She named the place. I knew it as a marshy stretch of country, bleak and windswept – the only border we shared with the Green Quarter.

'There must have been some kind of wall,' I said.

'There was. But it had a hole in it.'

'A hole?'

'A gap,' Marie said. 'I don't know what had happened. Maybe the wall had collapsed. Or maybe it was being repaired. I don't know. But there was definitely a gap. We couldn't believe it at first. After everything we'd heard about national security and the integrity of the state. We thought we must be seeing things.' Her eyes slanted towards the window – a thin stripe of grey-green sea, the grey sky above. She smiled. 'We walked towards it, and we walked really slowly, as if it was alive and we might startle it. Then we just climbed through.'

'Both of you?' I said.

She nodded. 'I remember standing on the other side. It looked the same, of course – but it *felt* different. Completely different. Like the moon or something. There was this moment when we looked all round and then our eyes met and we started laughing.' She shook her head, as if what had been stored there still astonished her. 'We jumped up and down and shouted things and danced, even though there wasn't any music. We behaved like mad people. You should have seen us.'

You should have seen us.

'Thomas?'

I jumped, the breath rushing out of me. Sonya stood in the doorway. She was naked, her face in shadow, one foot turned slightly inwards. I had gone so deep into my memory that I had forgotten where I was.

'I woke up and you weren't there,' she said. 'I thought for a moment you'd gone home.'

I smiled and shook my head. 'I wouldn't do that.'

She moved into my arms. 'You're cold.'

'I couldn't sleep, that's all.'

'You've been working too hard. When you come back, maybe we should go away – a long weekend . . .'

I held her tightly, kissed her hair.

'Come on, my darling,' she said. 'Come back to bed.'

On the Wednesday before I left for the Blue Quarter, I went for a walk, thinking I might sit somewhere quiet and read for an hour. I crossed the main road, making for the park that lay to the west of the office. Though it was overcast, the sky seemed to have retreated a great distance from the earth, and I had a feeling of lightness, almost of vertigo, as if there was too much space above my head, as if I might fall upwards. I passed through the park gates and took a path that curved around the south side of the lake. A blackbird spilled rapid, trembling drops of sound into the air. Something about the way a willow hung its branches over the water, leaving its trunk exposed, reminded me of a woman washing her hair in a sink. Odd thoughts. I stood still and stared up at the clouds, my eyes pushing into the greyness. I was trying to detect a surface, gauge a depth. Impossible, of course.

Following our lunch in Fremantle, Vishram had invited me back to his office, where he loaded me down with reading material. He always insisted on thorough preparation, no matter what the assignment, but I had never seen him quite so openly enthusiastic. As I turned to leave, my forearms already aching with the burden of articles, essays and treatises, he murmured, *Wait, Thomas, I forgot something,* and consulting his shelves again, he selected yet another volume, *Nightmare in Pneuma* by D.W.B. Forbes-Mallet, a high-ranking Green Quarter diplomat who had attended the inaugural cross-border conference. During the past fortnight I had got through a number of books – among them, an introduction to phlegmatic cooking called *The Cautious Kitchen*, with recipes for bread-and-butter pudding and fish pie, and a monograph on the mating habits of the sea horse – but now I had *Nightmare in Pneuma* tucked under my arm. Given the title, it was no surprise to discover that the first conference had gone badly wrong, with gangs of drunken Yellow Quarter delegates running amok in the streets, and a Green Quarter delegate jumping to his death from the roof of his hotel. He had been a colleague of the author's, and a good friend. It was almost as if the authorities had brought everyone together in order to illustrate the wisdom of their grand design, as Forbes-Mallet rather sourly observed.

I sat down on a vacant bench and stared out over the lake – the ducks with their black velvet necks and their enquiring heads, the colour of the grass enhanced by the cloud cover, the air shifting at my back . . . A young couple walked past, arm in arm, and I overheard a fragment of their conversation. *It'll be great,* the girl was saying. *You'll see.* The future tense, I thought. The tense that comes naturally to sanguine people. Though everything was normal, it seemed at the same time to be heightened in some way, not unlike the feeling one might have during an eclipse.

'How's the reading going?'

I looked up to see Vishram standing on the path, then I glanced down at the Forbes-Mallet, which lay unopened on my lap. 'It's going well,' I said, 'though I've only read about half of what you gave me, I'm afraid.'

'I did get rather carried away.' Vishram turned his eyes towards the sky. Were the atmospheric conditions affecting him as well? 'I was just going back to the office,' he said. 'Would you care to join me? Or perhaps you're not ready?'

'No, I'd be happy to join you.'

As we set off round the lake, I thought of our recent visit to Fremantle. It was now my conviction that Vishram had had affairs with several of the waitresses and, intending to draw him on the subject, I told him how much I had enjoyed the restaurant. We should go again, I said, on my return. Maybe next time I would try the famous *crème brûlée*, I added, remembering the white china pot that had been placed in front of him, the lid of melted caramel like a small round pane of amber glass. Vishram nodded, his usually opaque eyes lighting up at the prospect, but he seemed disinclined to speak.

Or perhaps not *affairs* exactly, I thought. Because, in the end, what the restaurant had reminded me of more than anything was a brothel – refined, discreet, infinitely sophisticated, but a brothel nonetheless – and I suddenly wondered if the whole establishment might not be a front, and all the talk of ambience and cuisine – of *crème brûlée*! – an elaborate euphemism, a code.

'And how's Miss Visvikis?'

Vishram's question dropped into my thoughts with a studied innocence, a certain delicious incongruity, and he smiled at me across his shoulder as though perfectly aware of the effect he had just created. As far as I knew, though, his many gifts did not include mind-reading. I had introduced him to Sonya at a party fund-raiser in August, and he had spent the best part of an hour discussing book-binding with her – or so he'd told me afterwards.

'She's very well,' I said. 'She's worried about me going away, of course. I think she's a bit jealous too, in a way.'

'That's only natural.' Vishram paused. 'Is she still working at the library?'

'Yes, she is. Though she'd like a change, I think.'

'Really?' Vishram lowered his eyes almost coyly. 'It just so happens that I'm looking for a research assistant.'

One of his impeccable eyebrows arched, as if he had just made a joke, but at his own expense. He was starting work on a new book, he told me. He had been commissioned to write the official biography of Michael Song.

'I can't think of a better person for the job,' I said.

Vishram thanked me for the kind words.

With so much of his time taken up by the Ministry, he went on, and by other related obligations, he doubted he would be able to carry out all the research himself. Perhaps I could mention it to Sonya, when I saw her next. He felt sure that she'd be equal to the task. Of course he wouldn't be able to pay very handsomely –

'I'll ask her,' I said. 'You never know.'

On Friday afternoon I reported to Jasmine Williams in Personnel for a briefing on my forthcoming trip. When I walked into her office she looked up and smiled. She had altered her hairstyle since I had last seen her, the neat cornrows drawing attention to the natural elegance of her head. Jasmine and I had gone out together for a while, when we were both trainees. She'd had a lovely unruffled quality about her, the ability to view any mishap with a kind of amused tolerance. She'd also had the most beautiful body I had ever seen, with breasts that tilted upwards, as if in eagerness, and skin that smelled like butter and sugar melting slowly in a pan. She had been posted to a branch of the Ministry up north, though, which meant we could only see each other at weekends, and after several months we had gradually drifted apart.

'So,' she said. 'This time it's you.'

'Yes.' I moved across the room towards her. 'I like your hair.'

'Thanks.'

As I lowered myself into a chair, there was a knock at the door

94

and Vishram appeared. 'I hope neither of you mind if I sit in on the meeting?'

Jasmine smiled at me again, a little more inscrutably this time. 'We don't mind, do we?'

'Not at all,' I said.

Vishram seated himself at the back of the room, against the wall. Crossing one leg over the other, he took off his glasses and began to polish the lenses. I would be issued with a standard business visa, Jasmine told me, valid for up to seventy-two hours. The visa permitted travel between the Red Quarter and the Blue Quarter, one journey in each direction. It was a stipulation of this type of visa that contact with local people be kept to an absolute minimum. Obviously the system worked on a trust basis – but then presumably I had earned that trust, she added with a glance in Vishram's direction, or I wouldn't have been selected in the first place. I should remember that the laws of both countries were equally specific about the dangers of psychological contamination. She need hardly say that the kingdom had been divided for its own good, and that it was in no one's interest to jeopardise twenty-seven years of comparative equilibrium.

'What about contact with other delegates?' I said.

'No restrictions.' Jasmine consulted her computer. 'We haven't mentioned medication.'

'Medication?'

'As you might imagine, things are a bit different over there. The pace of life is slower, but it's also more unpredictable. There's more indecision, more ambiguity. If you like, we can issue you with medication that will help you to adapt.'

'No, I don't think so,' I said.

Jasmine watched me carefully.

'I want to experience the Blue Quarter for myself,' I went on. 'I want to see it as it is. Not diminished in any way – or enhanced, for that matter.'

'All right.' Jasmine looked beyond me. 'Mr Vishram? Anything to add?'

Vishram held his glasses at arm's length to check the lenses for smears, but it seemed that he had done a good job. 'No,' he said, putting the glasses back on. 'I think you've covered everything.'

'Don't let the rules and regulations suffocate you, Tom,' Jasmine said. 'They're just there to provide you with a framework within which you can operate quite freely.'

'Hopefully,' Vishram said, rising to his feet, 'it will be an experience that you never forget.'

'You make it sound rather daunting,' I said.

Vishram merely smiled and turned away. On reaching the door, though, he paused, and I assumed he was going to offer me one last piece of advice or reassurance. Instead, he returned to an earlier and unrelated topic of conversation.

'Don't forget to have a word with Sonya, will you,' he said, 'or this wretched book of mine will never get written.'

THREE

I stepped out of the train just after midday on Monday. A shiver shook me as I stood on the platform, and I wrapped my overcoat more tightly around me. The cloth felt clammy to the touch. Though it prided itself on its spas, its Turkish baths, and its swimming pools, Aquaville had never enjoyed a healthy reputation. In recent years it had been ravaged by flu epidemics, and locals were always falling prey to arthritis and pneumonia. Some argued that the maladies originated in the phlegmatic character itself, its innate quality being cold and damp, but others believed that the Blue Quarter's first administration should shoulder the blame. In adding some two hundred miles of new waterways to the canals and lakes that existed prior to the Rearrangement, it stood accused of actually altering the city's climate. I felt fortified by the vitamin supplements Sonya had given me at the weekend. Even so, it would be a miracle if I didn't come down with something.

I had been told that a conference official would meet me, but I couldn't see anybody waiting at the barrier. Phlegmatic people had never been known for their efficiency – and besides, the train was at least an hour late. I decided to make my own way to the hotel. According to Jasmine, it was only ten minutes on foot. Picking up my case, I set off towards the exit. I had walked no more than ten yards when a man seemed to rise up out of the crowd beside me. He had moist pale-green skin and a dark pencil moustache, and his black hair had been smoothed down with some kind of oil or pomade. He thrust what felt like a postcard into my pocket.

'Something that might interest you.'

He spoke out of the corner of his mouth, his face angled away from me and lifted a fraction, as if he was scouring the busy concourse for someone he knew. Then he was gone – like a swimmer caught by a rip-tide, or a drowning man being taken down for the third time.

I walked on. The incident had lasted no more than a few seconds, and yet the contents of my mind had been upended. My thoughts flew past me in a jumbled state, like clothes in a tumble-dryer, and a light sweat had surfaced on my forehead and my chest. I didn't look at the card. I didn't even reach into my pocket to check it was still there. It seemed important to keep moving, to behave as though nothing had happened.

Outside the station the crowd thickened and grew sluggish, and I paused once again to take in my surroundings. The streets were narrower than I had expected, and many of the buildings had been allowed to fall into disrepair. Of the several hotels that I could see, for instance, only one – the Tethys – had been painted at all recently. There was a waterway to my right, with taxis moored against a floating wooden quay, but I decided to walk instead. I soon regretted it. I couldn't seem to synchronise my progress with that of the people milling all around me. They moved with so little purpose, with such a lack of certainty, that I kept colliding with them or treading on their feet. Once, I stepped aside to let a blind man pass only to stumble over an iron bollard and almost drop my suitcase in the canal. I'd not been hurt. All the same, I was beginning to wish I could sit down for a moment and close my eyes. I thought of Jasmine and her offer of medication. I would have swallowed something there and then, if I'd had it on me.

'Mr Parry?'

I looked round. A young woman with pale-blonde hair was hurrying towards me. In her hand she held a placard on which was scrawled T. PARRIE.

'Sorry I missed you at the station,' she said.

I didn't say anything. I had only just recognised the name on the placard as my own.

She talked on, a tiny muscle twitching under her left eye. 'Shall we walk? Or would you rather take a taxi? We can take a taxi if you –'

'Walking's fine,' I said.

She led the way, hesitating at several junctions, and even, once, taking a wrong turning, which meant we had to retrace our steps. She must have apologised at least a dozen times, her head sinking between her shoulders, her mouth curling at the corners in a hapless imitation of a smile. I would probably have fared better on my own – or no worse, at any rate. I still had a slight feeling of disorientation, though, and trembled every once in a while like someone suffering from a mild form of exposure, and when we finally got to the hotel, a majestic old building with wrought-iron balconies clinging to a mottled, off-white façade, I plunged into the lobby with a sigh of relief, as if I had been adrift on a stormy ocean for many days and had now, at long last, reached the safety of the shore.

'Welcome to the Sheraton, sir.'

I spun round. A middle-aged man in a pale-grey top hat and a tail-coat of the same colour had appeared at my shoulder.

'Are you here for the conference?' he said.

'Yes,' I said. 'Yes, I am.'

'My name's Howard. Guest Relations.' Clasping one hand in the other, he bowed from the waist. 'At your service, sir.'

'Thank you.' I attempted a modest bow of my own.

Howard waited until the young blonde woman had taken her leave, then his right arm described a generous arc in front of me, rather as if he were scattering rose petals in my path. I understood that I was being ushered towards reception. He gave the man behind the desk my name and informed him that I would like to check in. Eyebrows raised, the man consulted a computer screen and slowly shook his head. My room wasn't ready, he told us. Clasping his hands again, almost wringing them this time, Howard asked whether I would mind waiting in the lobby. Aware of his mortification, I didn't feel I could object. I sat down in an armchair and took out my guide to the Blue Quarter.

Every now and then I would lift my eyes and look through the window at the garden, where the flags of the four countries flew side by side on tall white poles.

As I was finishing a passage on the economy – verdict: permanently on the brink of collapse – I became distracted by a fidgeting at the edge of my field of vision. Looking round, I saw a short thin man rise from a sofa and walk towards me. His suit was the most peculiar colour – the fragile pale-blue of a blackbird's egg. He had a slight cough, I noticed, and the rims of his nostrils were chapped and red.

'My name's Ming,' the man said. 'Walter Ming.'

At that moment a large suitcase slipped from the grasp of a passing bell-boy. The case promptly sprang open, spilling its contents across the lobby floor, including somewhat bizarrely, a bottle of Tabasco sauce, which came to rest against the toe of my left shoe. The disturbance partially obscured the thin man's words, just as a clap of thunder might have done.

'Wing?' I said. 'As in bird?'

'Ming. As in dynasty.' He smiled mirthlessly.

I introduced myself, and we shook hands. Ming's palm had a dry, almost papery feel to it, and his black hair was thick and lustreless. Stooping quickly, I picked up the bottle of Tabasco and gave it to the flustered bell-boy.

'You just arrived,' Ming said.

I nodded. 'Yes.'

'Where are you from?'

'Pneuma,' I said. 'The Red Quarter.'

Ming had turned away from me. He was watching the bell-boy, who was trying desperately to force everything back into the suitcase.

'What about you?' I said. 'Where are you from?'

Ming didn't answer. In spite of his slight build, he seemed ponderous, like a city in which too much evidence of the past remains, and I thought of Cledge, the Green Quarter's capital, whose shabby low-rise tenements I could sometimes see from my office window if the air was clear. I was about to ask whether he was a melancholic by any chance when Howard appeared before me. My room was ready, he was happy to say. Shaking Ming's hand again, I told him that it had been a pleasure and that I was sure we would run into each other later on. I thought I could feel his curiously lifeless gaze resting on me as I moved towards the lifts.

On opening the door to my room, I was immediately struck by the oppressive quality of the furnishings, which had more in common with a museum, I felt, than a hotel. The sofa and the armchair were covered in a heavy plum-coloured brocade, and both the wallpaper and the curtains were dark-blue. My sense of claustrophobia was heightened by the bookshelves, which had been built into the wall on both sides of the bed and which were crammed with ancient, musty-looking hardbacks. In the middle of a stack of pillows and carefully positioned on a folded paper napkin was a complimentary chocolate in the shape of a smiling mouth. On the wall opposite the bed was a mural depicting a scene in which men in rowing-boats fished under a moonlit sky. I walked over to the writing desk. Here I found a bouquet of flowers and a wicker basket filled with fruit. A card from the organisers of the Sixteenth Cross-Border Conference wished me a rewarding and relaxing stay. I turned to the window. It looked west, over grey rooftops, the clutter only interrupted by the vertical spikes of a number of church spires. In the distance lay a smudged, uneven strip of countryside.

As I stood there, taking in the view, I remembered the man in the railway station – his sweaty pale-green skin, his oiled hair. The image had a surreal clarity about it, like the last fragment of a rapidly evaporating dream, something which, in the ordinary run of things, I would have automatically discounted or ignored. I slipped a hand into the pocket of my overcoat, half expecting it to be empty. There was something there, though – a sharp edge, a piece of card.

When I looked at the card for the first time I was slightly disappointed. I don't know what I had hoped to find. Something typical of the Blue Quarter, I suppose – a kind of souvenir. But this was nothing more than a flyer for a place called the

Bathysphere. It could be a new restaurant, I thought, or a bar. Or it might be a show. I studied the card more closely – the name and address written in dimly visible steel-grey, the background midnight-blue – then lifted my eyes to the window again. I remembered bathyspheres from adventure stories I had read when I was young. Round metal contraptions, large enough to hold a person, they were designed to be lowered to the bottom of the sea. A profoundly phlegmatic idea, then. Perhaps, after all, the flyer did typify the country I had entered. I wondered why the man in the station thought I'd be interested. Or did he hand out the cards indiscriminately to anybody who passed by? After staring over the rooftops for a while, I shrugged, then slid the card back into my pocket and forgot all about it.

The first event of the conference involved a visit to the Underground Ocean, which Vishram had alluded to, of course, and which the programme described as 'one of the Blue Quarter's most extraordinary attractions'. It would provide delegates with a chance to 'mingle informally' before the real business of the conference began. We were to assemble in the hotel lobby at three-thirty that afternoon. Transport would be laid on. As the programme breezily assured me, this was an opportunity '*not* to be missed!'. It would be followed by a cocktail party, which would be held in the Concord Room on the ground floor of the hotel from six o'clock onwards.

We gathered in the lobby at the appointed time, about forty of us. Several of the delegates had met before, it seemed, and were busy renewing their acquaintance, talking and nodding and laughing, while the rest of us stood in awkward silence, at slight angles to each other. Hotel staff were putting up decorations – blue streamers looping from one light fixture to another, and a sparkly golden banner above reception that said *Happy Rearrangement Day!* A portrait of the Queen gazed impassively down at me. She had been classified as a phlegmatic during the Rearrangement, and now, twenty-seven years later, she was still alive, having outlasted both her choleric husband and her melancholic eldest son.

A conference official finally arrived, and we were guided through the garden to the canal where a glass-topped barge was waiting for us. Climbing on board, I sat down next to a big pale man in a sports jacket. I had noticed him earlier, in the lobby, part of a group of delegates who had greeted each other like old friends. As the boat pulled out into the canal, I turned and introduced myself.

'Nice to meet you,' the man said. 'I'm Frank Bland.'

We shook hands.

'You seem to know a few people,' I said.

He grinned sheepishly. 'I've been on the circuit for a while.' He gave me a glance that slid sideways across my face, like an ice-cube on a mirror. 'You ever swum underground?'

I shook my head. 'I've never been here before.'

'It's something else.' He stared straight ahead, then nodded, as though his opinion needed reinforcing.

A woman with a microphone stood up and started pointing out the sights.

In less than half an hour we were drawing up outside an enormous rectangular building with a flat roof and no windows. It had the dimensions of a film studio or an aircraft hangar, and was painted a colour that reminded me of fired clay. A sign on the roof said THE UNDERGROUND OCEAN in huge white letters. Above the entrance, in blue neon, were the words *subterranean surfing*.

'One point two billion litres . . .' the woman with the microphone was saying.

Frank Bland leaned towards me until his mouth approached my ear. 'Quite a body of water,' he said, and then he nodded again and made his way down to the stern where he collected the surfboard he had brought along.

Once through the main door, we found ourselves in a large draughty area with a concrete floor. The air smelled of brine, and also, faintly, of disinfectant. I felt I had been taken to a down-at-heel municipal swimming-pool, or a brackish and slightly depressing stretch of coast.

Near the turnstiles we were met by a lifeguard. He wore a T-shirt and shorts, both blue, and his long hair was drawn back in a ponytail. In honour of our visit, the ocean had been closed to the general public, he told us. We would have the entire place to ourselves. He had a languid, absent-minded way of talking. I couldn't envisage him reacting quickly enough to save someone from drowning, but perhaps he was faster in the water than he was on land. Like a seal.

We followed him down four steep flights of stairs, then through several sets of double-doors, the last of which delivered us into a room where there was no light at all. We were standing on wooden slats – a boardwalk, presumably. When I lifted my hands in front of my face, though, they remained invisible. The lifeguard's voice floated dreamily above us. Any second now, he said, the scene would be illuminated, but first he wanted us to try and picture what it was that we were about to see. I peered out into the dark, my eyes gradually adjusting. A pale strip curved away to my right – the beach, I thought – and at the edge furthest from me I could just make out a shimmer, the faintest of oscillations. Could that be where the water met the sand? Beyond that, the blackness resisted me, no matter how carefully I looked.

'Lights,' the lifeguard said.

I wasn't the only delegate to let out a gasp. My first impression was that night had turned to day – but instantly, as if hours had passed in a split-second. At the same time, the space in which I had been standing had expanded to such a degree that I no longer appeared to be indoors. I felt unsteady, slightly sick. Eyes narrowed against the glare, I saw a perfect blue sky arching overhead. Before me stretched an ocean, just as blue. It was calm the way lakes are sometimes calm, not a single crease or wrinkle. Creamy puffs of cloud hung suspended in the distance. Despite the existence of a horizon, I couldn't seem to establish a sense of perspective. After a while my eyes simply refused to engage with the view, and I had to look away.

'Now for the waves,' the lifeguard said.

He signalled with one arm, and the vast expanse of water began to shudder. At first the waves were only six inches high, unconvincing and sporadic, but before too long a rhythm developed and they broke against the shore, one after another, as waves are supposed to. The lifeguard suggested we might like a swim. I rented a towel and a pair of trunks, but stopped short of hiring a surfboard.

Choosing a bathing-hut, I changed out of my clothes and then climbed down to the beach. I had assumed the sand would feel abrasive, like pulverised shingle, or grit, but much to my surprise it had the softness of real sand. Many of the delegates were already swimming, and the lifeguard was looking on, hands splayed on his hips.

He nodded at me as I passed. 'Enjoy your dip.'

The water was warmer than I had expected. Up close, though, it had a murky quality, and even in the shallows my feet showed as pale, blurred objects. I wondered how exactly one would go about cleaning one point two billion litres of water. I sensed the lifeguard watching me. Taking a breath, I dived through a wave, swam a few blind strokes, then let myself rise to the surface.

Once I was fifty yards out, I turned over and floated on my back, lifting my head from time to time to look towards the beach. At a glance, the sea-front looked convincing, with ice-cream kiosks and bathing-huts in the foreground and white hotels behind, but I knew that most of it was fake, a carefully contrived illusion. While I was still out of my depth, however, it seemed important to suspend my disbelief. When I started to doubt what I was seeing, a shiver veered through me – a strange, forked feeling that had nothing to do with being cold.

Later, as I dried myself at the water's edge, I saw Frank Bland again. He raised a hand as he ran past, his surfboard tucked under the other arm. He wore a pair of green-and-yellow trunks which emphasised the stocky pallor of his body. Plunging into the water, knees lifted high like a trotting pony, he threw himself face-down on his board and began to paddle with both hands.

On the basis of our brief acquaintance, I would have expected Bland to be an enthusiastic surfer, but not necessarily a gifted one. When he caught his first wave, though, he rode it all the way to the shore, showing a lightness of touch, even a kind of grace, which seemed at odds with his bulky physique. A group of delegates had gathered near me on the sand, and we all clapped and whistled as he stepped down into the shallows. Bland looked at us and grinned self-consciously. Then, furrowing his brow, he turned the board around and paddled out to sea once more.

As he came in again, he appeared to be travelling much faster than before. Knees bent, one arm extended, he cut across a wave's steep inner curve, the water tearing in his wake like ancient silk. Abruptly, he swivelled and sped off in the other direction. At the same time, a dark-haired man who was surfing near by lost his balance and toppled backwards into the ocean. Bland didn't see him until he surfaced, and by then it was too late. The leading edge of his board caught the man on the temple, and I saw the man go under.

The lifeguard rushed past Bland and hurled himself headlong into the breaking waves. Only seconds later, he was hauling the man up on to the beach. Blood spilled from a gash just above the man's hairline and slid over his face, the colour so intense, so vital, that it seemed to question the authenticity of everything around it.

Laying the man flat on his back and tilting his head, the lifeguard opened the man's mouth to check the position of his tongue. Just then, the man's chest heaved. The lifeguard turned him over, on to his side. The man coughed, then vomited some water on to the sand. I noticed a new silence and, glancing round, I saw that the ocean was quite motionless. They must have switched off the waves.

Frank Bland stood close by, head bowed. 'I didn't see him,' he was muttering. 'I just didn't see him.'

I went and stood beside him. 'It wasn't your fault, Frank.'

'He came up right in front of me. There was nothing I could do.' Bland's teeth began to chatter. I fetched a towel and wrapped it around his shoulders. Still looking at the ground, he nodded in thanks.

Meanwhile, the lifeguard was pressing a rag against the man's head to staunch the bleeding. At last the man's eyes opened. Rolling on to his back, he let out a groan, as though he suspected something might be wrong. He closed his eyes tight shut, then opened them again. They flitted across the bright-blue of the artificial sky.

'Where am I?' he murmured.

I arrived outside the Concord Room at ten-past six, but the party was already in full swing, people talking and laughing as if they'd been there for most of the afternoon. Large crêpe-paper models of our national emblems hung from the ceiling, each in the appropriate colour – red peacocks, yellow salamanders, and so on. I glanced down at my name-badge, making sure it was still securely fastened to my lapel, and then moved on into the room. I had just accepted a glass of wine from a passing waiter when Walter Ming walked up to me. He was wearing the same unusual pale-blue suit.

'We meet again,' I said.

'Just as you predicted.' His mouth widened in one of his trademark smiles, humourless and fleeting.

We shook hands. He didn't have a name-badge on, I noticed.

'I didn't see you at the ocean,' I said.

'I wasn't there.' Looking out into the crowd of guests, he sipped from his glass. 'I hear somebody died.'

'There was an accident,' I said. 'No one died.'

'Well,' Ming said, 'that's what I heard.'

'You don't happen to come from the Green Quarter, do you?'

'What makes you think that?'

'I don't know. Just a feeling I had.'

Ming nodded as if he understood such feelings, as if he often had feelings of that kind himself. 'Are you going to the club tonight?'

'What club?'

He reached into his pocket and took out a card that was identical to the one I had been given.

So, I thought. It was a club.

'I've got one of those,' I said. 'Someone handed it to me. A stranger.'

'Are you going?'

109

'I'm not sure. Maybe.' Actually I'd had no intention of going – not until that moment, anyway.

'I think you'd find it interesting,' he said.

'How do you know?' I said. 'You don't know anything about me.'

Ming looked at me. His eyes had the opaque, almost filmy quality of stagnant water. I could read nothing in them, and yet the look seemed significant. Muttering something about the need to circulate, he shook my hand, then turned and moved away into the crowd.

I finished my drink.

Ming had used the same words as the man in the railway station. Was that a coincidence, or were the two men connected in some way? Or – more sinister still – was I mistaken in thinking that Ming didn't know anything about me? Could he have been assigned to keep me under observation, for example, while I was attending the conference? If so, he clearly lacked finesse. If not, who was he?

'You look lost.'

I turned. A woman stood beside me, wispy grey-blonde curls hovering around her head like an aura. Her badge said *Josephine Cox – Conference Organiser*.

'Just thinking.' I gave her a smile that was intended to reassure her.

She led me across the room and introduced me to a group of delegates. Almost inevitably, we found ourselves discussing the incident that had taken place that afternoon. The injured man was Marco Rinaldi, a social historian from the Green Quarter. He had suffered a mild concussion, Josephine told us, as a result of which he was being kept in hospital overnight. He was going to be all right, though. He was going to be fine. Just so long as none of us thought it augured badly for the conference. I looked at her carefully and saw that she was only half joking. We all shook our heads, some less convincingly than others.

At one point I glanced around the room. There was no sign of the man in the pale-blue suit. It suddenly occurred to me that he might have been an intruder. After all, he hadn't been wearing a badge, and the name Ming – as in dynasty – could easily have been a fabrication. He had even managed to avoid telling me where he was from – on two separate occasions. I wondered about the level of security in the hotel. Should I call Howard and voice my suspicions? I faced back into the group of delegates. Wait a minute. Maybe I was overreacting. I nodded vaguely in response to something a bearded man was saying. I should relax, I thought. I should relax and enjoy my stay, as the note from the organisers had encouraged me to do.

That night Josephine took me out to dinner, along with John Fernandez, the bearded man, and two people he had met at previous conferences, Philip de Mattos and Sudhakant Patel. Fernandez was from Athanor, a major port in the Yellow Quarter. He worked as a shop steward in the Transport and General Workers' Union. De Mattos also hailed from the Yellow Quarter, though he was employed as a stockbroker on the Isle of Cresset, an offshore tax-haven. As for Patel, he came from just around the corner, as he put it. He had lived in Aquaville for the past fifteen years, where he practised alternative medicine – acupuncture and aromatherapy. It was an unlikely group, and on the way to the restaurant Josephine had told me – in strictest confidence, of course – that she was a little nervous at having two choleric men in her charge and hoped that I might help her keep the peace, but in the end her anxieties proved unfounded. We spent three hours together, and I didn't detect even a flicker of tension or unpleasantness. After dinner, the other men wanted to go to a bar they had heard about, and though tempted by their company, which was exuberant to say the least, I declined, thinking that an early night would stand me in good stead for the many surprises and excitements that undoubtedly lay in wait for me.

Back in my room, I switched on the lights. The dark furnishings and massed rows of dusty second-hand books closed around me. I sat on the end of my bed and looked at the mural – men fishing under a full moon. I had drunk wine with the meal, and then a liqueur, and I finally felt as if I was adjusting to my new environment. Somehow I didn't feel like sleeping, though. On a kind of impulse, I reached into my coat pocket and took out the card the man in the station had given me.

'The Bathysphere,' I said out loud.

It was a club, Ming had told me. In the city I came from, we had all sorts of clubs – dance clubs in Terminus, drinking clubs in Gerrard and Macaulay, strip clubs in Fremantle – and I had been to most of them at one time or another, but I knew nothing about clubs in the Blue Quarter. I glanced at the card again. Applied to a club, the name had a certain intriguing ambiguity, I thought, suggesting immersion in a foreign element, a descent into the deepest, darkest depths. Yes, there was definitely a hint of the illicit. If I went, though, I would be breaking the rules Jasmine had laid down for me. No contact with the locals, she had said. But what if I only stayed for an hour? How much damage could I really do? I'd have a drink – one drink – and see what was going on. I'd satisfy my curiosity. If challenged, I would claim to be meeting Walter Ming, a fellow delegate. Somehow, after all the equivocations and obscurities I'd had to put up with, it seemed only fair to use him as my alibi.

Smiling, I shook my head, then I reached for the phone and pressed the button that said *Guest Relations*. Howard answered. I asked whether he had ever heard of the Great Western Canal. Certainly, he said. It led out to the airport. I told him I would like a taxi, if that was possible. He didn't anticipate a problem. Replacing the receiver, I noticed that my heart had speeded up. As I turned back to the mural, one of the rowing-boats rocked quickly, the blink of an eyelid, and a fisherman toppled over the side, into the sea. I looked away for a moment, towards the curtained window. When I looked at the boat again, there was an empty space which I was sure had not been there before. But nothing else had moved or changed. I stared at the area of water into which the man had fallen. He failed to surface. Through the wall behind me I heard laughter followed by a burst of applause. Another hotel guest, watching television. Maybe I was more tired than I had realised. More overwrought. If I went out for an hour, though, I could still be in bed by midnight. Or, at the latest, one.

I passed through the revolving doors and down the front steps. Dwarf palms lined the footpath, and lurking in among the shrubs were urns on pedestals. The flags of the four countries stirred above me like huge birds stealthily rearranging their wings.

I emerged from the garden to find a taxi moored against the side of the canal, its engine muttering. It was one of the older boats, the cabin made of weathered blond wood, the bench-seats covered with imitation leather. I climbed on board and gave the driver the address of the club. He nodded lazily, then revved the engine. According to the licence displayed beside the meter, his name was Curthdale Trelawney. Dozens of charms and trinkets dangled from the narrow shelf above the helm. There were anchors, portholes and lifebelts, all predictable enough, but he had crowns too, and top hats, spanners and bibles and coins, the whole array glinting and swaying with the gentle motion of the boat. A superstitious man, Mr Trelawney.

I stared through the window as the taxi glided away from the hotel. Bunting had gone up on many of the big canals. Blue pennants seemed to be popular, or sometimes I saw a lantern in the shape of a sea horse floating high above the water. All the decorations had a faded, slightly weather-beaten look, which led me to suspect that they were brought out year after year. Trelawney drove slowly, absent-mindedly, but I found I was in no hurry. We were travelling through a city that was entirely unfamiliar to me. Well, not *entirely*. Since I dealt with people from the other countries most days of the week – on my computer, usually, or by phone – and since phlegmatics were generally believed to be harmless, I had assumed, despite what Jasmine had told me, that I would adapt to the Blue Quarter without too much trouble. I couldn't have been more wrong. During that short walk to the hotel, I had been overwhelmed by the strangeness of the place. It wasn't just the architecture or the dialect; it was something much larger and more abstract, like the look on people's faces, or the atmosphere itself. The citizens of

Aquaville seemed to equate existence with peril. They spent most of their time and energy trying to protect themselves – against the present certainly, against the future too, and even, perhaps, against the past. Thoughts of this kind had never entered my head before, but now, as a result of having to negotiate the streets and breathe the air, I was absorbing a little of the local people's trepidation, much as I had once absorbed well-being from Mr Page. I was even seeing figures move in paintings. Though, to some extent, it appeared to threaten or at least unsettle me, it was also proof of the theory I was going to expound in my talk on Wednesday, namely that the divided kingdom was self-perpetuating, and that the need for transfer and relocation would eventually die away. Each of the four quarters had already developed its own unique character and identity. In other words, although the idea of four types of people was fundamentally simplistic, there was a certain amount of self-fulfilling prophecy involved. Place someone in an environment for long enough and he starts to take on the attributes of that environment.

The taxi bumped against a row of car tyres, the engine noise subsided. We had stopped outside a tall stucco-fronted building that was set back from the canal. Wide steps led up to glass doors with vertical brass handles, and the words that featured on my flyer – T H E   B A T H Y S P H E R E – were spelled out in black block capitals on the white neon strip above the entrance. If I hadn't known the place was a club, I would have assumed it was a cinema, *The Bathysphere* being the title of the film that was showing. But there were no queues outside. I couldn't see any doormen either. There was no one around at all, in fact.

'Not much happening, is there?' I said.

My driver surveyed the building. 'What's it supposed to be?'

I told him.

'Maybe you're early,' he said.

Though I had my doubts about the club, I thought I should give it a try. After all, I had gone to the trouble of finding it.

'Could you come back later on and pick me up?' I said.

'How long are you going to be?'

I looked at my watch. 'Let's say an hour.'

'Fine by me.'

Once on the quay, I glanced behind me. In the boat's cabin, Curthdale Trelawney was lighting a cigarette. When he exhaled, the smoke unfolded against the dark glass of the windshield like a flower that only blooms at night.

The air roared and trembled as a plane went over, its wheels already lowered for landing. I adjusted my coat collar and looked around. Most of the buildings that lined the canal had once been business premises – factories, offices, warehouses – but they had long since been vacated. Bleak sodium lights stooped over a deserted towpath. The whole area had a forlorn, abandoned feel to it. I checked the address again – a nervous reaction, obviously, since the club's name was there above me in foot-high letters – then I climbed the steps and opened one of the glass doors.

The foyer was semicircular in shape. Its walls were red, with a gold picture-rail. The centre-light, housed in a black metal shade, cast a bright, unsteady circle on the carpet. In front of me stood an archway, sealed off by a velvet curtain. To my right, and built into the curve of the wall, was what appeared to be a ticket booth. A girl sat behind the perspex, reading a magazine. She had plucked her eyebrows into two perfect arcs, and her blonde hair shone. She glanced up as I walked over.

I took the card out of my pocket and showed it to her. 'Have I come to the right place?'

'Yes, you have. And that card means you get in free.'

'And it's a club?'

'That's right.'

'I'm not too early?'

She smiled. 'You haven't missed a thing.'

'Wonderful.' I hesitated. 'How long does it stay open?'

'You can leave any time you want.'

I tilted my head at a slight angle. 'I can't hear anything.'

'I'm sorry?'

'I can't hear any music,' I said.

She smiled again, more winningly. 'It's not that kind of club.'

Her answers seemed precise and clear, and yet she consistently told me less than I wanted to know. It was vagueness in a most sophisticated form. Though it did occur to me that I might have been asking the wrong questions.

'Which way do I go?' I said.

'Through the curtain, then round to the right.'

As I was turning away, one of the glass doors swung open, and I glanced over my shoulder, half hoping to see Walter Ming walk in. After all, there was a sense in which I needed him to justify my presence in this place. I could have bought him a drink. We might even have joked about the whole experience. But the couple who entered the foyer weren't people I knew or recognised. The man had an equine face and bad teeth, and his muscular figure was wrapped in a long, tight-fitting pale-grey overcoat with a black velvet collar. His companion wore a wide-brimmed hat at such an extreme angle that I could only see the powdered whiteness of her neck and the scarlet of her mouth. Her high heels were sharp as ice-picks. Well, I thought, at least I won't be the only person here.

I followed the directions the girl had given me and soon found myself in a narrow corridor that sloped gently downwards and to the left. Dim lights studded the walls at regular intervals, and there was the smell of warm trapped air. I had assumed the corridor would lead to a theatre of some kind, with rows of plush seating and a stage. I had been listening for the muted buzz of an expectant audience. Instead, I walked into a triangular room which had red walls and a black ceiling. In front of me were four doors, all painted pale-gold. To my right, on a simple wooden chair, sat a man in dark clothes. His hands rested on his lap, and his head was bowed, as if in prayer. For a moment I thought he might even be asleep.

'Choose a door.' His voice sounded automatic, almost pre-recorded. Presumably he had to say the same words every time somebody came into the room.

'What am I choosing between?' I asked.

'You're choosing without knowing what you're choosing. You're taking a chance. You're going into the unknown.'

'The unknown?' I said.

'You're free to leave at any time,' the man said in the same bored monotone. His head was still bowed, his hands still folded in his lap.

'So I just choose a door and open it?'

He nodded.

How does one choose between objects that appear to be identical? I had entered the realms of the arbitrary, the intuitive, and I didn't feel entirely comfortable, but I spent a while studying the room and in the end I found what I was looking for. At the foot of the second door from the right the carpet had been worn away, which led me to believe that this particular door was more popular than the others. Now, at least, I had something on which I could base a decision.

I opened the door and stepped through it, closing it carefully behind me as if I were a guest in someone's house. As I let go of the door-knob I became aware of a faint stinging sensation in my hand. Glancing down, I saw that I had scratched myself. Except they weren't really scratches. They looked more like pinpricks – four or five neat punctures in the centre of my palm. It must have been the door-knob. Some jaggedness or irregularity in the metal.

'Did you hurt yourself?'

I looked up quickly. A boy was walking across the room towards me. His fair hair glinted as he passed beneath the light that hung from the ceiling.

'Jones!' I couldn't believe that it was him. 'What are you doing here?'

He just smiled.

'Are you all right?' I said.

'I'm fine. Just like you said I'd be.' He took hold of my hand and turned it over. We both gazed down at my palm, the miniature beads of blood. His smile seemed to widen.

'Are you sure?' I said.

He was still looking at my hand. 'You shouldn't worry so much.'

They were the very words I had used a quarter of a century

ago. He had remembered them. I had so many questions, but they all merged, forming a kind of blockage, like leaves in a drain.

I stared at the top of his head. His hair had the gleam of beaten metal.

'What happens next?' I said.

And then it was as if I had blinked and missed half the evening. A girl stood in front of me. It was my sister, Marie – or rather it was a girl who looked just like her. Younger, though. Seventeen, eighteen. The age Marie had been when I first saw her.

'Where's Jones?' I said.

'Jones?' she murmured, lips slanting a little.

I shook my head. 'It doesn't matter. Jones is all right. Jones is fine.'

Her face slowly lifted to mine, as slowly as the sun crossing the sky, as slowly as a flower growing, and her skin glowed as if lit from the inside, and the whites of her eyes were the purest white imaginable. I became aware of a change in the temperature. The air in the room seemed warmer now, and it was scented too, not with perfume, though, and not with incense, no, with something sweeter, more indefinable, more rare – the breath of angels, perhaps . . .

I don't know how we reached the street. I simply found myself standing on the kerb, the girl beside me, her eyes as dark as liquorice or mink. My heart seemed to have swollen in my chest. My heart felt like a beacon, a source of light.

'How do you feel?' she asked.

'I've never been happier,' I said.

She took my hand and led me to a car.

'Is this yours?' I asked.

She didn't answer.

Before too long, we were moving along a straight road, our progress fluid, cushioned. She handled the car with great efficiency and deftness. Lights streamed past my window, all different colours.

'You drive beautifully,' I said.

She looked across at me and smiled. The space between us glittered.

'Where are we going?' And then, before she could reply, I said, 'I know. I shouldn't talk so much.' It didn't matter where we were going. Our destination didn't interest me at all. I just wanted everything to remain exactly as it was.

I wanted it to last for ever.

I stared out of the window, secure in the knowledge that she was still beside me. To look away from her felt like sheer extravagance. I was so confident of her presence that I could squander it.

The city faded. A glow in the rear window, a distant phosphorescence. I leaned forwards as the car took a series of long, sweeping curves at high speed. We seemed to be climbing, but I could see nothing through the windscreen, nothing except the headlights pushing into the darkness ahead of us. Every now and then a sign would loom up at the side of the road like a skeleton in a ride through a haunted house, only to fall away, insubstantial, obsolete. There was never a moment when I was frightened or even unnerved.

The girl didn't speak again. Once in a while she would glance across the magical secluded space inside the car, and the looks she gave me meant more than anything she could have said. Those dark eyes in the dashboard lights, that darker hair, the muted howling of the wind as we rushed on into the unforeseen, the incomparable – and then I was sitting next to a canal, a street lamp hanging over me, and everything plunged deep in a sickly orange solution, everything deformed somehow and yet preserved, as if in formaldehyde. I couldn't seem to focus properly. My throat contracted, and I coughed so hard that I thought I might vomit. I put my head in my hands and kept quite still. What had happened? I didn't know. I sat there until I felt the cold air penetrate my clothes.

At last I was able to look up. I was at the top of a flight of stone steps which led down into flat black water. Was it the Great Western Canal? I couldn't tell. There was no sign of the taxi. Perhaps I had fetched up somewhere else entirely. I risked a glance over my shoulder. No, there behind me was the tall white building. I climbed slowly to my feet, then stood still for a moment. The sweat had cooled on my face, and I felt more awake. My vision was sharper too. I made my way across the towpath to the club. When I tried a door, though, it wouldn't open. I tried them one by one, methodically. They had all been locked. I peered through the glass, but the lights had been switched off. All I could see was a dim distorted version of my own face. I banged on a door with the flat of my hand. Nobody came. What would I have said anyway? I went back to the bottom of the steps and gazed up at the façade. The white neon strip above the entrance was quite blank; the letters that spelled T H E B A T H Y S P H E R E had been taken down. It was only then that I thought to look at my watch. Twenty-past four. I let out a strangled cry and swung round, staring wildly towards the motionless canal, the empty buildings with their broken windows and their barricaded doors. I had to get back to my hotel – but how?

I began to run towards the city centre. A pain started up in my right side, and I slowed to a fast walk. My feet felt only loosely attached to my ankles. My throat burned. The conference would be starting in four hours, and I hadn't gone to bed yet. I didn't even know where I was.

A plane went over, tearing the clouds to shreds. I swore at it. The next time I looked up I saw a dimly illuminated sign that said TAXI. I burst through the door. The small office was filled with grey-skinned men smoking cigarettes.

'I need a cab,' I said.

Their heads turned in my direction, their lips purple in the drab yellow light. Somebody asked me where I wanted to go. The Sheraton, I told him. He named a price. It seemed expensive, but I agreed to it. In the circumstances, I suppose I would have agreed to almost anything. He consulted a clipboard which lay on the counter in front of him, then pointed at one of the younger men.

Twenty minutes later I was standing in my bathroom, staring into the mirror. It was hard to believe that I was back in the hotel, that I was safe. It had the banality of a true miracle. And the face that was looking at me didn't appear to have altered. The same wide, slightly furtive brown eyes. The same low forehead, two uneven horizontal lines etched delicately into the skin. I touched my hair where the sweat had darkened it, then I brought my hand down and turned it over so the palm faced upwards. Studying it closely, I could just make out five tiny marks.

At breakfast on Tuesday I sat with Frank Bland. He had called the hospital first thing, he told me. Rinaldi was feeling much better. He would be discharged within the hour. Bland celebrated by ordering smoked haddock, a basket piled high with toast and a large pot of tea. Later, we were joined by John Fernandez. When the waitress came, he wanted scrambled eggs and black coffee, nothing else.

'How was the bar?' I asked him.

He shrugged, then took his glasses off and rubbed his eyes. 'We were out till about two.'

'What about you?' Bland said to me. 'Did you get an early night?'

I smiled ruefully. 'No. Not exactly.'

Waking at seven, after less than two hours' sleep, my first sensation had been one of almost painful nostalgia. I had been part of something wonderful, but it was over. At the same time, I didn't know quite what to believe. It was possible that I'd been drugged. That would explain the exquisite clarity, and the way the minutes, even the seconds, had seemed to slacken and stretch out. And the nausea that came afterwards, it might explain that too. How much of what happened had been imaginary? And if it had all been imaginary, could it be imagined again?

'Parry?'

I looked up. Fernandez was staring at me.

'I didn't get to bed till five,' I said.

'*Five?*' Fernandez and Bland both spoke at the same time. People at the other tables looked up from their breakfast.

Fernandez was the first to recover. 'Where did you go?'

'I don't know,' I said. 'I'm not sure.'

Bland and Fernandez exchanged a glance.

'You know, you shouldn't be surprised,' said Sudhakant Patel, who had just arrived at the table. 'After all, this is the country of the mystical, the unex —'

'Oh, for Christ's sake,' Fernandez said. He produced a bottle of Tabasco from his jacket pocket and shook a few bloody drops on to his eggs.

The next few hours passed in something of a blur. I heard a phlegmatic delegate deliver a softly spoken and yet impassioned plea for the statue of the famous admiral to be removed from its column in no man's land and installed outside a maritime museum on the Blue Quarter's south coast, and though I acquitted myself reasonably well, I thought, making at least one contribution to the debate, my mind was restless and jittery throughout. I kept drifting back to the events of the night before. My gamble had paid off. I hadn't had any contact with the local population, not unless you counted the club's employees and the taxi-drivers. What's more, the experience itself had exceeded any expectations I might have had, so much so that all I could think about was going back again that evening.

When lunchtime came, I bought a map of the city from a kiosk in the lobby and took it into the restaurant with me, settling into a booth next to the window. I had just located the Great Western Canal and was following it with my finger when I sensed somebody at my shoulder. I looked up to see Walter Ming standing beside me. He had really surpassed himself this morning. He was wearing a green tweed suit with leather-covered buttons, a bright-yellow shirt and a knitted tie of an ambiguous brownish colour.

'Walter,' I said. Somehow I felt I was beginning to know him a little, even though we hadn't seen each other since the cocktail party.

He blinked. 'Mind if I join you?'

'Not at all.'

He glanced at the remains of my lunch. 'You know, before I sit down, I think I'll just go and get myself something to eat.'

While he was busy at the self-service counter, I folded up my map and put it away.

Ming returned with a white coffee and a bowl of rice pudding topped with two generous scoops of vanilla ice-cream. He took a seat opposite me, his eyes immediately sliding towards the place where the map had been.

'So,' he said, 'did you go?'

'Yes, I did.'

'How was it?'

I nodded. 'Like you said. Very interesting.'

He gave me a careful look, then turned his attention to his dessert.

'I didn't see you there,' I said.

'No. In the end I couldn't get away.'

I watched as Ming spooned rice pudding and ice-cream into his mouth. He had the unusual habit of biting his food up with his front teeth, which made me think of certain rodents. It pleased me to have noticed this about him. Though I had the feeling he possessed information to which I wasn't privy, I wanted him to realise that he, too, was under observation. It helped to redress the balance.

In less than a minute Ming had finished. He bent over his cup of coffee, took a quick sip and then sat back. 'Will you go again?' he asked.

'I'm not sure.'

'From what I hear,' he said, 'it can be a bit addictive.' He crushed his napkin into a ball and let it drop into his empty bowl. 'Well,' and he shifted in his seat, 'I probably won't be seeing you again.'

'Oh? Why not?'

'I've got to get back to work.' He rose to his feet. 'I had a half-day off, so I thought I'd look in on the conference. Get some ideas, some inspiration.' He smiled in that mirthless way of his, then we shook hands. 'It's been a pleasure meeting you,' he said. 'Enjoy the rest of your stay.'

From where I was sitting, I was able to watch him leave the hotel. Something about his manner failed to convince me. He didn't look like a person who was going back to work. Not that he faltered or dawdled. No, he walked at a steady pace, looking neither to the right nor the left. But there was *something*. . . Then I realised what it was. He looked as if he was walking *away* from an appointment rather than *towards* it. One hand in his jacket pocket, the other lifting casually to smooth his hair, he had the air of someone who had just relaxed. The job had been done, the mission had been accomplished. What job, though? What mission?

I glanced at my watch. If I didn't hurry, I would be late for the afternoon session. Far from making sense of the previous night's events, I had somehow managed to wrap them in extra layers of mystery. I felt like the fly that struggles to free itself from the spider's web only to discover that it is contributing to its own imprisonment. As I rose from the table, there was a moment when the floor appeared to be sloping away from me and it seemed I might be about to faint.

Should I or shouldn't I?

I stood on the front steps, under the awning, and looked out into the dark. It was ten o'clock in the evening, and it had been raining continuously for hours. A light mist curled and drifted on the surface of the canal. I had found a gap in my schedule that afternoon and slept for two hours, and I felt calmer now, more balanced. I put my anxious, befuddled state of earlier in the day down to simple exhaustion. After my nap, I had showered and dressed, then I had eaten a quiet dinner with Patel and Bland. Once the meal was over, I had excused myself; I had an event in the morning, I told them, and I needed to prepare (not entirely true: I had written my paper weeks ago). Now I was lurking outside the entrance to the hotel, trying to decide whether I could risk going to the club a second time.

A water-taxi drew up, and a young couple got out. Their coats held over their heads, they ran through the garden and up the steps, then pushed hard on the revolving doors that spun them, laughing and breathless, into the lobby. As I turned back to the canal again, still trying to make up my mind, I noticed someone sheltering in the shadows at the far end of the steps. The figure wore a long, pale, shapeless garment, a kind of cloak, and its face was hidden by a hood or cowl of the same colour. I knew instantly that this was one of the White People.

I had seen White People before – once at school, with Bracewell, and once with Victor, while out on a walk – but only from a distance. I remembered how Bracewell had pulled me away from a gang of boys who were taunting one of the poor creatures. He had been disappointed in me, assuming – wrongly, as it turned out – that I'd been actively involved. They were helpless, he said. They deserved better. I could still recall the rhyme the boys had chanted: *You don't belong/ You don't fit/ You're not a he/ You're an it.* Almost a decade later, on seeing a small group of White People on the cliff-tops, I had recited the rhyme for Victor, and he had winced. *Cruel*, he said, *but not wholly inaccurate.* They were society's untouchables, he explained on that occasion. The past had been taken from them, as it had been taken from everyone alive at the time of the Rearrangement, but these were people who had been either unwilling or unable to find a place in the future. They didn't fit into any quarter, he said, or any humour. They had ended up marooned between the old kingdom and the new one. Lost in a pocket of history. Once I joined the Ministry, I began to learn a little more about these strange nonentities. Known formally as achromatics, they were required to wear white because white had no status as a colour. Since they were perceived as having no character, they were deemed incapable of causing psychological damage, and as a result they were allowed to cross borders at will, to wander freely from one country to another. They were commonly believed to be both sterile and psychic – sterile because the idea of non-beings giving birth to non-beings was too bizarre to think about, and psychic because their apparent inability to speak had led to a reliance on other, more obscure forms of communication. Perhaps, after all, they had something to impart, and yet this had never really been acknowledged – except for here in the Blue Quarter, that is, where they were sometimes viewed as mystical beings or spiritual guides. In the Red Quarter, a far more secular environment, they could rely on charity: among other things, for instance, we had started a foundation that provided them with food and clothing. Throughout the divided kingdom they were, generally speaking, either tolerated or ignored, though in the Yellow Quarter, predictably enough, they were held in such low esteem that they were often treated as scapegoats.

I moved towards the figure slowly, so as not to frighten it.

'Do you need any help?' I said.

The figure looked round. It was a woman of about my own age. Though she had chapped skin and a runny nose, the expression on her face was remote and strangely benign, as if she had been contemplating an object of great beauty.

'You're wet through,' I said. 'Can I offer you some dry clothes?' I pointed to the revolving doors behind me. 'I have a room here.'

The woman took two or three steps towards me, and then stopped. Her expression hadn't altered, and I felt that I had now been incorporated into whatever she was thinking about.

'Come up to my room,' I said. 'I'll find you some –'

Before I could finish my sentence, she launched herself at me, almost knocking me off my feet. Her strength took me completely by surprise. I staggered, but remained upright. She had wrapped her arms around me, trapping my own arms by my sides, then she had pressed her face into my chest. She had gone quite still. It wasn't an assault, I realised, but an embrace, and I was reminded, for one brief, unnerving moment, of Marie.

'Oh dear.'

Howard had appeared on the steps. He began to try and free me from the woman's grasp, but she must have locked her hands behind my back. She had clamped her teeth together and turned her head to one side, her eyes fixed on some abstract point beyond my shoulder. There was a sense in which I had become incidental. She was clinging not so much to me, I felt, as to the idea of human contact, human warmth.

Howard moved round behind me. When the woman's fingers

were finally prised loose, she let out a bellow of distress and fell back, flushed and panting.

I looked at Howard. 'Can't we offer her some shelter?'

'I'm afraid it's against hotel regulations, sir,' he said.

I watched as the woman lumbered down the steps and along the flagstone path that led to the canal. She appeared to dissolve into the rain.

'Where will she go?' I asked.

'They have their places.'

I saw that Howard was trembling. 'Are you all right, Howard?'

'It upsets me too, sir.' He eyed my raincoat. 'Can I clean you up at all?'

I told him not to worry.

'You're sure?'

'Actually,' I said, 'there is something you could do for me. You could order me a taxi.'

Howard nodded, then withdrew into the lobby.

Standing on the steps, I could still feel the woman's grip around my ribs. She had left damp marks all down my front. I could even see the place where she had pressed her face against me, a stain with three segments to it – the imprint of her forehead, nose and chin. My raincoat had become a shroud. I stared out into the darkness. The force with which she had attached herself to me had been testament to her loneliness, her desperation. I was reminded once again of what Bracewell had said, that the White People couldn't help themselves, that they deserved better, and I rebuked myself for not having acted with more compassion.

By the time the taxi drew up outside the hotel, the rain had slackened off. The city seemed quiet, almost shocked, as if it had witnessed the entire episode and sided with the woman. Of the woman herself there was no sign. *They have their places.* I stepped down into the boat and gave the driver the address.

He frowned. 'What do you want to go all the way out there for? There's nothing out there.'

I didn't answer. Curiously though, his reaction provided me with exactly the kind of stimulus I had been waiting for. You're phlegmatic, I thought. What would you know? We were different people, the taxi-driver and I. We had different needs. A strong sense of conviction was flowing through me now. I could have been having drinks with John Fernandez, Philip de Mattos, and the rest of them. I could have been forging new contacts, furthering my career. Instead, I was in a water-taxi heading west, towards the airport.

There's nothing out there.

That's what you think, I thought with a smile.

Inside, it was all exactly as I remembered it. There before me was the foyer, half-moon-shaped, and decorated in flamboyant if slightly tattered red and gold, and there on the carpet lay the bright circle of light, trembling a little at the edges, and there in the ticket booth sat the girl with the blonde hair. I was filled to the brim with a joy which, even at the time, felt disproportionate. It was as though I had invested my whole being in this one image, and somehow, simply by walking in and seeing it, I had been repaid in full.

Well, not quite *in full*. There was still the pale-gold door, and what I would find when I stepped beyond it. I moved almost hungrily towards the ticket booth. The girl was wearing something different tonight, a silk kimono embroidered with exotic birds and trees. The backdrop was a landscape, lush mountains rising above calm bays, suns sinking heavily in skies of peach and lilac, and for a moment I was drawn into that world, and I was looking at the birds and trees from the other side, my face drenched in a lurid apocalyptic glow. The girl's voice came to me from everywhere at once, and across a great distance, like the voice of God.

'Can I help you?'

Feeling slightly dizzy, I took out my card and showed it to her.

'That was a special offer,' she told me. 'This time you'll have to pay.'

'That's all right.' I slipped the card back in my pocket. 'I'm just really glad you're open,' I said. And then, not wanting to appear eccentric or over-eager, I added, 'You must hear that all the time.'

She smiled uncertainly. I noticed how the sleeves of her kimono widened below the elbow, dark trumpets from which her arms emerged, like music. Her beauty was just the prelude to something even more exquisite. I looked away into the foyer, my happiness extravagant, baroque.

'You've been here before, then?' I heard the girl say.

Turning to face her again, I felt a momentary stab of disappointment. Somehow I had expected her to remember. 'I was here last night.'

'So you know where to go?'

'I thought you wanted me to pay.'

She laughed and shook her head, the light skidding off her hair. 'I don't know what's got into me today.'

I laughed with her. 'It's been an odd day for me too.'

She named an amount, and I slid the money into the shallow metal bowl at the base of the perspex screen. I took one final look at her, which she failed to notice, then I parted the velvet curtain and passed on into the corridor beyond.

When I reached the triangular room, the man in the black clothes stopped me by putting a hand on my arm. 'You'll have to wait.'

I sat down on the only other chair. The man was seated to my right. I hadn't looked at him properly the previous night. There hadn't been time. He had hooded eyes, which he kept lowered, and his hair was cropped so short that I could see his scalp. His face was made up of cavities and hollows, as if the bones had been broken and then imperfectly reset. Though his clothes looked new, they seemed dated, archaic. He was dressed like a footman, I thought, or notary – or even a church-warden. In his left ear he wore an earpiece, which would be how he received instructions from elsewhere in the club.

I looked still more closely.

His ankles, though long and spavined, were sheathed in expensive black silk socks. The ankle-bones protruded in the way that Adam's apples sometimes do.

A pulse beat patiently in the thick vein on the left side of his neck.

This was like no waiting I had ever known. I wasn't upset by the delay, or even curious. I simply assumed there must be a good reason for it. I felt physically comfortable, despite the cramped nature of the room and the hardness of the chair. Time was just a pool in which I happened to be floating. At one point I smelled violets. Not the real flowers, though. A synthetic version. They must have opened secret vents and released some kind of air-freshener into the room.

At last, and without looking up, the man signalled to me, a peculiar double gesture of his left hand, as if he were brushing cobwebs from in front of his face.

'You can choose a door.'

I chose the second door from the right. As my hand closed over the door-knob, I shut my eyes, and it wasn't Jones I saw but the girl who looked like Marie, her face lifting slowly to mine . . . I stepped through the doorway. This time I felt nothing. I glanced instinctively at the palm of my hand. There were no marks, no tiny punctures, no telltale beads of blood. Something opened in my stomach, bottomless, like an abyss. I was standing in a room I hadn't thought about in more than twenty years. There was my bed, the blankets and the eiderdown pulled back, part of the top sheet trailing on the floor. I had been sleeping in this room when the soldiers came, the beams from their torches lurching across the pale-blue walls. I had always slept here, even as a baby. The air itself seemed to remember me.

I moved into the alcove where the window was. Sunlight was falling on the copper beech in the front garden. I had climbed its branches so many times. I knew them off by heart. And the road beyond, I knew that too, its pavement smooth enough for roller-skates, and then the dark curving scar on the tarmac where a car had swerved to avoid me when I was six. I faced into the room again. Draped over the end of the bed was one of my father's old gowns from the university. I would put it on when I was pretending to be a vampire or a wizard. I ran my hand over the white fur collar, and a word appeared on my lips, familiar but magical: *ermine* . . . Smiling, I turned away.

On the mantelpiece was my favourite piece of rock. I had found it halfway up a mountain while on holiday. It had rained so hard that morning that the footpath had become a shallow stream. Veined with turquoise and tawny-gold, the rock looked valuable, like treasure. Back home, though, it dried out, quickly fading to a dull grey-green. My parents told me I should keep it in water – in a fish-tank, perhaps – then it would always look the way it had when I first saw it and I would never be disappointed, but somehow I had never taken their advice, and it had sat there above the fireplace ever since . . .

That dropping feeling in my stomach again, though steeper this time, and faster. I had been so startled by the room and then so caught up in its spell that I had overlooked the fact that it was just one fraction of the house, and that the bedroom door would take me to the rest of it, and that my mother and father might be somewhere close by. I stood still and listened. No voices came to me, and yet I had the sense that they were both downstairs. I thought I could hear the washing-machine, for instance. The whirr of it, then the shudder.

I opened the door, stepped out on to the landing. The dark wood of the banisters, almost black. The stairs, carpeted in pale-pink. And then the hall below, in shadow . . . There was another noise now, harsh and rhythmic. It was me, I realised. It was the sound of my own breathing.

'Matthew?'

My stillness seemed to thicken, to intensify.

'Darling, are you coming down?'

I couldn't see my mother, but I knew she would be standing by the kitchen door, the fingers of her right hand curled around the leading edge. She would be looking upwards, in the rough direction of my bedroom. Beyond her, the table would be set, with bread and marmalade, a pot of tea, and if it was the weekend my father would be there.

Though I couldn't move, I found my voice and called out, 'Coming.'

I felt so buoyant in that moment, so free, and I stepped back into my bedroom, thinking I would take one more look at it, only to be confronted by walls that were red and a ceiling that was black. I swung round. My bedroom was no longer there. The piece of rock, the gown, the window framing sunlit trees – all gone. There was only a row of pale-gold doors. I reached for the door that was second from the right, but a voice stopped me.

'Only one choice allowed.'

I turned to see the man in dark clothes sitting on his chair. 'What?' I said. 'You never told me that.'

The man rose to his feet. Standing only a few inches from me, he somehow gave the impression that he could expand rapidly to fill an enormous space. He was like something in its concentrated form.

'This way.' Taking me firmly by the arm, he propelled me through a curtain and out into an unlit corridor. *If only I had not turned back. If only I'd gone on across the landing, down the stairs . . .*

I stood on the towpath, my eyes angled towards the ground, one hand wrapped around the lower half of my face. The rain had stopped, but I could hear water everywhere, like a tongue moving inside a mouth.

A blast on a horn made me jump. I looked up. My taxi was still waiting, the small craft rocking and swaying in the wake of another boat. I nodded at the driver to let him know I was aware of him, but couldn't bring myself to leave.

In the end, though, there was nothing for it. I crossed the towpath and climbed down into the taxi. The driver turned in his seat with the self-righteous air of someone whose perfectly good advice has been ignored.

'You see?' he said. 'I told you there was nothing there.'

I had the feeling I'd been turning and turning in the bed for hours, but when I finally gave up trying to sleep and switched on the light I saw that it was only five-past one. Maybe I should try and read for a while – after all, the shelves on either side of me were full of books – or else I could go through my lecture one last time . . . I got out of bed and went into the bathroom. Leaving the lights off, I peered into the dim well of the mirror. My face floated there, not on the surface seemingly, but just below it, like someone underwater looking at the sky. As I stared at myself I heard my mother calling me again. *Matthew?* I had recognised her voice immediately. It was as much a part of me as blood or hair. Each layer of my skin had been inlaid with it. And it had sounded different to the voice I remembered from that night on the road, not piteous, not pleading, but tender, even, calm – the voice I had lived with, day in, day out, for years . . . I filled a glass with water, drank it down.

As I put the glass back on the shelf, loud laughter came from the corridor outside my room. I opened the door. There were five of them out there, arms round each other's shoulders – Fernandez, Bland, de Mattos and two I didn't recognise. Fernandez was holding a huge rabbit made of green crêpe paper. Bland appeared to have lost one of his shoes. When they noticed me standing in the doorway, their mouths opened wide, and they lifted glasses and bottles in a collective salute.

'It's the mystery man,' Fernandez said.

I grinned self-consciously and shook my head. *The mystery man.* That's what they had started calling me. Because I had gone to bed at five in the morning, and they still hadn't found out why. They staggered towards me, all at the same time, as if they had been pushed from behind. I took an involuntary step backwards.

'Sorry,' Bland said, 'but we're drunk.'

'I'd never have guessed,' I said.

They reeled back again, wheezing and chuckling, bumping against each other gently like boats in a harbour. Yes, they'd been drinking all evening, so many drinks, but now they were going to play cards. I'd play cards, wouldn't I?

'I'm not very good at cards,' I said.

'Well, you can watch,' de Mattos said. 'How about that?'

I thought about it. Probably anything was better than lying in bed and being unable to sleep – and besides, the idea of company appealed to me.

'All right,' I said.

With a resounding cheer, the five men swept me off down the corridor in my pyjamas and bare feet. Fernandez danced a celebratory rumba with the enormous bright-green rabbit. Bland offered me his one remaining shoe, which I graciously declined. They were going to Boorman's room, de Mattos told me. Charlie Boorman was the name of one of the men I hadn't met before. The other was Rinaldi. Marco Rinaldi. They were both miserable bastards, de Mattos said. You know, from the *Green* Quarter. From *Cledge*. Boorman and Rinaldi grinned queasily.

I noticed the surgical tape on Rinaldi's forehead. 'You're the one who had the accident, aren't you?'

'It wasn't an accident,' Rinaldi said. 'He did it on purpose. He was trying to kill me.'

I stared at him. 'Really?'

The others fell about laughing, Bland included.

Boorman's room was at the far end of the corridor. His bed hadn't been made, and empty beer bottles lay scattered about, together with dirty clothing, old newspapers and the remains of a meal.

'Talk about melancholy,' Fernandez said. 'Talk about fucking gloom.'

Bland and Rinaldi said they were going off to find some chairs. I looked at the wall opposite the bed. Where I had a mural of men fishing, Boorman had a beech forest in the autumn.

'Dangerous, that wall.' Boorman stood next to me, one hand resting heavily on my shoulder.

'What's dangerous about it?'

'See that tree?' He pointed, the tip of his finger revolving unsteadily, like a fly circling a light bulb. 'I pissed all over it.'

'I thought I could smell something,' de Mattos said.

'Woke up in the night,' Boorman went on, 'needed a slash. Thought I was outside, didn't I. Pissed on the first tree I could find.' His eyes squeezed shut, and he was shaking his head. 'Maid didn't like it.'

'What about this game?' Standing on a table, Fernandez was

fastening his rabbit to the centre-light with someone's tie. 'Are we going to play or not?'

Rinaldi and Bland returned with extra chairs, and the five men settled round the table. Sitting on the bed, looking over Boorman's shoulder, I watched as Fernandez shuffled the cards. He was due to speak tomorrow, after lunch. He would be discussing terrorism in his native Yellow Quarter, with special reference to the supposed links between various disaffected elements and the trade unions.

'I'm looking forward to your talk,' I told him when I caught his eye.

He grunted. 'At least someone's interested.'

The game began. They were drinking Boorman's brandy. Old, it was. Aged in special oak casks. I'd have some, wouldn't I? I said I would, secretly hoping it might make me sleepy. The green rabbit rotated solemnly above the table.

'We had a peacock too,' de Mattos said, 'but Rinaldi fell on it.'

'I just fell over. Squashed it flat.' Rinaldi looked at me. 'Nothing personal.' He glanced down, fingered his lapel. 'Lost my name-badge too.'

'Rinaldi's name-badge,' de Mattos said, 'it's not for people at the conference. It's so he knows who he is when he wakes up in the morning.'

The mention of name-badges reminded me of Ming, and when the laughter had died down I asked if anybody knew him. Fernandez looked blank. So did Rinaldi.

'He wears strange-coloured suits,' I said.

'I saw someone like that,' de Mattos said. 'What's his name again?'

'Walter Ming.' I had begun to see Ming's enigmatic behaviour as a kind of indecisiveness, and that, together with his persistent cough, led me to believe that he might come from the host nation, that he might, after all, be phlegmatic. 'I think he's from here.' I turned to Bland. 'But if that was true you'd know him, wouldn't you?'

'Maybe, maybe not,' Bland said. 'Our civil service, it accounts for something like three per cent of the population. There are thousands of us.' He threw down a card. 'What about him, anyway?'

'I don't know. He seems devious, somehow – and he keeps following me around –'

'Sounds like Rinaldi,' Fernandez said.

Rinaldi grinned uneasily, then put a hand over his mouth. Standing up, he lurched towards the bathroom.

'He's going to vomit.' Boorman hadn't taken his eyes off his cards.

'He always vomits,' Bland said.

A terrible noise came from behind the bathroom door, somewhere between a roar and a groan, as though Rinaldi was being tortured.

Bland looked across at me. 'Don't worry. It always sounds like that.'

'Rinaldi,' someone said.

There was a general shaking of heads.

A few minutes later I asked if anybody had been to a club called the Bathysphere. None of them had even heard of it. De Mattos wanted to know whether it had live girls. He knew a couple of places, if I was interested.

'It's not like that,' I said.

It was true, I suppose, that there had been an erotic edge to my first night at the club, but something else was happening now, something quite miraculous. I had gained access to a part of me that I had assumed was gone for ever. The club's name conveyed exactly what was being offered: a journey into the depths, a probing of the latent, the forbidden, the impenetrable . . . As for Ming, the suspicions I'd been harbouring now seemed ludicrously exaggerated and melodramatic. He was like the Blue Quarter, I decided, only in microcosm. He was fluid, elusive, a source of disorientation, but he didn't necessarily pose a threat. I was glad I had come to watch five drunk men playing cards. In an oddly paradoxical way, it had put everything in perspective.

At half-past two I thanked Boorman for the brandy, and though the others tried to talk me into staying I said goodnight and walked back down the corridor.

Sometime later, already curled up in bed, I thought I heard a person crash to the floor outside my room. There was a snort of laughter, then someone said, *Quiet!* I didn't really wake up, though, and the next thing I knew, the sun was slanting through the window – I must have forgotten to draw the curtains – and a maid was standing at the foot of my bed. She was sorry if she had startled me, she said, but she had knocked on the door – she had knocked twice, in fact – and there had been no reply.

That morning I decided to go and listen to Frank Bland, since his event immediately preceded mine on the programme. He arrived ten minutes late, his face drained of colour, his hands shaking as he fumbled among his papers. He had called his lecture 'Power and Energy: A Study of the Nature of our Borders', and though he lost his thread several times during the next half-hour he held my attention throughout since he was elaborating on what Vishram had talked about during our recent lunch together. The path taken by our borders had sometimes been determined by roads or rivers, Bland said, and sometimes by the boundaries of a country, a borough or a parish, but ancient ley lines had also played a part. To its immense excitement, the committee responsible for drawing up the borders had discovered that certain ley lines could have an adverse effect on the health of the people who lived within their sphere of influence. For centuries mankind had attempted to dissipate the hostile energy of these black streams, as they were known – there were a number of methods: the driving of iron stakes into the ground, the encircling of one's property with copper wire, the judicious placement of chips of jasper, amethyst, quartz or flint – but the architects of the Rearrangement had decided to harness it instead, to make it work in their favour. They had drawn directly and quite deliberately on the land's innate psychic strength, using spiritual power to reinforce political will. Maybe that helped to explain why so many phlegmatics believed that it could be fatal to cross a border, that certain borders could maim or even kill – unless, of course, one wore a copper suit or filled one's pockets with the appropriate crystals. Bland ended his talk by wishing those of us who had come from elsewhere a safe and pleasant journey home, and the ripple of amusement provoked by this remark shaded into warm applause as he thanked us for listening and began to gather up his notes.

I was just rising to my feet, preparing to move towards the podium, when Josephine Cox appeared at the microphone, Bland's last slide – a glowing chunk of amethyst – still showing on the screen behind her.

'I've got an important announcement to make,' she said.

I slowly sank back down into my seat.

'Mr Bland has been speaking of the possible dangers involved in crossing a border,' she said. 'What he doesn't know is that he's about to experience those dangers for himself – as we all are, in fact.'

She paused, seeming to relish our bewilderment.

'As you know,' she continued, 'today is Rearrangement Day. To mark the occasion, we have planned a special trip for you.' She consulted her watch. 'In just under three hours you will be flying to the city of Congreve, in the Yellow Quarter.'

She was now speaking into an intense silence.

Once in Congreve, we would be attending a grand firework display, she told us, and since fireworks were something the cholerics understood better than anybody else, it ought to be an unforgettable experience. Afterwards, a banquet would be hosted by the Mayor.

'Visas have been procured,' she said, 'and transport has been arranged. We've chartered a small plane, which will be leaving Aquaville at three o'clock. All you have to do is pack an overnight bag. Be back in the lobby no later than one-thirty.'

As she stepped away from the microphone, everyone in the lecture hall began to talk at once. It seemed I would not be delivering my paper after all. I slid my notes back into my briefcase, then I glanced at Charlie Boorman, who happened to be next to me. He raised both his eyebrows. I expressed surprise that the phlegmatics had been able to put together something so dramatic, so ambitious. He nodded in agreement, then leaned forwards and spoke to Rinaldi, who was sitting in the row in front of us. What I was actually thinking was that I had more or less adapted to life in the Blue Quarter, and that I didn't relish the notion of being plunged into yet another unfamiliar environment. Certainly it was the last thing I'd expected. Rinaldi turned to face me, as if he had just read my mind. There was an aspect of the phlegmatic disposition, he said, which we had either forgotten or overlooked. It was the most flexible, the most whimsical, of the humours – the most feminine, one might almost say. He didn't think an idea like this was particularly uncharacteristic, though he would be astonished, he added, if everything went smoothly.

'I think I'd better go and pack,' Boorman said.

I went to have a word with Josephine, who had been surrounded by the more anxious and excitable of the delegates. Her eyes glittered, and her frizzy hair appeared to have filled with static. She had pulled off a kind of public-relations coup. This was likely to be the most talked-about conference in years.

'Will we be safe?' one of the delegates was asking.

Josephine turned to him. 'Well, there has been some rioting –'

'*Rioting?*' The delegate's eyes widened.

'During the last few days,' Josephine went on, 'but it's mostly in the north, apparently. In any case, they often riot at this time of year. It's practically seasonal.' She permitted herself a small, vague smile, as though contemplating the behaviour of a wayward but cherished son.

When I was finally able to talk to her, she apologised for the seemingly impromptu and high-handed cancelling of my lecture. She had been determined to retain the element of surprise, she said. She hoped I didn't hold it against her. I would now be speaking on Thursday morning. It would be the last event on the programme, and everyone was very much looking forward to my contribution.

I took the lift to the seventh floor. They had already made up my room, a new chocolate mouth smiling at me slyly from the pillow. I opened my suitcase and started packing. After a while, though, I found my eyes returning to the mural. As usual, I scanned the blue-black water for the man who had fallen overboard. As usual, it yielded nothing. Then my gaze lifted an inch or two, and I noticed a stretch of barren coast beyond the rowing-boats. A small figure stood on the shoreline, looking out to sea. Was that him? Had he actually managed to reach dry land? Or had that figure been on the beach the whole time? I rose to my feet and moved towards the wall. Up close, the figure turned back into a smudge of darkish paint. It might have been driftwood, or a rock, or a heap of kelp abandoned by the tide. A lone siren spiralled up into the air outside my window. Still staring at the mural, I had an abrupt and pronounced sense of opportunity, as if there was something I ought to be doing, as if I ought to be exploiting the situation to my advantage. What, though? How?

I was looking round the room, hoping an answer would come to me, when the phone rang. I picked up the receiver. It was one-thirty, the receptionist informed me, and the delegates were about to depart for the airport.

'Please ask them to wait,' I said. 'I'll be right down.'

As we prepared for landing I saw Congreve below me, the city centre glittering in the gloom of the late afternoon like a solar system that had fallen from the heavens, like a grounded constellation, and then I was inside it, moving through it, buildings lifting steeply all around me, their upper storeys lost in the smoky, neon-saturated air. Seen at close range, they were less ethereal, more powerful; they seemed to emit pure energy, a deep turbine hum or murmur that I could feel in my rib-cage.

We were driving along a wide grand avenue, the traffic heavy in both directions, the pavements crowded. In the many-tiered emporia all the lights had been switched on, and I couldn't help but notice the variety of goods on offer, the sheer lavishness of the displays. At the same time, beggars sat hunched over on every corner, their dogs lounging sloppily beside them. Most of these beggars had hung cardboard squares around their necks on bits of string, and even from a distance I could read their sorry messages: STARVING or HELP ME or, in one case, with bitter sarcasm, SMALL CHANGE ONLY PLEASE.

Braking smoothly, the limousine turned off the main road and eased its way into a maze of narrow streets. Here, suddenly, were strip clubs, peep-shows and sex shops, all jammed together, all different flavours, like a box of candied fruits.

'A little tour,' our driver joked over the intercom.

We had entered Firetown, the red-light district. I had listened to relocation officers boast of their exploits on these streets – how young the girls were, what they could do – and as I stared through the window, the air seemed to pulse and glow, a livid blush of scarlet, pink and purple. Once, as we stopped at a set of traffic-lights, a fight broke out on the pavement beside us. A burly ginger-haired man fell heavily against the car's window, and the glass retained the print of his hand, as a cheek does when it's been slapped. One of my fellow passengers murmured in alarm.

'No need to panic,' came the driver's voice. 'It's reinforced.'

Not long afterwards, we pulled up outside the Plaza Hotel, and it was only then, with a sickening jolt, that I realised what our arrival in this new place actually entailed. *I had forfeited my last chance to visit the club.* We would be spending the night in Congreve, then returning to the Blue Quarter in the morning. A few hours later, my visa would expire, and I would have to leave the country. There would be no going back to the part of me that had been buried for so many years. There would be no more glimpses of that forgotten life.

A light clicked on in the limousine, and I saw myself reflected in the window. My face looked stiff, morose, vaguely ghoulish. I was in the Yellow Quarter for the first time ever, I had just arrived in one of its great cities, and yet I felt no elation. I didn't even feel any fear. I was trying to adjust to the sudden, arbitrary loss of all my hopes.

My mind lay soft and cold on the floor of my skull like a carpet of ash.

When I walked into my room, it recognised me. *Welcome to the Plaza, Mr Parry,* it said. *I hope you enjoy your stay.* I should have been ready for something like this, perhaps, since choleric people were known to be obsessed with technology, but such was the hectic nature of our schedule that I had no time to dwell on my surroundings. Five o'clock had already struck when I set my case down on the bed, and I was expected for drinks at five-thirty. The venue was a roof garden on the seventeenth floor. While at the party, we would be able to watch the firework display, which was due to start at six. I took a quick shower. As I got dressed, I caught a few minutes of choleric TV. They were showing a documentary about the Prime Minister, Carl Triggs, who was so fiercely patriotic, apparently, that he had taken fire-eating lessons. I watched some rare footage of a bare-chested Triggs demonstrating his prowess in the grounds of one of his palatial mansions, then I went into the bathroom to clean my teeth. When I returned, the commercials were on. At midnight there would be a programme which featured topless female mud-wrestlers competing for a huge cash prize. It was called *Rolling in It.* I threw on my tuxedo, gave my shoes a polish and by five-thirty-five I was stepping out of the lift and into a space that resembled a conservatory, exotic trees and shrubs massing beneath a high glass ceiling.

The men were dressed in lounge suits or formal evening wear. As for the women, they had chosen much more elaborate confections – one girl was wrapped in jagged swathes of red and orange taffeta, which made her look as if she was being burned at the stake – and their ears, necks, wrists and fingers were all heavily freighted with jewellery. I found Frank Bland in the shade of a palm tree, holding a cocktail. His dinner jacket clung to his midriff as tightly as the skin of an onion.

'Quite a place,' he said as I walked over.

'Does your room talk to you, Frank?'

'Good evening, Mr Bland.' He had put on a voice that was both disembodied and obsequious.

I nodded. 'That's very good.' Though everything was reaching me through a veil of quiet desperation, it was a comfort to see Frank Bland. In these altered circumstances, he felt like an ally. A friend.

He took a gulp from his drink. 'Did you hear me speak this morning?'

'Of course. I really enjoyed it.'

'Did I ramble?'

I thought for a moment. 'Yes, I suppose you did a bit.'

He laughed. 'It was one of the worst hangovers I've ever had.'

I wanted to thank him for shedding some light on a subject that intrigued me, but Boorman and Rinaldi wandered over and I lost my chance. Not long afterwards we were ushered out on to the terrace.

I had always loved fireworks – even the most modest sparklers delighted me – but the fireworks we saw that night, unleashed from the roof of a nearby building, were like nothing I'd ever seen before. The colours alone almost defied description. Instead of the usual sprays of red and green and gold, we were treated to the most delicate tinctures, the subtlest of hues – violet, burnt sienna, damask, eau-de-nil. And the fireworks themselves did not explode so much as unfold, like hothouse flowers opening their petals, but in fast-motion, bouquet after bouquet tossed carelessly into the dark. Later, various messages were emblazoned across the sky – 27 GREAT YEARS, THANKS CARL, and so on. The display ended in a riot of sound, the noise rebounding across the city, so deafening and persistent that it seemed the office blocks surrounding us might topple and the ceiling above our heads might shatter in a murderous cascade of glass. For a while I had forgotten how I felt, but then we went back indoors, and people turned to each other and began to talk, and the disappointment I'd been harbouring since the early evening rose inside me once again, swift and remorseless, like floodwater.

Josephine Cox came and stood in front of me, her face flushed. 'You don't seem very happy.'

So it was that obvious. Ever since I first set foot in the Bathysphere, I had been feeling scratchy, discontented. My initial experience had been the strangest mixture of the unexpected and the sublime, and it had stopped too soon, of course, and if I nursed a sense of regret about that shortfall the events of the second night had only compounded it, since I had dropped down deep into my past only to have the journey cruelly cut short. Then, a few hours later, Josephine's surprise announcement had cheated me out of my last chance to go back. But it wasn't just that. Those two nights had established a kind of precedent, and my life in the Red Quarter, the life I would soon be returning to, now seemed pallid, if not sterile, by comparison. Nothing that happened to me from this point on, I felt, could ever match what had happened to me in that club.

I summoned a feeble smile. 'I'm just tired, that's all.'

'I hope you're not too tired to enjoy the banquet,' Josephine said. 'I've put you on a rather special table.'

'What's special about it?'

She didn't answer. Instead, she placed one finger upright against her lips and lifted her shoulders towards her ears, then she moved off into the crowd.

Eleven o'clock was striking as I stepped into my room. I shut the door behind me and leaned back against the cool smooth wood. *Goodnight, Mr Parry*, the room said. *Sleep well.* Outside, in the street below, a siren squawked once, abruptly, and then went quiet.

It had been an awkward dinner. I'd been seated at the table of honour, next to the Mayor's wife. Dressed entirely in black, she had furtive eyes and though she wore expensive rings the skin around her nails was ragged. Between courses her clenched hands rested in her lap like two plucked quails. Trying to be diplomatic, I asked her about herself, but the answers I received were curt and dismissive. The only time she came alive at all was when she mentioned her sixth child, a son, who had been born the year before, and even then she sent a glance in the direction of her husband, seeking his approval, perhaps, or fearing his reaction. Halfway through dessert, she reached under the table, her head turned sideways, one ear only inches from her plate. I assumed she had dropped her napkin, and I shifted in my chair, ready to help her retrieve it. Then I saw that she had drawn her dress up, almost to her hips. Her unexpectedly voluptuous thighs, white as meringue, were darkened in two places by large bruises, both of which bore the imprint of somebody's knuckles. *Look what he does to me*, she said in a harsh whisper. She gave me a look of such fury that I thought for one surreal moment that I might be the culprit.

After the banquet, the Mayor himself walked up to me. We shook hands. He was a thick-set, fleshy man with a shaved head. Knowing what I knew, I found it hard to meet his gaze, but I suspected that he might be used to having people look away from him, that he might even see it as proof of his natural

147

authority, his manhood. *Thank you*, he said, *for taking such* good care *of my wife.* His lips parted on a set of strong, widely spaced white teeth. I had never heard gratitude so heavily laden with menace and innuendo. Just then, I thought of something I hadn't thought of in years. I remembered Pat Dunne in the border hotel the night before she crossed into the Yellow Quarter with Chloe Allen. I saw the heel of her hand slamming into the drinks machine. *You have to act like them,* she'd told me, *or you don't survive.*

I slowly levered myself away from the door and unfastened my bow tie. I was genuinely tired now, my fatigue given a sombre, despairing edge by the knowledge that I could have been in Aquaville, in a water-taxi heading west. I took off my tuxedo and threw it over the back of a chair, then squatted down and unlocked the mini-bar. Inside, I found two miniature bottles of brandy. I emptied one of them into a glass, then closed my eyes and brought it up to my nose. The smell instantly transported me to Charlie Boorman's room in the Sheraton – the unmade bed, the half-eaten meals, the green crêpe-paper rabbit revolving in the air. My eyes still closed, I drank. The first mouthful sent a thin blade of warmth through me. Brandy. It was the taste of the Blue Quarter to me now. It was the taste of the club with its velvet curtain and its blonde ticket girl. The taste of a gold door opening . . . *To speak to my mother, but not to be allowed to see her. To be so close to her, and then – and then nothing . . .* A low murmur came out of me, and I opened my eyes. Everything was edged in bright pale light. The Yellow Quarter. I finished my first brandy and poured the second.

Taking my drink with me, I walked into the bathroom and switched on the light. I put the glass on the shelf above the sink, next to my travel clock, then I examined myself in the mirror. The areas below my eyes seemed to have been shaded in, and the hollows in my cheeks had deepened. It made me think that the distance between myself and my shadow was narrowing, that I had begun to change places with my darker half. I was about to turn on the tap and drink a few handfuls of cold water when a sudden dull reverberation shook the room. Several things occurred at once. My clock tipped off the shelf and landed in the sink. The shower-curtain rattled on its rail. The mirror leapt in its chrome brackets, and then, almost as an afterthought, cracked down the middle, from top to bottom. My head divided into two sections that no longer quite fitted together. I thought fleetingly of stroke victims, and how one side of the face will often freeze or slip. My right hand lifted to my cheek, as if to check for damage. I picked up my clock and put it back on the shelf. 11:14, it said. And then, more than a minute later, 11:14. I still couldn't imagine what had happened.

A hush had fallen, and I had the sense that the reverberation had silenced everything that came after it, that it had robbed the world of all its sound. I stepped into the short passageway outside the bathroom. A pale smoke or powder had forced its way beneath my door. I stood quite still and watched as the particles settled on the carpet, a sprinkling of greyish-white, discreet but enigmatic, like a messenger who has been trusted with only part of the news. I moved to the door and pulled it open.

The air outside my room swirled with dust. To my left, about fifty yards away, my corridor met another. At the junction of the two I could see people rushing this way and that, their outlines hazy, their features smudged, as if they were in the process of being erased. Some had towels or handkerchiefs pressed to their faces. Others were doubled over, coughing. I heard the word 'bomb', and though I had never experienced anything like this before I replayed every detail of the last ninety seconds, and then I thought, *Of course. A bomb.*

I withdrew, closing the door behind me, and stood looking at my feet for a moment, then I moved on into the middle of the room. Again I stood still, my face lowered. I was seeing images, each of them deliberate, carefully chosen, pressed to my mind's eye like a licked stamp to an envelope. The hand splayed on the window of the limousine, Frank Bland crammed into his tuxedo. The bruises staining the thighs of the Mayor's wife, as if wild berries had been piled on to her lap. *Look what he does to me.* I couldn't marshal even one coherent thought.

A piece of paper whirred out of the fax machine and spilled languidly on to the carpet. It was blank. I put on my coat and picked up my overnight case, then opened the door again. By now, the vacuum that had followed the explosion had been filled with the constant shrill ringing and almost festive whoops of various alarms and sirens. I turned to the right, making for the emergency stairs.

Beyond the fire doors I came across the spindly, bewildered figure of Marco Rinaldi. He was wearing a red-and-white-striped nightshirt, and his eyelids were swollen with sleep. His black hair lifted above one ear in a single eccentric wing.

'I think I'm still drunk,' he said. 'What's going on?'

'There's been a bomb,' I said.

'A *bomb?*' He looked around, then back at me again, as though he expected me to offer him some proof.

We started down the stairs, Rinaldi leading the way. Our rooms were on the fourteenth floor. It would take a while, I thought, to reach ground-level. Every so often Rinaldi glanced at me over his shoulder, a nervous, enquiring look, and I would smile and nod. We passed the twelfth floor, the eleventh. By the tenth I noticed that my pace had slowed and that a gap had opened up between us. Other guests kept pushing past me. Part of my mind seemed to be examining the current situation from an entirely different viewpoint; it had begun to question my behaviour and was about to suggest alternatives. As we approached the eighth floor, two middle-aged men burst through the fire doors and out on to the stairs. *I can't find Angela,* one of them was babbling. *I can't find her anywhere. I've looked in her room, I've looked –* The other man took him by the shoulders. *John,* he said, *calm down. She's probably downstairs. She's probably waiting for us down there.* I stood stock still. My ambivalence had gone. Resolved itself. You have to use all this confusion and hysteria, I told myself. Use the dust, the hours of darkness, the uncertainty. *Use it.* No one will know what's become of you. They might think you're trapped under the rubble. They might think you're dead. They won't *know,* though. They won't be sure of anything. This is your chance, I said to myself. This is a *gift.*

Half a flight below me, Rinaldi had stopped as well. 'What are you doing?'

'I have to go back,' I said. 'I've forgotten something.'

'Go back? Are you mad?'

'I've got to. Look, you keep going. I'll see you outside.'

He hesitated, one hand on the banister, but I could tell from his snatched glances down the stairwell that he didn't relish the idea of waiting.

'You go on,' I insisted. 'I won't be long.'

'Be careful,' I heard him call out as I turned away.

Everyone apart from me was coming down, some of them bleeding, others white with shock. I met no other delegates, at least none that I recognised. It felt right to be going up again. Easier. As if, for me, the world had been upended.

The fourteenth floor was utterly deserted. Walking along the corridor, I thought the lights seemed dimmer. Dust in the atmosphere – or a partial power failure. I stopped outside my room and felt in my pocket for my keys. A draught edged past, and I could smell night air, the scent of fallen leaves. I entered my room, locking the door behind me. *Good . . . Good . . . Good*, the room said, and then fell silent.

I had lied to Rinaldi, of course. I had forgotten nothing.

I laid my coat on the bed, then reached for the remote. Surprisingly, perhaps, the TV still worked. A reporter was standing in front of the hotel. His voice had a thrilled, brittle quality about it – the voice of someone who was already an authority on something that had only just happened – and the wind ruffled the hair on his forehead in a way that made him seem dashing but vulnerable. He would probably be a celebrity by morning. The bomb had been left in a sports bag on the first floor, he was telling us. Thirty people had been admitted to hospital, some critically injured. As yet there were no fatalities. In a statement released a short time ago, the Black Square had claimed responsibility for the explosion. The notorious terrorist organisation had condemned the Rearrangement Day celebrations – twenty-seven years of shame, it had called them – and reiterated its determination to fight on, to bring about reunification. Carl Triggs had denounced the attack as 'a despicable and cowardly abomination'. The police suspected the existence of a second device – or, at least, they hadn't been able to rule it out. The entire area had been cordoned off.

I fetched my toilet bag from the bathroom, then went over to the wardrobe and lifted out the suit I had worn on the flight that afternoon. Laying the suit across the bed, I opened my wallet and took out the largest banknotes I had on me. I folded each note in half, lengthways, and then again, then I slipped my jacket off its hanger and, using a pair of nail-scissors, carefully un-picked two or three stitches from one end of the collar and slid the folded notes inside. I turned the collar down again and smoothed it out. It might have looked a little thicker than before, but I doubted anyone would notice. I put on the suit and reached for my overcoat. The clock next to the bed said ten-past twelve. I glanced at the TV. The reporter was standing sideways-on to the hotel. Half the front wall had dropped away, exposing the internal structure of the building. Rooms gaped out into the night. Wires dangled. How peculiar, I thought, that I was still inside.

Buttoning my coat, I crossed the room and unlocked the door. Out in the corridor nothing had changed. What I was con-templating was unthinkable – it went against all my principles, everything I had ever learned or held dear – but the disappoint-ment I had been dealing with all evening had not diminished, as I had hoped it might. If anything, in fact, it had intensified, gradually distilling into a kind of anguish. I had to return to that club in the Blue Quarter. I *had* to. Had I been finding out about myself, or just imagining things? I didn't know. Whatever the truth was, it had felt more real than anything had felt for ages. *I* had felt more real. Or more alive, perhaps. Yes, I would return, but under my own auspices. If I was caught, I would be charged under Article 58 of the Internal Security Act, an all-purpose clause that covered any action that could be seen to be 'under-mining the state'. I would be throwing away my career, my position – all those years. None of that appeared to bother me. I had always been renowned for my 'integrity' and my 'conscientiousness'. My 'sense of civic responsibility'. A strange, reckless delight swept through me at the thought that I would now be trampling on that reputation. For the second time that night, I set off towards the fire stairs, my heart like a bomb exploding endlessly inside my body.

As I reached ground-level, the power failed completely. In darkness now, I pushed through a sprung fire door, carpet replacing lino underfoot. A weak silvery light inhabited the corridor in which I stood, a kind of phosphorescence, as if sparks from the detonation had somehow been dispersed into the atmosphere. Though I could just about see, I had no idea which way to go. It was a vast hotel – five hundred rooms, someone had told me – and I had only arrived that afternoon. I hadn't had the opportunity to orient myself. Sounds came to me – the stammer of a helicopter, a man talking through a megaphone – but they seemed both distant and redundant. I chose a direction, began to walk. Once, I passed through an area of armchairs and plants, rain falling lightly on the plush upholstery, the leaves, and I looked up, expecting a glimpse of the night sky, clouds hovering, but the ceiling was still intact. The sprinkler system had come on, triggered by all the dust and smoke.

A few minutes later, and wholly by chance, I found myself outside the banqueting hall, the padded double-doors opening on air that felt dense, trapped, a fug of filter coffee and stubbed-out cigars. Standing just inside, I heard a peculiar rumbling noise. I moved cautiously out across the room, light catching on the rims of wine-glasses, the blades of knives, the mirror-panelled walls. A man had fallen asleep with his head resting against the back of a chair, his hands folded across his belly, his mouth ajar. When I shook him by the shoulder, his snoring seemed to concertina, one sound colliding with another in a sudden clutter of snorts and grunts. I shook him again. He murmured something, then slumped forwards on to the table. I couldn't just leave him. What if a second bomb went off? Also, I thought, more calculating now, my delayed departure from the hotel would look far less suspicious if I was seen to be bringing someone out. Putting an arm around the man's waist, I hauled him to his feet. He didn't struggle or protest. As we moved towards the FIRE EXIT sign, bumping between tables, he nuzzled affectionately into my neck, his breath warm and meaty as an animal's. We went up a short flight of steps, along a service corridor, then I pressed down, one-handed, on a horizontal metal bar and we were outside – cold air, voices, blue lights whirling.

Halfway down the alley, two firemen stopped me and I steered the dead weight of the drunk into their arms.

'I found him in the banqueting hall,' I said. 'I couldn't wake him.'

'We need to look at timings and schedules,' the drunk man murmured. 'Let me give you my card.' Eyes still closed, he chuckled to himself.

Showing the firemen my room key, I told them I was a guest of the hotel. I spoke calmly. In my suit and overcoat I must have looked affluent, respectable. They asked if I was hurt, and when I shook my head they waved me on.

At the end of the alley I ducked beneath a strip of yellow tape. The people on the other side of the police cordon were gazing past me, their faces brightly lit and utterly transfixed, as if a spaceship had just landed behind my back. I resisted the temptation to look round. I already knew what was there – I'd seen it on TV – and besides, I didn't want to run the risk of catching anybody's eye. I had to sink without a sound into the blue-black of the night.

As I moved deeper into the crowd, I wondered whether Rinaldi would be questioned by the authorities and, if so, what he would tell them. *Parry? He went back upstairs. He said he'd forgotten something. I don't know what . . .* Would he embellish his role at all? *I tried to stop him, but he wouldn't listen. He pushed me away. What could I do?* He might even become dramatic. *I didn't see him after that. I never saw him again* – In retrospect, I was glad Rinaldi was the last person I'd had contact with. Half-asleep, still drunk, dressed in a lurid nightshirt, Marco Rinaldi would make the most unreliable of witnesses. There would be layer on layer of ambiguity, plenty of room for doubt and speculation. I couldn't have planned it better if I'd tried.

Once I had put a certain distance between myself and the Plaza, I was able to slow down, feeling confident that I would no longer be recognised. The streets were full – I didn't think I'd ever seen such crowds – but none of the people who surrounded me had any idea who I was. There would be no chance meetings with old acquaintances or colleagues from the office, no voices calling out my name in disbelief. Though midnight had come and gone, the celebrations showed no sign of letting up, people shouting and dancing and fighting everywhere I looked, and the news of the bomb had just begun to filter through, which gave the atmosphere a feverish, chaotic edge.

I pushed my way into a bar, hoping for some respite, but here too I was buffeted, and it took me another quarter of an hour to get a drink. The TV in the top corner of the room had been tuned to a news channel, the volume turned up high. There, once again, was the hotel. I watched the injured being brought out on stretchers and loaded into ambulances. A section of the road that ran past the entrance had been buried under an avalanche of masonry and plaster, and we were shown endless close-ups of the rubble, among which lay an assortment of unlikely objects – an armchair, a vacuum-cleaner, three oranges, a doll (the camera lingered on the doll, of course). My brandy arrived at last. When I reached for the glass I noticed that my hand was trembling. Was it the fact that I had been in great danger, that I was, in some very real sense, lucky to be alive, or was it a response to the action I had subsequently taken? There was no way of telling. I drank half the brandy, which seemed to steady me a little.

Until the bomb went off, the notion of escape had not occurred to me – I hadn't even entertained it as a possibility – and yet, somehow, I found that I was already in possession of a strategy. Obviously I wouldn't be able to walk through a gap in the wall, as Victor and Marie had done. This was the Yellow Quarter, and the borders would be fiercely defended. No, I would make for one of the big northern cities – Burnham, Sigri, Ustion – and go to ground. I would become a student of choleric behaviour, learning rashness and belligerence, but all the while I would be working out how to return to the Blue Quarter. Only a moment ago my hand had been shaking, but now a thrill went through me at the sheer unimaginable magnitude of what I was doing. My thoughts had begun to startle me. Or perhaps I was just discovering new aspects of myself, qualities I hadn't realised I had. Sitting in that bar, not knowing where it was or even what it was called, I felt like a spy – glamorous, resolute, only dimly perceived.

By the time I left, it was after one o'clock in the morning, and slack columns of drizzle were slanting across the road like gauze curtains blown sideways by a breeze. There was almost nobody about. The weather must have driven everyone indoors. Moans and wails came from somewhere, and I paused, unable to decide whether the sounds were human or animal. It would be the tail-end of the revelries, I told myself. Things winding down, people who had gone too far. Turning my collar up against the rain and wrapping myself tightly in the folds of my coat, I set off in what I hoped was a northerly direction.

I passed along the damp dead streets of the business district, some of whose buildings I recognised from the drive in from the airport, then the road sloped upwards and I found myself on an elevated dual carriageway. Huge yards lay below me, filled with lumber and scrap metal.

Looking over my shoulder, all the brashness and glitter of the city centre behind me now, I saw a car come speeding up the fast lane. As I watched, it began to veer towards me. There didn't seem to be anybody driving. At the last minute, a woman's face rose into the windscreen, and I heard the tyres shriek as she applied the brakes. The car swerved out into the middle lane again, spun round twice, and then stalled, facing in the wrong direction, one of its elaborately spoked wheels resting on the central reservation. Its headlights angled sideways and upwards, almost quizzically, into the night. Fine rain fell through the beams, silent, sharp-looking, as if a tin of pins and needles had been emptied somewhere high up in the sky.

The door on the driver's side opened and an elderly woman climbed out. She wore a fur coat, and her pale hair had been pinned up in a tidy and yet complex bun. She appeared calm, if slightly indignant.

'What are you doing there?' she said. 'What do you want?' As though I had distracted her in some way. As though the accident were all my fault.

'Nothing,' I said stupidly. 'I was just walking.'

A car flashed between us, horn blaring.

She watched it vanish round a curve in the dual carriageway, then turned back to me. She seemed to have no sense that either she or her car might be in danger, or that they might present a threat to others. 'Yes. I see.' She passed one hand across her forehead, then lightly touched her hair. Her movements had the slow-motion dreaminess of someone underwater. 'Are you all right?'

'I'm fine.'

'Good. That's good.' She let out an unexpected husky laugh. 'Can I give you a lift?'

I asked her where she was going. Home, she told me. She lived in the suburbs. That would be perfect, I said, then glanced towards her car.

She read the look. 'I'm not drunk,' she said. 'I've just had a few champagne cocktails, that's all.' She saw that I wasn't entirely reassured. 'I was looking for my cigarette lighter. I dropped it on the floor.'

Perhaps I should hold the lighter, I suggested. When she wanted a cigarette, I would light it for her. She thoroughly approved of this idea.

Once she had turned the car around and we were under way, she asked me how I came to be walking along that stretch of road. She'd never seen anyone out there before. I felt an almost overpowering need to tell her that I'd been staying in the hotel that was bombed, but I knew it would be unwise. I had to try and keep my mouth shut, not give anything away.

'Cars,' she said. 'They always go wrong at the most inconvenient times.'

She had jumped to her own conclusions about me: my car had broken down and I'd had no choice but to abandon it. She glanced across at me. I nodded. It would be a miracle if it was still there when I got back, she said. The vandalism these days. Incredible. She shook her head. The diamonds she was wearing in her ears seemed to fence with the air, each glint of light as fine as the blade of a rapier. With crime so prevalent, I found it surprising she had offered me a lift, but perhaps I was part of a bargain she had made with fate that night. I was a risk she'd been required to take.

After a while she asked if I had the lighter handy. I held the flame up to her cigarette, and she inhaled. Smoke moved across the windscreen like ink in water. My eyes smarted, and I began to cough, but the woman next to me paid no attention. The city seemed endless, spreading out on all sides, in all directions. There was something careless about it. Something profligate. Her expensive car hurtled on into the dark, largely ignoring the white lines that divided one lane from another.

By seven in the morning I was standing outside a transport café on a country road. I had been lucky: I had covered a lot of ground and I hadn't got into any trouble. The aristocratic woman – Annette – had dropped me at a suburban petrol station. From there, I had hitched a ride in a lorry going north. The driver swore constantly at other motorists, and sometimes I thought I could see the violence rising off him like steam off a horse at the end of a long race, but he only spoke to me once, after about an hour, and that was to announce that he was stopping in a lay-by for a nap. I continued on foot. Cars and trucks slammed by, not even slowing down, and I had almost given up hope of another lift when a transit van came to a halt ahead of me, WE OF THE NIGHT painted on the back in silver and framed by a sprinkling of stars. The words unnerved me at first, but the man behind the wheel, Tony Spillman, turned out to be the sales director of a firm that manufactured beds. 'And I don't mind telling you,' he said before I'd even finished fastening my seat-belt, 'in a business like mine, I get into some *pretty interesting situations.*' With no encouragement from me at all, he embarked on a detailed account of his sexual exploits. I must have dozed off at some point, though, because the next time I looked at the clock on the dashboard it said a quarter to six and Spillman was telling me he'd have to let me out. 'Got a little detour to make – a breakfast meeting, so to speak . . .' and his head moved backwards on his neck, which gave him a temporary double chin, and his lower lip curved into a small plump shape, like a segment of tangerine.

I watched him drive away, the stars on the back of his van fading in the grainy light of dawn, then I turned and walked into the café. There were only two people in the place, both men. One huddled over a plate of bacon and sausage, the other was studying the sports pages of a tabloid newspaper. Not knowing when I'd have another chance to eat, I ordered a full breakfast. Neither of the men so much as looked at me. It was too early in the day for suspicion, or even curiosity.

Later, when I was paying my bill, I noticed a map of the region on the wall behind the cash-till and asked the waitress to show me where we were. She gave me a sharp look – maybe she thought I was trying to make a fool of her – then she put her finger on an area of pale-yellow. I murmured in disbelief. Despite the hours I had spent on the road, I was still no more than a hundred miles from Congreve. The lorry-driver had taken me north, I knew that much, but Spillman must have turned east while I was sleeping, and I'd ended up in a rural backwater, close to the border with the Green Quarter, which was no use to me whatsoever – though as I stood there staring at the map I began to see how it might work as a decoy. After all, who would suspect me of making for the Green Quarter? In short, my erratic route might actually throw people off the scent. From here, I could either continue north or double back. First, though, I would have to find a place to stay.

I asked the waitress if she knew of anywhere. There was a pub, she said. They might have rooms. She pointed to a small black box on a road that was even narrower than the one we were on. The junction looked about a mile away. I thanked her, then I buttoned my coat and left.

Outside, the sun had risen, but its rays were as colourless as panes of glass and I had to walk fast just to keep warm. I'd forgotten to give Annette her lighter back. I could feel its smooth shape at the bottom of my pocket.

As I approached the turning I saw a phone-box, and I had the sudden urge to call someone, so I could set a seal on what I'd done, so I didn't feel quite so alone. I stepped inside and put the receiver to my ear. The line was dead. I stared out across the road, the tops of the trees in sunlight, their trunks still plunged in shade. Who would I have talked to anyway? Marie? It was early. She would be asleep. When she heard the ringing she would pick up the phone that sat on her bedside table, next to the photo taken on a yacht when she was twenty-three – Marie in a pink bikini, laughing. *That's me, happy*, she had told me during my last visit.

Hello?

Marie? It's Tom. Did I wake you?

It doesn't matter. The sound of her turning in the bed, like surf. *Where are you?*

I can't say exactly. It's like you and Victor, though – what you did. It's like that. A pause. *I love you, Marie.*

She would be facing the ceiling, one forearm draped over her eyes. A smile at the corner of her mouth.

I always loved you, right from the beginning. Another pause, my mind drifting back. *I hated those people for making you feel bad.*

That was a long time ago.

I know. But you were so much better than they were.

A car rushed past, steel-blue, into the future.

I'll probably think I dreamt all this. I often have dreams about you, Tom.

I dream about you too.

Do you?

I couldn't have spoken to Marie, of course, not even if the phone had been working. Communication between the four

160

countries wasn't possible unless you went through official channels. But then I remembered the time I found Victor weeping over the death of his wife, and I wondered if there was a chance Marie had felt something while I was talking to her in my head. She might have woken suddenly and sat upright in her bed. Thinking of me, not knowing why.

I followed the narrow road for what seemed like hours as it climbed between rough pastures and drystone walls. Behind me, I could just make out the red roof of the café where I had eaten breakfast, the main road running through the middle of the valley like the spine in a leaf. Since I had started my ascent, there hadn't been a hint of any traffic, not unless you counted the wreck I'd seen, burned-out, windowless, abandoned in a ditch. The only signs of life were the fragile spires of smoke rising from chimneys in the valley's western reaches and, once or twice, from somewhere high above, the drowsy humming of a plane.

It was after midday when I came out at the top of the pass. A wide, shallow basin lay in front of me, a kind of plateau ringed by hills. In the foreground were a number of grey-and-white houses, one larger than the rest. Could that be the pub the waitress had spoken of? I hoped so. Cloud was moving across the sky from the north, a solid shelf or ledge of it. Whatever meagre heat the sun had brought would soon be gone. My limbs were heavy, my eyelids too. I could almost have slept standing up.

I forced myself onwards, each footstep sending a jolt through my whole body. Though I longed to reach the pub, the distance between us seemed to remain the same. Then, when I had almost despaired of arriving, I rounded a bend and there it was, only yards away. The chipped gold letters above the entrance said THE AXE EDGE INN.

I mounted the steps and pushed the door open. I'd walked into the public bar – a floor of stained wood, with chairs and tables to match. The air smelled of beer and green logs, and the horse-brasses pinned to the walls in vertical rows gave off a sullen gleam. A woman stood behind the bar, reading a note. Her hair was drawn back in a tight bun, which only served to accentuate the strong bones in her cheeks and jaw. When I asked if she had a room, she folded the note and put it in her pocket, then she came out from behind the bar and stood staring at me, hands on hips. She wore a white ribbed sweater, brown jodhpurs and a pair of tall, scuffed riding boots. Her face, which was lightly tanned, looked hard as a mask.

'I didn't hear a car,' she said.

'I don't have a car,' I said. 'I walked.'

Her gaze dropped from my face to my coat, then further, to my shoes. 'You don't look like much of a walker to me.'

I let out a sigh. 'Do you have a room or don't you?'

'All right, all right,' the woman said. 'Jesus.'

She led me through an archway and on into a second bar. On the wall hung a stag's head, a dented hunting horn and several framed black-and-white photos of men squinting on the tops of mountains.

'I don't usually have people staying,' she said, 'not this time of year.'

Winter, I thought. Business would be slow.

The woman reached over the counter and plucked a key from a metal hook. As I took the key from her, I had the distinct feeling that it was accompanied by a warning, unspoken, but quite palpable.

My room was small, with a low ceiling. The walls were stained with the bodies of insects that had been swatted during the summer months, their blood no longer red but dark-brown or dull-pink. I put my bag down at the foot of the bed and moved to the window. The land fell away in front of me, the coarse grass studded with boulders. Rain smudged the horizon to the east. I faced back into the room. There was a washbasin in one corner, and opposite the bed was a fireplace that had been boarded up. A tall wardrobe stood behind the door, as if intent on ambushing the next person who walked in. I placed my watch on the bedside table, then took off all my clothes and climbed between the sheets. The pillowcase smelled of mildew, but I laid my head against it anyway, and I remembered nothing after that.

I woke to raucous applause, people clapping and whistling. I couldn't see anything, though, nor, for a few moments, did I have any idea where I was. I reached out for my watch, which lay coiled on the table. The luminous green hands said ten to seven. Clutching the watch, I sank back among the blankets, my mind still stunned with sleep. Darkness had fallen outside. I let my eyes close, then forced them open again and swung my legs out of the bed. The cold air took hold of me, stippling my bare skin with goose-bumps.

As I rose to my feet, trying to remember where the light-switch was, a movement in the window caught my eye. Still naked, I went and looked through the glass. In the distance, perhaps a mile away, a monstrous creature glowed and flickered. A dappled brownish-golden colour, it had a long thick body and a tapering tail, and it was staggering, almost drunkenly, in the direction of the pub.

I found a light-switch by the door and turned it on, then walked over to the washbasin. I ran the hot tap. It coughed once, then shuddered, but nothing came out. I washed under the cold tap instead, bringing handful after handful of icy water to my face until I felt properly awake. I glanced at myself in the mirror. My eyelids were swollen, puffy, my forehead creased. How long had I been asleep? Five hours? Six? A towel in my hands, I returned to the window. The creature had edged closer. Its stubby head ended in a forked tongue which seemed to be licking at the night. I quickly threw on my clothes and went downstairs.

Both bars had filled with people, some dressed in army surplus, some in anoraks and wellingtons. Others wore fur hats with flaps over the ears. Several of the men had beards. Through the window I caught a glimpse of the woman I'd spoken to earlier. She was standing on the asphalt at the front of the pub, her legs astride, smoking a cigarette. I went outside and joined her. She continued to smoke, without acknowledging my presence.

'I saw something from my room,' I said. 'I thought I should tell you.'

'Did you?' Holding her cigarette at thigh-level, she stared out into the dark.

'It looked like a salamander.'

She said nothing. A thin spiral of smoke coiled upwards, past her sleeve.

'Is something going to happen?' I said.

'You tell me.'

'How could I tell you? I've never been here before.'

She looked at me sideways, steadily. She seemed to be debating something inside herself. Then she said, 'It's the burning of the animals.'

'I don't understand.'

'Every year, around this time,' she said, 'we burn the animals. We always do it in a different place, or the authorities would interfere. It's our little gesture of rebellion against the way things are.'

'I know about rebellion,' I said.

'You do?' Still watching me, the woman drew on her cigarette, then blew the smoke out of one corner of her mouth.

I found myself telling the woman who I was and what I had done. Perhaps I wanted to repay her for having been straight-forward with me, but there was also something about the harsh planes of her face and the toughness around her mouth that invited confidences. I was sure that her initial hostility was only caution blown up large. And so I told her everything.

Towards the end she nodded slowly. 'I heard about that bomb,' she said. 'Four people died.'

'I didn't know.' I looked up into the night sky. The dull pewter of the clouds had brightened to silver where the moon was trying to push through. 'There wasn't anything about me, was there?'

'You? No.'

'Good.'

She looked at me head-on for the first time, her eyes narrowing at the corners, and I suddenly felt delicate, almost breakable. 'So you're on the run?' she said.

164

I tried to smile. My mouth crumpled, though, which was something I hadn't expected, and I had to look away. 'Yes,' I murmured, 'I suppose I am.'

'You've chosen an interesting time to do it.' She threw her cigarette into the road. 'Let's go back inside. I'll buy you a drink.'

I had seen people drink heavily during the conference, Fernandez, Boorman, and the rest of them, but their drinking paled in comparison with the drinking I saw at the Axe Edge Inn that night, and I drank too, more than ever before, more than I thought possible. After I had been handed a double brandy by Fay Mackenzie – for that was the landlady's name – a friend of hers, Hugo, bought me another, then it was my round and I found myself embarking on a third. I always asked for brandy now. It had become my drink. I used it as a sort of touchstone, a way of throwing out a line from the immediate past to an uncertain future. Hugo had discovered I was a defector, as he called it, and he kept slapping me on the shoulder and offering me a top-up, even though my glass seemed constantly to be on the point of brimming over. He was also desperate to learn of my reasons for leaving the Red Quarter. '*I* know,' he exclaimed, his big straw-coloured teeth showing, 'you just couldn't take all that *contentment* any more, could you?' Clutching the side of his belly with one hand, like somebody with a stitch, he bent double, hugely entertained by his own joke.

Just then a fight broke out. The crowd parted, as though drawn to the edges of the room by some magnetic force, and two men staggered about in the makeshift arena, their arms wrapped around each other. They heaved and grunted, but neither could seem to gain the upper hand. I imagined for a moment that they were engaged in a form of primitive dance. At last one of them tore himself free and swung a blow. His fist circled the air like a wrecking ball, but demolished nothing, and as he tottered sideways, off balance, the other man clubbed him above the ear.

'This is what you came for,' Hugo bellowed. 'A bit of real life.'

About to disagree with him, I opened my mouth, but then I closed it again. I had always associated the Red Quarter with brightness, simplicity, a sense of hope. Oddly, though, I now felt as if these properties amounted to a superfluity of some kind, even a weakness. According to Galenic thought, blood was the only humour that had no particular quality when present in excess. Blood had to be looked upon as eucrasic or well tempered, and yet the world I remembered, the world in which I had lived for a quarter of a century, the world I'd turned my back on, didn't seem well tempered so much as over-sanitised, devoid of warmth and feeling, bland.

By now the two men were fighting on the tarmac in front of the pub, their struggle rendered more dramatic by the car headlights trained on them. I saw a third man with banknotes folded lengthways between his fingers like pieces of a dismantled fan. Bets were being placed on the outcome. Meanwhile, in the bar, a fair-haired man had stood up on a table and begun to sing. The tune was that of a traditional ballad, but the words belonged to a protest song. All people were different, he sang, but if one looked beneath those differences, all people were the same. We had to be allowed to live together, to complement one another. That was where true freedom lay. A subversive idea, of course, if not a kind of treason, and it was then that I realised exactly how far I had travelled in the last eighteen hours or so. The room almost burst apart as everybody joined in with the chorus, which demanded that we overthrow the current leadership. Even before the song had ended, though, there was a surge towards the door. When I asked Hugo what was happening, he looked at me over his shoulder, and his eyes had opened wide.

'The animals are coming,' he cried.

It was a sight I would never forget. On arriving at the pub that afternoon, the road outside had been deserted, even desolate, but people were now overflowing on to the verges and into the ditches, and judging by the lights that jumped and flickered in the distance, a good number were making their way across the fields. Fay Mackenzie came and stood at my shoulder. Four local communities took part in the festival every year, she told me. Each community was held responsible not only for the building of an animal, which had to be carried out in secret, but also for its delivery to the site that had been set aside for the burning. Her next words were drowned by the shrill cacophony of whistling and hissing that greeted the procession as it rounded a bend in the road just below us. All four creatures were made of papier mâché and lit from within, and the size of them astounded me. A rabbit took the lead. Despite squatting on its haunches, the rabbit must have stood at least fifteen feet tall, its head and body ghost-white with black patches, its ears laid flat against its back as if it had already learned of its impending fate. Its beady eyes looked frightened, blind. After the rabbit came a sea horse, which was even taller, its neat sculptured head on a level with the eaves of houses. Though it had been painted a delicate shade of lilac, the sea horse also seemed filled with a sense of foreboding. It was there in the recalcitrant curve of its body, and in the pouting of its coral lips. A peacock appeared next, its breast a deep enamelled blue. Its tail was on full display, dozens of eyes afloat on a glinting mass of turquoise, green and gold. To my surprise, I felt not even the slightest twinge of loyalty or pride. Taking up the rear – and here the whistles and hisses almost deafened me – was the salamander I had seen earlier. Up close, it was a terrifying vision, its long tongue lolling between toothless jaws, its short scaly legs grasping at the air. As it lurched past, people from the pub joined the procession, some carrying bottles, others holding torches. I followed, yet another glass of brandy in my hand.

Not far from the top of the pass, the crowd streamed left on to a narrow track that led down into a sort of rift or depression in the land. With steep grass slopes on three sides and a sheer dark wall of rock at the back, the site had all the qualities of a natural amphitheatre. Wooden platforms had been erected at the bottom, each with stacks of kindling underneath. The people gathered down there were singing the song I'd just heard in the bar. When they reached the end of it, they simply returned to the beginning again, the volume seeming to build with each rendition. By the time I completed my descent, I, too, knew all the words.

I pushed into the middle of the arena. The animals had already been hoisted up on to their respective platforms. Seen from below, they resembled the hideous creatures that appear in cautionary tales. I suspected that the children who attended the burning would have dreams about them afterwards. Or nightmares. If you didn't do as you were told, the salamander would come after you, its blunt jaws snapping at your heels. Or the ghostly rabbit with its blind pink eyes. These were the ogres in this part of the world. These were the bogeymen.

Sensing a shift in the crowd, I turned in time to see it parting. A dark-haired man strode towards the clearing, flanked by armed civilians in balaclavas. He was dressed in black tatters, as though he had just been pulled from a burning house; wisps of smoke rose from his clothes, and a trail of ashes glowed in the grass behind him. He began to mount a flight of wooden steps. On the ground below, his escorts formed a line, facing outwards, their semi-automatic weapons held diagonally across their chests. A hush had fallen. Just murmurs now. The man kept his back turned as he climbed. Only when he was standing beneath the salamander's fearsome jaws did he swing round. A loud gasp escaped from the crowd. A child began to cry. The man's face and hands were black, so black that I couldn't distinguish them at first. He opened his mouth as if to speak, but flames and smoke came out instead. Everything about him was black. The whites of his eyes, his teeth. Even his tongue. A wind sprang up. His charred rags stirred.

'I am the Master of the Conflagration,' he said slowly, his voice so deep and guttural that I imagined that his larynx too had been fire-damaged.

'Welcome,' the crowd said, sounding, by contrast, almost shy.

The Master paused for a moment, then he spoke again. 'If people tell us what to believe, do we believe?'

'No,' the crowd said, louder this time.

'If people tell us what we are, do we listen?'

The crowd shouted, 'No!'

I glanced over my shoulder. The field was full, right up to the top of the path. I could see heads silhouetted against the sky, and every face was turned in the direction of the Master.

'We know what we are,' he was saying, 'and we know what we are not.'

The crowd murmured in agreement.

'And what we are not,' he went on, 'we shall now, ceremonially, destroy.'

His right arm swept out sideways, then his left, and lighted coals flew in quick, bright arcs from both his sleeves. The crowd cried out with one voice, a voice in which I heard both rapture and alarm, then it burst into spontaneous applause. The coals had landed among the kindling, and the stacked wood beneath the animals had started to burn. But the Master of the Conflagration was gone. Though he didn't appear to have climbed down off the platform, he could no longer be seen. His bodyguards were leaving by a rough track that led up to the neck of the pass. Their dark clothes soon merged with the darkness of the field. Above me, the salamander began to creak and fidget as flames reached for its belly.

I turned to the man standing beside me. In the light of the blaze his face seemed to glisten. 'Where did he go?' I asked.

The man didn't take his eyes off the burning animals. 'This must be your first time.'

'Yes.'

The peacock's tail flared with a vicious crackle.

'Some say he's the leader of the Black Square,' the man said. 'Others say he's just a travelling magician.' The man turned to me, and the shadow of his nose lengthened across his cheek so suddenly, so markedly, that I flinched. The man grinned. 'You'll just have to make up your own mind.'

'It's you,' I said.

The man's grin widened. 'Is it?'

People scattered, screaming, as the salamander's head parted with its body and floated into the air, swept upwards by a blast of heat and held there for a moment, as if tethered. It swayed in the dark sky, leering at our upturned faces, then it was consumed by flames, its long tongue curling, shrivelling, blackening, and with one final lurch, in which it appeared to cast a poignant glance over its shoulder, recalling, perhaps, the journey it had undertaken earlier that evening, it crashed to the ground in a shower of sparks, leaving nothing but a heap of burnt paper and a scorched wire frame. I watched as several children ran over and poked at the corpse with sticks. Then, like many others, I turned and started back towards the road.

Afterwards I couldn't remember how we met, only that I was standing at the bar and that they were there as well, the three of them. Leon did most of the talking. He wore a leather jacket, and he had lined the lower rims of his eyelids with black kohl. The other man, Mike, had a spider's web tattooed on the side of his neck. The girl was called April. In her crimson headscarf, her frayed denim jacket and her knee-length boots, she looked faintly piratical. They lived in Ustion, Leon told me, which was sixty miles north, but they always drove down for the burning of the animals. You couldn't miss the burning.

Somehow it came out in conversation that I was thinking of heading that way.

'You want a lift?' Leon said. 'We're going there ourselves. Right now.'

Mike and April swallowed their drinks and placed the empty glasses on the bar. It all seemed to have been decided very quickly.

'Really,' April said. 'It's no trouble.' Gazing up at me, she linked her arm through mine.

'Well, if you're sure.' I drained my brandy.

'That's the spirit,' Leon said.

'Come on, Tom.' April pulled gently on my arm, and we walked out of the bar together.

Leon had a dented pickup truck with roll-bars at the front and an extra set of headlights mounted on the roof. For hunting, he explained. Before he could go into any detail, though, I realised I had left my bag behind. Saying I would only be a moment, I turned and hurried back into the pub.

Upstairs, when I switched the light on, my room appeared to

slip a little, like a picture dropping in its frame. Now that I had accepted Leon's offer of a lift, I was worried he might become impatient and go without me. And there was April too, of course – that tantalising look she'd given me, the way she'd called me 'Tom' . . . I packed as fast as I could and zipped my bag shut, then I hoisted it on to my shoulder and ran back down the stairs. I found Fay Mackenzie in the bar. I couldn't thank her enough, I told her, for taking me in, for treating me so well and, above all, for trusting me. Probably I said too much, my words tumbling over one another, but she only smiled at me and wished me luck. She wouldn't take any money for the room.

Outside, the air had thickened. The smoke from the burning seemed to have been driven down the hill, flakes of charred paper drifting past at head-height. My new friends were standing at the edge of the car-park, deep in conversation. Then one of them noticed me, and they separated, their faces turning towards me.

'All set?' Leon said.

I nodded.

He held the door open on the passenger's side. I climbed in first, hoping April would follow, but Mike got in next, leaving April to sit against the door. Leon went round to the driver's side. Once behind the wheel, he revved the engine, then let the clutch out fast. The truck leapt down the road that led away from the pub.

April leaned forwards and spoke to him. 'You drunk?'

'No drunker than usual,' he said.

I held my bag on my lap, aware of the men's shoulders on either side of me. It was cold in the truck, and the cramped interior smelled of oil and cigarettes. I watched as the headlights picked out one bend after another.

I turned to Leon. 'How far did you say it was?'

'Where to?' he said.

'Ustion.'

'I don't know. It's a way.'

He seemed to consider the question irrelevant, beside the point. My stomach tightened. I stole a glance at his profile,

171

hoping for some reassurance, but all I saw was a low, brooding brow, and teeth that slanted back into his mouth like a shark's – features I had failed to notice while we were talking in the bar.

After driving for five or ten minutes, Leon took a sharp right-hand turn on to a much narrower road. Mike and I were thrown to the left, and April cried out, then swore, as she was crushed against the door. Leon just laughed. The truck lurched and bounced over potholes, unseen branches scraping at the windows and the roof. As I peered through the windscreen, trying to determine where we were going, the road opened out into a wide apron of gravel and weeds. Our headlights swept over part of a building, and I caught glimpses of a turret and an ivy-covered wall.

'Where's this?' I asked.

Nobody answered.

Leon switched the lights and engine off, then opened his door and stepped out. April and Mike climbed out the other side. I hesitated, then I followed. We had parked next to a circular pond with a raised edge, the water hidden beneath a quilt of lily pads. I lifted my eyes to the building that lay beyond. The wings that extended sideways from the gate-house were topped by battlements, and the windows resembled those in medieval castles. I turned back to Leon, who seemed to have fallen into a kind of trance. His friends were standing near by, but facing in different directions, as though keeping watch. I wasn't sure why they had brought me to this place. I suspected I was becoming embroiled in some reckless agenda of theirs, as a result of which I might lose sight of my own.

'It used to be an asylum,' Leon said, 'but it was shut down years ago.'

The night was quiet and still. Moonlight coated everything.

I walked over to Leon. 'I need to get moving,' I said. 'Maybe you could tell me which way to go.'

He didn't take his eyes off the building. 'First you have to give us something. For our trouble.'

I stared at him blankly. 'Give you something?'

'Some kind of payment.'

172

Mike seized me from behind, pinning my arms, then Leon reached into my pockets and felt around.

'If it's money you want,' I said, 'it's in my wallet.'

Leon stood back. Behind him, April cut my bag open with a knife and started tossing pieces of my clothing on to the ground.

'There's nothing valuable in there,' I said.

Leon leaned in towards me again, blocking my view of the girl. 'You know it all, don't you?' A grey gleam on his sloping teeth. 'Actually, no, that can't be true,' he said. 'Because if you knew it all you wouldn't have got yourself into this situation in the first place.' I watched as he opened my wallet and went through the contents. He shone a torch on my visa, then on my identity papers, and let out a low whistle.

Still stooping over my bag, April looked round. 'What?'

'I heard he was from somewhere else,' Leon said. 'I just didn't know where.'

'Where's he from?' April asked.

Leon told her.

'What do you think he's doing here?' she said.

Still examining my papers, Leon didn't say anything.

April walked towards me. 'He could be a spy.'

I had applied the same word to myself only the night before, but in a purely romantic sense. Now, though, it was being used seriously, as an accusation.

'That's ridiculous,' I said.

Almost instantly there was an explosion in my head, and I dropped to the gravel, lights hanging in the left side of my field of vision like a curtain of garish elongated beads. Mike must have hit me.

As I lay there, April reached down and pulled off my coat. I made no attempt to resist. She put the coat on over her denim jacket, then paraded up and down in front of the pond as if she were on a catwalk. She was much shorter than me, and the coat's hem trailed along the ground behind her.

'You're spoiling it,' I murmured.

Mike's boot caught me just below the ribs. 'It's hers now,' he said. 'She can do what she likes with it.'

Lying on my side, doubled up, I felt the bile rush into my mouth. At the same time, I had the feeling that the episode was already over and that it could have been much worse. They had what they wanted – my money, my documents, my coat. Clearly, though, there was a kind of protocol involved. They couldn't leave until their superiority had been properly established. It was important therefore that I didn't draw any more attention to myself. Better to grovel, play dead.

It appeared to work. The next time I looked, they had their backs turned.

'I almost forgot,' Leon said over his shoulder. 'You go that way.' He pointed off into the trees.

April made a remark I didn't catch. The two men laughed.

Doors slammed. My head still resting on the ground, I felt the surge of the engine in my teeth, a vibration conducted by the earth, a kind of bass note. The pickup truck turned in a slow, tight half-circle and I was blinded for a second as its bank of lights swept over me. I saw myself as they must have seen me, a crumpled man, eyes shut to slits. The roar faded. For some time afterwards I thought I could detect the reverberation, but then I decided it was just one of the many layers that made up the silence – or even, perhaps, some residue from the bomb that had gone off, a memory that was physical, a tremor stored below the surface of my skin.

I lay there in the dirt like someone paralysed. There was even a part of me that wanted to go to sleep. They had taken everything – and yet, no, that wasn't quite true. At least I had those banknotes hidden in my collar. I would need them now. So why this sense of abandonment, this loss of all initiative? I could only think it was because I'd been attacked. Where I came from, things like that didn't happen.

The brandy was beginning to wear off, and my mouth tasted of cinders. I forced myself to sit up. The bead curtain still hung in my head, undulating slightly, as if somebody had just passed through it, and each time I took a breath a sharp blade seemed to pierce the left side of my chest. I had been hoping to continue on foot, but it was after midnight and I didn't know the exact nature of my injuries. It would make more sense to shelter in the asylum. Then, when morning came, I would reassess the situation.

I climbed to my feet and walked over to my bag. The sides had been slashed open, and my clothes lay scattered all around. I would only take what I could carry in my pockets – socks, a toothbrush, underwear. A sweater would be useful too, I thought. I removed my jacket, then pulled on the only sweater I had brought along, wincing as I lifted my arms above my head. I left everything else where it was. From a distance my bag looked cryptic, even faintly chilling, the sort of thing that leads people to believe in alien abduction.

Some gut feeling prevented me from trying the main entrance. Instead, I circled one of the towers and started down the left side of the building. There had been a path here once, but thistles and brambles had sprung up, and I had to inch forwards with my arms at shoulder-level and my elbows pointing outwards, like someone wading into cold water for a swim. The moonlight made space and distance hard to judge. A low branch almost took my eye out, and the backs of my fingers stung where they had brushed against blue-grey beds of nettles.

At last, towards the rear of the building, the undergrowth cleared, and I was able to approach a window. I began to hunt for a stone, kneeling down and running my hands over the ground, but I couldn't find anything, so I unlaced one of my shoes and, gripping it by the toe, swung the heel sharply against the glass. The splintering noise was so loud that I was sure a caretaker or night-watchman would appear. I held still and listened. Nothing except an owl deep in the woods behind me. Knocking the rest of the window into the room, I put my shoe back on and clambered through.

There was a smell of yeast. Methylated spirits too. I moved towards a doorway, glass snapping underfoot. Then on into a corridor. Much darker here. Gloss paint on the walls, the dim outline of a stainless-steel trolley. When I came to a staircase, I began to climb. Again, I didn't attempt to rationalise my decision. I simply assumed it was instinct, something primitive or vestigial kicking in.

In a small room on the third floor I found a bed, just a bare mattress resting on coiled metal springs, but a bed nonetheless, and for all my injuries, for all the exhausting twists and turns of the past day or two, I heard myself laugh out loud. The sound didn't last. The huge empty building dispensed with it, as though it were unsuitable, improper, a habit that had been discredited or lost.

On the far side of the bed was a wooden chair. Beyond that, the room's only window. The moon had lodged itself in the top right-hand pane, its bright face half-hidden by a strip of cloud. Lowering myself on to the bed, I reached out and touched the headboard. There were dark patches where the paint had been chipped away by inmates or intruders, the letters carved so crudely that they often overshot each other. I thought I detected a 'J', though, and I wondered whether it was to a place like this that Jones had been sent, and whether he had ever curled up on a mattress and tried to scratch his initials into part of a bed, or into a wall, and once again, despite all the time that had gone by, I felt for him. Then I remembered my first night at the club – Jones walking towards me, Jones unharmed. It was always possible that he'd survived, and even, maybe, prospered. And what of me? Would I prosper? Would I survive? I saw my bedroom, high up in the house, the copper beech outside, the road beyond. I'd had such a vivid sense of myself – just then, for those few moments. I had felt so present, so *alive*. And if I was here now, risking everything, it was because I was determined not to let that feeling go. I lay down on my side and, as I pulled my jacket over me and drew my knees in towards my chest, I found I had left the asylum, the Yellow Quarter too, and I was moving across the lobby of the club, one hand lifting to part the velvet curtain . . .

I woke several times that night. Once, the moon still hung in the window, though it had sunk into one of the lower panes. When I opened my eyes again, only seconds later seemingly, the moon had gone.

In all my dreams I was cold.

Towards dawn I heard a ticking somewhere outside. I rose to my feet and crept across the room. The door creaked as I turned the handle. All I could see when I peered to the left was a long corridor, like a tunnel, filled with milky light. I turned to the right. A dog stood twenty feet away, looking at me over its shoulder. It had small eyes and a blunt boot of a head. Some kind of bull terrier, I supposed. So pale, though. Unnaturally pale. I shut the door and leaned against it, my heart beating high up in my throat. I waited a few minutes, then I fetched the chair and wedged it beneath the door-handle. For the rest of the night I slept in snatches.

I woke and lay quite motionless, my breath showing against the wall like smoke. I pulled myself upright. My ribs had stiffened, but I didn't think anything was broken. On my temple a lump had formed, the same shape as the back of a teaspoon, and my left eyebrow had split open. The crusting of blood crumbled like earth beneath my fingers. I slipped my jacket on over my sweater, then let my eyes travel slowly round the room. Pale-green walls, floorboards painted grey. A window showing treetops and a cloudy sky. A cupboard. Bookshelves, but no books. Then I saw the chair tilted at an angle against the door. There had been a dog, I remembered. It had stared at me over its shoulder, its jaws set in a mirthless grin.

I began to look for something that might double as a weapon. In the cupboard I found some medical magazines, a plastic measuring jug and an empty pot of white emulsion. On the shelves, only a jam-jar filled with brownish liquid. There was nothing under the bed. In the end, I snapped one of the legs off the chair. It would serve as a cudgel. If I used the paint pot as a kind of gauntlet, I would be able to fend the dog off with one hand while I attacked it with the other. The whole thing seemed laughable – a charade, really – but how else was I going to protect myself?

I put an ear to the door. Silence. Hardly daring to breathe, I eased the chair out from beneath the handle and stood it behind me, then I opened the door. A lino floor stretching away. A scattering of leaves, fragile and ginger. Staying close to the wall, I set off along the corridor, the leaves exploding beneath my shoes. I hadn't noticed them the night before, but then I hadn't realised that if I made a noise I might put myself in danger. I reached the stairwell. Cool air slid up from below.

On the first floor I stopped again, imagining I'd heard a bark, though it was hard to tell above the fierce hiss of blood inside my head. I wondered how many dogs there were. It seemed unlikely there would be just one.

I didn't try and make it back to the broken window. Instead, I moved through the kitchens and on into the laundry. At last I found a door I could unbolt. Ducking under tangled washing-lines, I mounted a flight of steps and came out on to a terrace that ran the entire length of the back of the building. Fragments of shattered roof-tile lay about, and dandelions had sprung up in the cracks between the wide uneven flags. From the balustrade I could survey the grounds. A lawn and then a hedge, both overgrown. In the distance, a jagged, tree-lined horizon. The sky was still and grey, and pressed down like the soft pedal on a piano, deadening all sound.

I hurried away across the grass. Hunger gripped me, keen as loneliness. Beyond a high brick wall was a kitchen garden, and my spirits lifted, but everything in there had been neglected for too long. The leaves of cabbages had turned to ragged dark-green lace, while the rhubarb stalks were thick as builders' wrists. As for the apples, wasps had drilled them through and through. I managed to dig up two potatoes, which I wiped clean on my shirt-tail and ate raw. Later, on a spindly tree by the far wall, I found a single pear. I plucked the fruit from its branch and studied the speckled skin, as if for instructions, then I bit into it, and the flesh, though hard and bitter, had a curiously refreshing quality. All the same, I couldn't rid myself of the feeling that I might have eaten something that was supposed to be orna-mental.

I emerged from the garden and climbed a grass slope, making for the cover of the trees. Once there, I stopped and took a final look at the place where I had spent the night. It struck me as odd that the asylum hadn't been put to better use – choleric people were meant to be so dynamic, so resourceful – but perhaps, in the end, the four countries didn't vary as much as was commonly believed. Perhaps our famous differences were no more than convenient fictions. I was aware that my thoughts were taking a new turn, and wondered if I had been influenced – contaminated, some might say – by Fay Mackenzie and her friends. Before I could reach any conclusions, I saw a white dog come lumbering round the edge of the building, its blunt muzzle close to the flagstones, as though following a scent. I could delay no longer. Keeping a firm grasp on the chair-leg, I set off into the woods.

After walking for some time, I stepped out on to a ridge, and there below me, to my astonishment, lay the border. From my vantage point I could see over the wall into the countryside beyond – its fields, its hawthorn hedges, its narrow twisting lanes. For a moment I thought I was looking at the Blue Quarter, but then I remembered it hadn't featured on the map in the café at all. The border with the Blue Quarter would have to be at least an hour away by car, and we hadn't been on the road for more than five or ten minutes. Leon and his friends had told me we were driving north, to the city where they lived, but actually we must have driven east. It was the Green Quarter that I could see. Those people had not only robbed me, they had lied to me as well. Maybe that was why they'd been laughing just before they left.

Tired and disconsolate, I sat down at the foot of a tree, laying my eccentric weapons on the ground beside me. It was a typical rural border, with a single concrete wall reaching away in both directions. There were no watch-towers, no death strips. No men with guns. A set of tyre-tracks ran parallel to the wall, worn in the grass by regular patrols. It made me think of the section of border that Marie had talked about. *We thought we must be seeing things. We just climbed through.* I couldn't see any gaps or holes in this wall, though – and, even if there had been, it wouldn't have done me any good. I hadn't the slightest desire to enter the Green Quarter. There was nothing for me there.

Still, after a while, curiosity got the better of me, and I started down the hill. A few minutes later, I was standing in the shadow of the wall, and I saw at once that it was both immaculate and unassailable. No flaws or blemishes. Not even any cracks. The wall had been built to the standard height, with a smooth rounded lip at the top, a kind of overhang. It offered no handholds or footholds – no purchase of any kind. I placed my palm against the surface. It was cold as a gravestone. It promised death. Even here, under an innocuous November sky. Even here, in the middle of nowhere. I stood back. What now?

At that moment I heard a faint buzzing noise, not unlike a power drill or an electric razor. I looked northwards along the track. A motorbike came slithering and sliding over a rise in the ground, and as it drew nearer I saw that its rider was wearing the uniform of a choleric border guard, the black rainproof jacket trimmed with yellow piping, the gun strapped into a yellow holster.

The motorbike stopped beside me. I hadn't moved. The guard switched off the engine, then he removed his helmet and placed it on the petrol tank in front of him.

'Hard to talk with one of those things on,' he said.

'I imagine,' I said.

The guard had cut himself shaving, and the small circle of dried blood on his chin gave him an air of vulnerability. His black hair had been flattened by the helmet. I was reminded, incongruously, of the places in fields where people have had picnics or made love. Now that I was facing the danger I had hardly dared to picture, I felt curiously calm, and on the edge of a powerful and unforeseen hilarity.

'What are you doing here?' the guard said.

'Just out for a walk,' I said.

'You're not thinking of –' His eyes darted towards the top of the wall.

I smiled. 'Climbing over? How could I?' I held my arms away

from my sides, to demonstrate my innocence, the fact that I had nothing to hide.

'You'd be surprised,' the guard said.

Removing his leather gauntlets, he took out a pouch of tobacco and some rolling papers, and then embarked on a story about a man called Jake Tilney who had been transferred to the Yellow Quarter when he was in his forties. Though he seemed, outwardly, to be settling into his new life, Jake never stopped trying to find a way of returning to the Green Quarter, which had been his home before. At last he came up with something so obvious, so straightforward, as to merit the word genius. He designed and built his very own pocket ladder. It had an extension capacity of eleven and a half feet, which was the exact height of the wall, but it folded into a metal rectangle that measured no more than twelve inches by eighteen and weighed less than a bag of sugar. One day Jake travelled to a remote section of the border. Alone and unobserved, he assembled his ladder and climbed to the top of the wall, then he simply pulled the ladder up after him, placed it on the other side and climbed down again – and all in less than sixty seconds, or so he maintained in his statement.

'He was caught,' I said.

The guard nodded.

When Jake Tilney appeared in front of the tribunal, claiming that he belonged in the Green Quarter, the judges laughed at him. In the very manner of his escape attempt, they said, he had proved beyond a shadow of a doubt that he was unqualified to live there.

Perhaps if you had done something less practical, they said, *less daring* –

But then it wouldn't have worked, Jake cried.

The judges exchanged a knowing glance.

Jake was transferred back to the Yellow Quarter. Two years later he died of a heart attack, a common cause of death for those of a choleric disposition. His ladder, now known as the Tilney, won him a posthumous award for significant achievement in the field of industrial design.

'A cruel irony,' I said.

The guard nodded again and looked at the ground, his roll-up dead between his fingers. He was not at all the kind of brute or bully I would have expected to encounter at the border. Though he seemed a little indiscreet – should he be telling me about escape attempts? weren't all those details confidential? – I felt he was a man I could get along with. I offered him a light, which he accepted.

'There is another possibility, of course,' he said, removing a strand of tobacco from his tongue. 'You could have something hidden in the grass. Or up there' – and his eyes lifted to the ridge behind me – 'among the trees.'

'Like what?'

'Like maybe a pole,' he said. 'As in pole-vault.'

I raised my eyebrows. 'I would never have thought of that.' And it was true. I wouldn't.

'We had one of those last month. Ex pole-vault champion. Fellow by the name of Alvis Deane.'

'Can't say I've heard of him.'

'Well, nor had I, to be honest.'

'Did he make it?'

'Yes and no.' The guard fell silent. The art of suspense appeared to come naturally to him. 'There was something on the other side,' he said, tossing the soggy stub of his roll-up into the grass. 'A greenhouse.'

I imagined the scene. 'Noisy.'

'And painful,' the guard said. 'He broke his pelvis and both his legs. An elbow too, if I remember rightly. And there were severe lacerations, of course.' He shook his head.

It had all been going so easily. We were like two men talking in a pub, so much so that I had been lulled into believing that the guard could be disarmed by the mere fact of conversation, that any suspicion he might normally have felt in a situation like this could be overridden, and that, in no time at all, I would be allowed to continue on my way without further ado. During his most recent silence, however, his eyes had been roving across my suit, which was creased and stained, and he gradually assumed a resigned, almost forlorn expression.

'I'm afraid I'm going to have to search you,' he said.

'In case I've got a ladder on me?'

Smiling bleakly, the guard stepped off his motorbike and heaved it up on to its stand. 'Could you empty your pockets?'

I did as he asked, producing the lighter, my toothbrush, some loose change, a pair of underpants and some socks.

'Nothing else?' he said.

'That's it.'

The guard pushed his hands into all my pockets, much as Leon had done a few hours earlier. Then, like a customs officer, he ran his hands over the outside of my clothes, along both my arms, down both my legs. Up close, he smelled of wintergreen, as if he might be carrying a sporting injury. I looked beyond him, at the wall, its smooth blank concrete unable either to help or to remember.

At last the guard stood back. 'You don't appear to have any papers.'

'No,' I said. 'Well, I was attacked, you see.'

'Attacked?'

'Three people in a pickup truck. They attacked me. They took my papers and all my money. They took my coat as well.'

'You're aware, of course,' the guard said slowly, 'that it's a criminal offence to travel anywhere without your papers?'

'I just told you. They were stolen.'

We weren't like two men in a pub any more. The mood had altered, the sense of common ground had dropped away. A hierarchy had been established in its place. The guard was beginning to work himself up into a state of necessary indignation. He might even achieve outrage. And if that happened, I would be in trouble.

You have to act like them.

I snatched up the guard's helmet and hit him full in the face with it. He cried out. Hands covering his face, he sank to his knees and toppled sideways, bright blood dripping through his fingers. I took the gun out of its holster and used the butt to smash the radio, then I hurled the gun over the wall. It landed on the other side with a dull thud like ripe fruit dropping from a tree. No greenhouse there, then. I grabbed my possessions and stuffed them back into my pockets. As I turned away, the motorbike fell over, crushing one of the guard's legs. He cried out again, even louder this time. I hesitated for a moment, then I started running.

I leaned against a tree at the top of the hill. My mouth tasted of tin, and I felt sick. I had never hit anyone before. Maybe that was why. Down below, the guard was on the ground, the motorbike still lying across his leg. My mind began to spin, hurling out thoughts the way a lawn-sprinkler hurls out water. A motorbike like that might weigh as much as three hundred pounds. It would be hard to shift. There was even a possibility that his leg was broken. Without a radio he wouldn't be able to raise the alarm, in which case he'd have to wait until a colleague came along, and that might not be for hours. Still, it was only a matter of time before word got out. *There's a man on the loose. He's wearing a dark suit. He's not carrying any documents.* A pause. *He could be dangerous.* With a hollow, frightened laugh, I turned and plunged into the woods. I couldn't form a coherent strategy as yet. I was simply trying to put some distance between myself and what had happened.

Half an hour later I waded out of waist-high bracken and on to a farm track. On the far side, behind metal railings, was a field of green wheat. A light wind blew. The wheat ears swayed. It was peaceful, but suspiciously so, as though the crops hid an entire battalion of soldiers. When the signal was given, they would all rise up, the barrels of their rifles trained on my head and heart. As I started along the track, I tried to put myself in the guard's position. There he was, trapped under his motorbike, and with a bloody nose into the bargain. It was an absurd predicament. Humiliating too. Would he be prepared to admit that someone had hit him in the face with his own helmet? Imagine the teasing that would go on at his local barracks! Imagine the nicknames he'd be given! *Helmethead, Nosebleed. Arse.*

Rounding a bend, I saw a five-bar gate ahead of me. A country lane beyond. My mind was still whirling with theories, hypotheses. What if the guard claimed that his bike had skidded in the mud? What if he pretended that he'd never even set eyes on me? I began to see how his discomfiture might work in my favour. It seemed conceivable that I might not be reported after all – in which case I could return to the Axe Edge Inn, where Fay would help me.

I looked up into the sky. The clouds had thinned, unveiling a strip of the purest pale-blue. I could be in the bar by lunchtime, and think of the tale I would be able to tell! I vaulted over the gate and, buttoning my jacket against the wind, set off along the lane with rapid, determined strides.

It looked exactly like a crime scene. The pub had been sealed off with bright-yellow plastic tape, the words POLICE – DO NOT CROSS repeated every few feet in black. Two of the downstairs windows had been smashed, and the car-park glittered with broken glass. A plank had been nailed at an angle across the front entrance. There were dark stains at the edge of the road. I couldn't tell whether it was oil or blood. As I stood there, I noticed something glinting in the ditch. At first I took it for a coin, but then I bent closer and saw it was a ring. Though made from silver, it was uneven, almost crude, and it had blackened here and there, either with neglect or age. On the inside an intriguing inscription had been carved into the metal, with an anchor to separate the first word from the last. *So you don't drift too far*, it said.

I had just slipped the ring into my pocket when I heard a whirring sound, and I looked round to see a bicycle come freewheeling down the hill towards me. I recognised the rider as the fair-haired singer from the night before. When he saw me, he braked and sat astride his bicycle, one foot resting on the pedals, the other on the ground. He had a gash on his cheek, and three of his fingers had been bound with tape. I asked him if he had seen Fay Mackenzie.

He looked past me, at the view. 'She's been arrested.'

'What happened?'

'There was a raid.' He looked at me again. 'Who are you, anyway?'

I told him roughly what I had told Fay, adding that I had been attacked and robbed shortly after leaving the pub. Fay was the only person I could trust, I said, and I needed her help.

'She's the one who needs help,' the man said. 'I hate to think what they'll do to her.'

Midnight was striking, he told me, when they heard engines snarling on the hill below the pub. The lorries were enough to scare you in themselves – enormous military vehicles with searchlights mounted on the top, their wheels the size of tractor wheels, thick shapes carved into the tyres for grip. The police were members of a special riot squad, armed with rubber bullets, tear-gas and electric cattle-prods. At least thirty people had been arrested, and many more were injured. The Axe Edge Inn had been officially closed down until further notice.

'But why?' I said. 'What's the reason?'

'They don't need a reason. They can call it anything they want.' He glanced at his taped fingers. Then in a bitterly ironic voice, he said, 'I expect we were jeopardising national security.'

'You got away, though.'

'I was lucky.'

The world seemed to flatten, to spread out sideways. With Fay gone, I had no one to turn to – unless . . . Into my head floated the image of a large bearded man dancing with a bright-green rabbit.

John Fernandez.

I remembered that he lived in Athanor, the Yellow Quarter's biggest port. As good a place to disappear as any. Ports were heterogeneous, chaotic, filled with strangers. If I went to Fernandez, though, would he hand me over to the authorities? Somehow I couldn't imagine it. I hardly knew the man, and yet I had spent enough time in his company to realise that he was something of a maverick. Despite his bulky, shambling presence, he had a quicksilver quality. A conventional reaction could not be relied upon, which in my current predicament could only augur well, I felt. In the end, it had to be a risk worth taking.

I asked the fair-haired man where the nearest railway station was. He pointed back the way I had just come. It was fifteen miles, he said. Maybe more.

'I'd like to buy your bicycle,' I said.

The man laughed.

'I'll give you a good price.' I took off my jacket and, reaching into one end of the collar, eased out a banknote and held it up.

'That would buy you three of these,' he told me.

'Yes or no?'

The man shrugged. 'Please yourself.'

Handing him the money, I took the bicycle and swung my leg over the crossbar. 'Well,' I said, 'I suppose I should be going.'

Hands on hips, the man was shaking his head. Clearly, he couldn't quite believe the direction that events had taken.

'Safe journey,' he called out as I rode away.

The wind roared in my ears, and the air was so cold that tears slid sideways into my hair, but I felt liberated, almost giddy. I began to sing. I had no words, only a melody, and though the piece sounded familiar I couldn't place it. That didn't stop me. I sang until my throat hurt. At first I assumed it was something to do with Victor, a favourite tape of his, but two hours later, when I drew up in front of the station, my mind seemed to open, revealing a door standing ajar and a landing beyond, not L-shaped like the house on Hope Street, but wide and spacious, with a hallway below, and light showing through the dark bars of the banisters ... Could I be remembering music my parents used to play after I'd been sent upstairs to bed?

Athanor shocked me with its brazen air of dereliction. I suppose the name had led me to expect a wondrous place, a place of magical transformation, and yet, as I emerged from the gritty gloom of the railway station and started walking down one of the port's main thoroughfares, I saw stretches of barren land sealed off by wire-mesh and wooden hoardings, whole sections of the city laid to waste, whole streets demolished, gone. At one point I passed a pub that stood entirely on its own, defiant yet piteous, like the last remaining tooth in a punch-drunk boxer's mouth. In the years prior to the Rearrangement the city would have gone under completely were it not for all the money made from drugs, and traces of that warped energy were still visible in the developments along the docks, the casino complexes and the flyovers that swooped dizzily through the centre. Still, the city seemed defined by omissions, by absences. *Athanor: an oven used by alchemists.* I couldn't imagine all this grime and decay turning to gold, at least not in the near future.

Not long after arriving, I saw a group of ten-year-olds with voices like crows and no eyebrows, soft drinks in their hands, and bags of crisps, and mobile phones. Over the choppy paving-stones they came, with predatory speed, only fanning out and flowing round me at the very last minute. One of them lifted the flap on my jacket pocket, his fingers deft as a gust of wind, but it was just habit, a kind of reflex. He had already scanned me as a prospect and rejected me. With hindsight, I was glad I had left my bicycle at the station. I was glad too that my overcoat had been stolen. As it was, the gang never guessed that I had a small fortune sewn into my collar, nor that a silver ring hung on a piece of string around my neck. I touched one hand to my bruised forehead. Oddly enough, the fact that I'd been attacked now stood me in good stead. It made me more authentic, less visible. I could imagine tourists flying in to Athanor with stick-on stitches and fake scars in their luggage, as one took sun-cream to the beach, for protection. *Want to enjoy your stay in the Yellow Quarter? Want to blend in? Make sure you look badly beaten up! Choose from our unique range of cosmetic wounds and injuries!*

In a street not far from the cathedral I found a pub called the Duke's Head. The walls were the colour of raw liver, and the wood floor was strewn with cigarette butts. It was Friday night, and people stood three or four deep at the bar. A mosaic of faces, everybody talking. The air mostly smoke. When I got close enough, I sat on a stool and ordered a double brandy. It was a cheap make, and the first taste sent a shudder through me. I held still and stared between my knees, hoping I wouldn't bring the drink back up, but then I felt the warmth hit my stomach and begin to spread.

The journey to Athanor had gone smoothly – that is, until a woman got into my carriage. She had a boy of about four with her, and he had noticed me immediately. Children are like the police, I thought. No one can make you feel guilty the way a child can. Standing on his mother's lap, the boy had levelled a finger at me. *What's that?* The woman glanced in my direction. *That's a man.* The boy hadn't seemed at all convinced. In an attempt to deflect any awkwardness, I asked the woman what his name was. *Thomas,* she said. *That's my name,* I told her. *Did you hear that?* the woman said to the child. *The man's called Thomas, just like you.* The child shook his head. *No,* he said. I smiled at the woman and shrugged good-naturedly, then I stared out of the window, pretending to take an interest in the scenery. *What's that?* Strange how appropriate those words seemed. With his innocent yet merciless gaze, his almost feral intuition, the boy had seen me for what I was – at large without papers, stateless, no longer properly a person.

Putting my drink down, I asked the landlord whether it was possible to make a call. He directed me to a pay-phone in the corridor that led to the toilets. The phone-book had been torn in two, but luckily the front half had survived. I ran through the 'F's. There he was, the only FERNANDEZ J. in the book. I memorised his address – 176 Harbour Drive – then returned to the bar and ordered another brandy. When the landlord brought me my drink, I asked if he knew where Harbour Drive was. He couldn't think, but an old woman with a black eye-patch overheard and answered for him. Take a left out of the pub, she said, and then keep walking for about a mile. I'd see the road on my right. There was a chippie on the corner. I thanked her, and she promptly banged her glass down on the bar in front of me. She wanted a large vodka, with no ice. I bought her one. When she had swallowed it, which only took a moment, the glass hit the bar in front of me again. I smiled at her and shook my head, then I finished my brandy and eased down off my stool. As I turned to go, the woman put her face close to mine and lifted her eye-patch to reveal the scarred and hollow socket underneath. I pushed through the crowd to the door, then I was outside.

From the fish-and-chip shop Harbour Drive sloped upwards, becoming steadily more prosperous. After half a mile the road levelled out, and it was here that I found number 176, a detached house with a garage. I walked in through the front gate, climbed the steps to the porch and pressed the bell. The house looked closed up for the night. Even the stained-glass fanlight above the door showed only a faint glimmer from inside, as if a single lamp had been left on at the far end of the hall. I hoped John Fernandez hadn't gone to bed. I pressed the bell again.

'Who's there?'

I jumped. It was Fernandez, and yet I had heard no footsteps, nor had I noticed any lights go on. Was it possible that he'd been watching out for me? Had he somehow known that I would come?

I put my mouth to the letter box. 'It's Thomas Parry. We met at the conference.'

A moment of absolute stillness, then two locks turned and the door swung inwards. We stood facing each other, in near darkness. Fernandez was wearing the same black-rimmed glasses he had worn on the night of the card game.

'What are you doing here?' he said.

'Could you let me in?' I said. 'I'll explain everything.'

He looked over my shoulder, scanning the street, then looked at me again. For a few tense seconds I thought he might turn me away – he would have been quite capable of such a reaction, I was sure – but finally he stood aside, and I stepped past him, into the hall. He closed the door and fastened both the locks.

'I was just going to bed,' he said with his back to me.

'I'm sorry,' I said. 'I had nowhere else to go.'

I followed him through a door on the right side of the hall. He told me to watch my head on the way down. At the bottom of the stairs we turned left into a long low-ceilinged room with a mustard-coloured sofa at one end and a desk with a swivel chair at the other. In the middle of the room two armchairs faced each other across a shag-pile rug. Dark-brown curtains hid the windows. On the desk, in an ornate silver frame, was a black-and-white photograph of a woman in her late twenties or early thirties. She had thick dark eyebrows, creamy skin, and black hair that curled in beneath her chin.

'My sister used to have hair like that,' I said.

Even as I spoke, I was overwhelmed by sheer exhaustion. Sinking into the nearest chair, I leaned my head back and closed my eyes. I gripped the arms of the chair like someone bracing himself for take-off. Like someone afraid of flying.

'I should tell you,' I said. 'I'm here illegally.'

I opened my eyes again. Fernandez seemed to stand out against the furnishings, almost as though he had been superimposed.

He moved over to the desk and opened the deepest of the drawers. He took out a bottle of whisky and two glasses. 'The night the bomb went off,' he said. 'You disappeared.'

'What happened to the conference?'

'It was suspended. We were all sent home.'

I gave him an abbreviated version of what I had done during the hours immediately following the explosion.

'And you've been missing ever since?' he said.

'Yes.'

I watched him carefully. This was the moment I hadn't been able to predict, or even imagine. Either he would think of an excuse to leave the room, and then he would go upstairs and call the authorities, or he would – he would what?

'Drink?' Fernandez held the bottle out towards me.

I shook my head. 'Thanks. I've had enough.'

He poured himself a single measure, then placed the bottle and the unused glass on the desk and stood facing the curtains. 'How did you know?'

'Know what?'

'About me.'

'I didn't.' I paused. 'I don't.'

'No one told you anything?'

'No.'

'Strange,' he murmured. 'I had the feeling you'd seen through me. Something you said, I don't remember what. Or it might've been a look you gave me.'

'I had the feeling there was something unpredictable about you,' I said. 'When I thought of you this morning, when you came into my head, somehow I couldn't imagine you turning me in. So here I am.'

'You took a pretty big risk.'

'I know. I seem to have been doing that lately.'

Fernandez flashed me a look over his shoulder. I ought not to be glib or flippant, I realised. I had almost certainly endangered him by coming to his house. Him and whoever he lived with. That woman in the photograph, perhaps.

'I had no choice,' I said. 'You were the only person I could think of.'

'What do you intend to do?'

'I need to get back to the Blue Quarter.'

'The Blue Quarter? Why?'

I had known that he would ask that question – or that someone would – and yet I hadn't been at all sure how I was going to answer. I leaned forwards in the chair. 'Remember the club I asked you about?'

'What club?'

I started to describe the Bathysphere and what had happened there. I told him how I seemed to have crossed a kind of border in myself, and how, for the first time, I'd had a real sense of the person I used to be, the person I was first, before everything changed, and as I was talking I realised something extraordinary. I had always seen the moment when I was lifted out of bed as a birth, but actually the opposite was true. The cold hands, the bright lights – my parents grieving . . . I had died that night, and I'd been dead ever since. And now I was trying to do something about that. What was this whole journey in the end but an attempt to bring myself back to life?

'I've been dead all this time,' I said, laughing, 'and I didn't even know it.'

Fernandez studied me for a few moments, then he finished his drink and set the glass down on the desk. 'You're tired.'

'Yes. Very.'

'You'd better stay here tonight. You can sleep on the sofa.'

I was about to thank him when I heard a creak on the stairs outside the room. We watched in silence as the door-handle tilted towards the floor. A small face appeared round the edge of the door and gazed at me.

'My daughter,' Fernandez said.

I let my breath out slowly. 'I didn't know you had children.'

'Two.' He walked over to the little girl and lifted her into his arms. 'Come on, Rosie. I'll take you back to bed.' Her solemn dark-brown eyes still trained on me, she rested her head against her father's shoulder.

Before he left the room, he told me to stay where I was and not make any noise. There should be some bedding in the cupboard, he said. The toilet was outside the door. He'd come and get me in the morning.

Later, as I lay beneath a couple of rough wool blankets, I heard a ticking and though I knew there must be a clock in the room it was the pale dog that I could see, patrolling the corridors of the asylum, blunt head lowered, jaws ajar . . .

Somebody let out a cry, and I sat up quickly, blinking. The centre-light had been switched on.

A man with a black beard and glasses stood by the door with a tray. 'You shouted so loud,' he said, 'I almost dropped the whole thing.'

'I'm sorry. I was asleep.' I pushed the blankets to one side and put my feet on the floor.

He set the tray down beside me. He had brought me a cup of coffee, a plate of scrambled eggs and some toast.

'Is it late?' I asked.

He told me it was after ten. He had waited until his wife and children had left the house, not wanting them to know that I was staying.

'What about your daughter?' I said.

'Luckily she's always making things up. When she said there was a strange man in the basement, my wife just told her to get on with her cereal.'

'I'm sorry to have caused you all this trouble.'

He glanced at me over the top of his glasses, as if he suspected me of sarcasm, but I pretended not to have noticed, and he looked away again. He had made a few calls, he told me. While I ate, he outlined what he'd been able to arrange. A boat was leaving the north docks at four o'clock that afternoon, bound for the Blue Quarter with a cargo of religious artefacts. Once it reached its destination, however, I would be on my own. Usually, customs officers were paid to turn a blind eye, but there hadn't been enough time to set up anything like that. He couldn't guarantee I wouldn't be arrested as soon as I stepped out of my container.

'Container?' I murmured, still dazed by what he had just told me. All I had expected from him was a temporary refuge, the chance to catch my breath. Now, suddenly, I was on my way to the Blue Quarter.

'Keep eating,' Fernandez said. 'We have to leave soon.'

When I had finished my breakfast, he took me up to a bathroom on the first floor, where I had a shower and a shave. He left some clean underwear and socks outside the door. Though I had questions for him, somehow I didn't feel I could ask. He was doing so much for me. Curiosity would seem like a form of ingratitude.

Dressed again, I went downstairs and waited in the kitchen. The air still vibrated with the presence of his wife and children, the silence so recent that it had yet to settle properly. I glanced at the remains of breakfast – a slice of toast with a bite taken out of it, small pools of milk in the bottom of bowls, the rim of a white cup smudged with lipstick. A home, a family, routine – all things that people took for granted, and yet they had never seemed more inaccessible to me, or more unlikely. I felt a stab of nostalgia as I stood there, then a loneliness. Was it because I was looking at the kind of life I had been denied, or did I wish I could simply abandon the difficult course I had taken and somehow attach myself to all this security, this warmth? Maybe both were true. But perhaps it was also true that nothing of any value could be achieved without a measure of apprehension and regret.

Given that the authorities might already have issued a warrant for my arrest, Fernandez thought it best if I remained out of sight for the duration of the car journey, so I wedged myself behind the two front seats and let him cover me with some newspapers and an old blanket. I didn't speak until we had been driving for several minutes, but then I couldn't hold back any longer.

'You said last night that you thought I'd seen through you,' I said. 'What did you think I'd seen?'

A snort of disbelief came from the driving seat. 'You really expect me to tell you that?'

'Why not? You've got nothing to lose.'

He stayed quiet for a while. I assumed he had decided not to answer.

'What was so clever about the way they divided us,' he said at last, 'was that it more or less guaranteed that we would hate each other. I can't help feeling a kind of contempt for you, for instance. It might be because of what you're doing, and the effect it has on others, but it might simply be because of who you are. I'm from the Yellow Quarter, and you're from somewhere else. That's probably enough. And yet, to answer your question, I'm one of the few people who believe in that great pipe dream, that we should be able to live in the same country. All of us. You, me – even Rinaldi.' He allowed himself a brief wry laugh. 'Then I see myself succumb to prejudice, and I realise how insidious it is, how easy . . .'

It was silent except for the ticking of the indicator. I chose not to say anything. The honesty and bluntness of what I'd heard had caught me unawares. I hadn't expected Fernandez to be so open, but perhaps, with me hidden, he felt alone in the car. In a sense, then, he was talking to himself.

'It's like racism, really, if you think about it,' he went on. 'I don't mean the old racism. That's dead and gone. I'm not interested in the colour of someone's skin. It's their thoughts that bother me. The new racism is psychological. What's strange is, we seem to need it – to thrive on it. If we don't have someone to despise, we feel uncomfortable, we feel we haven't properly defined ourselves. Hate gives us hard edges. And the authorities knew that, of course. In fact, they were banking on it. They force-fed us our own weakness – our intolerance, our bigotry. They rammed it down our throats.' He paused. 'They took the worst part of us and built a system out of it. And it worked –' He blasted his horn, then swore at another driver, but it was the authorities that he was angry with, and clearly he was also angry with himself.

'You asked me what I thought you saw,' Fernandez said. 'I'll tell you. I thought you realised I was bluffing, or even double-bluffing – my talk on terrorism, and so on. I thought you knew I was against the system. I even suspected you might pity me because I was so obviously fighting a losing battle, and I hated you for that. And I thought you could feel me hating you.'

'I felt something,' I said. 'Not that, though.'

'I was classified as choleric,' Fernandez said, 'which is something I dispute, of course, something I resent as well, and yet I seem to be getting more and more choleric with every year that passes. It's ironic, don't you think?'

I didn't answer.

'What about you?' he said. 'Where do you stand?'

'I'm not sure. What I'm doing, it's not really political. It's more –'

'Everything's political.' The car lurched as Fernandez braked. 'Keep quiet for a moment.'

I heard him wind his window down and speak to somebody outside, then he shifted into gear and drove on.

'I'm not sure you made the right decision,' he said eventually.

'How do you mean?'

'Maybe, when the bomb went off, you should have gone home like the rest of us. Maybe you should have thought things through.'

'Maybe. I don't know.' I paused. 'No, I don't think so.'

As a result of what had happened in the club, something entirely unexpected had risen up inside me. On returning to my hotel room after leaving Rinaldi on the stairs, there had been a moment when I wanted to fling my head back and give vent to a strange wild laughter. I hadn't known what lay behind that sudden exhilaration, only that it felt like the dismissal of everything that didn't matter and the embracing of all that was vital and true. I had been sure of myself in a way that was both abstract and unprecedented and, in spite of all the difficulties I had run into since then, that sense of certainty had grown stronger.

'No,' I said again, more firmly. 'I had no choice.'

'Well, anyway,' Fernandez said, 'it's too late now.'

When I got out of the car, I saw that we were parked in the corner of a large warehouse. I paced up and down to try and work some feeling back into my legs. After a while, a man in blue overalls came over, wiping his grease-stained hands on a rag. 'That's the one, Mr Fernandez,' he said, pointing to a pale-orange container. Then he slid his eyes across to me. 'They lift that container, you'd better be holding on to something. They're not exactly gentle.' He flicked his lank, thinning hair back from his forehead. 'Maybe try and wedge yourself among the statues.'

'What statues?' I said.

The man just sniggered. I watched as Fernandez went round to the back of his car and opened the boot, then I looked at the container again, its exterior scarred and battered. 'Are you going to lock me in?' I asked.

'The door's got a bolt on it,' the man said, 'so it can be opened from inside as well as out. I'd stay inside if I was you. Stuff shifts about. You start walking around the hold, you could get crushed. Also, the guys that run the boat don't know you're there. They're not going to like the idea of a stowaway.'

So I was a stowaway now. I was becoming more illegal by the minute.

'How long's the voyage?' I asked.

'Eighteen hours. Maybe more. Old tramp steamers, it's hard to say.'

Fernandez returned with two blankets and a plastic carrier bag. 'Some food for the journey,' he said. 'And you'll need the blankets. It'll probably get cold in there.'

The man in the overalls stood some distance from us and began to gnaw at his fingers. Every so often he would lift them away from his mouth, nails curling in towards the palm, as if to admire his handiwork.

I looked at Fernandez. 'I don't know how to thank you for all this.'

'I'll be glad to get rid of you,' he said. 'You people who don't know what you're doing, you're dangerous. You destabilise things.'

'I thought that's what you wanted.'

'You people.' Fernandez shook his head. 'You always have to have the last word, don't you?'

There were smells first of all – salt water, rust and then, surprisingly, fried food. I waited for the darkness to ease a little, to reveal something of the interior, but nothing changed. I heard Fernandez drive away – at least, I assumed it was him. My ears still rang with the dull clang of the door slamming. Minutes went by. The darkness was no less dense. I didn't panic, though. Instead, a certain unanticipated relief came over me. It's strange how our reactions can startle us. But perhaps relief made sense. I had been living a life sustained almost entirely by adrenalin, and obviously there was a part of me that viewed the next eighteen hours as a respite, a kind of breathing space. Also, I was bound for the Blue Quarter – and far sooner than I could ever have hoped or imagined. I still couldn't quite believe what Fernandez had done for me.

The man in the overalls had shut the door on me so quickly that I had had no chance to inspect my surroundings. To allay any fears or uncertainties that might beset me later on, I decided to do some exploring. I took one step at a time, fumbling at the air with hands I couldn't see. Having located the wall of the container to my left, I began to follow it, but I hadn't gone far when I came up against an obstacle. Taller than I was, wider too, this would be one of the statues the man in the overalls had mentioned, but since it had been wrapped in protective sheeting I wasn't able to guess who it was. To its right stood another statue, equally well protected and equally anonymous. I stepped to the right once more and found a statue whose arms stretched out in what I took to be a gesture of supplication. A saint, presumably. Which one, though, I couldn't possibly have said. To the right of this third statue there was only air, and I walked forwards again. In nine steps I had reached the far wall of the container. I turned to my right. As I groped my way towards the next corner, my foot caught on something and, bending down, I found a coil of slightly oily rope and several small cylinders or tubes, all roughly the same length. When I realised what they were, I laughed softly to myself. I'd had a lighter on me the whole time – the one that belonged to Annette. Feeling stupid, I brought it out of my coat pocket, then flipped the lid open and thumbed the flint. The flame only lit the area immediately around me, but I could see the rope now and the cigarette butts. There were some white cartons on the floor as well. A couple of dockers must have eaten a takeaway in here, then had a smoke. Holding the lighter at head-height, I saw how the rope had been used to lash the statues together. Solid and yet ghostly, oddly menacing, the wrapped shapes occupied at least two-thirds of the container, which left me a narrow right-angled space, a sort of corridor, in which to move about..

After a while I heard a man shouting instructions close by, his voice accompanied by a high-pitched electric whine, then a loud grinding sound came from below me and the entire container shifted to the left. I pocketed the lighter and sat down, wedging my back against the wall and bracing my heels against one of the ridges in the floor. The container instantly lifted off the ground. I assumed it was being transported from the warehouse to the quay. We stopped again, and I heard more shouting. There were various knocks and bangs on the roof, then the container was hoisted into the air where it swung from side to side, tilting a little. I gripped the legs of the statue nearest to me and kept my feet braced against the metal ridge.

Though I did my best to prepare myself for the container's arrival in the hold, the sudden impact jarred my spine. I was aware too of the disparate pieces of bone that made up my skull; somehow I could feel all the joins. And the loading hadn't finished yet. Shortly afterwards, another container was lowered on to the roof above me with a brutal resounding clang. Now I knew that the containers were being stacked on top of each other, and that mine could well be on the bottom, I felt a flicker of claustrophobia. Once the ship was moving, it might be wise, I thought, to unbolt the door, if only to have an idea of how the cargo had been arranged.

In the meantime my thoughts turned to John Fernandez. Despite his contempt for me, which he had done nothing to conceal, and despite his habitual gruffness, I realised I was missing him. He was the person I felt closest to in all the world. I had tried to explain myself to him, and even though he hadn't really understood, let alone approved, he still knew more about me than anybody else I could think of. It was pathetic, perhaps – he would surely have thought so – but true nonetheless.

A loud rumbling began, and the wall behind me started to vibrate. The ship's engines. Soon we would be heading out to sea. I sat on the floor with one blanket folded under me, the other draped over my shoulders. Night wouldn't have fallen yet, but it was already cold. I opened the bag Fernandez had given me. Inside, I found a slice of pizza. I took a bite. Chorizo or pepperoni. I ate half of it and saved the rest. There was a banana too, a packet of biscuits and a Thermos flask. I unscrewed the flask and brought it to my nose. He had made me coffee. I poured myself a cup, then drank it straight down. I didn't care if Fernandez despised me. My gratitude still stood. He had chosen not to turn me away, though it would have been well within his rights to do so. Instead, he had offered me food and shelter, and we had talked without evasion, without pretence. It was hard to believe that I would never see him again. I only hoped I hadn't compromised him in any way, him and his family.

The floor of the container was plunging and tilting now, and the statues were straining at their ropes. We must have sailed beyond the harbour wall. Using my lighter to locate the door, I began to work the bolt up and down to loosen it. As the door opened, the noise level rose. Clanking, hissing, drumming. In front of me was a container identical to mine. No more than eighteen inches separated the two. The man in the overalls had advised me to stay hidden, but I couldn't have got out, not even if I'd wanted to. I put my head into the narrow gap. Though the containers had been set down in rows, the distances between them varied, making a network of irregular corridors or aisles. A naked bulb in a wire cage protruded from the side-wall of the hull, but the light in the hold was dingy, thick and yellowish. It seemed to ooze from the bulb like some sort of discharge. I looked the other way. Another corridor, but crooked, cramped. The reek of diesel oil and rust and brine. It was a grim place, brutal as a dungeon. Needing to urinate, I aimed into the space between the two containers. When I had finished, I bolted the door and lay down on the folded blanket, then I covered myself with the second blanket and tried to doze.

The unrelenting din of the engines, the see-saw motion of the floor beneath me, the pitch-black and the cold . . . I would lie on my side until it froze, then I would turn over. I did this again and again. In the end I must have slept, though, or else I had one of those visions that sometimes grace the edge of sleep. I was crouching in the shade at the side of an old house, and the garden beyond was so drenched in sunlight that it looked ethereal, almost transparent. Then I was on my feet and running. Round the crumbling, rose-hung corner of the house I went, and out on to a lawn where grown-ups were sitting on the ground, legs folded under them, or standing about with glasses of wine. I ran headlong into my mother's skirt, which had huge flowers all over it, and reaching up – she must have been kneeling now, or bending down – I put one of my hands to her face, and we looked into each other's eyes, and she was nodding and smiling as if to say, *There you are, I was just wondering*, and then I heard the groan of metal being wrenched apart, and I turned quickly to see what it could be, only to lose my balance, fall, roll over . . . I woke in darkness, one elbow in a puddle. The container, I thought. I was in the container. But what was that awful sound I'd heard, and how had I come to be thrown across the floor? Had I been walking in my sleep? From somewhere high above came the sound of men shouting. Though I knew next to nothing about ships, the urgency and desperation in their voices didn't exactly reassure me. The engines had stopped too, and I could hear a noise I couldn't remember hearing earlier, a kind of rushing. I began to struggle with the rusty bolt. At last it slid sideways in its bracket, and the door banged open. Things had changed position since the last time I looked. The boat must have run aground, or hit something. Luckily, the container opposite me had shifted backwards a little, and I was able to drop down into a small, wedge-shaped gap. From there, I edged along one of the aisles, aware that if anything moved again I would be trapped or crushed. I had to walk uphill to reach the side of the hold. Glancing behind me, I saw water flooding greedily into the spaces between containers. I imagined for a moment that I heard voices pleading, but I could only think it was the sigh of machinery that had been shut down, the gasp and murmur of pistons cooling, and I turned and hurried towards the nearest flight of stairs.

I climbed through a metal doorway, almost as though I were emerging from a picture frame. The two men standing on the deck were grappling with each other, but when they sensed my presence they stopped and gaped at me, their heads twisted in my direction, their hands still clutching at each other's throats. I glanced over the guard-rail at where the sea should have been. A dense white fog pressed in all around me.

One of the men broke free and took a step towards me. He was wearing a red baseball cap with the brim flipped back. 'Who the *fuck* –'

'Did we hit something?' My voice sounded muffled, as if I were still inside the container.

The man in the baseball cap hurled himself at me with such power that he appeared to have been propelled. Taking fistfuls of my jacket in his raw hands, he began to shake me. 'Who *are* you? What the *fuck* are you doing here?'

His lower lip had deep vertical cracks in it, and his breath smelled sour – a mix of fish and beer. Though he didn't seem to be any taller than I was, he loomed above me, forcing me backwards and downwards, and for a moment I didn't understand what had happened to my sense of perspective.

Then I realised that the deck itself was sloping.

'Are we sinking?' I said.

The man threw me away from him so fiercely that I staggered against the bulkhead. 'Get a dinghy,' he yelled at his colleague. 'There's got to be some kind of dinghy.'

The other man, freckled and ginger, with a pale mouth, stared at him for a few long seconds, and then yelled back. 'I already – fucking – told you –'

I moved sideways to the rail. The sea had appeared just a few feet below, opaque and colourless, ominously still. As I stood with my hands on the rail, the boat creaked, and then a shudder passed through it, and I thought of the moment when a slaughtered animal drops to its knees, that sudden fatal heaviness, that somnolence . . .

Water swirled across my shoes.

Then I was beneath the surface, with no idea which way I was facing. I couldn't see or breathe. There was a sound in my ears like someone turning over in a bed. I reached up with both hands, tugging at the water. I kicked and kicked. My foot struck something that seemed to give, and one of my shoes detached itself. I imagined it dropping away into the dark, the laces still tied in a neat bow. It looked unhurried, leisurely, almost weightless. A feather would have fallen faster. My shoulder knocked against a solid object, but I fought to get past it, upwards, always upwards. At last, when I no longer believed it possible, I burst out into a small round space. Whiteness enclosed me on all sides. Air wrapped itself around my skull like a cold rag.

'Hello?'

I had shouted, but my voice was swallowed by the fog. There was no point calling out. I tried to think instead. It was already light. A new day. Even if it was only dawn, the ship would have been under way for fifteen hours. We should be somewhere off the coast of the Blue Quarter – but where exactly? Which direction was the land? And how long before I succumbed to fatigue or hypothermia?

Just as panic was rising through me, I was struck a firm blow on the side of my head, behind the ear. Crying out in shock as well as pain, I swung round in the water. Jesus was floating on his back beside me. His mournful eyes, his crown of thorns. His arms lifting vertically into the air, the tips of his fingers lost in fog. I began to laugh, then stifled it, not out of respect, but simply because it sounded inappropriate, even sinister, in the small dead patch of water we were sharing. I reached out for the statue and held on. It was larger than life, at least eight or nine feet long, and carved from solid wood. It would take my weight quite easily.

The first time I attempted to clamber on, the statue rolled in the water, and I fell back. This kept happening. The white paint they had used for the raiment was slippery as ice. In the end, sapped of nearly all my strength, I heaved myself across the legs and hung there, like a pannier slung over a mule. I was cold now, and my head ached, but at least most of me was out of the water. I waited a few minutes, then I clawed my way up on to the statue's chest and sat facing the feet, the bearded chin behind me, the outstretched arms on either side.

Once, I thought I heard someone call out. I answered with a cry of my own, but there was no reply. The silence descended again, padded, claustrophobic.

Maybe I dozed off, my head resting on my knees, or maybe I blacked out, I couldn't have said. The next time I glanced up, though, the fog had cleared. I had expected bits of wreckage to be drifting about close by, but there was only the whiteness of the sky and the greyness of the sea, heaving and empty, drab. I felt exposed. Defenceless. I swallowed once or twice, then gripped the statue's arms. What had become of those two men? Had they drowned? My narrative had blurred patches, jump-cuts, pieces missing. I rubbed at my eyes, then looked over my shoulder and saw a slab of muddy green on the horizon.

Land.

I began to try and steer the statue in that direction. I had to lie face-down and use my hands as paddles. I paddled hard, but when I lifted my head and squinted beyond the statue's toes it didn't seem as if I'd made much progress. Still, the exercise had stirred my blood, warming me a little.

Time passed. The sun burned with more conviction, showing through the cloud cover as a sharp-edged silver disc. Though I had stopped paddling, the wedge of land appeared to have grown in size. Either currents were ferrying me shorewards, or else I had latched on to an incoming tide. Staring at the land, where low cliffs were now visible, their brows fringed by wiry scrub, I coughed twice and nearly vomited. I was hungry – ravenous, in fact – but the remains of my provisions were in the container. I didn't even bother to go through my pockets, I knew they would yield nothing. I fell to paddling again, if only to distract myself.

As I floated a few yards out, I heard a bell tolling, the sombre notes resonating across the lazy, almost oily waters. Perhaps, after all, I had drowned, just like the other two. Perhaps I was arriving at my own funeral. I slid down off the statue and waded through the shallows to the beach. Using my last reserves of strength, I hauled the statue on to a steep bank of grey and orange pebbles, where it lay on its back, appealing to an utterly indifferent sky. The land felt unsteady beneath my feet. I sat down, forearms on my knees, and gazed at the waves from which I had been delivered. Something was rocking on the swell out there, something that gleamed in the dull light. The minutes passed, and it drew closer. At last I recognised the swollen golden belly. Jesus wasn't the only one to have escaped from the hold of that tramp steamer. Buddha had freed himself as well, and he was making his own way, patient and unruffled, to the shore.

A crunching sound came from further up the beach, and I glanced over my shoulder. A man in dark-blue robes was striding towards me. His tall scarlet hat had the look of a bishop's mitre, and in his right hand he held a long stick or staff that curled at the top like a fern. A crowd of people followed in his wake – maybe as many as a hundred, maybe more.

I tried to stand, but all the power drained out of me. The sky lurched sideways. Darkness poured into the corners of my eyes. The man bent over me, bright colours flashing from his ring finger like shafts of sunlight glimpsed through trees.

L ying in bed with blankets drawn up to my chin, I was looking at a ceiling, delicately vaulted, white as chalk. The smoothness of the surface made it hard for me to focus, so I turned my head to the right. Set deep into the wall was a single window, its tiny panes framing a sky of blended grey and gold. There would be a garden out there, I thought, a place where one could read or dream. I turned my head the other way. The man from the beach was sitting on a chair beside the bed. He was clean-shaven, with high cheekbones, and his shorn black hair showed traces of silver. He was still wearing his blue robes, but his mitre was resting on his lap.

'How do you feel?' he said.

'I don't know. Weak.' Actually I felt like a child who had been sick for a long time – or perhaps I was being distantly reminded of my boyhood, the lost years, an illness I had concealed from myself. 'Are you a bishop?'

The man smiled faintly, lowering his eyes. 'In a manner of speaking.'

There was a stillness about him, as if he had retreated from the outer edges of his body into a place that was private, inaccessible.

'When we found you on the beach,' he said, 'you needed medical attention. We brought you back here, dressed your injuries –'

'I was injured?'

'You must have hit your head. You don't remember? You were suffering from exhaustion too.'

'Were there any other survivors?'

'Not that we know of.'

The man reached behind him for a glass. I should drink, he said; it would help me to sleep. I lifted my head off the pillow, and he held the glass to my lips. I had swallowed half the medicine when a panic began to unfold inside me, heat flooding across my skin.

'Is this the Blue Quarter?' I said, looking up into his face.

He nodded.

I sank back with a sigh. Sleep took me.

A bell hauled me to the surface once again. This time a woman was sitting beside the bed. Something about her complexion, some papery quality it had, made me think she must have suffered. She wore her brown hair cut short, like a boy. A book lay open on her lap, the words arranged in blocks. Poetry, I thought. Or hymns.

'Were you one of the people on the beach?' I asked.

She looked up at me and smiled. 'Yes, I was there. We were all there.' She closed her book. 'You probably don't realise this,' she said, 'but you have performed a kind of miracle by coming here. You've saved the whole community.'

Ever since the vernal equinox, she told me, they had been waiting for a sign, something that would confirm the fact that they were living in the right way, that they had chosen the correct path. All summer they had watched the skies, but they had seen nothing out of the ordinary – no comet, no shower of meteors, no eclipse. In the gardens and the orchard everything grew as it had always grown, the fruit trees bearing fruit, the soil yielding a rich variety of vegetables; eggs were provided by the hens, milk by the goats, honey by the bees. Had times been different, they would have given thanks for this abundance. Instead, it had only caused anxiety, as though the gods of nature were procrastinating, as though they had already made up their minds but couldn't work out how to break the dreadful news.

Then, early one morning, a young member of the community had been walking along the cliffs when she noticed what appeared to be a wooden figure in the waves below. She ran back to the main house, where she reported the sighting to Owen Quayle, whose community it was. He led his followers down to the coast to witness the sign for which they had all been waiting with such eagerness and trepidation. It was more conclusive than they could ever have expected. The figure the girl had seen was just one of many figures washed up on the beach that day, and the manner in which they had chosen to manifest themselves – dislodged, toppled, overturned – allowed of only one interpretation. They were false gods. They no longer deserved obedience. They should be summarily cast out.

'And it was you who delivered the sign to us,' the woman said, 'in person, as it were, and for that we're profoundly grateful.'

'I was shipwrecked,' I said.

Smiling, she shook her head. I had been too literal. I hadn't understood that facts were only the servants of some far greater message. 'So long as you remain here,' she said, 'you'll be treated as an honoured guest, a benefactor.'

I lay back, trying to make sense of this strange information. 'I've talked too much,' the woman said. 'You should rest now.' She rose to her feet and moved across the room. Then, with one hand on the door, she turned to face me again. 'My name's Rhiannon, by the way.'

For days, it seemed, I slipped in and out of consciousness. Usually, when I came round, there would be people in the room, and they would ask me how I felt or whether there was anything they could do for me. I didn't always have the strength to answer. I would close my eyes, surrender to the bed's embrace, my body without weight or substance.

I couldn't even be sure, at times, if I was awake or asleep. Once, at night, I became convinced that I was lying on a car seat with a warm rug over me. Through the window I could see black trees rushing past at a steep angle. Above them was the sky, paler, and in much less of a hurry. Stars showed dimly. My parents had been talking in hushed voices, but now they were silent. Soon my mother would look round. I would pretend to be asleep. She would reach down and adjust the rug, then gently brush the hair back from my forehead. It felt like the beginning of a holiday – or it could have been the end, the long drive home . . . Another time I sat up to get a drink of water, and there on the bedside table were the cigarette-lighter and the silver ring – all that these people had found on me, presumably, when they took me into their care. I picked up the lighter and ran my thumb across the flint. To my amazement it produced a flame.

Occasionally I would hear laughter coming from outside, or footsteps, or snatches of conversation, and I remembered what I had read about phlegmatic people, that they were 'dulcet' or sweet-tempered, but not necessarily equipped to deal with life's many tribulations, and gradually I became curious about this community that I was supposed to have saved. I began to question Rhiannon, who seemed to be in charge of my recovery. She told me I should speak to Owen, the man in the blue robes. As founder of the Church of Heaven on Earth, he would be able to give me the answers I was looking for. When I felt well enough, she would arrange an audience.

'The Church of what?' I said.

She smiled, the dry skin creasing at the edges of her eyes.

'It's true that we call ourselves the Church of Heaven on Earth,' Owen Quayle said, 'but I don't want you to get the wrong idea. We don't pretend that things are perfect here. The name expresses an aim – or a yearning, perhaps – not a fact.' He gestured towards a crystal decanter. 'Can I offer you a drink?'

'Yes,' I said. 'Thank you.'

I adjusted my shirt collar, which chafed a little. I was dressed in clothes Rhiannon had laid out for me, my own having been ruined by the sea, apparently. On leaving my room that evening – the first time I had ventured beyond the door – I followed her across a cobbled yard, then down an unlit path and out on to a wide two-tiered lawn. To the left of us was a walled garden. To the right lay a swimming-pool, drained for the winter. The lawn swept up to the back of a large country house whose many windows glowed in the dusk. The place had once belonged to an arms dealer, Rhiannon told me, and, before that, to a duke. She took me as far as the door of the library. *Go on in*, she said. *You're expected.* It was a comfortable room, filled with well-worn furniture, oriental carpets, and reading lamps with green glass shades. Three walls were lined with books, and against the fourth, between a pair of heavily curtained windows, stood a leather-topped writing desk and a chair whose cushions were moulded to the shape of Owen Quayle's body.

When we were settled on adjacent sofas with our wine, he began, in concise and elegant language, to explain the precepts on which his community had been founded. They believed in God, not as a judge or an avenger, but in the abstract sense, as the seed from which the universe had grown, the source or fount of all existence. They were prepared to accept Jesus Christ too, though they saw him as a teacher rather than a divinity; in their opinion, he was simply a man who had encouraged people to treat each other well. They didn't believe in the resurrection or the life everlasting, and they rejected the notion of an immortal soul. All life was here, on earth. Though they had set themselves apart, on this remote property, they weren't puritans or ascetics. Far from it. The purpose of their 'church' – a word they used in the loosest sense – was not to renounce the world but to savour it, to relish it – to embrace it in all its rich variety. If they had an aim, it was probably happiness, which they tended to define negatively as freedom from distress and pain. In philosophical terms, the system with which they identified most closely was that of Epicurus, whose teachings could be summarised, Owen thought, as follows: to live in tranquillity, to appreciate the gift of life, to have no fear of death. It was an approach that was at once spiritual and rational. Respect remained a fundamental principle, as did a sense of awe and wonder, but faith didn't really play a part.

'In that case,' I said, 'why did you need a sign?'

Owen nodded, as if he had known such a question might be coming. At that moment, however, we were interrupted by a knock on the door. A man with a shaved head announced that everything was ready, then withdrew. Owen turned back to me.

He would be more than happy to continue our discussion, he told me, but it seemed that dinner was served.

He rose to his feet and, reaching for his tall scarlet hat, fitted it carefully on to his head. With his mitre and his robes, it was possible that he had gone too far, but I wouldn't be the one to say so. Where would I have been without him and his followers? If he wore elaborate clothes, it must be because he thought that there was a place for ritual and hierarchy, that they were things that made people feel safe.

Though Owen wasn't looking at me, he appeared to feel my gaze on him and to have a rough idea of what I was thinking. 'I don't always dress so formally,' he said, 'but tonight's a special occasion, as you're about to find out.'

The following morning, after breakfast, I went for a walk. In the daylight I could see that they had put me in a stable-block which, like the main house, had been built from limestone, austere and grey. Though it was only a few weeks until Christmas, the sun was shining, and a haze that felt autumnal clung to everything I saw. Tranquil pathways led between high hedges. Lawns were silvery with dew. I passed a lake with an island in the middle, then climbed unsteady steps into a wild meadow. In the distance a black cat picked its way through the tall grasses, setting each paw down with the utmost care, as though the ground were mined. From where I stood, I saw how a ridge encircled the house on three sides, hiding it from the world. The tension and anxiety I had felt while staying with Fernandez had lifted away, and I was filled with a new optimism. Against all the odds I had made it to the Blue Quarter. The crossing had been unorthodox, to say the least – perhaps they all were – but the border was behind me now, and I could start thinking once again about what it was that I wanted to attain. I couldn't help but believe that there would be less resistance from now on, less danger, that things would, in general, be easier. The essential nature of the people in this country dictated it.

At the top of the meadow, I looked back towards the house,

remembering what had happened the previous night. Once we had left the library, Owen escorted me down a corridor and into a room that was entirely dark. Before I could voice my bewilderment, I was blinded by a sustained flash of electric light. When my eyes had adjusted, I saw that I was standing on a dais at the far end of a dining-hall. In front of me were dozens of faces, all lifted in my direction, all applauding me. Owen put a reassuring hand on my shoulder. These would be the people I had seen on the beach, I realised. These would be the members of the Church of Heaven on Earth.

'We have gathered here tonight, as you know,' Owen began, 'to honour an unexpected guest –'

A ripple of amusement washed around the room.

'Unexpected, but certainly not unwelcome. In fact' – and here he couldn't resist a smile – 'it might have been nice if he had come a little sooner.'

Loud laughter greeted this.

'It has been a troubled year for all of us, but now, thanks to the man standing beside me, I think I can honestly say that we feel better in ourselves. Now, thanks to him, our life can go on.'

The hall erupted in cheers and whistles.

Owen lifted his hands in an appeal for quiet. 'Let's raise our glasses to this long-awaited messenger – our saviour, you might even say – Thomas Parry!'

I smiled as I started up the hill. Although I had felt humbled by the reception, fraudulent too, in some respects, I had thought it only polite to respond to Owen's speech with a few words of my own.

'Thank you.' I cleared my throat. 'I'm afraid I don't know very much about your community. I'm not even sure I share your beliefs. To be perfectly honest, I don't know where I am at the moment –' My opening remarks had created a slightly awkward silence, but now I heard laughter swooping through the room, the exaggerated laughter that often accompanies a release of tension. 'But I do want to say one thing,' I went on. 'You took me in and showed me kindness, and, in my situation, that was more than I could ever have expected, and I simply want to thank you for that.' My voice had begun to shake, which surprised me, and I found myself adding, 'Really I'm just happy to be alive.'

A standing ovation followed. Embarrassed, I looked away.

Owen approached me again, and I thought I saw both fondness and compassion in the smile he gave me. I had surprised him too, perhaps. In a gesture I scarcely recognised, I took his right hand in mine and placed my left hand over it. It wasn't a handshake so much as a way of demonstrating the sincerity of what I'd said.

I came out on to the brow of the ridge and set off along a path that led to the sea. In half an hour I had reached the cliffs. Far below, the waves threw themselves languidly against a strip of mud-coloured sand. There was an eerie quiet down there, a sense of lassitude, and even though the sun still shone I had the impression that something had leaked out of the day. Whatever had been easy-going and benign was gone.

I found I was thinking about John Fernandez – the speed with which he had arranged a passage for me, his apparent familiarity with procedures which, to many, would have seemed baffling, not to say perilous. And he had mentioned bribing customs officers as well. He worked for the transport union, of course, but still . . . I had read enough relocation files to know that smugglers operated up and down the coast, trafficking in human beings. There were always people who wanted to cross illegally from one country to another. They just had to pay the going rate. Did Fernandez run a business like that? Had I turned, unwittingly, to one of the few who could actually get me out? He hadn't asked for any money, though. When I arrived outside his house, he'd been standing in the darkened hall, behind the door. Was I something Fernandez had been waiting for, or even dreading? Was I his day of reckoning? In which case he'd got off lightly, maybe.

Then I remembered the voices I thought I'd heard, and it occurred to me that there might have been stowaways in some of the other containers. Unable to unbolt their doors, they had been calling out for help, their cries muffled by the metal walls and by the rush of water through the hold. No, no. Surely someone would have mentioned it. That docker in the overalls – or Fernandez himself . . .

I stepped back from the cliff-edge, took the dank air into my lungs. It seemed difficult in this place even to breathe. Perhaps it had been a mistake to come down to the sea. I would head east along the coastal path, then circle back towards the house. It was almost midday now, and Owen had asked me to join him for lunch.

When I knocked on the library door, I was greeted by the shaven-headed man from the night before. He was Owen's personal assistant, he told me. Unfortunately, Owen had been called away unexpectedly. He was very sorry. I was shown to a table by the window. There was a plate of freshly cut sandwiches for me and a jug of lemon barley water. If I needed anything else, the man said, he would be in the next room.

After I had eaten, I wandered into the conservatory where I found Rhiannon sitting in a wicker chair, doing needlepoint. She was working on an image of a woman and a small boy. Dressed in sandals and brightly coloured robes, they were walking hand in hand along an unpaved road. There were olive trees behind them, and stark white hills.

'I don't know if I'd have the patience for that kind of thing,' I said.

She looked up and smiled. 'It's Epicurus and his mother. She was a fortune-teller. He used to travel from house to house with her when he was young.' She reached into her bag for a new ball of wool. 'It's for Owen's birthday.'

She had reminded me of something that had been bothering me. 'You know, I still don't understand why you were looking for a sign,' I said.

She laid her needlepoint aside and ran a hand slowly through her hair.

'In January,' she said, 'one of our members committed suicide. He had only been with us for a month. We thought we could help him, but he was too unstable. He would have been better cared for somewhere else – a hospital . . .' She sighed, then

217

leaned forwards in her chair. 'Well, anyway, after Kieran's death – that was his name – a shadow fell over the community. It was as if something had been lost. An innocence, perhaps. Nothing bad had ever happened here before . . .

'The sign was Owen's idea. If we were going to change the atmosphere, he told us, we would have to look outside ourselves. Something special was needed – some symbolic event or ruling. We were quite prepared to abide by it too. If the sign had gone against us, we would all have had to leave.' She stared out across the garden. 'I don't know where we would've gone, though.'

I followed her gaze. Two girls were playing badminton on the lawn, laughing whenever they swung at the shuttlecock and missed.

'How did all this begin?' I said.

She had never heard the whole story, she said, but she would tell me what she knew. When Owen was in his twenties, he had owned several factories that made pre-cast concrete. He had been wealthy even then, apparently. But the Rearrangement had turned him into a multimillionaire. He won a contract to act as sole supplier to the governments of all four countries. Uniformity of product was vital. Every wall that was erected had to look the same.

'A concrete millionaire?' I said. 'I'd never have guessed.'

Rhiannon shook her head, as though she too found it hard to believe.

The authorities were always telling Owen that he was helping to create a better world, she said, that his name would go down in history, and so on, but he soon began to feel uncomfortable. He must have noticed how much misery was being caused, and he must also have realised that, for large sections of the population, the most powerful symbol of that misery was the concrete that he had himself supplied. He stopped going in to work, hoping the business would collapse, but it had become so established that it more or less ran itself. There was only one course of action left. He sold everything – the factories, his town house, the lot – and moved to the coast. He went from being a dynamic, glamorous industrialist to a man who grew tomatoes and read books about comparative religion. He still enjoyed company, though. Friends came to stay. Then friends of those friends came. One day he looked around and saw that he was living in a community. It hadn't been planned, or even thought about. It had happened organically. And, purely by chance, their way of life was perfectly in tune with the phlegmatic temperament. They understood the need for sanctuary, they rejected materialism without being puritanical, and with their emphasis on gratitude and celebration they were able to channel or harness all manner of emotion. People heard about the community, and it spoke to them, and they began to arrive on the doorstep.

'And they're still arriving,' Rhiannon said, 'even now.'

'By sea as well as land,' I said lightly.

'Actually' – and she gave me a smile I couldn't fathom – 'I think you'd fit in rather well.'

My eyes drifted beyond her. The girls had disappeared, leaving their rackets lying on the grass. The lake beyond was motionless.

'In the end, there's something about this place,' Rhiannon said. 'I don't know what it is. An absence of pressure, I suppose. A sense of acceptance.' She smiled again, more openly this time. 'A kind of peace.'

The unearthly stillness that had troubled me during my walk turned out to have been the prelude to a change in the weather. That night a storm blew in, gale-force winds rushing through the courtyards and passageways of the house. Sheet lightning lit up the sky every few seconds, making the clouds look like stage scenery, artificial and melodramatic. After dinner I retired to my room with a book I had borrowed from the library, an essay on gardens by someone called Sir William Temple. As I lay on my bed reading, a lamp on beside me and the rest of the room in darkness, the door came open. At first I thought the wind must have forced the latch, but then I saw a figure silhouetted against the steel-grey light in the yard outside.

'Rhiannon?'

'It's not Rhiannon.'

A girl crossed the room with a tray. She had brought me a herbal infusion that smelled a little like warm grass. I didn't think I'd seen her before – unless, perhaps, she was one of the girls who'd been playing badminton. The silk dress she was wearing came down to her ankles, but it showed off her forearms, which looked slender, almost golden, as she reached into the fall of lamplight to pour the tea. Her dark-brown hair was so long that it hid her shoulderblades. She couldn't have been more than eighteen or nineteen.

'I was the one who saw you first,' she said.

'I'd been wondering who it was,' I said – though, in truth, I had done my best to put the events of that particular day behind me.

She looked away into the room. 'I'm often out there early. It's a beautiful time. That morning, though, I saw something on the water, a figure that had arms, a face. Then I saw you crouching on top of it, all huddled up. I ran back to the house. I don't think I've ever run so fast.'

'I heard a bell tolling as I was drifting in towards the beach,' I said. 'I thought it was a funeral. There was a part of me that thought I must have died.'

She glanced at me sideways. What I had just said seemed to disturb her. Outside, the wind swelled, surging against the walls.

'How long have you been here?' I asked.

'About a year.'

'And will you stay?'

'I don't know. I'm happy at the moment.' She moved her shoulders, as if to rid herself of the burden of having to decide too soon. 'Would you like to go for a walk?'

She saw me hesitate.

'It's not raining,' she said. 'It's not even cold.'

I closed my book and put it down.

She led me through the stable-yard, then along the side of the conservatory whose sheets of glass creaked under the gale's weight. We crossed the lawn at the back of the house. In Owen's library, the curtains had been drawn against the storm. After circling the lake, we entered a wood on the edge of the property.

Lightning flared. High wrought-iron gates stood on the path ahead of us, forbidding as a row of spears. Any sound they might have made as we hauled them open was drowned by the trees hissing and thrashing all around us. We began to climb upwards, over rugged ground, and soon the house had shrunk to a collection of frail yellow lights afloat in a swirling blackness.

Before long we found ourselves on a headland, its cropped grass the colour of slate when the sky lit up. Only now did the wind reveal its true power, gathering the girl's long hair and lifting it away from her neck until it flew at right angles to her body. Her exhilarated laughter was snatched from her mouth and carried off into the night. I watched the silk of her dress ripple against her belly and her thighs, and I imagined that, if I kissed her, her breath would taste fresh and slightly bitter, like the petals of chrysanthemums. I remembered the tea that she had served with such care, then carelessly abandoned, tea which would be cold by now, and I thought how young she was, how little lay behind her, how far she had to go.

She had brought me to a part of the cliffs I hadn't visited before, and I could hear the sea below, boiling and roaring on a steep bank of shingle. The waves didn't break so much as shatter. We leaned into a wind that seemed to want to fling us to the earth. Once or twice, miles out, sheet lightning flashed, and I could just make out the clouds massed on the horizon, their furious shapes, their ripped and jagged edges, like molten metal left to cool.

The girl linked her arm through mine and pointed to the east. 'Look that way,' she shouted.

For a moment, though, I couldn't take my eyes off her face, which was so eager, so elated. It was one of the purest things I'd ever seen.

She tightened her grip on my arm and pointed again. 'Keep looking.'

And then it happened. White water came leaping from the ground in front of us, rising high into the air, only for the wind to reach out and bend it sideways. Now I could see the blow-hole in the cliff-top, just a few feet from where we stood.

The girl leaned close to me again. 'There's a cave down there. We swim there in the summer. When it's calm.'

'I'll be gone by then,' I said.

But she had already turned away, and didn't hear.

My door was open, and a triangle of early morning sunlight stretched out on the floor, as white and pristine as a sail. Since my suit was beyond repair, I was wearing the clothes Rhiannon had found for me, which would in any case be more appropriate for the kind of travelling I had in mind. Before throwing the suit away, I'd checked the jacket collar, but the banknotes had been reduced to a pulp. I was broke. If I was to reach Aquaville, I would either have to walk or hitch.

The room darkened. Rhiannon stood in the doorway, holding a knapsack. 'You're leaving,' she said.

I nodded. 'I think it's time.'

'So you know about our visitors?'

'What visitors?'

She stepped inside and closed the door behind her. The day before, Owen had been interviewed by two officials from Customs and Excise, she told me. They suspected there had been at least one survivor from the boat that had recently gone down just off the coast. If the person or persons in question were illegal immigrants, as appeared to be the case, they would have to be apprehended and taken to a detention centre where their true status could be established.

'He didn't mention me,' I said, 'did he?'

'He said he'd seen some statues on the beach, but that was all.'

'Did they believe him?'

'I think so.'

'I'm sorry. I should have told you.'

'There was no need. As far as we're concerned, it doesn't matter where you're from. You're the reason we can go on living here. We're hardly going to hand you over to the authorities.'

'All the same, it's best I leave as soon as possible.'

'I'm afraid so.' Rhiannon reached into the knapsack and handed me a wallet. 'Owen had a collection for you.'

The wallet was stuffed with notes of all denominations, and plenty of loose change. 'This is a lot of money,' I said.

'He didn't want you to leave empty-handed, not after what you've done for us.' She passed me the knapsack. 'A few things to keep you going.'

I shook my head. 'You didn't need to do all this.' Then I remembered the principles on which the community had been founded. 'Thank you,' I said. 'For everything.'

She smiled. 'Are you ready?'

Aware that the house might be under observation, she took me along a series of overgrown paths that would see me safely off the property. As we came through a wooded hollow, I heard the stuttering of rotor blades.

'That's probably them now,' she said.

She held quite still and listened, then she moved on up the slope. I followed her. The chatter of the helicopter faded.

We scaled a fence, then struck out along one edge of a field. When we arrived at the stile in the corner, the land unfolded in front of me, sleepy and unspoiled. This was as far as she could go, Rhiannon said. In the knapsack I would find a detailed map of the area. For the first few miles, I should keep to footpaths and bridleways. She doubted the Customs and Excise people would be looking for me there.

I thanked her again. We embraced quickly. Stepping back, I saw that her face had altered, as if the bones had shifted a fraction.

'Think of us sometimes,' she said.

With those words, I felt she had given something away – something she'd wanted me to see all along, perhaps, but hadn't wanted to spell out. I had thought of the Church of Heaven on Earth as a kind of cult, though it was actually more like a charity. Owen had created a place in which he could try and redress the damage wreaked by the division of the kingdom. Losses could be overcome there. Injuries could heal. Maybe that was what Rhiannon had meant when she said I would fit in. Maybe that explained the unfathomable smile. She had identified me as a casualty, not of the shipwreck, but of an earlier catastrophe – the

Rearrangement – and if times had been different, who knows, I might even have stayed on. How had she been wounded, though? What was the origin of the pain I thought I'd seen in her? I turned to speak to her, but it was too late. She was already halfway across the field.

Though it was almost December, the air had a sweet burnt smell, and the sky was tall and blue and empty. The recent storm had blown the clouds into a different part of the world altogether; all that bad weather had piled up somewhere else. I had the feeling that my life, too, had been swept clean, put in order. I walked northwards through open, undulating country. To the east I had a view of a ruined castle. Beyond it, a finger of water pointed inland. An estuary, I thought, or possibly the sea.

After a couple of hours I paused for a rest. In the knapsack Rhiannon had given me, I found some mineral water. I drank half of it, then consulted the map. Now that I had money, of course, I could afford a train. I decided to make for a town to the north-west, whose station was on the main line to the capital. Even if I kept to the footpaths and bridleways, as Rhiannon had advised, I should be able to get there in two days. I would be thirty miles from the coast by then, and breaking cover ought not to be a problem. Pleased with my strategy, I tucked the map and water-bottle back into the knapsack and hurried on.

Once, as I climbed down into a gully, I heard the helicopter again, though it was only a subdued grinding in the distance, little more than a vibration. I saw it too, above the treetops, heading busily in the wrong direction.

By the time I stopped for lunch I must have walked ten miles. A kind of heath spread out all round me, pine trees relishing the sandy soil. Gorse clung to the ground in strands like natural barbed wire, and every now and then my trouser-legs would snag on its sharp spines. Unpacking the knapsack, I discovered hard-boiled eggs, crusty rolls filled with slabs of cheese, several apples, a bar of chocolate, and a second bottle of water. As I ate and drank, I checked my position on the map. I was in a white space, between two rivers. Ahead of me lay an area of downland, the hills topped with ancient forts and barrows, the valleys housing villages with quaint, humorous-sounding names. The going would be more arduous, but at least I ought to be able to find a place to stay. I finished the bread and cheese, then ate an apple. I kept the rest of the food and water for later on. My energy renewed, I set off again, determined to make full use of the daylight.

That afternoon I passed through several farms, every one of them abandoned. The houses had been boarded up, and the cattle sheds were empty, ghostly places, doors hanging off their hinges, hay strewn haphazardly about. Not long before the Rearrangement, disease had swept the countryside, and huge numbers of livestock had been slaughtered and then burned. The farmers had never recovered. A substantial percentage of the Blue Quarter's population had been vegetarian for years.

Imagine my surprise, then, when I saw a large flock of sheep about a mile to the west. As I watched them move across the wide green flank of a hillside, though, I realised they weren't sheep at all but people – White People. It was astute of them to favour the Blue Quarter. They would be treated kindly here; in some areas, in fact, they would be revered, or even worshipped. I had always felt a good deal of sympathy for them, a feeling that had only been enhanced by my encounter on the front steps of the Sheraton, but I had never really believed in their so-called powers, preferring to find rational explanations for their some-times mystifying, almost supernatural behaviour, and I remem-bered a story Marie had told me, one from which we had drawn quite different conclusions.

The incident occurred during Victor and Marie's walking tour of the Red Quarter. They had been in the far north at the time. Instead of slavishly following the border, they decided to scale a ridge that ran parallel to it. The ground had been marshy at first. After a while, though, it turned into high pasture, punctuated by pale-grey boulders. The ridge was further away than it had looked, but they had started now, and both father and daughter agreed that nothing tried the patience more than the process of having to retrace your steps. They would reach the ridge, they said, even if it killed them. And it almost had.

They toiled onwards, upwards. The grass became a steeply sloping field of stones. No sooner had they arrived at what they had imagined to be the summit than another summit would appear, one which, until that point, had been concealed by the angle of their ascent. To make matters worse, a mist had drifted in behind them, obscuring the route they had taken. They peered at the ridge. It had transformed itself into a crest of ominous black rock. They glanced at each other. On they went.

In another hour they had reached the top. They couldn't see for more than a few feet in any direction, and their clothes were soaking wet. Still, they celebrated by sharing a cup of coffee from their flask.

What happened next was something Marie hadn't been able to explain. The mist seemed to give in front of her, and in this opening she saw a footpath curve off through a kind of meadow. She took a few steps towards the opening, so as to have a clearer view of the path, some clue as to where it went. When she glanced over her shoulder, Victor had disappeared. She couldn't believe it. Assuming he must be behind her, she whirled one way, then the other. There was no one there. The mist closed in around her. She called his name softly, almost experimentally, but there was no reply. She shouted as loud as she could. Her voice refused to carry. Her sense of isolation was so acute that, paradoxically, she felt haunted.

She returned to the patch of ground where she'd been standing when she last saw him. The rocks looked different. She thought about crying, but managed to resist it. She had no idea what to do. The mist thinned. A bronze light fell. Looking up, she saw a group of figures dressed in white. One of them detached himself from the others and approached. His face was blurred with a growth of beard, and his black hair hung down to his shoulders, its knotted strands festooned with burrs and leaves and bits of bark. He stood sideways on to her and gestured with one hand. He wanted her to follow him. She realised she wasn't frightened, and this surprised her.

226

The figures moved effortlessly across the rough terrain. She tried to draw level with them, hoping to get a look at their faces, hoping to talk to them, but no matter how quickly she walked they contrived to keep the same distance ahead of her. And then she forgot all about them because she saw Victor sitting on the ground beneath a stony ledge. She hurried over, knelt beside him. He had fallen, he said, but he didn't think he'd hurt himself. His eyes were bright and pale. *Did you see them?*

She nodded.

White People. He had been about to launch into a discourse on their behaviour when he noticed one of them standing near by. *Come on. He wants to take us down.*

They followed the white figure until the border appeared below them. When they looked round to offer thanks, they found that they were, once again, alone.

To Marie, the story was a confirmation of the White People's uncanny psychic skills, but my scepticism remained intact. They had been able to lead Victor and Marie down from the ridge because they were acquainted with out-of-the-way places. It was in places like these that they had been forced to live their lives. Also, they didn't want other people intruding, perhaps. Victor and Marie had strayed on to their territory, and the two of them had been gently but firmly escorted away from it.

I watched the cloaked figures vanish into the shelter of a wood. Though I didn't think I would need rescuing that day, the knowledge that I had set eyes on them gave me the feeling that nothing bad could happen, or if it did, then it wouldn't be anything that couldn't be remedied, and maybe, in the end, that was all people meant when they talked about unusual powers.

I stayed in a village pub that night. My only anxiety was that the authorities would have alerted rural communities for miles around, and that people would be on the look-out for strangers, but nobody even gave me a second glance. The next day I set out early and made good progress, arriving at the station towards four in the afternoon, just as the rain came down. I bought a one-way ticket to the capital.

When the train pulled in fifteen minutes later, I chose a seat by the window, facing forwards. My carriage was nearly empty. It was a Friday, I realised, and most people would be travelling in the opposite direction, going to the country for the weekend. Opening my wallet to check on the state of my finances, I noticed a piece of plain paper hidden in among the banknotes. *Come and see us in the summer*, it said. *I'll take you swimming*. Under the two lines of looping handwriting was the imprint of a girl's lips, the colour of crushed raspberries. She hadn't signed her name. She hadn't needed to. As we walked back to the house, her hair had flown into my face, half blinding me. She had laughed and then apologised, plucking the long, sweet-smelling strands out of the dark and twisting them into a knot. We had parted in the stable-yard, outside my door. The summer . . . Words like that had no significance for me. I couldn't imagine where I'd be in six days, let alone six months.

I looked at her mouth again, the pattern of white lines as distinctive as a fingerprint. So intimate, that mouth – and the waxy fragrance of her lipstick lifting off the paper . . . Although she had brought me tea less than forty-eight hours ago, I felt I was thinking back to an event that had taken place in the long-distant past; it seemed exaggerated, almost apocryphal, even though nothing had happened. I imagined trying to tell the story to somebody – Vishram, for instance. *There was a storm that night. A gale. I was in my room, reading a book. At first I thought the wind had blown the door open, but it was a girl . . .* And Vishram would smile in that patient, knowing way of his, and he would say, *You slept with her*. And I would say, *No, I didn't. That's the whole point*. Vishram would shake his head at what he would undoubtedly see as slowness on my part, a wasted opportunity.

I settled back in my seat. The rain was still falling, each drop wriggling diagonally across the outside of the window. The telegraph poles slid by, their wires sinking, rising, sinking. When I thought of Vishram, he seemed too vivid a concoction, somehow. His suits shimmered. His nails were as dark as dried rose petals. He didn't walk, he floated. He was extravagant, improbable, a character enlisted from a dream. It occurred to me that I had forgotten to let Sonya know about his offer of a job – and he'd been so insistent. Ah well. Tired after the day's exertions, I leaned my head against the head-rest and surrendered to the rhythm of the train.

On waking, I saw that I was no longer alone. A girl was sitting on the other side of the carriage, reading a newspaper. She must have boarded the train while I was sleeping. She was smartly dressed, in a tailored black jacket and wide black trousers, and on her feet she wore a pair of men's brogues, also black. She had hair the colour of copper wire, or bracken, and curious heavy-lidded eyes, and her face was covered with freckles to such a degree that she gave the impression of having been camouflaged. I was still studying her when she looked up from her paper and met my gaze.

She took a fast, shallow breath. 'Don't I know you?'

'I'm sorry?' I said. 'Do you mean me?'

'Yes.' She smiled quickly. 'Sorry. It's just that I thought I'd seen you somewhere before.'

'I don't think so.'

'You'd remember my face, I suppose,' she said lightly.

'Yes.'

'It's striking.'

'Yes, it is.'

'People often say that about me.' Her voice was still light, objective. 'I'm "striking", apparently. I always have the feeling it's just another word for odd.'

I laughed. 'Where do you think you might have seen me?'

She turned in her seat and looked directly at me. Seen straight on, her face had even more power to unnerve. The way her eyelids lowered over her eyes, the distance between her cheekbones, the strong line of her jaw. Above all, her mouth, which was incongruously voluptuous, the top lip carved with delicate precision, the bottom lip succulent and drowsy. And then the freckles – as if she'd hidden herself behind a kind of veil or screen and was watching me through it. Taken all at once, these features gave her a look that was poised somewhere between

229

the sensual and the menacing. I had never seen a face quite like it.

'I'm not sure,' she said after a while. 'In Aquaville, I think.'

'I've only been there once, and that was for a conference.'

'Was it about two weeks ago?'

'Yes. The Cross-Border Conference. It was held at the Sheraton.'

Now she was laughing. 'I was there.'

'No,' I said. 'Really?'

'Every night they put a chocolate on my pillow,' she said. 'It looked just like a smile.'

'That's right.' I had forgotten about the chocolates.

'And then there was that trip to the Yellow Quarter. I had such a bad feeling about it. I didn't want to go.'

'You weren't hurt?' I said. 'In the bomb, I mean?'

She shook her head. 'I was dancing at the time. There was a disco in the basement. Flaming something. We were all evacuated on the spot. What about you?'

'I was in my room when it went off. I got out down the fire stairs.'

She folded her newspaper and put it on the table in front of her. 'I must have seen you at one of the parties,' she said. 'Or perhaps I heard you speak. I don't think we actually met.'

'What were you doing there?'

'Oh, nothing very important. I was just an observer.' Looking down, she pinched the crease in one of her trouser-legs between finger and thumb and let it go again. Then she glanced at me quickly, so quickly that her hair still hung in her eyes. She used both hands to tuck it back behind her ears. 'So what are you doing now?'

I had been wondering whether we would get to this point and what I would say if we did. After all, I had no idea who she was, this girl with the unique face and the disarming manner. She could have been anyone. In the event, the long hesitation worked in my favour.

'Listen, if it's confidential,' she said, 'I completely understand.

230

It's just that you don't often see people from the Red Quarter all the way out here.'

So she did remember me. Before I could say anything, though, she spoke again.

'You seem very much at home, if you don't mind me saying so. I mean, I would never have guessed, not if I hadn't seen you at the conference.'

'No, I don't mind,' I said. 'In fact, it's strange, but that's exactly how I feel. Almost as if –' I cut myself off, wary of giving too much away. 'Of course there are things I could never get used to.'

She nodded vigorously. 'Of course.' She reached for her purse. 'I'm just going to the buffet. Can I get you anything?'

'I'll come with you,' I said.

At the buffet I asked if I could buy her a drink. A brandy would be good, she said. Rather than returning to our seats, we took our brandies to a table in the dining-car. The girl's name was Odell Burfoot, and she seemed eager to talk.

'It must be extraordinary,' she said, 'crossing borders like you do.'

'I haven't really done very much of it . . .'

'No, but still. How does it feel?'

'It's such a big thing, isn't it? I mean, it's something you're not even supposed to think about.' I paused. 'When it actually happens, it's almost impossible to separate all the things you've been told you're going to feel, or imagined you might feel, from the actual feeling itself. Does that make any sense?'

The look on her face, though neutral, appeared to intensify, as if her heart rate had accelerated or her temperature had just gone up. 'Yes,' she said, 'I think it does.'

'In the end, you're doing something you never thought you'd do. So there's excitement, but there's fear too. I don't think that would ever go away.'

She smiled at me with her eyes, but said nothing.

We flashed through a country station and on into the dark. As I sipped my brandy, I thought back to the conference. I tried to place Odell at one of the events or functions, but her face refused to float up into my memory. Another face came floating up instead.

'Do you remember somebody called Walter Ming?' I said. 'He was at the conference too. His hair looked like a wig, and he wore the most peculiar suits.'

She laughed. 'Poor Walter.'

'You met him? What did you make of him?'

'Why do you want to know?'

'I'm not sure. I suppose I thought there was something suspicious about him.'

'I think he was just lonely. He asked me out to dinner, but I said I was busy. He was rude to me after that.'

Lonely? It had never occurred to me that Ming might be lonely.

'I saw the two of you together,' Odell said. 'You talked to him, didn't you?'

'Yes. A couple of times.'

'He seemed really taken with you. Maybe he'd never met anyone like you before.'

'You think so?' All I could remember was how offhand and aloof he had seemed, and how slippery. 'How odd that you were there – that you saw it all . . .'

She finished her drink, then glanced out of the window.

'Aquaville,' she said.

I climbed down from the train. There, once again, was the station concourse, with its sluggish crowds and its posters advertising remedies for colds and flu. To think of how nervously I'd surveyed the scene when I arrived back in November! Imagine how I must have stood out! This time, though, I was dressed in phlegmatic clothes, phlegmatic shoes. This time, against all the odds, I looked the part. What had that girl said? *You seem very much at home, if you don't mind me saying so.* I hadn't minded at all. In fact, it had bolstered my confidence. And yet, as I hesitated on the platform, I half expected to feel a hand plucking at my sleeve, and when I swung round, there he would be, the man I'd seen before, with his slicked-back hair and his

232

damp greenish complexion, something of the gambler or the ticket tout about him. He would be facing away from me, of course, pretending to consult the departures board, its litany of cancellations, and I would hear the words – *something that might interest you* – then he would slip a card into my pocket. Instead, it was the girl with the freckles who circled round in front of me. She had put on a black cloche hat and a long dark coat whose hem brushed the tops of her carefully polished brogues. She had the severe, otherworldly look of a lay preacher. For the first time I felt a flicker of recognition, as though, at some point in the past, I had smelled her perfume as she stood beside me in a lift, or caught a glimpse of her reflection in a mirror as she walked behind me, but the flicker stubbornly refused to resolve itself into anything more definite.

'Well,' she said, 'I suppose this is goodbye.'

'Yes.' I shook hands with her.

'Are you going to forget me again?'

'Probably,' I said.

We both laughed.

She thanked me for the drink, then turned away.

As soon as she had vanished into the crowd I felt desolate. Foolish too. Why had I let her go so easily? I should have arranged another meeting – a walk, maybe, or dinner. This was my new life, after all, and I had enjoyed her company. But then, almost immediately, I had the disturbing sensation that the encounter hadn't taken place at all, that I had invented the whole thing, right down to her freckles and her bracken-coloured hair, right down to her name – Odell Burfoot – so awkward, like somebody talking with a mouthful of stones . . . Or, if it *had* happened, it was already fading. Even the one moment of physical contact – the handshake – was beginning to seem ephemeral, as if I had shaken hands with a figment of my own imagination.

A dense fog had descended on the city. The passers-by looked shadowy and incomplete, mere sketches. The weather couldn't have been more appropriate. I would be able to make my way through the streets without the slightest fear of being recognised. I only wished I had something warmer to wear. Perhaps, in the morning, I would find a charity shop or a fleamarket and buy myself a second-hand coat. How easy to allow that thought to form, how natural it seemed, and yet, at some point between now and tomorrow, I would be turning the handle on that pale-gold door, and then – and then what? I didn't know. I had hopes, of course, but that was all. I couldn't possibly have predicted what I'd be feeling in twelve hours' time.

Opposite the station were three high-class hotels – the Aral, the Tethys and the Varuna. I remembered their ornate, decaying façades from my previous visit, but with my limited finances and little or no idea of what the next few days might bring, I decided it might be prudent to economise. I turned right, then right again, away from the city centre, opting for the maze of obscure canals that lay to the west of the station. Within minutes, I found myself in a different world – rubbish bags dumped everywhere, the scuttle of rats, and a smell that was almost sweet, like rotting celery. Wooden boards had been nailed over the ground-floor windows of all the houses. Once, I was able to peer between two slats that had come loose. The dark glint of floodwater, a framed photo of three children floating on the surface . . . Further on, a crudely painted arrow pointed to a basement. A palm-reader known as Undine plied her trade down there. I pictured Undine as a fat woman in a rowing-boat, which she would steer from one room to another using a frying pan or a spatula or the lid from an old biscuit tin. I hurried on, passing beneath the tattered awning of a fish restaurant. Sooner or later I was bound to find a cheap hotel, the kind of place where they wouldn't care about documents or think it untoward if someone had no luggage.

As I crossed a metal footbridge, I looked to my left and saw a pale-blue neon sign fixed vertically to the front of a building and glowing weakly through the fog. HYDRO HOTEL, it said. Then, in smaller horizontal letters, *vacancies*. The canal was so narrow that there was only room for a path along one side, the houses opposite sliding straight into the water like teeth into a jaw. I retraced my steps and turned along the path, pausing when

I reached the hotel entrance. The lobby had a beige tile floor with a strip of orange carpet running up the middle. Reception was a hatch cut in a chipboard partition. I pressed the buzzer on the counter. Behind me, on a drop-leaf table, stood an aquarium. I put my face close to the glass. A single goldfish was swimming upside-down among the weeds.

'You know anything about fish?'

I straightened up. The hatch framed a woman, middle-aged, with dyed blonde hair and fleshy arms. *Aquaville* was printed on the front of her white T-shirt in silver script, as if a snail had crawled across it in the night.

'When they swim upside-down like that,' I said, 'it means they're dying.'

The woman nodded gloomily. 'Oh well.'

'Have you got a room?'

I told her I would be staying for two nights and paid in advance. This would establish my respectability, I thought, and stop her asking any awkward questions. She handed me a key. It was on the second floor, she said. At the front. Thanking her, I set off up the stairs. When I had rounded the first corner, I allowed myself a brief smile. Documents hadn't even been mentioned.

My room smelled of cologne, something lemony, as though it had only recently been vacated. Either that, or nobody had cleaned. I walked into the bathroom. At first I thought the washbasin was cracked, but then I realised it was a black hair, six inches long. I flushed it down the toilet. Back in the room, I stood at the window, staring out into the fog. For days, if not for weeks, I'd hardly dared to think about the city in case all my attempts to return to it were thwarted. But I had managed it. Everything I wanted was no more than a few light steps away. Her hand resting on my forehead, her skirt a blur of brightly coloured flowers. *There you are* . . . A motor launch passed by below, its engine beating like a bird's heart, soft and rapid.

That evening I ate dinner at the restaurant I had seen earlier. Called, rather touchingly, My Plaice – a fish which, as it happened, did not feature on the menu – it was a small, chaotic establishment where each new arrival was treated as an almost insurmountable catastrophe. My waiter, a bony, long-fingered man in his late twenties, seemed threatened by every word that was addressed to him. When I ordered fish of the day, for example, and a carafe of dry white wine, he just stared at me, his forehead pearled with sweat. Surprisingly, the food was quite good, and I lingered over it, exchanging a few words with Mr Festuccia, whose 'plaice' it was, and accepting a liqueur on the house. By the time I paid my bill it was almost eleven o'clock.

I asked my waiter to call me a taxi, but he gave me a look of such consternation that I instantly revised my request. Did he know where I could find transport at this time of night? Yes, he knew. I'd just have to let him think for a moment. Fingers in his mouth, he squinted at the ceiling. Yes, he'd seen a taxi-rank, he said finally. In the direction of the railway station. Five minutes' walk. Well, maybe seven.

Once outside, I walked as fast as I could. I saw no point in delaying any longer. I seemed to have been waiting an eternity for this moment without ever knowing whether it would actually arrive. Now, at last, it was just a matter of a taxi ride. The city was still wrapped in fog, the light of the street lamps blurred as candy-floss. As I turned into a narrow passage that linked two canals, a door slammed open and a man whirled out on to the pavement with such velocity that I assumed he'd just been forcibly ejected from the house. We collided. He almost fell. As we muttered our apologies, I caught a glimpse of him. Something vulpine about the face, something canny. A quarter of a century collapsed in a split-second.

'Cody!' I said.

'What? Who are you?' He pushed his face close to mine, and I smelled his breath, sugary and yet corrupt, like over-ripe fruit. He must have been drinking for hours. Days even.

'We were at Thorpe Hall together. I sat next to –'

Gripping my sleeve, he led me down a cul-de-sac that was still more narrow and obscure, then pushed me into a doorway. 'What's your name?'

'Then or now?'

'Now,' he hissed. 'Now, of course.'

'Thomas Parry.'

'And before?'

'Micklewright. Matthew Micklewright.'

'You really expect me to believe this is a coincidence?'

I laughed. 'What else?'

His head swivelled towards the alley, as if he had heard something. He kept one hand on my chest, though, pinning me against the door. We remained in that position for at least a minute. I could probably have freed myself, but I chose not to. He turned to me again. 'We could go somewhere,' he said, 'if you've got time.'

'Yes,' I said. 'All right.'

He stepped away from me, sliding both hands into his trouser pockets. Though he was still staring at me, his face seemed to have been decanted of all expression, like someone daydreaming. For the first time he was thinking back, perhaps, trying to place me. I straightened my jacket, brushed myself down.

'Are you still called De Vere?' I asked.

'How do you know that?'

'Bracewell told me.'

'Bracewell . . .' He looked off down the cul-de-sac to where a cat crouched by a dustbin, its eyes lustrous and flat.

We didn't say much after that – at least, not for a while. De Vere jerked his head and started walking. Over bridges we went, through a housing estate, across a park. Every now and then he would give me a rapid sideways glance. He still appeared to suspect me of some kind of trickery or subterfuge.

At last we reached a building whose double-doors were paned with frosted glass. De Vere knocked twice. A stooping grey-haired man let us in. The interior was poorly lit, the floor bare concrete, the walls pale-blue to waist-height and then cream beyond. The man locked the doors behind us, grumbling about the weather. As we set off down a corridor, I thought I could smell chlorine.

'A swimming-pool,' I said.

'Used to be,' De Vere said. 'It's a bar now.'

We passed through another set of double-doors and into a vast dark hall that was lit only by candles, the air filled with the murmur of people talking in lowered voices. Glass-topped tables had been arranged on the floor of the pool. More tables stood around the edge. The fact that it had been drained was supposed to be a political statement, De Vere told me, a slight sneer on his face. Clearly he thought such gestures either immature or futile.

There were no free tables in the pool itself, so we sat above it, near the diving-board. I studied De Vere as he ordered drinks, large ones – gin for him, brandy for me. He looked pretty much as I remembered him. He had the same unusually red lips and cocky features, and he gave off the same subtle aura of debauchery – or perhaps it wasn't quite so subtle any more, I thought, as I noted the faint but uneven growth of beard, the stained teeth, the eyes that looked bloodshot, almost infected. He had acquired a curiously indefinite quality. I could see the boy he used to be, but I could also see the old man he was going to become. He was like somebody trapped between different versions of himself, unwilling – or unable – to decide between them.

Our drinks arrived. De Vere snatched up his gin and drank half of it straight down, then he apologised for his behaviour in the alley.

'You did seem a bit nervous,' I said.

He let out an explosive sound that was only distantly related to laughter. 'Do you have any idea what's going on round here?' He watched me across the candle flame, the shadows shifting on his face. 'No. Probably not.' He drank from his glass again, ice-cubes jostling against his teeth.

The authorities pretended to be initiating transfers, he told me, but what they were actually doing was throwing people into prisons or detention centres, or even, and here his voice trembled, into unmarked graves.

'It's true,' he said when he saw my reaction. 'At least one person I know has disappeared. Because he spoke out. Because he said it was wrong, the way our country's organised, and that no government should have the right to –' He shook his head, as if it was useless to go on about such things, then he finished his drink and stared fiercely into the empty glass.

'It doesn't sound very phlegmatic,' I said.

'You don't have to be strong to abuse power. You can abuse it out of weakness or insecurity. Out of fear. We've had so many governments during the last decade that every new one spends most of the time looking over its shoulder, trying to consolidate its position – using whatever means it can.' Once again, he saw the expression on my face. 'You think I'm exaggerating.'

I didn't say anything.

'Do you still live in the Red Quarter?' he said.

'It's where I've been living,' I said, 'yes.'

'Well, let me tell you something,' he said. 'It's happening there too.'

I started to remonstrate, but he talked over me.

'Maybe not the killings, but the arrests, the imprisonment without trial, the interrogations. That's why we all have an Internal Security Act. That's what it's *for*.' He looked at me and shook his head again, as though he couldn't believe my naivety. 'Why do you think you have the same leader year after year?'

'Maybe people are happy with the way things are,' I said quietly.

'*Happy?*' He almost choked on the word. Then he beckoned to the waiter and ordered two more drinks.

'I don't know how you know all this,' I said.

'Because I talk to people,' he said. 'Because I listen. Because I don't go round with my head buried in the sand.'

We sat in silence until the waiter brought our drinks. This time I paid.

I glanced down into the pool where a young couple were sitting at a table, kissing. 'So you knew about Bracewell.'

De Vere looked up slowly. 'That's not his name.'

'Maclean,' I said. 'How did you find out?'

'A policeman I was having sex with told me.' He stared at me, chin lifted, and I caught a glimpse of Cody, the boy I used to

239

know – his combative spirit, his iconoclasm – then he looked down and began to fidget with his plastic swizzle-stick. 'I used to have a thing about policemen in those days. Border guards as well. Maybe it was the uniforms – or maybe it was as close as I could get to being somewhere else.'

The policeman in question was one of the people who had found Maclean. Haunted by the case, he had given De Vere a graphic description of the mutilated body, as if by recording every detail he might exorcise himself.

'He even told me about –' De Vere broke off. He wiped at his nose savagely with the palm of his hand. 'Fuck,' he said. 'Fuck it.' He wiped at his nose again, then his eyes, and then sniffed loudly. 'What did you have to turn up for? What are you doing here, anyway?'

I was silent for a moment.

Then I spoke again. 'So you were sent to the Yellow Quarter?'

'I spent eight years in the Yellow Quarter. Now I'm here. They don't seem to know what to do with me. Can't make up their minds.'

'And he knew you were there?'

'Maclean? Yes, he knew.' De Vere's face twisted, and he looked away. 'He wanted to join me. He wanted to be with me. That's why he tried to escape.' De Vere laid his hand flat on the table, the palm facing down. The way he was staring at it, it could have belonged to someone else. 'He never stopped loving me – did he?'

'No,' I said. 'He talked about you all the time.'

With a single violent gesture, De Vere reached into his pocket and tossed something on to the table. The object behaved much as a dice would have done, only it seemed heavier, clumsier. When it came to rest, I saw it was his wedding ring. I remembered Bracewell telling me that they had both thrown their rings into the moat. Was that a lie, or had De Vere gone back later and fished his out again?

'Crazy, isn't it,' he said. 'It's just the wheel-nut from some old bastard's car.'

'It's more than that,' I said.

He eyed me sceptically. I was presuming to speak for him, and I didn't have the right. With an impatient sound, half sigh, half snarl, he snatched up the ring and thrust it back into his pocket, as if he hated himself for keeping it but couldn't help himself, then he reached for his glass and swirled the contents. 'Another drink?'

Wondering how late it was, I risked a look at De Vere's watch. He noticed.

'I'm sorry,' I said. 'There's somewhere I've got to be. I mean, I don't –'

'Yes. Of course.' He jumped to his feet, rocking the table. His drink toppled over. 'Sorry to have kept you.'

'No, wait. I didn't mean –'

But he was already brushing past me. By the time I twisted round in my chair, he had disappeared through the double-doors at the far end of the pool. Somehow, I felt I could still see him, though – his tousled red-brown hair, his tight, hoisted shoulders, the worn-down heels on his shoes.

When I left the bar moments later I half expected to find him on the towpath, pacing up and down, or scowling into the canal. He would still be smarting from what he would have perceived as an insult, but I was ready to apologise. I had been insensitive, unthinking. Also, I wanted to have the chance to explain myself. If I told him what I was doing, I was sure that he would understand. But he had gone. I listened for his footsteps, called his name. Out in the fog somewhere was De Vere, who I hadn't seen for twenty-seven years.

I waited ten or fifteen minutes, but he didn't return. I had lost him, probably for ever. Even an unexpected stroke of luck – a water-taxi gliding out of the fog with its 'for hire' light on – couldn't lift my spirits. I flagged the taxi down. It cut its speed and drifted towards me. In a listless voice, I gave the driver the address.

'That's quite a way,' he said.

'It's all right,' I said. 'I've got money.'

I stepped down into the cabin. Everything I touched was damp and slightly sticky. If anything, the fog had thickened since the early evening, and the taxi's engine had a flat, dead sound as we pulled out into the canal. There wasn't a single second during that long ride out to the club when I didn't regret my tactlessness.

I suppose I should've known that something would go wrong. There had been any number of warning signs, not least De Vere with his sinister disclosures. I was dreaming of a reunion, though, a kind of homecoming, and when the club's white stucco rose out of the murk, lights burning in the ground-floor windows, my excitement was so great that I didn't doubt that it was all about to happen. I didn't really notice the figures standing on the towpath, let alone grant them any particular significance. I paid the taxi-driver. My hands shook so much that I almost dropped my wallet in the canal. There were no thoughts of a journey back to the centre, no thoughts of anything beyond this moment . . . Only when I approached the club did I realise that the figures were all dressed identically, in dark-blue tunics, and dark-blue hats with black plastic brims, and that their eyes were trained exclusively on me. They were police, of course. One of them stepped forwards, flipping open a small notebook. 'Thomas Parry?'

I didn't answer. Clearly they had been patrolling the quayside for some time. They had an excitement that was all their own – the thrill of a tip-off, a stake-out, a possible arrest. Their bodies trembled with stored tension.

'You're to come with us,' the man with the notebook told me.

To have travelled so far, to have got so close – and now this . . . I hadn't even considered such an outcome, and my reaction was suitably incongruous. I laughed out loud.

'We're taking you to the Ministry,' the same man said, 'for questioning.' His voice had tightened. He nodded to one of his colleagues, who grasped me by the upper arm and tried to steer me towards a waiting motor launch. I immediately shook him off. I had never been able to bear the feeling of being held like that.

'First I have to go into the club,' I said.

The man with the notebook shook his head. 'We've got our orders.'

'Please,' I said, 'it won't take –'

'It's orders,' one of the others said. 'It's not up to us.'

The inside of my head buzzed and flashed, as if something in my brain had blown. They were about to deny me the very thing that I'd been looking forward to, the thing I wanted most in all the world. I pushed past them, making for the entrance, and was aware, for a few moments, of people shocked into unnatural shapes.

Before I could reach the door, though, two of them grabbed hold of me. Then the third joined in, his notebook fluttering clumsily to the ground. As we struggled on the steps, one of the glass doors opened and the blonde-haired girl looked out. She was wearing her kimono with its pattern of exotic birds and trees, and her eyebrows, lifted a little in surprise, were plucked into two fine arcs, as usual. In order to recreate the experience of my other visits to the club – or to reproduce the same level of intensity, at least – I had always felt that conditions had to be similar, if not identical, and the blonde girl's presence there that night, the fact that she would have been sitting in the ticket booth when I walked in, only added to the fury with which I resisted all attempts to restrain me. I was told later that I seemed to possess an almost superhuman strength, and that, if there hadn't been three policemen at the scene, and if one of them hadn't been a famous wrestler when he was young, I might actually have got away.

We passed beneath a bridge and swung sharply to the left, the canal splitting wide open in our wake, waves slapping against the sheer dark walls of town houses and then rebounding. The massive bulk of the Ministry towered above us now, its eaves all but shutting out the sky. Though it was after two in the morning, lights still showed in several of the windows. It could be a twenty-four-hour job, working for the government. Nobody knew that better than I did.

I was escorted to a room on the first floor where two men were waiting for me. One wore glasses with no frames, his brown eyes floating beneath the lenses like a pair of sea anemones. The other man had the fleshy but solid build of a field athlete. Running along the far wall of the office was a soundproofed window that overlooked an indoor marina. The water was lit from below, an eerie jewelled green, and various small craft were going silently about their business.

The man with the glasses installed himself behind a desk. I took a seat in front of him. The other man lowered himself, grunting, into a swivel chair some distance to my left. We spent the first half-hour establishing the facts – name, address, occupation, and so on. As for the date of my arrival, I had entered the Blue Quarter on Monday the 7th of November, in the morning, and my visa had expired three days later, on the 10th. I had been at large, illegally, for about two weeks.

At one point the man to my left leaned forwards. 'Thomas Parry,' he said in a thin, high-pitched voice that sat awkwardly with his muscular physique. 'You know, I'm not sure I didn't speak to you once, on the phone.'

'Maybe,' I said.

'There's something I don't understand,' the man with the glasses said. 'Why did you *return* to the Blue Quarter?'

'There's no point trying to explain,' I said.

'No point?'

'You wouldn't understand.'

The ferocity of what had flashed through me on the towpath seemed to have burned out entire circuits in my head. Only a kind of numb, childish truculence remained – but that seemed justifiable. I was once again the boy who had been abducted in the middle of the night, the boy who had been removed from his home against his will, only this time my feelings were right there on the surface.

'If you hadn't been arrested,' the man with the glasses was saying, 'what would you have done? What would you have done tomorrow, for example?'

I shook my head. For some reason I remembered Chloe Allen

in that moment – her mockery of all authority, her cheek, the sweet smell of her breath through the van's wire-mesh . . .

'You know what you are?' I said with a smile. 'You're drones.'

During the silence that followed, I happened to glance upwards. Slabs of reflected light from the marina were undulating on the ceiling. Distracting, hypnotic, oddly sensual, it was almost as if a belly dancer was performing in the room.

'Drones,' I said again.

The man with the glasses wanted to know who I had come into contact with since arriving in the Blue Quarter for the second time. He would be needing a list of names and places, he said – an inventory, in other words, of every one of my encounters. I brought my eyes back down from the ceiling. I didn't have the slightest intention of betraying Owen or Rhiannon – or any other member of the community for that matter. No one was getting any names and places out of me.

'Well?' said the man with the glasses.

I had been in a shipwreck, I told him. I had nearly drowned. On reaching land, I had been exhausted and bewildered. I'd had no idea where I was. Though I had almost certainly met people, I didn't know who they were or where they lived.

But he would not give up. 'What about the route you took?'

'What's wrong with you?' I shouted. 'Are you deaf?'

Taking a deep breath, then letting the air out through his nose, the man shut down his computer. He glanced briefly at his colleague. The fleshy man's face showed no discernible expression.

Even though I couldn't recall any of the people to whom I had been exposed, the man with the glasses said, it was likely that I had been contaminated as a result. He would therefore be recommending a series of tests to determine the exact nature and degree of that contamination. He consulted his watch. Testing would begin at midday.

I slept poorly that night. Each time I woke up, my pillow would be hot, and when I lifted my head all I could see was a pale oblong hanging in the darkness. Guards had shown me to a small windowless room – a 'secure unit', as they called it – in the basement of the Ministry. There was a narrow bed, with sheets that smelled sharply of bleach, as though certain of my predecessors had soiled themselves. There was also a sink and a toilet, both made of metal. In the top half of the door was a single pane of reinforced glass. Once I had established where I was, I would turn my pillow over, cool side facing up, and then lie back. So the authorities had finally caught up with me . . . I couldn't work out who the informer was. The woman who ran the hotel, perhaps. Or that sweaty waiter at the restaurant. Or perhaps De Vere had had good reason to be paranoid: if the police were keeping him under surveillance, as he suspected, then they couldn't have failed to notice me. I remembered De Vere's missing friend and wondered if I should be frightened.

Thoughts came to me one at a time, with no great urgency.

At midday I was taken to a room that resembled a laboratory. There were no windows here either, just pale-green walls and the steady rush of air through ventilation grilles. A technician asked me to remove my shirt, then she proceeded to wire me up to a number of machines. I was being put through various psychological tests, she said, but they would be monitoring my physiological responses at the same time, everything from heart rate and blood pressure to galvanic skin response, muscle tension and brain activity. Data of this kind added to the clarity of the picture that emerged.

I nodded.

'We do pretty much the same where I come from.'

Though she gave me a smile, she didn't seem remotely interested in the fact that I'd been involved in work that was similar to hers.

I spent most of the day in that room. To start with, I took a test designed to map out the basic structure of my personality. This was followed by a written paper, comprising several hundred true/false statements, which would allow the authorities to make predictions about my future behaviour. Later came the visual tests. In responding to a series of pictures, I would unconsciously reveal the kinds of ways in which I interacted with the world around me. In the middle of the afternoon I was allowed an hour's break, during which I ate lunch in the Ministry canteen.

After the break, my levels of fear, anxiety and depression were assessed. Finally, towards seven o'clock, I was moved to a different room. I noted the seascapes on the walls, the scatter cushions, the stacks of monthly magazines. The atmosphere had been carefully constructed so as to prevent subjects feeling nervous or threatened. In the subsequent 'diagnostic' interview I was required to react to a sequence of questions and statements which were intended to tap into my emotions. My responses were so full of anger that I felt transparent. I couldn't pretend the anger wasn't there, though, and I couldn't seem to disguise it either.

By the time I had completed everything that was asked of me, it was late in the evening and I could hardly keep my eyes open. They took me back to my room. I didn't have much of an appetite, but they brought me supper anyway. Not long afterwards I went to bed. My tests would be processed overnight, they had told me, then I would see a psychological assessment officer who would inform me not only of the findings but of any action that might be taken as a result.

Since they had such a dramatic effect on people's lives, and since they dealt with these people face to face, psychological assessment officers were routinely subjected to considerable levels of pressure and stress, and it was no wonder, perhaps, if they were prone to delusions of grandeur, and no wonder if, from time to time, they became brittle and over-sensitive. Like plants growing in rarefied conditions, they tended to assume unusual or even distorted forms, and Dr Maurice Gilbert, whom I saw at five o'clock the following afternoon, was no exception. He had the doughy, etiolated look of someone who seldom ventured outdoors. Only his hair had flourished: glossy, thick, oxblood in colour, he wore it swept back and a little too long, a sure sign that it was a feature of which he was inordinately proud.

'It's not often,' he mused from behind his desk, 'that somebody leaves the Red Quarter for the Blue Quarter. I mean, why would anyone do that? Life's supposed to be so harmonious over there, so full of purpose and good cheer – so perfect . . .'

I let my eyes drift past him to the window. The blinds had been lowered, though, and the slats were tilted shut. There was no view.

'But perhaps it's *too* perfect,' Gilbert continued. 'Perhaps one craves a little discord, a little mess. Perhaps, in the end, we tire of harmony.' He adjusted one of his gold cufflinks, then leaned back in his chair. 'You know, I've often thought that I belonged in the Red Quarter, but the results never came out quite right. It's almost as if the tests we use aren't capable of picking up the nuances that make us what we are, as if our methods of assessment simply aren't *fine* enough. Have you ever had that feeling, Mr Parry, that our procedures, our techniques, are failing us?'

I thought at first that he might be trying to trick me into admitting something, but then I realised that the question had been rhetorical. Wholly preoccupied with himself, Gilbert was in love with the sound of his own voice, and he would need nothing from me except an occasional prompting.

'It sounds strange to say it,' he went on, 'possibly even a touch arrogant' – and his eyes veered towards me, and he let out an abrupt, abbreviated sound, not unlike a dog's bark – 'but we *know* ourselves, don't we? Surely we know ourselves better than all this' – and he looked around the room – 'all this cumbersome machinery with which we surround ourselves?'

I smothered a yawn, but once again I chose not to reply. My patience was running out. I didn't know how much more of Gilbert I could stand.

'*However*,' he said, and he rose to his feet with a finger raised, as if warning me not to jump to any conclusions, and then began to pace up and down in front of the drawn blinds, 'the machines, the tests, the inventories – they're all we have at the moment, poor creatures that we are. At times, you know, I can't help feeling that we live in an impossibly primitive age, and that future generations will look back at us and laugh.' Staring at the carpet, he shook his head and smiled ruefully. 'Still, that's the way the system works – at this point in history, anyway – and if I find it primitive, well, who am I? Who's going to listen to me?'

'Nobody,' I said.

Gilbert's head came up sharply, and his eyes narrowed a fraction as he peered across the room at me. Until that moment, for reasons I didn't completely understand, he had been treating me as an accomplice, a kind of ally, but now he saw that I was actually the enemy. I watched him return to his desk and flip through my case notes. I could restrain myself no longer.

'Look, it's obvious you're going to send me to the Yellow Quarter,' I said, 'so why don't you stop playing games and just get on with it?'

Gilbert had paused with the corner of a page between finger and thumb, and he was looking up at me. The lower half of his face appeared to have swollen slightly, as though he was concealing an entire plum inside his mouth.

'The Yellow Quarter?' he said. 'Oh no. We're not sending you there.'

They had ushered us on to a coach, fourteen of us, all adults, and we were heading east along the Orbital, an old motorway which circled the four capitals and which was only used by vehicles in transit. Sitting across the aisle from me was a woman of about my own age, perhaps a little older, her clothes expensive but severe, like those of a solicitor. In the bus station she had cried openly, her whole body shaking, but there had been another woman with her, a counsellor of some kind, and I hadn't wanted to interfere. Though she didn't appear to be crying now, she had one hand over her eyes. The other was loosely closed around a tissue.

I leaned towards her. 'Are you all right?'

Keeping her hand where it was, she nodded.

I faced the window again. They had classified me as a melancholic, which was ludicrous, of course, but what did you expect from a bunch of Blue Quarter officials, known as they were for their endless vacillation and incompetence? Though I was beginning to question the way things were organised, there were times, I noticed, when I fell back on prejudice. I remembered what Fernandez had said about the system, how it was rooted in a form of racism and how it drew all its strength from our weaknesses, and I thought he might well be right about that. That doctor had really tried my patience, though. When he finally deigned to let me know where I was being sent – and he did it smugly, oh so smugly – I completely lost my temper, calling him all sorts of names.

This outburst only confirmed his diagnosis, and he was almost nodding and smiling as he watched me, which infuriated me still further. I kicked my chair over, then I grabbed my file and hurled it across the room. Gilbert lowered his eyes and shook his head, as if he had just received news of the death of a distant relation. The only time I brought him up short was when I started telling him how vain he was, and how I'd like to cut off his hair, hack it all off and set fire to it. He had looked quite shocked for a moment. Then the security guards arrived.

Yes. Well.

My anger had died down since then. There was no going back to the club, I knew that now, and I would be fooling myself if I thought any different. I would have to make do with what I already had, a few brief glimpses of a buried past – the house I had lived in, my mother's voice, my face pushed against her skirt . . . I wasn't always sure if I was remembering, or just imagining, and in a way it didn't matter. The point was, the fragments *felt* authentic. They felt *real*. In the absence of so much, they were something I could turn to when I needed to, something I could count on.

'Would you do me a favour?'

It was the woman sitting opposite me. As I glanced over, she brought her hand down and pressed her crumpled tissue to one eye, then the other.

'Of course,' I said.

'Would you hold me?' She was looking down into her lap. 'Just put your arms around me,' she said. 'Please.'

I was glad she had asked, though I couldn't have explained why exactly.

When I sat beside her, she turned to me clumsily, almost blindly, and laid her head against my chest, both hands clasped beneath her chin. I put an arm around her shoulders and drew her close. She murmured, but I didn't think she had spoken; it was the sort of sound people make just before they fall asleep, part pleasure, part relief. And then she did fall asleep, her breathing becoming coarser and more regular, her right arm reaching across my chest in a gesture that would have seemed too intimate had she still been conscious.

We left the motorway at an exit marked *Cledge East*, the slip-road leading directly to a checkpoint. The Green Quarter guards scarcely even glanced at our papers, their lax, fatalistic approach to security reflecting the fact that they were quite accustomed to the sight of new arrivals. The melancholic humour was associated with old age, so there was something logical, if not inevitable, about being transferred here. It was like a kind of natural progression.

Shortly after crossing the border, the woman woke up and lifted her face to mine, her eyes wide open but entirely blank. 'I don't know who you are,' she said.

'You're safe,' I said quietly. 'Go back to sleep.'

She muttered something I didn't understand, then her head dropped back against my shoulder, and her breathing deepened once again.

We meandered through the outskirts of Cledge – shops boarded up, street lights out of order – and before too long the city was behind us. On we went, past little restless towns. It was late now, almost one in the morning, but lamps still burned in many of the windows. This was a land much troubled by insomnia.

And then the spaces between towns began to widen. The road sliced unsentimentally through flat fields. There was nothing there, nothing to see, only the night rushing towards the coach's windscreen, and the shrinking tail-lights of overtaking cars. My right arm was trapped behind the sleeping woman's back, and I had to keep adjusting its position so as to keep it from going numb.

The brakes hissed. Our driver stood up and stretched, then he switched all the lights on and took down a clipboard from the rack above his head. Groans came from passengers who had just been woken up. We had stopped outside a semi-detached house, its front door open wide. The spill of light from the hall revealed a couple of brick steps, a concrete path and part of a rockery. In the foreground, by the gate, stood a large woman in a quilted housecoat and a pair of fluffy slippers.

The following people were to leave the bus at this point, the driver told us. He read out three names, one of which was mine. Everybody else should stay in their seats, he said. He read the names again, then lifted his eyes and looked down the aisle.

I tried gently to disentangle myself from the woman, but she sat up quickly, blinking. 'Sorry to wake you,' I said. 'I have to go now.'

'Oh. Yes. Of course.' Her hand skimmed lightly over her hair, touching it in several places. She seemed brisker, more business-like. Even more of a stranger.

'Will you be all right?' I said.

She nodded. 'I'll be fine. And thank you for –' She broke off, not knowing how to complete the sentence. As I rose to my feet and reached up for my bag, she caught hold of my wrist. 'I'm Iris,' she said. 'Iris Gilmour.'

I told her my name, then wished her luck.

'And you, Thomas,' she said. 'Good luck to you too.'

Stepping out of the bus, I felt a chill in the air and saw how the breath of the other two men ballooned in front of their faces. The sky had the hard, cold lustre of enamel. I knew then that we had come a long way north.

I turned towards the house. On one of the gateposts was an oval of wood, its varnished surface ringed with bark. *The Cliff,* it said. I smiled grimly. You'd think they would have banned names like that, along with all the bridges and high buildings. I waited for the other men to introduce themselves to the woman in the housecoat – the taller of the two was called Friedriksson, the other one was Bill something – then I walked over and held out my hand.

No sooner had I told the woman who I was than she began to shake her head. 'No, no,' she said. 'There must be some mistake.' She turned her back on me and walked a few paces up the street.

I asked the coach driver what was wrong. Her husband had been called Thomas, he told me. He'd been run over a few years ago, and Clarise had never really recovered. We stood about on the pavement, the four of us, uncertain what to do. At the end of the street, beyond a row of black railings, I could see a park. Birds were beginning to fidget in the trees. Dawn could not be far away.

Clapping his hands and then rubbing them together, the driver said he should be going. He was behind schedule, he said. He wasn't addressing anyone in particular, and nobody responded. I watched the door slot hydraulically back into position as he settled himself behind the steering-wheel. The coach reversed into a nearby side-street and then pulled away, Iris Gilmour's face floating in the dark window like a moon trapped in a jar. When she gave me her name, there had been such intensity in her, such earnestness, as though she feared that I might be the last person ever to hear of her, and that if I didn't remember her no one would. The coach reached the corner, tail-lights blushing briefly, then it was gone.

'Not right,' I heard the woman murmur.

I glanced at Friedriksson, but he just shrugged and looked off towards the park, as if he was expecting someone to come for him. The other man had his back to me. He must have been feeling the cold because he was hugging himself. I could see the tips of his fingers on either side of his rib-cage.

In the distance a cock crowed, raucous and yet forlorn.

At last the woman blew her nose, then she looked at us over her shoulder, her face puffy and tragic. We followed her indoors. I waited in the hallway while she took the others down to the basement. The house smelled like a cheap hotel. Armpits, cigarettes and gravy. The stair-carpet had turned pale down the middle, its pile almost worn away, and the paint had chipped off the banisters, revealing the wood beneath. When the woman returned, she locked the front door, then led me up the stairs, letting out a faint but urgent grunt with every step.

Once she had showed me to my room, which was on the first floor at the side of the house, she went downstairs again, muttering something about the television. I said goodnight and closed my door. The room was small and square, almost exactly the same dimensions, curiously, as my room in the house on Hope Street. A single bed had been pushed up against the left-hand wall, and an armchair was wedged into the gap behind the door. A chest of drawers doubled as a bedside table. On the wall above the bed was a painting of a clown with a fistful of wilting marigolds. Putting my bag down, I went to the window and looked out. A yard, a wooden fence. A mangle. The sky was a grey lid on the new drab world to which I had been delivered. Once, as I stood there, a light came on in the bathroom of the house next door, a burst of yellow behind a pane of blurry scalloped glass, and then, perhaps a minute later, it went out again, and everything was the same as before. Lowering myself on to the edge of the bed, a great burden of familiarity settled over me, as though I had already spent long years in the room. I seemed to be looking back on something that hadn't happened yet – my own existence, endless and unvarying. Was the Cliff, with its ominously precipitous name, the place where it would all, finally, come to an end?

Five men were already installed in the house when I arrived. The room below mine was occupied by a man with an unlined, almost childish face whom everyone referred to, mysteriously, as Marge. A sour-looking ex-town-planner called Martin Horowicz lived across the landing from me. His room looked out over the street. He appeared to have a fixation on Clarise Tucker, the landlady, but she was at least twice his size and had no trouble fending him off. She kept two rooms at the back of the house, both of which were painted pastel colours and filled with soft toys. Sandwiched between my room and that of the town-planner was a young man by the name of Aaron Moghadassi. I rarely heard him speak. Every now and then, while sitting at the kitchen table or in the lounge, he would bring his right hand slowly up out of his lap. He would examine the palm, then the back of the hand, then the palm again, and he would frown, seemingly baffled by the fact that they looked different. An old pot-smoking carpenter by the name of Urban Smith had made his home in the attic. The fifth man, Jack Starling, had moved into the converted outhouse. With the three new arrivals – myself, Lars Friedriksson and Bill Snape – the house was full.

To begin with, I kept to myself, never leaving my room except at mealtimes, or when there were chores to be done, but gradually I ventured out into the common parts of the house. I encountered despondency and gloom, which was only to be expected, but I also encountered merriment, and some, like Clarise, veered wildly between the two. I had thought, on first meeting her, that she was large, but she was actually a woman of such vast proportions that she was as wide when viewed sideways-on as she was from the front or back. She tended to raise the subject herself, and usually with hilarious results. 'Why, I'm practically *square*!' she shrieked on one of the first evenings I spent downstairs. 'Yes, you *are* square,' Jack Starling agreed. 'Like a plinth.' He grasped his chin between finger and thumb in a parody of thoughtfulness, and then added, with a sly glance in Horowicz's direction, 'Now what are we going to put on top of you?' They had all howled with laughter, Clarise included.

Most nights, after supper, she would switch on the imitation coal fire in the front room, draw the brown velour curtains and gather us around her – 'my boys', as she called us. We would fog the air with cigarette smoke and down Jack Starling's lethal home-made beer, and Urban Smith, who had a fine baritone voice, would entertain us with his extensive repertoire of morbid songs, or Lars Friedriksson would read excerpts from the autobiography he was writing, a work that wasn't remotely amusing in itself but was rendered so by his unbelievably earnest and lugubrious delivery. Later, one of the men would start complaining with great relish about something or other – we all enjoyed a good moan – or else somebody would embark on an anecdote, and what anecdotes they were, riddled with mythomania and self-delusion. Since we were living in the Green Quarter now, these stories often hinged on some misfortune or disaster, and long before she retired to bed, Clarise would have tears in her eyes. She would not be the only one. The combination of her infectious sentimentality and the potent home brew was enough to bring anyone's emotions to the surface. I didn't take up smoking, but I drank and wept with the rest of them, and I laughed the peculiar, giddy, almost hysterical laughter of the melancholic.

Of all the tales that were told, none was stranger than Marge's, and I heard it not in the front room but privately, during a walk through the neighbourhood. One afternoon in the middle of December I was returning from the town centre, where I had just collected my weekly allowance, when I spotted him on the road ahead of me. Drawing closer, I saw that he was clutching at a tree-trunk with both hands and squinting upwards through the branches. He seemed apprehensive, if not actually frightened. I stopped a few feet away and asked if I could help.

'Help?' he said. 'I don't know. I'm not sure.' His eyes wobbled a little as he brought them down from the sky. 'What's that sun feel like?'

'It feels good.'

'Is it warm?'

'No, not very.'

'Oh.' If his face looked unnaturally youthful, his voice sounded like that of a much older man, the tone uncertain, tremulous.

I asked him whether he was going back to the house.

'I'd like to, yes,' he answered mysteriously. As he spoke, the sun slipped behind a cloud. The day darkened. 'Quick,' he said. 'No time to lose.' He started up the road, bending forwards from the waist, his badly darned elbows jabbing at the air.

I watched for a second or two, then followed.

'You're Marge, aren't you,' I said when I had caught up with him.

He gave me a doleful glance. 'It's supposed to be a joke.'

'I don't get it.'

'They haven't told you?'

'No.'

He shook his head. 'That Horowicz. He thinks he's so clever.'

As we hurried back towards the Cliff, Marge told me some-thing of his life, often stopping in mid-sentence to scrutinise the sky. Once, when the sun broke through unexpectedly, he looked wildly about and then flung himself beneath the bench in a bus shelter, where he lay quite motionless, eyes staring.

His real name was Brendan Burroughs, he said, and for as long as he could remember he had believed that he was made of butter. I thought I had misheard him, but I chose not to interrupt. Instead, I just watched him carefully, as before. That was why people called him Marge, he was saying. They thought it was funny. He had always known he was different, though, right from when he was a small boy, but he'd never found a way of telling anyone back then, not even his parents. *Especially* not his parents. If they had learned the truth about him, how could they have looked their neighbours in the eye? They would have been so embarrassed. He had been forced to live in a kind of solitary confinement, with no one to turn to for comfort or advice. He'd had to take great care at all times. In the summer, for instance. He shuddered. How he used to dread the summer! When it got hot, he would seek out the coolest places – the garden shed, the cupboard under the stairs, the cellar. Sometimes, when his parents were out, he would empty the fridge and climb inside. The presence of other butter on the shelves reassured him. His mother opened the door once when he was curled up in there. She screamed and dropped the bowl of trifle she was holding. He could still remember the look of all that sponge and jelly on the floor. As if something had been slaughtered. She asked him what he was doing. *I don't want to go bad*, he said. It was as close as he ever came to revealing his secret.

Chunks of white sunlight had appeared on the street ahead of us, and Brendan had to be circumspect, avoiding the bright areas as a child avoids the cracks between paving-stones. Climbing down into a strip of scrubby parkland, we followed a shallow gully for a while, the stream at the bottom coated with a frothy brownish-yellow scum. Sometimes the stream would burrow under a road, and we would join up with it on the other side. Above our heads the clouds seemed to be merging into a single gloomy canopy. Relieved, perhaps, Brendan became talkative again. He spoke about the dangers of winter – open fires, hot-water bottles, central heating . . . Once, when he was a teenager, he had accidentally leaned against a radiator and he had felt the backs of his thighs start to melt.

'You can't begin to imagine,' he said darkly, 'what that feels like.'

I agreed that I could not.

'Where were you before this?' I asked him.

He had spent most of his life in the Blue Quarter, he told me. They had seen his reticent behaviour as evidence of passivity. His caution they had taken to be indecisiveness. No one had ever suspected him of being melancholic – well, not until the greaseproof-paper phase began. That was four or five years ago. He had started wrapping himself in greaseproof paper before he went to bed. He thought he would stay fresher if he dressed like that. Looking down, he grinned and shook his head. He'd really given the game away, hadn't he?

When I asked if he felt he was in the right place now, he nodded. He was more likely to be understood in the Green Quarter, he thought, than anywhere else. There were others like him – or not dissimilar, anyway. Also, people were more inward-looking, less meddlesome. They tended to ignore you. Except for Starling, that is. The other day Starling had come at him with a lighted match, the bastard.

As I followed Brendan up the path to the front door, he thanked me for keeping him company. He had enjoyed our talk, he said, but now, if I would excuse him, he thought he would go up to his room and lie down. He was feeling a bit soft around the edges, a bit rancid.

Shortly afterwards, I was formally incorporated into the household, and in a manner Brendan would himself have recognised. One night, as we were eating supper at the kitchen table, Horowicz turned to me. From now on, he declared, I would be known as Wigwam. 'Why Wigwam?' he said before I could open my mouth. 'Because your initials are T.P.' Despite the laughter that accompanied this declaration, the name stuck. I became Wigwam – or Wig, for short – not just to Clarise, for whom it was a huge relief, since she'd never been able to bring herself to use my first name, but to all the men living at the Cliff, and even, after a while, to myself.

Christmas was coming, Christmas in the Green Quarter, an event that filled the entire population with fear and dread. Everybody was aware of the statistics: some people would commit suicide, some would sink into severe depression, and so on.

'There's only one way of dealing with it,' Clarise told me on a dark December morning as I was helping her with lunch. 'Get drunk, then go to sleep.'

'With a bit of hanky-panky in between, maybe,' Horowicz said.

He was leaning in the kitchen doorway, just a few feet away from her. The space between them filled with the glint and glitter of his small sharp eyes.

But Clarise didn't even look up from the shortcrust pastry she was rolling out. 'No hanky-panky,' she said. 'Not for me. Not any more.'

Without another word, Horowicz rounded the table, hauled the back door open and slammed it shut behind him. A bird flew diagonally across the window like something chipped off by the impact.

Clarise turned to me. 'You see? It's starting already.'

Wind flooded round the edges of the house, making the lights in the kitchen flicker, and for a few moments the spirit of Christmas was in the room with us, glowering and baleful – pitiless.

Some years there would be three or four men who she felt might try and do away with themselves, but the only person who troubled her this year was Aaron. Did I know him? I shook my head. I'd had very little contact with Aaron. Whenever I spoke to him, he would look at me much as a statue might, with blank eyes. I had assumed he was heavily medicated, a fact which Clarise now confirmed. All the same, she was going to put a camp bed in his room, she said, and she wanted the rest of us to take turns sleeping in there, just to keep an eye on him.

That week, we drew numbers to see who would spend which nights in Aaron's room, each number representing a date between Christmas Eve and New Year's Day. Much to the relief of the other men, I was lumbered with twenty-five.

We sat down to Christmas dinner at half-past three. Afterwards, we gathered in the front room, which had been decorated with sprigs of holly and bunches of cheap balloons, and Jack Starling, who wasn't one to miss an opportunity, served a punch that he had concocted especially for the occasion. I never found out what the ingredients were, but within an hour Lars had passed out under the tree – somebody tied his ankles together with tinsel so he would trip over when he stood up – and Bill Snape, a man known for his scholarly ways and his reserved demeanour, was attempting a headstand on the top of the piano. I had been watching Aaron surreptitiously ever since breakfast. He had drunk almost nothing. Once the meal was over, he sat on the sofa examining the two sides of his hand, his air of studiousness contrasting oddly with the yellow paper crown he was wearing.

Towards eleven, with the party in full swing, Aaron went upstairs. I waited a couple of minutes, then I followed. Though Clarise was already pretty far gone, she caught my eye and nodded in approval. When I opened Aaron's door, a wedge of light from the landing showed me that he was lying on his back in bed with his eyes open and his hands behind his head.

'I'm sleeping in here tonight,' I said, 'if that's all right.'

He let out a quietly mocking laugh. 'Make sure I don't kill myself.'

I decided not to respond to that.

'Last night it was Starling,' Aaron said. 'He was so drunk I could've done it ten times over.'

I closed the door, then took off my clothes and got into the camp bed. Downstairs, in the front room, Urban Smith was singing 'In the Bleak Midwinter', a carol that could easily have been the Green Quarter's national anthem.

'I still think about her all the time,' Aaron said after a while.

'Think about who?'

'Lucette.'

She had been his fiancée, he told me. He had loved her bony wrists and the way her knees almost knocked together when she walked. She had been clever too. A mind so sharp you could cut yourself on it. One night, while they were sleeping, policemen had burst into their flat. He would always remember the sight of Lucette struggling, half-naked, in the arms of strangers. One of them pointed a finger at him and said, *Stay*. As if he were a dog. The shame of it, that he couldn't rescue her, protect her. The immense, excruciating shame. He hadn't seen her since that night, but he knew she would never forgive him for not coming to her aid.

'There wasn't anything you could have done,' I said.

'I could've tried.'

'It wouldn't have made much difference.'

'It would to me.' Aaron lay still for a moment, then I heard his bedclothes rustle. I sensed that he had turned to face the wall.

I stared up at the ceiling, sleep eluding me. I had been at the Cliff for almost a month now, and though I had settled into the rhythms of life in the house my nights hadn't been particularly restful. I woke too often, and had too many dreams. I would be walking through an empty building or caught in two minds on a street corner, or I would be running along a towpath, but whatever the location there was always something missing, something I had to find. I began to write my dreams down in a small green notebook, as if the process of transcription might reveal their truth, as if, once the dreams had been recorded, once they had been *retained*, they might be persuaded to give up their meaning. Sometimes I had the feeling that I cried out, as I had cried out when I stayed with John Fernandez, but in the morning nobody mentioned it, not even Horowicz, who slept in the room opposite mine. I wasn't alone, perhaps. We were all troubled, it seemed, in one way or another. Once, I heard my own name being shouted in the middle of the night – *Tom? Tommy?* – and I sat upright in my bed and answered, *Yes?* but then I realised it was Clarise at the far end of the landing, Clarise calling for her dead husband in her sleep.

'It's never the things we do that we regret the most,' I said. 'It's the things we didn't do. Or haven't done. Or can't.'

I heard Aaron's head turn on his pillow, but he didn't say anything, and a curious, almost savage impatience took hold of me.

'You know, there's nothing particularly special about you,' I said. 'You're just like all the rest of us. We're all the same. Not because we're melancholic – whatever that means – but because we're haunted by the lives we could have had. The lives we never had a chance to live.'

I wasn't talking to Aaron any more. I wasn't even aware of him in the room – or even of the room itself. The air above my face vibrated like a cloud of midges. I remembered how I had tried to explain myself to Fernandez, and how, simply by talking, I'd made new discoveries about myself. Though Fernandez had listened, he had, in the end, become exasperated with me. *You people who don't know what you're doing.* Or perhaps it was because I had turned up on his doorstep. Because I'd seen through him, as he put it. But yes, I must have sounded delirious, frenetic. I had been suffering from shock, of course – I'd cut myself loose, left everything behind – and there had been exhaustion too. Now, though, I had more clarity. The authorities had deprived me of a life that was mine, and mine alone. They hadn't asked my permission or given me a choice. They'd just taken it. By force. In a sense, then, I had been murdered. How I wished I'd shouted that at Dr Gilbert. *You murderer!*

A glass smashed one floor below.

I listened to the yelling and the helpless laughter, then I listened to people staggering to bed, doors slamming shut, the throaty flushing of the lavatory, and when all that eventually died down, I listened to the window creak with cold and the air sigh in and out of Aaron's lungs. Thinking back to the night of the bomb, the moment I disappeared, it seemed to me that what I'd done was both defy those in power and take a kind of revenge on them. It had been my way of saying, *No, I* won't *accept what you offered me. And no, I'm* not *going to be grateful.* Finally, after twenty-seven years, I had asserted myself. Twenty-seven years! That's how long it takes sometimes. To make the connections, to determine what you feel. To *realise*.

Aaron fell asleep, and then, perhaps an hour later, so did I, and by the time I woke again, at nine in the morning, Aaron was already dressed and standing at the bedroom window, watching the snow.

A white Christmas, the first in many years.

And nobody had killed themselves.

In fact, nothing terrible happened, not unless you counted the bizarre events of Boxing Day night. Sometime towards dawn on the 27th I was woken by shrill screams coming from below. As I opened my door, Clarise thundered past in her quilted housecoat, a beige eye-mask pushed high up on her forehead. I followed her down the stairs and into the kitchen where we found Brendan Burroughs stretched out on the table, his naked torso slathered in flour, sugar and raw eggs. Starling and Horowicz were standing over him, beating him with wooden spoons.

When Clarise finally found her voice, she asked the two men what in the world they thought they were doing.

'What's it look like?' Horowicz said.

'I don't know,' Clarise said. 'I've no idea. That's why I'm asking.'

Horowicz came round the table and stood in front of her, his body swaying, and he spoke very slowly, as though he thought she was stupid.

'Can't you see?' he said. 'We're making a cake.'

In the New Year I began to go for long walks after supper, partly because I wanted to escape the endless drinking sessions in the front room, which left me feeling irritable and jaded, but also because I was finally becoming curious about the town to which I had been sent. Iron Vale was famous for its trains. It was here, once upon a time, that locomotive engines for the entire country had been manufactured. During the last two decades, however, the foundries and rolling mills had closed, and all that remained of the glory days was the railway station, which stood high on a ridge with its own ornate red-brick clock tower. Certainly Victor would have known about the town, and during my first desultory walks I often felt his presence quite distinctly, Victor as a young man, his big head topped with unlikely corrugations of black hair, his eyes pale with enthusiasm.

I quickly settled on one or two favourite routes. I would often make my way out to a piece of flat land that lay at the edge of a housing estate. It was the strangest place. There were roads and pavements, there were street lights too, but there were no buildings. The roads turned corners, linking up with one another, forming orderly rectangles and squares, and yet the areas of scrub grass in between, where the houses should have been, were strewn with rubbish – umbrellas, condoms, microwaves. Crows sat on top of every street lamp like memorials to some dark event. I suppose the council had simply run out of money, but it always looked to me as if something sinister or supernatural had occurred. Other times I would wander out into the country, to a village a couple of miles south of where we lived. I would walk over an old stone bridge and down into a churchyard that stood right on the river. Though small, the church was exquisite, its walls built from a mixture of red and white sandstone, most of which had been quarried from the river bed itself, while the bridge, with its elaborate arches, seemed to hark back to a more dynamic era, when local people had been full of energy and aspiration. On my first visit I entered through a heavy iron gate that groaned loudly on its hinges. Moving among the tombs, I found the most beautiful surnames – Story, Eden, Raine. Towards the rear of the church, where the property had been allowed to go to seed, the dead became anonymous, their dim brown slabs illegible and tilting haphazardly among the weeds and tall grasses. Even here, though, there was a sense of release, a feeling of having been freed from time's net. This wouldn't be such a bad place to be buried, I thought. The river's constant presence near by. Trees shifting in the breeze that lifted off the water. And, in the distance, a long low ridge – the moors – on which, that very afternoon, unearthly bright-orange sunlight fell. No, not a bad place at all.

One January night, standing in the middle of the bridge and looking down into the churchyard, I saw three scraps of white in the darkness. At first I couldn't decide what they were, then one of the scraps shifted, developing a head and arms, and in that same moment I remembered someone telling me that White People were often to be found in cemeteries. Various theories had been put forward, the most obvious being that they instinctively identified with dead people. After all, one could argue that White People were dead too. Dead in the eyes of the authorities, at least. Bureaucratically dead. As I watched, the three figures moved behind a row of yew trees, then they appeared again, their white cloaks showing in stark relief against one of the grander tombs. Thinking it might be interesting to observe them at close range, I crossed the bridge, swung a leg over the churchyard wall – the gate would have made too much noise – and stepped down into coarse grass. I wasn't sure why I was so curious, or what it was I hoped to learn. I felt compelled, though – guided even. It was as if my body comprehended something that my mind did not.

I crept slowly forwards, crouching among the gravestones. I imagined this would be, among other things, a test of their psychic powers. Would they detect my presence? And if they did, what then? My heart beat harder, as though there was the possibility of danger. As I reached the yew trees, the moon rolled out into a patch of clear sky, and I saw them ahead of me, passing through a gap in the fence at the back of the cemetery. Now, perhaps, I could close the distance between us. I ran to the fence, then knelt in the shadow of an overgrown holly bush to catch my breath. I could hear them on the other side. There weren't any words, just odd little grunts and snuffles. No wonder some people thought of them as animals.

I stole a look over the fence. Clouds hung before me, rimmed in silver. To my right was the bridge, the black river flowing underneath. I lifted my head a fraction higher. There they were, below me. They had removed all their clothes, and they were standing in the shallows, two men and a woman. Pale as stone or marble, they looked like damaged statues, half their legs gone, the tips of their fingers too. They began to wash themselves. They didn't hurry, despite the fact that it was winter, and I wondered whether they had lost the ability to feel the cold, along with everything else. The river swirled around their knees with the dark glint of crude oil. I was struck by how methodical and self-contained they were. Their nakedness had no sexual overtone. In fact, they behaved as unselfconsciously as children. There was also an understated dignity about the scene which I found strangely poignant, and which gave me the feeling, just for a moment, that I was looking at a painting. These people had nothing – nothing, that is, except their freedom, the license to go wherever they pleased . . . As I watched them, an idea occurred to me. I wouldn't do anything just yet, though. No, I would wait. I needed to think things through. Prepare myself.

I had been standing by the fence for about five minutes when the woman's body stiffened. She had been bent over, scooping water on to her back, first over one shoulder, then the other, but now, suddenly, she had frozen, one hand braced on her thigh, the other still dangling in the river. Her head turned towards me. My chest locked, all the breath held deep inside. I didn't think she'd seen me. She acted more as if she'd picked up the scent of something foreign, something that didn't belong. Her eyes still angled in my direction, she slowly straightened up and, tilting her head sideways, wrung out the thick cable of her hair. Black water spilled from between her hands. Without even exchanging a glance, the two men stopped washing and began to wade towards the bank.

I ducked down, then hurried off through the churchyard. I wasn't embarrassed, or even afraid exactly – Victor had always maintained that White People were peaceful and harmless, and that people only feared them out of ignorance – but at the same time I didn't want to risk a confrontation. Vaulting over the wall, I kept low until I reached the far end of the bridge. There was nobody in the river now, and the cemetery lay quiet and dark and still. They must have fled along the bank. I glanced at the watch Clarise had given me for Christmas. Twenty-five to twelve. It had been time for me to leave in any case, or she'd start worrying. She could never rest easy in her bed until she was sure that all her boys were home.

On arriving back, I saw that the downstairs lights had been switched off. I unlocked the front door, locked it again behind me and was just making for the stairs when a figure stepped away from the banisters.

'You're up to something, aren't you?' Horowicz's face rose out of the grey gloom of the hall.

'I've been out for a walk,' I said, 'as usual.'

He gave me a knowing look, then laughed softly, cynically, and shook his head. 'You can't fool me, Wig. I've been watching you.'

After a brief silence, I moved past him and started to climb the stairs. When I reached the landing, he was still standing in the hall, looking up at me, his eyes glinting in the half-light like a drawer full of knives.

In recent years, Iron Vale had become home to the Museum of Tears, and it was the inalienable right of every melancholic, no matter where they might live, to have a sample of their tears stored within the museum walls. All you had to do was write to the curators, enclosing proof of identity. They would send you an air-tight glass vial, no bigger than a lipstick. The next time you cried, you collected your tears and transferred them to the vial. Some people waited for an important event – the death of a loved one being the most obvious, perhaps – but it was up to you to choose which aspect of your melancholy nature you wanted to preserve. When it was done, you sealed the vial and returned it to the museum, where it would be catalogued and then put on display, along with millions of others.

One evening towards the end of January, we were sitting in the front room, all nine of us, when Horowicz launched a vitriolic attack on the museum. He thought it self-indulgent, overblown – a total waste of tax-payers' money. What was there to look at? Row after row of tiny bottles, each containing more or less the same amount of more or less the same transparent fluid.

You could hardly call it an *attraction*, he said. If anything, there was something repellent about the whole idea.

Clarise let him finish, then slowly shook her head. 'You don't understand,' she said.

Horowicz's eyebrows lifted. When someone started complaining, people generally joined in, and the level of complaint would escalate. The sessions would go on for hours, becoming ever more self-righteous and extreme. But not tonight.

'Think about happiness for a moment, Martin,' Clarise said. 'Can you remember being happy?'

Horowicz let out a snort, as though he found the question absurd.

There was a fundamental problem with happiness, Clarise went on, quite unperturbed. Happiness had a slippery, almost diaphanous quality. It gave nothing off, left nothing behind. Grief was different, though. Grief could be collected, exhibited. Grief could be *remembered*. And if we had proof that we'd been sad, she argued, then we also had proof that we'd been happy, since the one, more often than not, presupposed the other. In preserving grief, therefore, we were preserving happiness. The Museum of Tears stood for much more than its name might initially suggest. It wasn't just to do with rows of identical glass bottles – though that, in itself, said a lot about equality, if you thought about it. It was to do with people trying to hold on to such happiness as they had known.

Her eyes returned to Horowicz, who was staring at the carpet. 'But maybe you don't know what that feels like,' she said. 'Maybe you've never lost someone. In which case, though it sounds odd to say it, I'm sorry for you, I really am.'

'I know what it feels like,' he muttered.

Later, Clarise expanded on her thesis. She believed the museum was both a testament to individuality and a collective ode to the country in which we lived. We were all unique, she said, and yet we shared a common humanity, a common humour. I had never heard her so impassioned, so articulate.

'And there's also the little matter of immortality,' she went on. 'It's hard to resist, the offer of immortality.' She sent a sideways look at Horowicz, who reached for his beer and drank quickly. 'I wouldn't be surprised, Martin, if you didn't end up in there yourself one day.'

He shook his head savagely but unconvincingly.

'I'm in there,' Jack Starling said.

I watched Horowicz's top lip curl. He would view Starling's announcement as tantamount to a betrayal.

'The night my still exploded,' and Starling turned to Clarise, 'remember? Half the outhouse went up with it. I shed a few tears over that, I can tell you.'

'What, and you kept them?' Horowicz's voice was acidic with disbelief.

'You know, you're right,' Starling said, still speaking to Clarise. 'I can walk into that museum and look at my tears and it all comes back to me, that first batch of sloe gin I made, and the nights we had on it, those brilliant nights, and you know the really strange thing?' He put down his glass so as to make the point more emphatically. 'That little vial, it's like a miniature. The vial's the gin bottle, and my tears, they're the gin. It's like the whole thing's there, the whole memory, only tiny.'

Smiling broadly, Clarise told him he had just summed it all up, everything she'd been talking about, then she turned to me and asked if I'd been to the museum yet. I shook my head.

'You should go,' she said.

A few days later I walked down into the town. The museum stood on a narrow street, directly opposite the public library. Looking at the staid red-brick façade and the antiquated ventilation units, I guessed that the building had once housed municipal offices – the council, maybe, or the gas board. A modest brass plaque had been bolted to the wall, just to the left of the double-doors: *The Museum of Tears – Please ring for entry.*

Although I had gone along with what Clarise had been saying that night, I hadn't known what to expect from the museum, or even why I was there, really, but I found a stillness settling over me as I ventured into the first of the rooms. All these people reduced to a few ccs of salty water, as if a kind of essence had been wrung from each of them. Was Marco Rinaldi here? What

273

about Boorman? I wandered dreamily from floor to floor. Apart from the museum guards, I had the vast place to myself.

The glass vials were arranged in three parallel rows at shoulder-height, and underneath each of them was a rectangle of white card indicating the donor's name and date of birth (and, if necessary, death). In themselves, the vials had a somewhat medical aura. They reminded me of test-tubes and, by association, of hospitals and laboratories. In the manner of their presentation, though – the careful labelling, the fashionable austerity – I detected more than a hint of the art gallery. And yet the interior itself, its ambience, had something in common with a school – the grey-blue walls in need of redecoration, the dark, slightly greasy parquet floors. Research, creativity, nostalgia . . . In the end, the museum displayed characteristics of so many different kinds of institutions that I was no longer sure how to behave or what to think. There was something inherently awkward, or inchoate, perhaps, about the whole experience.

After half an hour I felt I had seen enough, and I walked back towards the stairs that led to the exit. I was passing through a perfectly innocuous room on the second floor when my eye happened to fall on a name I recognised. *Micklewright.* The air around me appeared to sag and then fold in on itself. I looked away from the wall and blinked two or three times, then I looked back again. The name was still there. In fact, the name was there twice: *Micklewright, Sally*, and then, right next to it, *Micklewright, Philip.*

My mother and father.

A trap-door opened in me somewhere and my heart dropped through it. My hand over my mouth, I sank on to the ottoman in the middle of the room.

My mother and father. My parents.

I had thought of them so seldom during the last twenty-seven years. Partly this had to do with survival. If I'd thought of them, I wouldn't have been able to go on. I'd had no choice but to put them behind me, out of sight. Partly, also, it came down to the image I carried in my head of two people standing on a road in the middle of the night. Her bare feet, his sleepy face – rain slanting down . . . It was so timeless, so static. So complete. As the years went by, it had taken on an eternal unyielding quality, like a cenotaph, and it had been impossible for me to think around it, impossible for me to remember, or even imagine, anything that had happened before that moment. Then came my visit to the club, exposing the need in me, the ache – the hollowness that lay beneath a life so seemingly well ordered, even charmed. When I stepped through that pale-gold door, something had given in me. Fragments of another life had been released. There had not been much, and it had come so late, so very late, but it had altered me for ever. Everything I had built had been revealed for what it was – mere scaffolding. Everything would have to be remade.

I stood up again and went over to the wall. This time I noticed the dates beneath my parents' names. They were both dead. I tilted my head to one side, as if I needed another angle on what I was being told. As if that might help me to comprehend. My father had died first. My mother had survived him by eight years. Neither of them had lived to a great age. My father had been fifty-nine, my mother sixty-three. Had they been melancholic all along, or had they been transferred at some point, as I had? What was their story? I had no way of knowing. Since the vials were exhibited in strict chronological order, the two belonging to my parents must have arrived at the museum simultaneously. It was quite conceivable then that they had been crying at the same time – possibly for the same reason – and that those were the tears they had chosen to collect. I wondered if they had been thinking of the boy they'd lost. I wondered if they'd ever forgiven him for turning away from them. Or perhaps they hadn't even noticed. All they had understood, in their confusion, in their distress, was that their only son was being taken from them. Gazing at their remains, I felt instinctively that they hadn't tried too hard to stay alive, that they had given up, in other words, and I couldn't really say I blamed them.

So the museum was a graveyard too.

I stared at the names and dates until they blurred. I hadn't found my parents – not really. Perhaps they had been present for a few minutes, while I was sitting, head lowered, on the ottoman, but now they had disappeared again. All in all, it hadn't been much of a reunion. I reached up slowly with one hand.

'No touching, please.'

I looked round to see a museum guard standing in the doorway to the room. My hand dropped to my side. The guard nodded and moved on.

Out on the street again, I felt as though years had gone by. I wouldn't have been surprised if the library had been knocked down and new buildings had been erected in its place.

I walked back to the Cliff, the air glassy, dazzling.

When I opened the door, Clarise was standing at the far end of the hall. She asked me whether I would like a cup of tea. She was just about to put the kettle on, she said. I shook my head, then stepped sideways into the front room. I heard her come after me.

'What is it, Wig?' she said. 'What's the matter?'

'This is a terrible place.'

'Here?' Clarise's face whirled like a clumsy planet, taking in the mould-green three-piece suite, the velour curtains, the gas fire with its tile surround.

I shook my head again.

A boy could balance on one leg for hours. A man could make a book from his wife's shoes. A couple could stand on a road in the middle of the night and call their son's name, only to have him turn his back on them. Candles burned in windows all year round, memorials to those who had gone but were not dead. There were very few who didn't live in the shadow of some separation or other. The divided kingdom was united after all, by just one thing: longing.

I sank down among the sofa's sagging cushions. Clarise sat beside me. I told her that I had visited the museum and that I had found my parents, my real parents, but then my voice began to tremble and I couldn't carry on. The grief had been stored inside me for too long. It hurt to bring it out. Clarise took me in her arms and held me against her. I smelled the wool of her cardigan,

276

and her face powder, and the oil at the roots of her hair. My whole body jerked, as if caught on a fisherman's hook.

'There, there,' she said. 'Let it out.'

And though I was crying I learned something about myself just then. I saw it clearly for the first time. I had never been sanguine – at least, not so far as I could remember. No, wait – that was wrong. I had been sanguine until the moment I was classified as sanguine, but all my happiness had ended there, and all my optimism too. Ever since that night, the only thing I had ever really wanted was to find my way back. I was like someone who has died and can't let go, someone who wants desperately to rejoin the living. And it wasn't possible, of course. It wasn't even possible to remember, not really – or rather, there was a limit to what could be recovered. None of that mattered, though. It was enough to believe, enough to know. That my parents had mourned me while they were alive. That they had died still missing me. That they had loved me.

Clarise held me close and said the same words over and over. *Let it out. Let it all out.*

As February began, gales swept the length and breadth of the country, causing untold damage. Several people were killed by falling trees. In the south a headless man was seen speeding down a village high street on his bicycle. He had been decapitated by a flying roof-tile only seconds earlier. The freak conditions and unusual sightings sparked off the kind of doom-laden apocalyptic talk that wouldn't have been tolerated even for a moment in the place I came from, though I found myself susceptible to it, perhaps because I was waiting for circumstances to favour me. As a result of what had happened to me during the previous month or so, a certain threshold had been crossed, a decision had been reached, but everything now depended on the White People, and they seemed to have vanished without trace. Weeks had elapsed since that night in the graveyard, and I hadn't so much as caught a glimpse of them. The only advantage was that Horowicz had lost interest in me. Whenever we spoke, which was rarely, he would berate me for my apathy, my fecklessness, almost as though he was trying to goad me into an action that he could then expose, condemn. I still went for walks after supper. On returning to the house, however, I would often join the others for a drink in an attempt to dull my frustration, to anaesthetise myself.

One Thursday evening I was on my way upstairs to change – Urban Smith was taking part in a talent contest in the local pub that night, and some of us were going along to support him – when I chanced to look out of the landing window. Across the street, beneath the drooping branches of a magnolia, stood a man in a white cloak. The tree had flowered early, and the man blended with its creamy blooms so perfectly that I had almost failed to notice him. I steered an uneasy glance over my shoulder. The landing was deserted, all the bedroom doors were closed. Somewhere below, I could hear Urban doing his voice exercises. Quickly, I went through my pockets. All I had on me was a cigarette-lighter, my dream notebook and a key to the front door. I had some money too, saved for precisely this eventuality. Round my neck was the silver ring I had found, which I now regarded as a sort of talisman. I couldn't think of anything else I might need. I looked out of the window again. The man was still standing in the shadow of the magnolia tree. I thought of Victor and Marie lost in the mist and shivered. I didn't know if I should feel apprehensive or reassured. I checked the time. Twenty to seven. What with the excitement of the competition, I doubted anybody would notice my absence, and if Urban won and the men drank enough of Starling's latest brew, a lethal poteen, then it might easily be morning before they realised I was gone.

My abrupt departure would not come as a surprise to every-one. Clarise had treated me so kindly that I had felt duty bound to let her in on at least part of the secret. I had waited until it was my turn to help her with the dinner. On the night in question, I stood at the kitchen sink, washing spinach, while she sat at the table behind me and coated veal in egg and breadcrumbs. The men were out somewhere, playing darts. Only Lars Friedriksson had stayed behind, and he was in the basement, poking, two-fingered, at his ancient portable. Though he had already written a thousand pages, he claimed that he had hardly scratched the surface. He would not disturb us.

'I'll be leaving soon,' I said.

Clarise's wide, unblinking eyes veered towards me.

'I'm not going to give you the details,' I said. 'I just want you to know that it'll happen sometime in the near future.'

'You can't leave,' she said, 'not unless they relocate you. It's not allowed.'

I couldn't help smiling. She only ever invoked the law out of anxiety or panic.

'I'm telling you now because I don't want it to upset you,' I said. 'I wouldn't want you to think' – and I paused – 'that I had come to any harm.'

'Are you so unhappy here?'

I went over, took her hand. 'You've been good to me, Clarise. I owe you a lot. It wouldn't be fair if I did it behind your back. You mustn't try and stop me, though.'

She looked up at me, tears beginning to fill her eyes. 'Where will you go?'

'It's better you don't know. And anyway, it might all go wrong, in which case I'll end up here again.'

She tried to smile through her tears, which were dripping off her cheeks and down into the breadcrumbs. Later that evening, at dinner, Bill Snape would tell her, in that precise, fastidious voice of his, that although the veal was delicious she had, in his opinion, used a little too much salt.

Yes, she would realise what had happened, I thought, as I turned from the window, and I knew I could trust her not to give anything away. She had even promised to wait a few hours before she informed the authorities.

I managed to reach the kitchen without running into anyone. The lid vibrated gently on a saucepan of root vegetables and chicken bones, stock for a risotto Clarise would be making in the morning. I opened the back door, then eased it shut behind me, and I was just setting off along the narrow passageway that led to the street when a voice called my name. Brendan Burroughs was standing by the outhouse. He had one hand cupped in the other, and his chin had moved into the air above his right shoulder, as if he had to peer round a corner to see me. He asked where I was going.

'A walk,' I said. 'To clear my head.'

'Aren't you coming to the pub?'

'Maybe later on.'

'Tell you what,' he said. 'I'll come with you.'

'No,' I said.

'Yes, I'd like a walk. My head needs clearing too. And, after all, moonlight can't hurt me, can it?' He took several rapid steps in my direction, half tripping on a drain in his eagerness to join me.

I took out my lighter and struck the flint. A flame sprang up between us. 'Didn't you hear me, Brendan? I said no.'

Shrinking back, his mouth opened in a crooked, incredulous grin. He couldn't believe I'd done such a thing. I wasn't Starling or Horowicz. I wasn't cruel like them.

'Wig,' he said, his voice balanced precariously between pleading and reproach.

'No.' I snapped the lighter shut again. With one last look at him, a steady look, to show him that I wasn't joking, I turned away.

When I stepped out on to the pavement, the space beneath the magnolia tree was empty. I looked left, then right, just in time to see the cloaked man shamble through the gate and down into the park. I risked a glance over my shoulder. Brendan was still loitering in the shadows at the side of the house, one hand clasping the other, hoping that I might relent.

'No,' I said.

Once I was safely out of sight of the Cliff, I broke into a run. I had waited so long, and it might be weeks before another chance presented itself. I needn't have worried. When I reached the black railings I could see the man below me, beneath the overhanging trees, his pale cloak appearing to hover in the gloom.

He followed the polluted stream for a while as it wound

behind the backs of houses and under roads, then he turned to the south, using a maze of lanes and alleys I had never been along before. He seemed to know the town in such detail – its recesses, its hiding places. I realised that if I'd seen so little of the White People recently it was because they had mapped out an alternative geography. Their existence lay parallel to everybody else's.

At last he stepped out on to a road I recognised. It led downhill past a school, fetching up close to the river. His hood had fallen back, and the light from a street lamp caressed his bare head as he passed beneath it. No more than fifty yards separated us, but he didn't appear to have noticed me. Was he preoccupied, or merely simple? I couldn't have said. It would be a kind of suicide, what I was about to attempt, but at the same time it would be a transformation – another life entirely. The White People were treated either as scapegoats or as deities, depending on the territory into which they wandered, and this, I thought, was the basic yet paradoxical truth about them, namely that, although they had been certified as non-persons, they had access to a far wider range of experience than the rest of us. We were limited, imprisoned, but they walked free. Another life indeed . . .

The man reached a junction and seemed to hesitate. To his left the road angled back into the centre of Iron Vale, while to the right it ran out into the country, passing through the village with its graveyard and then on towards towns that were famous for their racecourses. On the far side of the road was a thinly wooded area, the treacly blackness of the river just visible beyond. Although it was still early, not even eight o'clock, very few cars were travelling in either direction, and there was nobody out walking – nobody except us, that is. I hoped he wasn't thinking of meeting up with others like him. My plan would only work if he was on his own. Instead of making for the graveyard, though, as I had feared he might, he crossed the road and disappeared into the old dark trees that lined the pavement.

I stood on the kerb, exactly as he had done. If I kept quite still, I could hear people weeping. I wanted to dismiss it as my imagination, but then it occurred to me that the sound might be happening inside my head. It might be my own grieving that I could hear – for those who had been unable to protect me, and those I myself, in turn, had been unable to protect. The sorrow I had always known about was more in evidence these days. It was as if I lived in a house that had a stream running under it. There wasn't a moment when I didn't feel the damp. At the same time, high in the air above me, traffic-lights were swaying on their slender wires, and I knew that it might just have been the wind. It might have been the wind all along. Maybe the man in the cloak had heard it too. Maybe that sound, and nothing more than that, was what had held him on the pavement for so long.

Once across the road, I found a narrow lane that led through a picnic area and then on down a gentle, curving incline to the river. Tables and benches, all built out of wooden slats, had been arranged among the trees. The moon had risen, bright and swollen, gleaming like an heirloom, and the short grass was crazed with the shadows of bare branches, shadows so black that the ground seemed to have cracked wide open. I glanced up. There he was, ahead of me, unmistakable in white, and quite alone. He followed the lane to where it became a car-park. Though he wasn't hurrying, he appeared determined, as if he had a purpose. They weren't supposed to be capable of that. I dropped back, allowing a distance to open up between us. It didn't seem likely that I would lose him, not here.

Beyond the car-park was a concrete embankment that over-looked a weir. The man stood at the railings, staring out over the river. Above the weir the water was smooth and dark. A notice warned of strong currents, hidden dangers. Further down, the river narrowed a little, its surface becoming ruffled. Part of the river bed on our side had been exposed, forming a beach made up of grassy banks, stretches of mud, and big white stones. After a few minutes the man clambered down off the embankment and on to the river bed. I was still standing at the edge of the car-park, beneath the trees. The wind lifted. The branches' shadows swung and shuddered on the ground before me, which made me feel unsteady on my feet. To my right, where the railings were, something knocked and clanked. I watched the man pick his way across the stones. I decided to wait under the trees until I discovered what his intentions were. There would be nowhere for me to hide down there.

At last he arrived at the water's edge, a ghostly shape against the river's glinting blackness. He started to undo the buttons on his cloak. This was better than I could have hoped for. I kept my eyes on him, watching his every movement. The wind slackened again. I realised that I was breathing through my mouth. Under his cloak he was wearing a collarless shirt, split open down the front, and a pair of long johns. He stooped to untie his laces. There was something infinitely touching about the way he conscientiously pushed each of his socks into the appropriate boot, as if somebody had taught him how to get undressed, as if, once upon a time, somebody had cared for him. You rarely thought of childhood or upbringing when confronted with the White People; they appeared to have emerged, fully fledged and yet unformed, into the world. Removing his undershirt and then a vest, he placed them on top of the cloak. Finally he peeled off the long johns. He stood on the mud in his underpants, his body wide and solid, hands dangling on a level with his thighs, and once again he seemed to be debating something inside himself, then he began to wade into the water. In that moment he became the same as anybody else, waving both arms in the air as he struggled to stay upright. When the blackness reached his knees, he crouched quickly and slid forwards, chin raised, moonlight silvering the flat plane of his forehead.

Leaving the cover of the trees, I crept out along the embankment and then climbed down to the river bed. At the pressure of my foot the mud belched softly, and a smell lifted past my face, a cloud of something rank, primeval. I started to move gingerly towards the place where the man had left his clothing. Once, I stopped, looked up. The river ran from right to left, all kinds of notches cut into its shiny surface, and the man's head bobbed there, among the reflections, a small pale globe with careless dabs of black for hair and mouth and eyes. Then he began to swim in my direction. He must have noticed me at last. His arms beat fiercely at the water, white splashes showing in the darkness like matches being struck repeatedly against the side of a matchbox but never bursting into flame. I undid my jacket, took it off.

The man hauled himself to his feet, then staggered out of the water. His chest heaved with the exertion of his dash to the shore, and his underpants had slipped low on his left hip, revealing a smudge of pubic hair. By the time he reached me, I too had stripped down to my underwear. My shoes stood on a rock, the contents of my pockets placed near by. The man had come to a halt in front of me, no more than a few feet away, his chest still rising and falling.

'I want you to take my clothes,' I said.

The man tipped his head to one side, as if intrigued, or charmed.

I offered him the clothes I was holding. He stepped back. One of his feet sank deep into the mud, and he almost lost his balance. When I took his arm so as to steady him, his features seemed to scatter on his face. Air whistled past his teeth. His arm was cold and heavy.

'I don't mean you any harm,' I told him.

Looking down, he lifted his foot out of the mud. An extravagant sucking sound accompanied the movement, and he grinned at me, a wide gap showing between his two front teeth. The strangest smell came off him. Bitter, like the milky sap in the stalks of bluebells.

'There,' I said.

I looked over my shoulder, scanning the embankment for signs of life. I saw nothing, no one. All the same, I couldn't afford to waste any time, not if my plan was going to succeed.

I pushed my clothes against his chest. 'Take them. Your life will be much easier.' Bending swiftly, I picked up his vest and put it on.

The man was clutching my clothes now, but he hadn't looked at them at all. He was still staring at me, transfixed. His mouth had fallen open, and his eyes had the dull flat shine of porcelain. A single drop of water hung from the lobe of his left ear like a pearl. Hung and hung. Then fell.

I slipped his undershirt over my head and pulled on the long johns, then I reached for the cloak. Fingers stumbling, I did up the buttons. The cloak weighed more than I had anticipated, and it was damp from lying on the river bed. That odour of bluebell sap again. I dropped my few possessions into the pocket at the front, then slid my feet into the man's boots and tied the laces. I kept thinking that he would intervene, but he seemed paralysed. Then, as I turned away, a hoarse bellow came out of him. He had flung my clothes to the ground. I began to run. The boots were a size too big and the cloak swirled around my ankles. I floundered in the mud, expecting to be brought down from behind at any moment.

At last, and breathing hard, I levered myself up on to the embankment. Only then did I glance round. The man had not moved. My clothes still lay beside him in a small shapeless mound. Once again I heard him bellow, an inhuman noise, like a cow being butchered. I had wanted the exchange to benefit us both, but clearly it would take more than a new set of clothing to improve his lot. I had deceived myself. It occurred to me that I had done a kind of violence to him, and that I might, eventually, have to pay for this. Stealing one last look at the half-naked figure, as though to fix in my mind the debt I owed him, I turned and began to walk back through the trees.

SEVEN

S treet lamps hung above the tarmac, buzzing. If I hadn't known better I would have said that they were living things and that the rest of the world was dead. I looked both ways, then stepped out into the road. Halfway across, my boot caught in the hem of the cloak and I went sprawling. My clumsiness was greeted by a blast from the horn of a passing car. The mockery had begun, and it didn't feel unwarranted. I already seemed to have altered in some indefinable way. It wasn't the weight or the smell of the cloak. It wasn't even the sheer unfamiliarity of such a garment. It was more as if I had entered a tradition, and the clothes themselves were imparting something of that responsibility, that lore, as a crown does when it is lowered on to the head of a king. In donning the cloak, I had parted company with the person I used to be without knowing quite who or what I was going to become. When I reached the far side of the road I stood and stared at the cracks between the paving-stones. They looked precise but temporary, as though they had been drawn in pencil. As though they could be rubbed out. There was something frightening about that, but something exhilarating too. Like turning your hand over and seeing that all the lines have gone. The world could disappear. I could disappear. A blank slate everywhere I looked. Staying close to the wall, I moved off down a quiet residential street.

You would think I would have realised sooner, but it was almost midnight before it occurred to me that I had nowhere to go. I had failed to work out any of the practical considerations.

Where would I sleep? What would I eat? I found myself in a cobbled alley by the station, its clock tower lifting high above my left shoulder. There were railway tracks behind me, on the other side of a wooden fence. In front of me stood a terrace of red-brick houses. They faced away from me, their back yards silent, their garages locked up for the night. On top of the walls, glass splinters glittered where they had been embedded upright in cement. Each street light cast its own sullen dark-yellow glow. I was cold now, and tired. Teeth chattering. I could see Clarise Tucker's front room with its tatty velour curtains and its misshapen furniture, coils of smoke unwinding from the ends of cigarettes, the air clouded with the pungent, yeasty fumes of Starling's beer, and then, having climbed the stairs, I saw my single bed, and the reading lamp behind the door, its shade cocked like a bird's head, and my book lying open on the chair, a book I would never finish now. Who would have thought I would miss that tiny, dingy room on the first floor of the Cliff? Who would have thought I would miss any of it? But a loneliness had risen up in me, keen, abrupt, and disproportionate, somehow, and it kept on rising, a sense of the smallness of my life, a rapid ebbing of conviction, and I stood on that bleak lane, beneath piss-yellow lights, and bellowed, and, much to my surprise, I sounded exactly like the man whose clothes I'd taken. A window grated open, and a woman shouted back. *Some people are trying to sleep.* I walked on, teeth clicking in my mouth like dice in a cup, no destination in my head.

All night I kept moving, aimlessly, hopelessly, my feet adrift in a stranger's boots. All night I oscillated between moments of elation and longer stretches of despair. The town offered neither shelter nor guidance, and by half-past three I had come full circle. The station loomed before me once again, with its forbidding brickwork and its draughty doorways. This time I walked in. The concourse was brightly lit and quite deserted. No trains were due for hours. I stood outside a photo booth and, staring into the mirror, practised the faces for which the White People were renowned – the rounded, vacant eyes, the slack, half-open mouth. I made a few attempts at their trademark grunts and mumbles. The sounds boomed around and above me, the empty concourse acting as an echo chamber.

I was about to move on when a short bald man in a uniform burst out of one of the offices and collided with me. It was entirely his fault, and yet he swore and lashed out at me, the back of his hand catching me above the ear. I stepped backwards, laughing. So this was how it was going to be! My laughter had no effect on him. In fact, I wasn't even sure he noticed it. He had hit me without looking, without so much as checking his stride, and I'd been unable to ward off the blow. My cloak was made out of a heavy, hard-wearing material, some kind of hemp or jute, and the slits for my arms were difficult to find in a hurry. Had this been done deliberately, to keep White People powerless? I also wondered about my overall reaction. If the man had been a little less distracted, would he have thought my behaviour untypical?

I had only been living as one of the White People for a few hours, but I could already see that I was lacking certain vital qualities and skills. In shedding the superfluous, they had reduced themselves – or been reduced – to some sort of residue or essence; their so-called emptiness was actually a distillation, a form of knowledge. I wasn't acquainted with the labyrinth of pathways and alleys through which they moved with such apparent freedom and authority, and if I didn't find out about them soon I would become too visible, I would begin to arouse suspicion. My only option was to attach myself to a group of genuine White People, and quickly; I needed to hide among them, learn from them. If I really wanted to step outside the system, if I wanted to be rid of it entirely, I would have to forget myself – everything I was, or ever had been. I would have to enter the fold in reality that the White People inhabited. Eyes of the dullest porcelain, and a black hole for a mouth. Words all swallowed up. Head like a guest-house for the wind. That sentence of Pat Dunne's had stayed with me, but it had never been more relevant: *You have to act like them, or you don't survive.*

I didn't sleep at all, and yet afterwards, when I thought back to that first night, I came across blank patches, like periods of unconsciousness, where I couldn't recall what I had done. There seemed to be no clear sequence of streets, just this place, and then another place, and then another place again, as if, like a giant, I had moved by leaps and bounds. Sometimes a place occurred twice – the river, the museum – which led me to suspect that I was clinging to small pockets of familiarity. Or else I had found myself in one of the circles of hell, perhaps, condemned to repeat myself . . .

By first light I was walking in a poor part of town, north-east of the station. A council estate had been built out there, among the weeds and puddles. White gulls whirled, screeching, above mounds of rubbish. I had been thinking it might be wise to hide myself away before too long, but then a small boy emerged from between two walls of pebble-dash and as I watched him turn in my direction I had a flash of inspiration and fell into step with him.

'Morning,' I said.

The boy stopped and stared. 'You can talk.'

'You won't tell anyone, will you?'

He weighed his decision, then shook his head. 'No.' He squinted up at me. 'Can you say anything else?'

I noticed an old man cycling along the road towards us. 'Not now.'

The man pedalled into the estate, leeks and sticks of celery poking out of the wicker basket lashed to his handlebars.

The boy was called Felix – an unusual name for a melancholic, I thought, though I chose not to comment on it – and he was on his way to the market to do some shopping for his mother. I asked if I could tag along. He didn't see why not. He took me to a muddy expanse of wasteground where a number of vans stood about with their doors flung open. Traders in cheap leather jackets bent into the interiors, unloading endless brightly coloured streams of second-hand clothing. We moved on past stalls selling electronic goods, jewellery, shoes, kitchen equipment, old war medals, and even live birds in cages, arriving eventually at an area where one could buy fresh produce. While Felix queued out the front with all the women, I scavenged round the back. I came upon a box of badly bruised pears, several of which I was able to devour before the stall owner chased me away. A few minutes later I salvaged four tomatoes from a pile that had been dumped on the ground, and then, even better, I discovered a heap of unshelled peanuts and the wrinkled tail-end of a salami. I ate half of what I had found and stored the rest in the pocket of my cloak.

When Felix appeared again, he was loaded down with bags. He wondered if I'd be willing to help him carry them. Fortified by my rudimentary breakfast, I said I would. As we trudged back along the main road, he asked whether I had a name. People called me Wig, I said. I told him how it had come about. He nodded soberly and said he thought it was a good name, under the circumstances.

As we turned into the estate where he lived, I decided it was time to ask the question that had been on my mind for much of the night. Did he have any idea where I could find others like me? His forehead crumpled, and he walked more slowly, staring at his shoes. He was giving the matter serious consideration, as I had suspected he might. Under the flyover, he said at last. The one out by the kennels. He had seen some White People there. Or try the railway line, he said. Going north. At his front door, he asked if I wanted to come in and rest. There was only his mother, he said, and she always got up late.

'Better not.' I put a hand on his shoulder. 'I enjoyed meeting you, though.'

'Thanks for helping, Wig,' he said. 'I couldn't have done it by myself.'

'If anybody asks about me, don't say a word. All right?'

He tucked his lips into his mouth, then nodded.

'It's our secret,' I said. 'Promise?'

'I promise.'

I ruffled his hair and told him to look after himself, then I turned and walked back to the pavement.

When I reached the corner of the street I heard a voice call out. Glancing round, I could see a face showing above the dark wooden fencing. He must have climbed on to a dustbin. I waved to him, and he waved back, his hand moving so fast that it became a blur.

Felix.

I don't know how I got through that day. I was so tired that I kept tripping over and though I'd stuffed bits of newspaper into the backs of my boots so they would fit a little better I already had blisters on both heels. Taking the advice I had been given, I followed the main branch of the railway line out to the north end of town – to no avail. The flyover didn't yield anything either, only a torn, stained mattress and a circle of black ashes, the remains of someone's fire. Every time I saw white, my heart jumped, but it was always just a man opening a newspaper or a woman hanging out a sheet, and afterwards fatigue would reclaim me. Each new false alarm took something out of me, depleting me still further.

Towards the middle of the afternoon I was on a railway bridge out near the unfinished housing estate when I happened to stop and lean on the parapet. I was only going to pause for a while before I continued on my way, but there below me, seated on a grass embankment, were three of the people I had been looking for – two men and a woman. Were they the same three that I had seen washing in the river? I had to assume so. In which case I was doubly relieved they hadn't noticed me that night. After all, this was my chance, and it seemed unlikely I would get another. The authorities would know of my disappearance by now – Clarise would have to report me, if only to protect herself – though I had spent a good part of the day trying to keep that thought from entering my head, since it would have done nothing for my rapidly dwindling morale.

I clambered over the fence. One of the men heard me and turned to watch, his jaw revolving, as I edged side-footed down the bank. A goods train approached, its trucks loaded with sand and gravel. By the time it had gone past I was standing beside the White People, attempting to replicate the unnatural complacency I saw on their faces. In front of them, on a sheet of wrinkled brown paper, they had laid out a few chunks of white bread and a fatty cooked meat that might have been pork. Both the men were still eating. I took some peanuts out of my pocket and placed them on the paper, then I added a couple of tomatoes. One of the men, the dark one, looked up and nodded. I nodded back. The other man appeared to smile at me, though it could have been wind. He had pale eyebrows, and cheeks that looked grazed. The inside of his mouth seemed raw too, with chipped teeth and swollen gums, and he chewed gingerly, wincing as he did so. The woman opened one of the peanuts and ate the contents, then she thumped the ground beside her with the flat of her hand. I sat down next to her. She nodded and stared out over the railway line, her eyes misting over. A humming sound came out of her, a series of monotonous notes that didn't resemble any tune I'd ever heard. After a while she reached for a chunk of bread and pushed it into my hand. I took it from her and bit into it. It shattered between my teeth. Using saliva, I turned the fragments into a kind of paste, then swallowed hard and got it down. It must have been days old. I watched as the woman sorted through the meat, flicking it this way and that with the backs of her fingers. In the end she chose a piece that was mostly fat and handed it to me. Warts clustered on her knuckles, and the lines of her hands were inlaid with dirt, but I was past caring. I had eaten nothing since my foraging behind the market stalls just after dawn. As I chewed on the pork fat I transferred my gaze to the man sitting furthest from me. With his knotted black beard and his weather-beaten skin, he had the air of a prophet who had just walked out of the wilderness. His eyes were strangely matt and dusty-looking, as though, like blueberries or grapes, they were covered with a kind of bloom. I could see how the lost or the gullible might want to follow somebody like him.

Once they had finished eating, the woman wrapped the remainder of the food in the brown paper and tucked it out of sight beneath her clothes, then they set off along the embankment. I went with them. They didn't appear to find my attachment to them at all unusual or suspicious. The weather was still and grey, oddly dreamy and exhausting. I had the feeling time had been suspended. Or perhaps it was place that seemed different, as if I were being shown things through a series of artfully positioned mirrors, as if the world, while looking just the same, were actually reflected, diluted, a distant cousin of itself. Once, I closed my eyes, and I would have lost my footing and gone tumbling towards the railway line had the bearded man not seized my arm at the crucial moment. I nodded, grunted. He let go of my arm and then moved on. Curiously, I felt the incident had lent me a certain credibility.

Towards evening we took refuge in a warehouse that backed on to the railway. On the top floor, in the corner, were three primitive beds built out of whatever came to hand – cardboard, polystyrene, scraps of rag and plastic. I watched my companions prepare themselves for sleep, two of them curling up on their sides. The man with the sore mouth lay on his back with his arms crossed on his chest, as though clutching a valuable possession. Their breathing slowed and deepened. I needed sleep too, more than anything, but first I had to make myself a bed. I walked down to the far end of the warehouse and started to hunt around for suitable materials. The building creaked gently as the light faded. Pigeons murmured on window-ledges.

That night a harsh, shallow panting woke me. As my eyes adjusted to the dark, I saw that the woman was sitting on top of one of the men. They were both still dressed. She had her hands laid flat on the man's chest, and her head was thrown right back. Light caught on her teeth. It was the bearded man who was underneath her, the one I thought of as the prophet.

A train let out a long, mournful whistle.

I turned over and went back to sleep.

For the next few days we kept moving, sometimes basing ourselves in the outskirts of Iron Vale, sometimes traversing the town centre, but always using routes that meant we passed virtually unnoticed. I had found some old bandages in a rubbish bin behind the hospital and bound my feet in them, which made walking easier, and my blisters slowly hardened and healed. I was becoming used to the cloak too, managing the armholes with greater dexterity, and tripping far less often. There were times when I felt I was back in my childhood, dressed up like a vampire in my father's cast-off gown . . . We generally slept at dawn, and then again in the afternoon, and never for more than four or five hours at a stretch. I gave myself up to their rhythms as one might surrender to an ocean's currents. In a sense, I was deferring to their experience. After all, it was their life I was living, not mine. At first I assumed the constant movement was dictated by the search for food and shelter. Later, though, I realised it served an end in itself. If they had become nomadic, it was because they didn't want their presence to weigh too heavily on any one section of the population. They were acting out a simple desire for anonymity and peace.

One evening we camped by the river, underneath a bridge. I had caught a chill that day, the first of many. As I sat close to the fire, trying to warm myself, the bearded man took hold of my wrist. He was peering at my watch. When I undid the strap and handed the watch to him, he placed it on the ground and reached for a piece of brick that lay near by. He carefully tapped the brick against the face until the glass disc shattered, then he tossed the brick to one side and bent over the watch, so close that his beard folded in the dirt. One by one, he began to pick out the tiny fragments of glass. He might have been removing lice from the head of his own child. His shadow leapt and ducked on the concrete stanchion behind him. Once all the glass was gone, he snapped off the two hands and threw them over his shoulder into the dark. He examined the watch again, then nodded and passed it back to me. The whole operation had been conducted with such serious intent and absolute precision that I had no choice, I felt, but to strap the watch on to my wrist again, as if it had just been mended. Later, as I curled up by the fire and closed my eyes, I saw the episode as an initiation ceremony. From now on I would be wearing a watch that didn't have any hands. I had joined a people for whom time had no relevance at all. Even they appeared to be aware of that.

On the fourth evening, after our usual sleep, we set out along the east bank of the river, heading in a southerly direction, and I sensed a different mood, nothing so definite as a purpose, just the feeling that there had been a shift of some sort, a change of gear. After a while we arrived at an allotment, and my companions began to gather vegetables which they stored in the pockets of their cloaks. I did the same. The White People had no concept of property or ownership. If the man whose clothes I'd taken had been upset, it wasn't because he thought the clothes belonged to him, but because he didn't recognise what he'd been given in return. He'd been reacting not to loss but to the unknown. There were occasions, I suppose, when White People would be caught. They'd be accused of theft, but the word would have no meaning for them, nor would punishing them have much effect. Punishment only works if its relationship to the offence is clear. That night, though, we got away with it. A scarecrow watched us, its arms stretched wide as if to acknowledge its ineptitude, its face even blanker and more ghostly than our own. When we had filled our pockets, we moved through a gap in the hedge and on across the countryside.

I wondered whether they would ever realise I was an impostor. Surely, at some point, I told myself, their sixth sense would let them know. But then it occurred to me that they might actually be incapable of suspicion. To be suspicious, one needs a context or a precedent, and the White People had no understanding of either. The past meant nothing to them, and without that kind of framework suspicion simply couldn't arise. Like children who had never grown up, the White People were sealed in an eternal condition of trust. As they floated ahead of me in the half-light, I was struck once again by their complacency, their good nature. They seemed so affable, so unruffled, so oddly content with their lot – and this despite the way society often mistreated them. They did not have an aggressive bone in their bodies. Luckily, they had learned to organise themselves into groups, responding to some deep-rooted instinct that told them there was safety in numbers. Could that be why they had accepted me so readily, why they had not, as Fernandez would have put it, seen through me? Because I'd made them stronger? We walked on in single file, the night wind pushing against our faces, and although I thought of Clarise and her boys from time to time I was glad to be leaving Iron Vale at last.

By my calculations we had been travelling for about a week when we came down out of the hills on to a plain, mist afloat in the dark fields, the bare trees loud with crows and magpies. Before too long, I saw signs informing us that the border lay just a short distance ahead, but we hurried on, unfaltering, the wet grass drenching the hems of our cloaks. We appeared to be about to cross into the Yellow Quarter, and at a point some eighty or ninety miles north of the place where I had attacked the guard. I had already been to the Yellow Quarter once, and I had no desire to repeat the experience, but I couldn't part company with the White People. They were my passport, my camouflage; it would be a while before I had the confidence to strike out on my own. An expedition into choleric territory had only one advantage that I could think of: nobody would be looking for me there – or, if they were, then they'd be looking for a civil servant in a suit, and I had shed that version of myself whole lifetimes ago.

As we drew closer, it began to rain. I remembered my trip with Dunne and Whittle, and how the Yellow Quarter's notorious commercialism had spilled over into the strip of sanguine land adjacent to the wall. There was none of that here. A community had grown up around the checkpoint, but there were no souvenir shops, no theme hotels. I saw an off-licence, a cut-price supermarket and a few drab streets of terraced housing, net curtains in all the downstairs windows. Some of the kerbstones had been painted a defiant patriotic shade of green.

The guard on duty waved us through without even bothering to glance up. Though I knew he must have seen us coming, I was disappointed all the same. I had wanted him to look deep into my eyes and be deceived by their apparent emptiness. One wall lay behind us, but a second loomed a hundred yards away, its concrete scarred and pitted like the back of an ancient whale. Head bent against the rain, which was falling more heavily now,

I followed my companions across the mud of no man's land. A ditch ran down the middle, with strips of sand on either side. There were searchlights on metal poles and rolls of razor wire. It was the first time I had crossed a border illegally. Actually crossed it. My cloak had soaked right through, weighing me down, and it was tiring just to walk. Up ahead, I saw a long, low shack raised up on breeze-blocks. This would be a guardhouse for Yellow Quarter personnel. I doubted we would have such an easy time of it with them.

When we drew level with the shack, the door swung open, just as I had feared, and an armed guard motioned us inside. We climbed into a large rectangular room that had a floor of mustard-coloured lino. Fluorescent tubes fizzed on the ceiling. A row of cubicles had been built against one wall. This was where the body searches would be conducted. At the far end of the room hung a detailed map of the entire region, the border marked by a wide green-and-yellow stripe criss-crossed with black. A grey metal desk stood near by, cluttered with computers, faxes and phones. It was hot in the room. The air smelled of sweat and damp cloth.

The guard who had let us in remained by the door. Three more guards stood in a tight cluster with their backs to us. They broke apart and turned towards us, muttering and cursing. They had been checking the lottery results, it seemed, and none of them had won. The guard holding the newspaper rolled it into a cylinder and swatted the palm of his hand with it.

We stood in the centre of the room while they fanned out in front of us, each guard approaching from a slightly different direction, as though they were each preoccupied by a slightly different aspect of our appearance. Their behaviour struck me as both patronising and sardonic. They were playing on the fact that interest was something we weren't used to and didn't deserve, and in doing so they were establishing their own superior status as a species. They wore crisp, pressed uniforms, the dark-green fabric trimmed with bright-yellow epaulettes, which crouched on their shoulders like tropical spiders. Guns lolled in polished leather holsters, truncheons swung seductively at hip-level. Although I had only been with the White People for a short time, I was overwhelmed by how perfect, how immaculate, the guards looked. I don't think I could have spoken, even if I'd wanted to.

The one with the rolled-up newspaper seemed in artificially high spirits, so much so that I wondered whether he was on amphetamines. He darted towards the man with the sore mouth and made as if to strike. The man ducked, hands up about his ears, and then let out a moan. One of the other guards mimicked him – the ducking, then the moan. His colleague with the paper laughed out loud and wheeled away, his eyes glancing off the rest of us.

Hanging my head, I saw that water from my cloak had collected in a dark pool around my feet. As I watched, it found a gradient in the floor and crept away from me in one thin stream.

'Hello. Somebody's pissed himself.'

The rolled-up newspaper cannoned into the side of my head. I hadn't even seen it coming. My right ear buzzed. The man standing next to me, the bearded man, was told to get down on all fours and drink. I watched as he knelt in front of me and tried to lick the water off the floor.

'One of them's a woman.'

Silence fell so emphatically that I could hear the rain falling on the roof, a beautiful and inappropriate sound, like a herd of wild horses galloping across open country. All three guards had gathered round the woman. She was staring into the middle distance. Maybe she thought she could hear horses too. Until that moment I had somehow assumed she was in her late-thirties or early-forties, but now, in the glare of the guardhouse, I saw she was probably no more than twenty-five.

The guards began to squeeze the woman's breasts, which made her writhe and squeal, and only encouraged them to go further. Two of them held her by the arms while a third started rubbing between her legs. The man with the sore mouth had wandered over to the window, and he was staring through it at a section of the wall. I looked down at the bearded man, still kneeling at my feet. Though he returned my gaze, his veiled eyes showed nothing.

As the woman squirmed, something fell from beneath her cloak and rolled across the floor. It was a large carrot. The guard with the newspaper picked it up. 'Fuck me. She's got her own vibrator.' He tossed the carrot to one of his colleagues. 'You know what to do.' The guards dragged the woman over to the desk. Shoving the phones and faxes to one side, they pushed her on to her back and held her down. They lifted the cloak over her head, then forced her legs wide open and ripped her sodden underclothes apart. Her thighs were red and chapped. As I turned away, the woman let out the most peculiar noise, a kind of long, shuddering sigh.

'Think she's enjoying it?'

'Of course she is. Just look at her.'

I hadn't wanted to watch, but once or twice I glanced in that direction, and I realised that I was smiling. It could only be nervousness, I thought, or fear.

The guard with the paper noticed and moved towards me. 'Like it, do we?' He brought his face so close to mine that I could smell the coffee, black and bitter, on his breath.

I grinned like the idiot I was supposed to be.

He reached up with one hand and pushed his fingers into my mouth. 'Nice teeth.' His tongue slipped out, blind and fat and glistening. He licked my lips and, sighing languorously, turned his eyes up to the ceiling. Then he danced backwards, burst out laughing. 'Where's that carrot?'

A shrill ringing cut into the silence.

One of the guards let go of the woman and picked up a phone. 'Yes?' He listened for a second or two, then shouted across the room. 'Lieutenant, it's for you.'

The guard leaned close to me again. 'It's for me.' He lifted both his eyebrows twice, quickly, and swung away. Shaking now, I watched him take the call. After a while, he wrapped his free hand over the receiver and spoke to his two colleagues in a brisk, clipped voice I hadn't heard until that moment. 'Get rid of them.'

We were pushed out of the guardhouse and down the steps,

the door slamming behind us. Seconds later, it opened again, and something flew in a brief bright arc over our heads. I watched the woman retrieve the carrot, wipe it clean and return it to a hidden pocket beneath her clothes. She saw me looking and nodded, as if to let me know that what she was doing was only right and proper. Still trembling, I stared at the ground. The rain had eased just when I wanted it to come down harder than ever. I wanted to feel the water crashing against my skull. I wanted to be able to lift my face up to the sky and have the rain wash off every trace of that guard's tongue.

I remembered Frank Bland talking about the borders that had been built on negative ley lines – black streams, he had called them – and how the trees and plants in those areas sometimes displayed warped or stunted growth. If people crossed such a border, he had claimed, their health could be adversely affected. If people *worked* there, though, day in, day out, then surely the effects would be that much more pronounced. Did Frank's theory explain the scene I'd witnessed in the guard-house? Or was it our freedom that incensed them so? Yes, we were outcasts and rejects, but at the same time we could go wherever we pleased; moreover, in being cut loose from society, we had been liberated from the pressures and responsibilities of daily life. Perhaps, at some deep level, people were envious of that. Hence all the persecution . . . As I stood there wondering, I felt a surge of malignant energy in the air around me and I glanced at my companions to see if they had noticed, but their faces looked the way they always looked – complacent, unaware.

The bearded man had already moved beyond the barrier into the Yellow Quarter, and the other two were following behind. I set off after them. They didn't appear especially troubled by their ordeal. Even the woman seemed quite unconcerned. Was that because they had become accustomed to abuse? Had they, in some obscure sense, prepared themselves, conscious that it was the Yellow Quarter they would be dealing with? Or were they simply incapable of feeling? And, if so, had they been incapable of feeling all along? Was that part of what made them who they were? Or had they gradually been rendered numb by the endless horrors to which they had been subjected? I looked at the man walking ahead of me, his teeth and gums so ravaged that it often hurt him to eat or drink. On those days, the woman would chew up food for him and spit the pulp into his mouth, like a bird feeding her young. I shuddered to think how he might have come by such injuries. The hardest part of all, however, was not having a voice. I couldn't ask them questions. I could express no sympathy. What did they think – if anything? I would never know.

For the rest of that day we moved with real urgency, and I wondered whether there might not, after all, be some desire on the part of my companions to put distance between themselves and what had happened at the border. At the same time it implied a knowledge of the territory. We had entered a place where one did all one could to avoid confrontation. To convey a sense of purpose, even to look as though one had a destination in mind, was to engage in a form of self-defence.

We had crossed into the northern reaches of the Yellow Quarter, which was less densely populated, but we still couldn't seem to get away from the roads, at least not to begin with. We walked on grass verges, in ditches, along hard shoulders, and the traffic hissed past us, endless traffic. People would blast their horns at us, or wind their windows down and jeer, and once a can of beer came cartwheeling through the air and struck the bearded man on the point of his elbow. After that, he held his arm across his chest, but he wore the same expression as before, his chin lifted upwards and a little to one side, his dusty-looking eyes unfocused, as if he was listening to distant music.

By late afternoon we were approaching the outskirts of a city, the main road lined with car showrooms, designer-clothing outlets and fast-food restaurants. Our shadows appeared on the pavement before us like dark predictions. I looked over my shoulder. The sun had dropped out of a mass of shabby cloud, giving off an orange light that seemed unnatural, diseased. It was time to sleep. We started searching the yards and alleys behind the shops for bedding. We found several sheets of plastic in a skip and shook off the rainwater, then we carried them into the corner of a car-park and settled in the long grass up against a wire-mesh fence. I listened to the lorries pulling in – the clash of gears, the sneeze of brakes – and heard the drivers shouting at each other, trading insults and dirty jokes.

Over the past few days, as we journeyed south-east across the moors of the Green Quarter, then west towards the border, I had been observing my companions and I had begun to form a theory. I had noticed certain sounds recurring, and made a point of recording how and when they were used. Created almost exclusively from consonants, they had an abrupt, glottal char-acter. The sound 'Ng', for instance, was used in relation to the man with the sore mouth, and I wondered if this might not be a name the White People had given him. Once I'd had that idea, I turned my attention to the bearded man and quickly discovered a sound that was applied to him, a sound best represented by the word 'Ob'. Likewise, 'Lm' was often employed around the woman, its comparative softness a subtle, almost poignant acknowledgement of her gender. Since crossing the border that afternoon, I had started using these curious sounds myself, tentatively at first, but then with increasing confidence, and I was usually rewarded with a grunt or a glance or a jerk of the head. Once, in response to my use of the word 'Lm', which I pronounced Lum, the woman came out with something that sounded like 'Gsh'. Later, the bearded man used the same sound when looking in my direction. Could it be that I had a White name now?

The woman, Lum, was leaning over me, shaking my shoulder. It didn't seem possible that I had slept, and yet the sky behind her head had the murky burnt-orange glow of night. I sat up and looked past her. The other two were already awake and on their feet, Neg urinating through the wire-mesh fence.

To the north of the city we stumbled into an area of heavy industry. The landscape was strewn with the tangled paste jewellery of chemical plants. All those buildings ticking, humming, breathing. All those strings of pearly lights. And white smoke blossoming in tall chimneys, like stems of night-scented stock. Beauty of a sort, but poisonous. We didn't cover the miles with our usual efficiency. We kept tripping on debris piled up at the edge of the road, then Lum fell into a narrow culvert and damaged her leg, and we had to take turns supporting her. That slowed us even more. We slept again at dawn, as always.

The next night we left the road for an unpaved track. As we came over a rise, I heard a strange, inhuman squabbling, and there before us lay an enormous rubbish dump with hundreds of gulls wheeling and swooping, fighting over scraps. We forced an opening in the corrugated-iron fence and began to circle the dump in a clockwise direction. On the far side, out of sight of the entrance, a bonfire had been lit, its flames sending handfuls of red sparks into the air. The woman murmured and, looking away to my left, I saw a group of pale figures emerging from a wood. By the time we reached the fire, there must have been thirty of us. We had gathered in the same place, at more or less the same time, and yet, so far as I could tell, nothing had been arranged or discussed. There had been no communication – at least not in the ordinary sense of the word. It seemed like evidence of the telepathic powers that I had always been so sceptical about.

They sat themselves down all round the fire, and I sat with them. They nodded, muttered, scratched themselves. They prodded at the fire with bits of stick. In the side of the dump, which lifted above us like a tattered cliff-face, pieces of silver foil winked and glittered. A litre bottle was passed from hand to hand. The fumes that rose from the neck smelled floral, but the taste reminded me of gin, and I imagined for a moment that I was back in Clarise Tucker's front room, sampling one of Starling's deadly new concoctions. Between random bursts of animation, when the White People would either grunt or moan, a silence would fall during which they stared into the fire, apparently lost in thought. I didn't understand what they were up to. It was like an assembly, a convocation, but of the most eccentric kind. Though our numbers had swelled, I felt more exposed, more of an outsider, and I found a stick of my own and stirred the embers in an attempt to disguise my growing sense of awkwardness.

And then, in a flash, I had the answer. *They were sending pictures to each other in their heads.* They were showing them to each other as you might show photographs, except they were doing it telepathically. How did I know this? Partly it was intuition. But also, if I concentrated hard enough, if I blocked out the rest of the world, I seemed to see images that I could not explain. They were only fragments – a burning house, a frozen lake, a naked man sat backwards on a horse – but they came from somewhere quite outside my own experience. It was another form of communication, a different language altogether, and yet, given time, I felt I could become fluent. Then, perhaps, I would receive whole sequences of images. Meanwhile, I was a mere novice, with no real contribution to make. I was the person who nods and grins, even though he hasn't got the joke.

They stayed awake all night, only dozing off when the first blush of colour appeared in the eastern sky. In the middle of the day we moved on, travelling due north. I counted thirty-four of us. There were no children. Was that a coincidence, or was it true what I had heard, that White People were sterile? Certainly all the ones I had come across had been born either before or possibly during the Rearrangement, which lent weight to the view that they were the fall-out from that radical exercise in social engineering. The Rearrangement had been a kind of controlled explosion, sending a white-hot flash through the heads of everybody living in the country at the time. The vast majority had recovered, adapted, tried to make it work in their favour. But there were some who had been less fortunate. Their minds had been scorched; their thoughts had turned to cinders. That, at least, was the general consensus. Although I could see a certain logic in the sterility argument – how could life be created by people who were not themselves, supposedly, alive? – it also seemed rather too convenient, a piece of sophistry or wishful thinking on the part of those for whom the White People were an embarrassment. For if fertility had been destroyed, along with language and character, then the White People would die out. They would no longer be able to act as reminders of the system's cruelties and its shortcomings. There would be no exceptions to the rule.

That afternoon, as I watched Neg inspect a cracked wing-mirror that he had picked up at the dump, I realised I had seen his face before. Not literally, of course. But I remembered that Jones had had the same expression, or lack of it, when I found him standing on one leg in that gloomy passageway. Jones had been a White Person before anybody even knew White People existed. He would have to have been one of the first. If Jones was still alive, he would probably be living among the White People, just as I was. How strange to think that I could run into him at any moment!

After walking for several hours with a strong wind at our backs, it began to look as though we were making for a blighted area known as the Wanings. The provincial capital was Pyrexia, a city that manufactured chlorine, plastics and petrochemicals. The Yellow Quarter's leadership had recently declared the Wanings to be ungovernable. I had heard stories of atrocities from various relocation officers, though none of them ever claimed to have actually set foot in the region.

By the middle of the fourth day we had reached a high, barren moor. The wind had died down, and the sky, which was overcast, seemed suspended just above our heads. If you touched the clouds they would be soft, I thought, like the breast of a bird. On we went, still heading north. Our cloaks whispered across the heather.

In the late afternoon we hauled a dead sheep out of a disused mineshaft. Luckily, it hadn't started rotting yet, and we roasted the carcass over a peat fire. Our bellies full, we slept for longer than usual. It was almost light before we set off again.

Although we tended to keep to the high ground, out of sight of human habitation, we would sometimes climb down to a road and look for animals that had been run over. We found plenty of rabbits and even, once or twice, a pheasant. We carried a supply

308

of stale bread and raw vegetables with us, but the roads became, for a while at least, our chief source of food.

We had no choice but to sleep in the open. Every six or seven hours we would huddle down, packing ourselves tightly together, like children playing sardines.

Time began to blur.

Once, we had to cross an eight-lane motorway. I heard it long before I saw it, a sustained but airy roar that I mistook for a waterfall. A man was hit by a truck that day. I watched his body spin, then crumple. He was dead when I reached him, one side of his head grazed and bloody, his spine smashed, the pulse in his neck nowhere to be found. The truck hadn't even slowed down. We laid him on his back on the hard shoulder. Curiously, his hands were still moving, folding inwards, as if he wanted to touch the inside of his wrists. A woman tried to arrange blades of grass across his face, but the slipstream from the traffic kept disturbing them. In the end we had to use a piece of shredded tyre instead.

Beyond the motorway the land turned bleaker still. Only the wind and the clumps of blackened heather and the shifting pale-yellow grasses. The further north we went, the more use we seemed to be making of the daylight hours; we had removed ourselves from society to such an extent that we no longer needed to hide. Also, there were the mineshafts, which would pose a threat if we were travelling at night. And I had seen notices warning of unexploded ammunition. At some point in the past the area must have been used as a firing-range.

I suppose we must have been in the Yellow Quarter for about ten days when we scaled a stony ridge and then came to a halt, a wide shallow valley sprawling before us. A single road ran across the land from north to south. I couldn't imagine who it might be for. The military, perhaps. To the west of the road lay a stretch of ground that seemed to have been dug up or turned over, and a crowd of White People had gathered there. While it looked as though we might have reached our destination at last, I couldn't see anything in this desolate place to justify the long and perilous journey we had just undertaken.

We began our descent, and before too long we were on the valley floor ourselves. The White People were not in the habit of exchanging greetings. There was no embracing, for instance, no physical contact. They stood in front of each other or beside each other in a muted show of acknowledgement, or else they circled one another with their eyes lowered and their hands fidgeting among the folds of their cloaks, as if overwhelmed by a sudden attack of nerves. I could never tell whether they were renewing their acquaintance or meeting for the first time.

I walked over to the muddy area I had seen from the ridge. It was the rough size and shape of a swimming-pool. Tyre tracks led from the road to one of the longer sides. At the far end, I saw a man on his knees. I moved towards him, curious, but not wanting to intrude. Every now and then he would lean forwards and lay his cheek tenderly against the earth. When I reached him, I nodded and murmured, an all-purpose mode of conduct that I had picked up from my three companions. The man ignored me. Staring out over the land, I thought I understood. Something had happened here.

I returned to the main group. Lum and Neg had built a small fire by the roadside. Potatoes nestled among the embers. I squatted down and hunted through my pockets, bringing out apples and red peppers that I had found at the back of a village supermarket several days before. I also produced a few muddy beetroot, stolen from someone's kitchen garden. Lum placed the peppers round the fringes of the fire so they would sear. Neg bit gingerly into one of the apples. As for Ob, he was gazing into the distance with his usual mystical intensity.

Most of the White People had set up camp by now. Some even owned billy cans in which they were heating water or broth. The curved shape of the valley amplified our murmurs. Once we had eaten, though, a hush settled over us, a silence that had the patient, reverential quality of a vigil. The air itself appeared to have tightened as if, like a crisp new sheet, it had been snapped out over the mattress of the earth. I wrapped my cloak around me and lay down.

When I woke it was dusk, and our fire had burned low, the

mound of grey ash delicately embroidered with scarlet threads. As I tried to rub some feeling back into my legs, I looked up and saw a full moon balanced on the ridge above me, a moon so huge that I imagined for a moment that both the land and all the life in it had shrunk. The colour, too, astounded me. A lavish, creamy pale-gold, it had the gleam of antique satin or newly minted coin. Glancing round me, I saw that people were rising to their feet as if they had just received a signal.

I watched them move towards the rectangle of earth. Arranging themselves around the edge, they started taking off their clothes. I had no choice but to join them and do the same. Once undressed, we stepped out on to mud that had a particular coldness of its own – far colder, somehow, than the grass, far colder even than the air. Our flesh gave off the pale, almost transparent glimmer of a puddle when it freezes. The people nearest me were scooping up the mud and plastering their bodies with it, their faces too. As I bent down, a light seemed to flare inside my head, and I saw a lorry reversing towards a wide, deep trench. Its tail-lights glowed, then faded. Glowed again. Then the back end lifted on hydraulic rods, and the load began to spill . . . All this I received in a split-second, then it went dark again, and there was only my bare arm reaching out and the mud below, and the hairs rose on my skin, but not with cold.

I started covering myself, then stopped, aware of a sound coming from the people gathered round me. They were calling out, not to each other, but to some larger thing, or even to the void, perhaps, their voices tentative, enquiring. Slowly the volume grew, the voices becoming less distinctly individual, less obviously human. I thought of a swarm of bees, a reverberation that was partly music, partly noise, and I found that I had been caught up in it and that my voice had merged with theirs. I was ridding myself of burdens I had been carrying for years – the collusion, the deceit, the lies I had told to others, and to myself as well; everything was being dumped on this rectangle of ground, and I could leave it here, I could leave the whole lot here. The sound made earth and air vibrate, and that was all we were just then, a single voice raised against the elements, a resonance, a kind of harmony.

When I woke the next morning, I didn't know what to believe. Were the images I had seen the product of my own fevered imagination? Or could it be that I was beginning to receive the pictures that the others were receiving? Was I gradually gaining access to their peculiar, unspoken language? If my vision of the night before could be relied upon, it looked as if White People had been slaughtered in their hundreds and then buried here. I hadn't actually seen the bodies tumbling out of the truck, but somehow I knew that that was what had taken place. We were camped on the edge of a mass grave. In covering themselves with mud, the White People had been remembering their dead, and the chilling, unearthly music had been both requiem and homage. If that was true, they were more conscious of the past than people said.

Another possibility occurred to me. Though I had been living among the White People, I hadn't actually become one, and that had given me the license to create my own mythical version of their lot, which wasn't something they were necessarily capable of doing themselves. After all, if my own feeling of release was anything to go by, then the removal of their white clothes and the smearing of themselves with mud might simply have been their way of ridding themselves of the abuses to which they had been exposed, a ritual that enabled them to go on living as they did – from hand to mouth, from pillar to post. When the singing came to an end, we had walked down to a brook that ran between two banks of heather. Stepping into the ice-cold water, we had washed off the mud, then put our cloaks and boots back on, and I remembered how clean I had felt, how light, how free.

As I packed up our few remaining provisions and scattered the last embers of the fire, I decided that it didn't much matter where the truth lay. They could have been reliving the agony of those who'd gone before or shedding pain they had themselves endured. The ritual lent itself to a number of interpretations. In the end it seemed likely that it was part of a process of purification and renewal. It was also part of their own unique culture, which was relentless in what it required of them. To suffer. To continue.

Just as they didn't greet one another, so the White People didn't say goodbye. There was no leave-taking, not even so much as a backwards glance, only a gradual dispersal, a miniature diaspora. Along with Ob, Neg, and Lum, I joined a group of about twenty others, setting off in a north-westerly direction that would bring us, sooner or later, to the sea. Lying a few miles offshore were several holy islands, most of which belonged to the phlegmatics. Some distance further north, the border with the Green Quarter came curving round to meet the coast. I wondered which of these destinations the group had in mind.

The land quickly became harder to negotiate, the fells much higher and topped with splintered crags, the woods thornier, more dense. Though deserted, the moors had had their dangers, but the country we entered that day felt all the more hazardous for being populated. As we passed through a village during the afternoon we were pelted with manure and bits of coal by a horde of vicious, foul-mouthed children, and then a bucket of slops was tipped from an upstairs window. We suffered cuts and bruises, nothing more serious than that, but I still thought we should be circling places like these, especially since the terrain now offered so many opportunities for concealment – or else we should hurry through on light feet, while everybody slept. I had no say in the matter, though. There didn't seem to be any decision-making as such. There was only a momentum, which was neither questioned nor explained.

Some miles beyond the village, the path we were following began to loop back on itself as it coiled down into a gorge. Far below, I heard the breathy race of water. Growing sideways out of walls of rock were trees whose branches had the look of flayed limbs, the flesh stripped away, the sinews and tendons all exposed. From somewhere to the south came a muffled roll of thunder. On reaching the floor of the valley, we crossed a stretch of spongy turf to the edge of a river, its waters running thin and green across great beds of pale stones. I watched as my companions settled on the ground. Some dozed off almost immediately. It was strange how their expressions never altered, their faces as blank when conscious as they were in repose. Lum sat on a bank below me, studying the crooked gash on the front of her calf. The wound was black with dried blood, but I knew it to be free of infection; I had cleaned it myself only a day or two before. We exchanged a glance. When I looked into her eyes I was aware of neither emotion nor intelligence. My gaze could find no purchase. Instead, it travelled on into a kind of dizzying infinity.

I lay on my side, facing the river. The cold seeped up into my hip. I turned over, on to my back. These days I could sleep almost anywhere; I could even sleep if I was shivering. Once it was dark, Lum came and lowered herself on to me. Opening my underpants, she coaxed me into her. She began to move up and down, slowly at first, then faster, more rhythmically, her hands spread on my chest, her teeth clamped on her bottom lip. Afterwards she fell asleep beside me. Her breath smelled of onions and sour milk. Though I was tired, the rush of water kept me awake, and when we struck camp several hours later I didn't feel as if I had slept at all.

It seemed we had chosen to ignore the one road that led through the region, and for once I approved: we were in the heart of the Wanings, and it paid to be cautious. Still, there were repercussions. One of our number was attacked by a feral cat, which tore at his throat and hands. We bound his lacerated flesh as best we could, with strips of cloth and crushed dock leaves. Later, we found our way blocked by a rock-fall, and we were forced to retrace our steps. With its steep climbs and its sheer drops, the land itself appeared to be against us. The injured man wouldn't stop whimpering. A few more miles of this, I kept telling myself. Just a few more miles.

Towards dawn we filed down a farm track into a clearing. I saw no dwelling of any kind, only a barn and a wrecked white car. The wheels had been removed, and the sockets that once held its headlights were empty. I walked over to where Ob stood. He was staring at the barn door. A rat had been nailed to the wood in a manner that made me think of crucifixion. I heard a steady crashing noise behind me and turned quickly, thinking people were coming through the undergrowth, but it was just the rain. A few of us took refuge in the barn. There was nothing much inside, only straw bales piled against one wall and some broken tools. The rain drew a heavy curtain over the doorway. I made a bed out of several old sacks and tried to sleep. The world beyond the barn was murky, indistinct.

Only seconds later, it seemed, I woke to see men standing in the entrance. Shotguns lounged in the crooks of their elbows. Their hat-brims dripped. Without saying a word, they hoisted their rifles and fired over our heads, and the air filled with sawdust, feathers and straw. I managed to roll sideways and duck through a gap in the wall where a board had come loose. Outside, I found Neg and Ob. As the three of us plunged back into the rain-soaked trees, Lum rose up out of the bracken where she'd been hiding. We moved deeper into the woods. All sounds came to me through a loud, insistent buzzing. It was hours before I could hear properly.

We didn't sleep again that day. Though we were able to link up with some other members of our group, there were, ominously, fewer of us than before. For the first time I sensed a loss of heart. Our supplies were running short. Every time our clothes dried on us, the clouds would open, drenching us in seconds. We could find neither food nor shelter. We continued to move in a north-westerly direction, but there was a drifting quality about our progress that did nothing to reassure me.

In the afternoon the clouds thinned to the west, and the sun slanted through at a low angle, its white light laying the landscape bare. The rest of the sky hung above us, a weighty, marbled grey. It seemed likely that the rain would sweep down again at any moment. As we rounded a bend, with farm buildings on our left and dark woods bristling to our right, a kind of stockade showed about half a mile ahead, the top as jagged as newspaper torn against the grain. What could it be for? Why block a thoroughfare like that? Drawing closer, I lifted a hand to shade my eyes. In the pale glare of the sun the structure stirred and shifted, and now, at last, I could see what it was, not a stockade at all, not a barrier, but a line of people stretched across the road. A cry went up. I turned around. Neg stood motionless, his eyes pinned open, his skin congealed. The sound he was making was like no sound I had ever heard before, no consonants this time, just a note, soft and yet high-pitched, monotonous, and I was suddenly aware of my spine, the entire length of it, like something hard and cold inserted into me against my will.

I started running. Then we were all running, fifteen or twenty of us, our cloaks flapping round our legs. The road offered no hiding place, no protection. We made for the woods instead. A grass track led off to the right, trees closing overhead. We stumbled, fell. We scrambled to our feet. We were ungainly, almost comical, like a flock of birds that has forgotten how to fly.

Turning, I saw Neg behind me. His mouth gaped open, a black hole ringed by mangled gums and stumps. He had been beaten once before, somewhere down south. I knew that now. They had threaded his teeth into a necklace and hung it, bleeding, round his neck. His own teeth. They'd made earrings too. He had showed them to me in a picture, flashed from his head into mine. I watched him run. He seemed to be leaning backwards, both hands clawing at the air as if it were in his way. Beneath his clothes, his breasts and belly hurled themselves about. He was carrying too much fat. One look at him, and you knew he was done for.

They'd been waiting for us. Dusk hadn't fallen yet, and us in our white cloaks. A cruel colour, white. No mercy in it. We had passed through a village only minutes earlier, its doors and windows shut. Eyes to keyholes, though. Curtains twitching. Then a crowd of figures looming, the winter sun behind them. Men mostly, though I saw women too. And children. Heads shaved on account of lice. Or was it the custom in these parts, to shave the heads of children? They must have been told of our approach. They had weapons. The kind of things you end up

316

with when you don't have too much time. A bicycle chain, a tin of paraffin. A scythe.

Once, I could have reasoned with them, perhaps. I had the words back then, the charm. Not any more. Only noises issued from me now. I could do a cow in labour, rain on leaves. I could do a foot sinking into a bog. None of that would be much use. But even if I'd talked fluently, I doubt they would have listened. They'd worked themselves up to something, and they weren't about to be denied.

I looked for Neg again. He'd fallen back. I heard him calling me – Gsh? *Gsh!* – but I faced forwards and ran faster. Trees jumped out at me. Trunks moist and black as if they had risen from a swamp, roots like tentacles. My breath burned in my throat. Soon, please God, it would be dark.

In my veins my blood was chasing its own tail.

A shriek came from somewhere, and I turned. They had him now. I heard them laughing as they ripped his clothes with vicious downward movements. In the half-light his naked body had the texture of a mushroom. The delicate, creamy underside – the stalk. They bound his wrists behind him with fencing wire, his elbows too, then they stood back. His eyes were closed, and his feet stamped up and down in the mud, but in slow-motion, almost tenderly, as though he was trampling ripe grapes. Making wine. They unleashed one of their hunting dogs, a blunt-looking thing, all jaws and shoulders. It tore at his genitals, and then, when he pivoted in agony, his buttocks, then his genitals again.

It's hard to run with your hands over your ears.

Was I complacent once? Was I too full of myself? I don't know. I don't remember. If I was, I regret it. I take it all back.

I denounce myself.

One of our number had been set on fire. No, more than one. Deep in the woods, white birds were sprouting bright-orange crests and wing-feathers.

On I went, the spit thick in my mouth. Trees jolted and staggered as ships' masts do in a storm. The earth heaved, threatening to unburden itself of all its darkest mysteries. Any moment it would vomit blood-stained treasure, murder weapons, human bones. It was just me running, though. Just me running. The world stood still like someone frightened or amazed.

Over to my left I saw a woman go down, two men in hunting clothes on top of her, their mouths split open, red and wet and grinning. You'd think somebody had taken an axe to their faces. One of the men had pulled the woman's head back by the hair, as if she were a horse and her hair the reins. Her throat stretched tight against the air, the crown of her head almost touching her shoulderblades. Was that Lum? I couldn't tell. In any case, I didn't want to see what followed. It would be worse than I could possibly imagine. There were more of my companions among the trees, most of them with dark figures fastened to their heels or curved against their backs. We were trying to outrun our shadows.

I'm not sure how I came to lose my balance. In taking my eye off the path for a moment, I missed my footing, perhaps. Then I was rolling and sliding down a steep bank that was slippery with mud, wet leaves and ivy. Down I tumbled, branches whipping at my face and arms. A tree brushed one of my legs aside. I even turned a somersault, the sky whirling like the skirts of a woman doing some old-fashioned dance. At last I reached the bottom. I lay on my back next to a track, my heart about to spring from between my ribs, the breath crushed out of me. I stared at the bare branches laid out peacefully against the clouds. All the cries came from high above me now. I got to my feet. My leg hurt, but not too much. I didn't think I'd broken anything. On the other side of the track were more trees, then a river, and in the wide green field beyond I saw a building that had the look of a ruined church or priory. As I stood there, uncertain what to do, the sky appeared to shift and then disintegrate. Out of a heavy charcoal greyness, something incongruously light and soft began to fall.

Snow.

It was as though bits of us were falling through the air. Bits of who we were. A snowflake landed on my sleeve and promptly vanished. If the snow settled, I would vanish too. A disappearing trick. This was more luck than I could ever have expected. Just then, though, I heard a shout. Several figures had paused on the ridge above me, motionless and wizened. They were staring at me through the snow, one in a cap with ear-flaps, one in fatigues. A third was looking back over his shoulder, his arm raised, beckoning. I hurried across the track, then climbed down to the river's edge, its water the colour of beer, its flow interrupted here and there by smooth round boulders. Weeds stretched full-length beneath the surface like a drowned girl's hair. I began to splash through the shallow water, my boots skidding on the smaller stones. I was alone, I realised, alone for the first time in I didn't know how long. I felt a flicker of something against my stomach walls.

On the far side, hoof-prints showed in the mud. Sheep, I thought. Or deer. This was where they'd come to drink. A bank rose in front of me, red earth bound in roots. Above it, outlined against the sky, I saw a battlement. I climbed the bank and found myself in the lower reaches of a field. There was no cover here at all. I glanced over my shoulder. Two men were scrambling down the slope towards me, cursing as their feet caught in the brambles. One had a pitch-fork and a coil of rope. The other was carrying a pair of shears. At least they didn't have a dog. I couldn't explain the calm that welled up in me just then. Was it the snow, which was falling still more thickly now, flakes the size of oak leaves sticking to my cloak? Or did I have an inkling of what was about to happen?

As I set off across the field, a girl jumped out in front of me. She seemed to have appeared from nowhere. I let out a cry. She put a hand over my mouth, then placed one finger upright against her own. Her face was covered with freckles. I'd never seen so many. She gave me a queer blurred smile.

'This way,' she whispered. 'Quick.'

She wasn't one of them. She was somebody else.

Thank God for that. Thank God.

EIGHT

She ran ahead of me, her hair and coat-tails flapping. Snow poured into the gap between us. We passed to the left of a church, its roof partly gone, its stone floor open to the sky. There were other buildings, ancient-looking, some with walls still standing, some torn down to their foundations. Through a hedge and into a garden, the grass waist-high. Buildings here too. More recent. Tall chimneys, narrow windows. All in a state of disrepair. I looked round, eyes half-closed against the swirling snow. I thought I could hear men's voices, but the men themselves weren't visible.

We had reached the back of a house, the whole wall hidden behind a screen of vines and creepers. The girl heaved on a door and pushed me inside. Brick steps led down to a cellar. The smell of cold ashes and mouse-droppings. The faintest memory of candle wax. She motioned for me to follow, then parted a frayed curtain to reveal a second door, the wood untreated, dark as peat. She bolted it behind us and started up a narrow staircase. I could only tell where she was by listening to her footsteps on the bare boards. Once, a light flared in my head and I saw a hand splayed on the earth, pale as something that had just been disinterred, and I knew that it belonged to Lum, even though I couldn't see any other part of her.

At last we came out into a room with a low ceiling and a single round window. There was no view, only a tangle of greenery, the snow a constant slanting movement just beyond. Again the girl bolted the door behind us, then she went to the window and put her face close to the criss-crossing bars. I squatted on my haunches, my heart beating so hard that it seemed to shake my whole body. Blood sizzled in my ears. They were still out there, all the rest of them.

The girl turned from the window. 'Do you know who I am?'

I stared at her. It had gone all blank inside me. All hollow.

'You don't remember me, do you.'

What was she saying?

'Can you talk?' She moved towards me, knelt in front of me. I felt her eyes searching my face. All hollow. Just a space. 'It doesn't matter,' she said. 'It's not important.'

I'm sorry, I said inside my head.

'Don't cry,' she said. 'You're safe now. You're going to be all right.' She placed her hand over mine. I was aware of its weight, its heat. 'They'll never find us here. It's too rundown, too overgrown. There are too many rooms. They'll lose interest. I know what they're like.'

That's not what I'm frightened of, I said inside my head.

She couldn't hear a thing, of course, and yet she held herself quite still as she looked at me, and her look didn't waver, not for a moment. She didn't even seem to blink. She had lines in the thin skin below her eyes, which made me think that she had slept too little in her life, or seen too much. 'You really don't recognise me, do you?' She tucked a strand of her bracken-coloured hair behind her ear. 'Well, maybe it's no wonder,' she added, half to herself.

Faint cries reached me from outside. The window was a mouth belonging to someone in great pain.

'Listen to me,' the girl said.

I was receiving images of mud and roots, a clearing in the woods, and all from ground-level, as if my face had been forced sideways into the dirt. Men stood round me, a boy too. Thick fingers held his shoulder. A dog panted in my ear, its breathing coarse and hot. Far above me, out of reach, I saw a tree's branches shifting against a darkening sky, and it was beautiful up there, and quiet, a kind of paradise. I was seeing through the eyes of one of my companions, a person was calling out to me, and there was nothing I could do.

'Listen,' the girl said.

And she began to speak to me. She had been with me all along, she said. She had made her share of mistakes. She had been too slow sometimes, too indecisive, which was only to be expected, perhaps, and once or twice she had lost me altogether. But when I slipped just now. When I fell. That was her. She'd pushed me.

What are you saying? I said inside my head.

There had been someone right behind me, she told me. One of them. I shouldn't worry, though. Everything would be fine now. She was going to take me home. That was why she had appeared. That was what she did.

I still didn't understand.

Later, she withdrew into the middle of the room, an elbow cupped in the palm of one hand, the fingers curled against her chin. She needed to go out for supplies, she said. I would have to stay put. I wasn't to leave the room, not under any circumstances. She moved towards a second door, which I hadn't noticed until that moment. Still sitting on the ground, I drew my knees up to my chest, then laid my forearms over them and lowered my head.

'That's right,' she said. 'You rest for a while.'

The door closed behind her. Her footsteps receded.

As soon as she had gone, I began to doubt her existence. She seemed so convenient – too good to be true. Had I invented a saviour for myself? Was the only kindness imaginary?

Dusk crept into the room as though it, too, were seeking refuge.

The last of the light picked out a cobweb, its fragile hammock slung high up in one corner. The smell of earth grew stronger, earth that had never seen the sun.

When I finally heard noises, I flattened myself against the wall, expecting men with weapons. The door opened. The girl backed into the room. She had a rucksack over her shoulder, and she was dragging some lengths of material. Velvet, she said. She thought they might have been curtains. She had found a few hessian sacks as well. If we used the sacks as a kind of mattress, she said, we could pull the curtains over us like blankets and it might just be enough to keep us warm. She was sorry she'd been so long. She hoped I hadn't worried.

While I arranged the bedding on the floor, she opened her rucksack and unpacked a wedge of cheese and a loaf of bread with a jagged crust. There was also a brown-paper bag filled with apples, some pickled onions in a jar and a flask of wine shaped like a teardrop. We could not risk a candle, she said. Someone might see it from outside. We made do with the dim glow that filtered through the window, starlight reflecting off the snow.

She watched as I washed the food down with gulps of rough red wine.

'Good,' she said. 'That's good.'

After we had eaten, she wrapped up the rest of the food and put it in her rucksack, which she hung on a nail behind the door. Undoing my boots, I climbed into the bed and lay down on my side, one hand beneath my cheek. I was still receiving pictures. They belonged to the operating theatre or the mortuary, the bloodshed casual, plenteous. My whole body flinched each time they came.

She gave me something she called dwale. She kept it in a small glass bottle that she wore on a cord around her neck. The liquid tasted of alcohol and stale herbs. It would help to calm me, she said. I watched her settle beside me, on her back.

Night had filled the room. The darkness of her face against the lesser darkness of the air. Her even breathing. A silence had descended, a silence that didn't necessarily mean peace. Through the window came the smell of snow. Clean, vaguely metallic. Like stainless steel.

My mouth had dried up. I had no spit.

Though the cries had stopped, I could still hear them.

I was exhausted, and yet I couldn't seem to sleep – or if I did drift off for a while I was always on the verge of witnessing some terrible atrocity, violence the like of which I had never imagined before, let alone encountered. In my dreams people kept telling me not to look. If I didn't look, they told me, I would be all right. But I couldn't help looking. There was a part of me that was inquisitive, perhaps, or weak-willed, or even missing altogether. I was the woman who became a pillar of salt. The warrior who turned to stone.

All night she lay beside me, and I drew comfort from the warmth and nearness of her body. When the cold of the floor rose up through the layers of sacking, I pressed myself against her, the backs of her thighs on my lap, her hair in my mouth. She didn't seem to mind. As for me, I was used to sleeping next to strangers. I'd been doing it for weeks.

At some point she realised I was still awake and started telling me a story.

'The night you were taken from your family,' she said, 'was the night I came into the world.'

I stared at her, wondering how she knew that, but she didn't notice. She was looking at the ceiling, her profile showing as the finest of silver lines.

She had been born on a houseboat, which was where her parents had lived back then. Her father worked as a lock-keeper. At midnight, when she was five hours old, she had opened her eyes for the first time. It had been snowing all evening.

It was raining where I was, I said inside my head.

Her mother wrapped her in a shawl and held her up to the window. She had watched the snowflakes come showering out of the sky like white flowers, snowflakes landing on the canal and vanishing. She had no memories of that night – her parents had told her about it later, when she was older – but she sometimes wondered whether that was where it all began.

Where what began? I said inside my head.

The first time it happened, she had been standing on the towpath. She remembered the warm air on her bare arms, the drowsy sound of bees humming. It must have been summer. She couldn't have been more than four or five. A dandelion floated out over the still green water. She had only stared at the delicate, almost transparent ball of seeds for a few moments, but when she returned to herself again she was standing on the other side of the canal. She had a tickle in her nose, as if she might be about to sneeze, and both her feet were wet. She began to cry. Her father appeared on the deck of the houseboat, his face the colour of a peeled apple. *How did you get over there, Odell?* She had no words for what she'd done.

After that, she kept ending up in strange places. She learned to look forward to the lost seconds, the thrilling, inexplicable journey from where she was to somewhere else. She would feel powerful yet passive. Years later, she had the same sensation on a funfair ride, the way the car whirled her backwards in a tight curve, a motion that was slow at first, oddly hydraulic, then high-speed, blurry, irresistible. She couldn't always regulate it, though, certainly not in the beginning. Sometimes it took her by surprise, like the afternoon she stepped outside during a gale and her mother found her as the sun was setting, two miles down the towpath and halfway up a tree.

Under the velvet my body jerked, tension leaving my muscles at long last.

One day she went walking with her parents in the fields near the canal. The wind was blowing hard again, and she had lifted her arms away from her sides and leaned against it, as if it were a wall. Then she was gone. Her parents had been looking at her when it happened, waiting for her to catch up with them. In the next moment they heard her calling from the far end of the field. Though it scared them half to death, it also came as something of a relief. In the past they had often been at a loss to explain her movements, but now, perhaps, they had an answer. She should protect her gift, they told her. Keep it to herself. She did the opposite, of course.

I was falling away. Sinking. A light object dropping through thick liquid.

The trouble was, she had never been popular at school. Her looks seemed to unnerve people. They could never tell what she was thinking. To try and win them over, she started doing tricks. Once, while in the company of two girls from her class, she used a gust of wind to transport her from the school playground to the roof of the bicycle shed. *Up here*, she shouted. *I'm up here*. The girls wouldn't have anything to do with her after that. They claimed she'd hypnotised them. All they would talk about was her weird eyes. Green, they said, but black too, somehow, like fir trees planted too close together. Black like a forest. And her face as well, the freckles. It made them think of one of those road-signs in the country that people have fired guns at –

I woke to see bright fragments lying on the floor. Despite the barred window and its mask of vines and creepers, the sun had managed to penetrate the room. I turned in the bed. The girl's eyes slid open.

'You slept,' she said.

I sat up and yawned, the memory of her story still with me. It seemed to have been addressed to the naive or credulous side of me. It appeared to be testing my ability to suspend my disbelief. But maybe that was the whole point. She had claimed to be capable of extraordinary things. I was supposed to have faith in her.

She had been out, she said, just before dawn. The men had gone. As for my friends . . .

I rose to my feet and walked into the corner of the room. I found a cobweb that spanned both walls and pushed gently at the sticky threads. They had surprising resilience. Behind me, the girl had fallen silent, aware that I had heard enough. When she spoke again, she approached the subject from a different angle.

We would have to lie low, she said. Let things settle. In the meantime, she had a change of clothes for me. It wouldn't be wise to be dressed as one of the White People, not at the moment. If I wanted to wash, there was a water-butt outside. I turned to face her. She was sitting on the faded velvet, lacing up her boots.

Yes, I said inside my head. *I'd like to wash.*

She handed me a bag containing the clothes, then she unbolted the door. I followed her down the staircase and into the cellar. While she looked outside, to make sure there was nobody around, I stared at the walls. I'd just noticed the graffiti. Genitals, both male and female, all highly exaggerated.

'Originally this would have been a guest-house for the priory,' the girl said. 'Later, it became the vicarage. The vicar was moved out during the Rearrangement.' She was standing just inside the room, shaking water off her hands. 'After he went, the place was taken over by the military. They trained border guards here. You can see what kind of people they must have been.' Her eyes drifted across the walls without showing any expression. 'I don't know why they left. Maybe the novelty wore off. It's been empty for a while now.' She glanced at me. 'You go and wash if you like. I'll wait here.'

The hinges let out a croak as I pushed the door open.

It was the most perfect morning. Beneath a blue sky the snow had the restrained glitter of caster sugar, and it lay evenly on everything, the branches of the trees half white, half black. The air had absolute clarity and crispness; simply to stand and breathe felt like a luxury. I thought I could hear the trickle of a stream, but it might have been the river on the far side of the field – or perhaps the snow had already started melting. There was a tension to the stillness, as if the beauty of the day could not be sustained for long.

I moved to the water-butt and stripped off my white garments. Spattered with mud, ashes and dried blood, they stood out quite distinctly against the snow. I kicked off one boot, then the other. They lay there awkwardly like a pair of crows that had been shot in mid-air and then plummeted to earth. Bending over the barrel, I brought handful after handful of water to my face. The cold made me gasp. My skin stung. The ring that hung around my neck knocked against the barrel's lip as I leaned forwards. My fingers soon went numb. I took care not to lift my eyes towards the ridge. I didn't want to think about what had happened there.

I dried myself on my undershirt, then dressed in the clothes the girl had given me – jeans, a black sweater, thick wool socks and a cheap brown leather coat. I felt in my cloak pocket. It was empty. The key to the front door of the Cliff was gone. So was the lighter and the book of dreams. I must have lost them when I fell. Still fastened to my wrist, though, was my watch, the one that didn't tell the time. I pulled my boots back on, then folded up the cloak.

When I walked back into the cellar, the girl glanced round, and a single ray of sun reached through a broken pane high in the wall, lighting up her face. I understood what her classmates had meant about her eyes. They were neither black nor green, and yet both colours were involved, somehow.

'Let's go back up,' she said. 'I'm starving.'

Like peasants from another period of history, we breakfasted on bread, cheese, pickled onions and red wine. While we ate and drank, the girl outlined her plan. We were deep in the Yellow Quarter, so there was no easy option. If we travelled south and luck was on our side, we could reach the Red Quarter in four or five days. It might be dangerous, but it would be better than heading east and crossing into the Green Quarter, where the authorities were probably still looking for me. Also, we would only have to cross one border, not two. We would have to pretend to be a couple, though. A choleric couple. Had I seen how they behaved? No? Well, the beauty of it was I didn't need to talk. The kind of man she had in mind was more likely to hit a woman than speak to her. The women tended to nag and moan, while the men just grunted or read the papers.

'That's all you have to do,' she said. 'Ignore me. You can do that, can't you?'

I nodded slowly. Of course I could ignore her. I didn't know her. When we first arrived in the room, she'd asked if I remembered her. What was that about? I still had no idea.

After breakfast she suggested a game of draughts to pass the time. I scratched out a board on the floor with a stone while she went to look for objects we could use as pieces. She returned with some chunks of burnt wood and fragments of stained glass, all of which she had collected in the church. We played for most of the morning, and I didn't win once.

In the middle of the day she had to go out again for provisions. I lay down on the bed and tried to sleep. It was a

331

way of protecting myself from the images that were appearing in my head, images that were graphic, almost medical. Also, if I stayed awake, I would only worry. What if something were to happen to her? I didn't believe I could survive by myself. Not out here. Without her, I would be dead – or worse.

I slept fitfully, but the images still came, disguised as dreams.

She returned with cold sausage, bread, pickled cabbage and more red wine, but she seemed different, more preoccupied, and we ate in silence. The light gradually faded, the room darkening long before the world outside.

When we had finished, she asked me if she should go on with her story. I nodded, and she picked up exactly where she'd left off.

Ignoring her parents' advice, she carried on performing for other children in the hope that they would become her friends, but her gift just frightened or bewildered them. She was lonelier than ever. And then, one morning, she received an official-looking letter. Her father opened it and read it first. 'They know,' he said.

'Know what?' she said.

Her father handed her the letter. She was required to appear before a tribunal, not locally, but in the capital, two hundred miles away. She couldn't tell what the charge was – the summons contrived to be both menacing and utterly inscrutable – but she knew she was guilty.

On the appointed day she caught a train to Aquaville, her parents' reproach clearly audible in the rhythm of the wheels on the track: *If only you'd listened – if only you'd listened . . .* If only I'd listened, she thought as she climbed the steps to the Ministry, her mouth dry, her heart stumbling inside her. She was convinced she was about to be severely punished. Borstal at the very least, maybe even a prison sentence.

A government official escorted her to a grey door high up in the building. He turned the handle, then stepped aside to let her through. On entering the room, she saw a man sitting behind a desk. In front of him was a piece of moulded plastic with the name *Adrian Croy* printed on it. The man was alone, which disconcerted her. She had been expecting a judge and jury, something that resembled a court of law.

'Ah, Miss Burfoot,' the man said.

Adrian Croy was a slight, dapper man with wrists as narrow as school rulers. His hands twirled and fluttered when he spoke in such a way that she imagined he was simultaneously translating what he was saying into sign language. She felt clumsy in his presence, as if surrounded by bone china.

'You probably think that you're in trouble.' He was looking at her in a manner that did not endear him to her. She saw amusement and curiosity. A kind of craving too. 'You have crossed the border illegally,' he said. 'Twice.'

She sighed. It was true. She had done it as a dare to herself, just to see if it was possible. Then she had done it again, to make sure the first time hadn't been a fluke. She hadn't meant anything by it. 'I knew you'd find out,' she said.

'Oh yes, Miss Burfoot, we always find out.' Croy leaned back in his seat and studied her. 'We would like to offer you a position.'

'A position?'

'A job.'

'I've never had a job,' she said, 'except for working on the canal.'

Croy allowed himself a small, neat smile. 'I'd hardly call that making good use of your particular skills.'

They weren't going to punish her. They were giving her a job instead. She could scarcely believe her luck.

I shifted uneasily on the bed of sacking and old velvet, reminded of a certain sunlit afternoon, Diana smiling at me across the rim of her wine-glass, the word 'immunity' suspended seductively in the air between us.

'I was so innocent,' Odell murmured, half to herself.

Me too, I said inside my head.

At the age of seventeen she had come to an arrangement with the authorities. She was paid a modest retainer, and reported to Croy twice a month. Sometimes he would brief her on a specific job – surveillance, usually – but more often than not he would attempt to justify their shadowy activities. At some point, though, the talk would always gravitate towards the nature of her gift. When she told him what she could do – somehow, with Croy, she couldn't seem to help bragging about it – the black parts of his eyes would widen, and his hands would move more dreamily in front of him, like objects in space. He would claim that she was part of a tradition that dated back thousands of years. In her, he would say, one could see the true flowering of the phlegmatic character – adaptability, yes, but taken to extremes. He had theories about her too. In his opinion, she didn't actually *become* invisible. She simply *appeared* to do so. He called what she did 'escaping notice'. Frankly, it would bore her having to listen to all this, but she tried not to show it. She had to keep reminding herself that this dainty, middle-aged man was dangerous. If he were to turn against her, he could make things difficult for her. And so it paid to keep him sweet. Aware of this, she always played a little vaguer, a little more *spiritual*, than she really was.

'Tradition?' she said once. 'What tradition?'

He beamed. Her unworldliness never failed to delight him. 'The shape-shifter, the psychopomp,' he said. 'The seer.'

'What's a psychopomp?' This time she was genuinely curious.

'They're spirit guides,' Croy told her. 'They pilot dead people to their place of rest. They oversee the process whereby souls are purified, transformed.' He paused. 'I suppose you could say they teach the craft of dying.'

On another occasion he startled her by proposing that they should become a magic act. 'Burfoot & Croy,' he said. 'Can't you see it?' His right hand slid sideways across the air in front of him, palm facing outwards, fingers uppermost and slightly curled, as if to enclose an exotic painted sign. She smiled but said nothing. He had such peculiar fantasies. Was he really suggesting that they should run away together, or was it just another test? She could never quite be certain. If she hadn't been so strange-looking, she would have said that Adrian Croy was in love with her.

For all his ambiguities, though, and despite the power he

wielded over her, they were, at some fundamental level, of one mind. Yes, she had crossed borders illegally, but that didn't mean she wanted them removed. Far from it. Without borders they would return to the chaos of a quarter of a century ago. Without borders they would find themselves living in what used to be called, laughably in her opinion, the 'united kingdom' – a kingdom united in name only, a kingdom otherwise characterised by boorishness, thuggery and greed. She had no desire to live in a place like that. The Blue Quarter might be deficient in some respects, she said, but at least those who lived there were socially aware and ecologically responsible, prizing gentleness above aggression and spiritual development above material success, and on the whole she wanted to preserve things pretty much the way they were. She just liked to bend the rules once in a while, that was all.

'I still cross the border illegally from time to time,' she said. 'You know what I tell them now, if they find out?'

I lay still, waiting for the answer.

'I tell them I'm practising my craft. That's the kind of language they understand.' She fell silent. 'I'm not breaking the law,' she said after a while. 'I'm doing my duty.' And she laughed softly, delighted by her own capricious logic.

Odell shook me out of a deep sleep, letting me know that it was dawn. I had a feeling I hadn't had since I was a boy – a panic that uncoiled slowly as a snake, a powerful dread of what the day might bring. I wished I could have stayed in bed or hidden somewhere. I wanted it all to be over. She shook me again. I sat up, blinking. A weak light leaked through the window, grubby as the skin on boiled milk. Birds fumbled in their nests. I pushed my feet into my boots and pulled on the stiff leather coat. We ate the few scraps left over from the previous night's meal, sharing the inch of red wine in the bottom of the bottle, then it was time to go.

I followed Odell through the second of the two doors and into a small high-ceilinged room. The only piece of furniture in there was a wardrobe, its mirror-panelled door ajar. Our figures crept across the glass, furtive as thieves. On we went, through other, larger rooms, most of which showed evidence of looting. Paintings had been removed, leaving ghostly after-images. Wallpaper had been defaced or gouged. In one room a fire had been lit in the middle of the floor, and I imagined I could smell it, the air inlaid with a thin blue seam of smoke. We stepped out on to a landing, its uneven boards sloping away from us, slippery with light. Pinned to a door at the far end was a life-size black-and-white picture of a soldier with a gun, concentric circles radiating outwards from his heart. There were holes in the paper, and the wood. At the head of the stairs I stooped and peered through a diamond-paned window. Pines lifted before me, their red-brown trunks showing dimly through the mist. To my surprise, the snow had melted. The land looked waterlogged and drab.

Downstairs, in the hall, wooden chairs were arranged against opposing walls, making me think a party had been held here once. Trainee border guards would have cavorted with girls from nearby villages, the guards resplendent in their dress uniforms, all pressed serge and polished brass, the girls in short skirts and white stilettos, their bare legs marbled with the cold. I could almost hear the live band with its thrashing drums, its raunchy lead guitar. Odell led me across the hall and down a passage. Then, as we passed through yet another door, the space seemed to explode above my head. We were in a church. The roof must have been sixty feet high, and the nave could have held a congregation of many hundreds. Here too, though, the vandals had been at work. Pews had been upended and set on fire. Windows had been smashed. The stone flags underfoot were crunchy with stained glass – the blue of saints' robes, the yellow of their haloes, the green of a green hill far away. I noticed some incongruous additions to the church's interior – relics of the military occupation, no doubt. Leaning non-chalantly against the font was a motorbike, its back tyre flat. Further up the aisle, empty bullet casings and beer bottles lay scattered about. And there were even more recent intrusions: a pigeon chuckled in the organ loft, and on the altar steps some sheep had deposited their neat but convoluted droppings, each of which looked exactly like a small black brain.

We left through the sacristy. Once outdoors, I paused and looked around. Some fifty yards ahead of me was a drystone wall, and on the hillside beyond were the evergreens I had seen from the landing. Behind me rose the great hunched back of the church. A few traces of snow lingered under trees and bushes, and against the base of north-facing walls.

As I stood there, Odell stepped in front of me. 'Your face is all wrong.'

I stared at her, perplexed.

'You look as if you've never been here before,' she said, 'as if you come from somewhere else. They'll notice that immediately. You can't show any surprise or curiosity. I want you to look fed up, long-suffering. We're a couple, remember, and we don't get on.'

I nodded. *All right.*

'Show me,' she said, 'before we go any further.'

I pushed my hands deep into my trouser pockets, then I scowled. I could feel the skin buckling on the bridge of my nose.

'That's more like it,' she said.

We passed through a wicket gate and set off along a footpath. On my shoulder was a bag that held my cloak and undergarments. Without them, I wouldn't be able to cross back into the Red Quarter. If we were stopped and searched, Odell was going to claim that they were trophies from the recent hunt, as was the watch I was wearing, the one that had no hands. She would tell the story with relish, how we had chased the White People through the woods, how we had terrorised and raped and butchered. I had become so carried away, she would say, that I had completely lost my voice. When she first suggested this strategy, I felt something contract inside me. She noticed the look on my face and said simply, 'Do you want to get out of here or don't you?'

We climbed over a stile and down into a country lane, then walked on, side by side, in silence. Stone walls hemmed us in.

We passed barns of corrugated-iron, some faded red, some green. Once, the sun broke through, alighting on a piece of rough pasture to the north-east of us, the land all round still deep in shadow. Like a memory of happiness, I thought, that single illuminated field. Like the bits of my life that had been given back to me . . . We were quiet for so long that I almost forgot the role I was supposed to be playing, but then I saw a man come hobbling towards us. Chained to his wrist was a hawk, its head sheathed in a leather hood.

As the man approached, Odell began to grumble. 'How much further? My feet ache.'

I chose not to answer. Instead, I gathered a ball of phlegm into my mouth, rolled it on my tongue, then fired it past the end of her nose and into the ditch.

She grasped me by the sleeve. 'I said, how much further?'

I shook her off and lengthened my stride, giving the man a curt nod as he passed by. The man grunted in reply. I watched him move on down the road, a stocky figure dressed in brown, the bird of prey so motionless that it could have been stuffed. Knowing it was alive beneath that hood sent a shiver through me.

'Good,' Odell said. 'Just right.'

To the south the landscape brooded. The sky had lowered, and the air above the hills was smeared with rain.

By the time we reached our first village, something unexpected had occurred. My mood had soured. I was in a bad temper after all, a genuine bad temper, which meant I no longer had to worry about standing out.

As soon as we entered the village, Odell said, 'I thought you told me we were there,' and she stopped in the middle of the street and put her hands on her hips. 'You fool,' she said, 'you stupid fool. Hey!' And she grabbed me by the upper arm.

I'd always hated being touched like that. Swinging round, I raised my fist as if to strike her. At the last minute, though, I turned aside and slammed my hand into the front wall of a house. I watched the grazed skin ooze blood, then whirled away from her and stormed up the street, scattering the chickens that darted, cackling, across my path. I might even have trodden on one of them. I felt something squirm out from under my boot, but I didn't bother looking down.

'Oi,' said a woman in an apron. They were probably her chickens.

I glared at her, and she sprang back into her doorway as though pulled from behind by an immensely powerful hand.

Rage surged through me. Such a rage.

The air filled with the jangle of fairground music, and I turned to see a white high-sided van grinding its way up the street, a loudspeaker bolted precariously to its roof. Every so often, the driver interrupted his music to proclaim the delights of his hams and sausages, his tongue. Odell stopped the van and bought a few items, then it passed me and dipped down an incline to the village green. A crowd had gathered there, beneath a large, gnarled oak, and once the racket the van was making had died away I could hear the shrieks and squeals of children. There must be an attraction of some kind, I thought. A juggler, perhaps. A puppet show.

As I drew nearer, Odell caught up with me and took my arm. 'No,' she muttered. 'Keep going.'

This time I didn't shake her off. Something in her voice told me she wasn't acting. She led me down the road, past grim, grey houses, their windows either too low or too high, and oddly asymmetrical, as if only dwarves and giants lived inside. Before long, the village was behind us, and the children's cries had faded into the distance.

'It was nothing you need know about,' she said.

The smell of melted snow on the grass verges, the sky above the fields grey and pale-yellow.

After a while two men in work clothes appeared on the road ahead of us. I pushed my hands into my pockets, feeling the rips in the lining. Each new encounter was a test of our authenticity, our nerve, and I couldn't help but believe that, sooner or later, we would be found out.

The men slowed as they reached us.

'Seen the heads?' said the shorter of the two.

'We just came from there.' Odell pointed back along the road. 'There's three of them. All bitches.'

The short man laughed lasciviously. He looked at his companion, eyes like bits of wet glass, then the two of them moved on, quickening their pace.

I waited until they were hidden by a bend in the road, then I went and leaned on a farm gate. I had received an image of a woman. Ears and nose cut off. An apple wedged into her mouth as if she were a suckling pig. *Seen the heads?* I retched once or twice, but nothing came up. Cold sweat all over me.

Odell laid a hand on my shoulder. 'I'm sorry you had to hear that. It was the only way.'

I know, I said inside my head. *I understand.*

Do you want to get out of here or don't you?

It was dark by the time we entered the next village, but Odell made no attempt to find a room. It might have been the ginger-haired twins sitting on a bench outside the post office, one gnawing avidly at his thumbnail, the other aiming a kick at a dog as it loped by, or perhaps it was the fat woman in her front garden who took one look at us, spat sideways and withdrew into her house. This was a sour embittered place, a place that had turned its fury against itself, and it would have no patience with the likes of us.

We had reached the edge of the village and were beginning to prepare ourselves for a night in the open when we saw a caravan parked in the corner of an orchard, a white shape seemingly afloat among dock leaves and thistles. Odell forced the door – a sharp dry snap, like the cracking of a nut – and we climbed inside. The curtains were already drawn, but a faint glow eased through the frosted-plastic sky-light, just enough to see by. There were cushioned bench-seats, ideal for sleeping on. There was even a sink, with running water. We fastened the door, using a metal catch. If anyone came, Odell said, we would escape through the window at the back.

Though she had promised me nothing but tantrums that day, she had broken her own rules within the first few hours. She had

340

been aware of my fragile state, I think, and whenever we found ourselves alone she would link her arm through mine and tell me how well I was doing. Once, as we stood beneath a tree, sheltering from the downpour that had been threatening all morning, I turned to look at her. I had no memory of ever meeting her before, or even seeing her, but that now seemed irrelevant. In the tarnished half-light of the storm her eyes had taken on the strangest colour, a new commingling of green and black, ambiguous but vivid, and the breath stalled in my throat. All of a sudden I wanted to touch her. Did she guess what I was thinking? Possibly. Because she chose that moment to announce that the rain was letting up and it was time to push on.

By late afternoon we had left the Wanings behind. In a sense, though, we had merely swapped one set of dangers for another. The Wanings may have lapsed into anarchy, but we had just as much to fear from the so-called forces of law and order, whose reputation for corruption and brutality was common knowledge. As the sun was setting, we saw our first roadblock. Fortunately the two officers were facing the other way, questioning a man on a bicycle, and we were able to slip behind a hedgerow and flatten ourselves against the ground. As their jeep finally roared past, a cigarette butt landed in the grass no more than a hand's width from my right elbow. Though it had been discarded, it continued to smoulder, all the virulence of the Yellow Quarter concentrated into that stubborn quarter-inch of ash.

Following a meagre supper in the caravan, Odell began to talk. Before too long, she said, we would be passing through built-up areas. Things would move faster, and I would have to be ready to act decisively. If we got into any kind of confrontation, for instance, I should leave immediately. Just leave. If we already had a place to stay, I should go back there. Lock myself in. If not, I should wait near by. She would extricate herself. That was her speciality. If for some reason she failed to reappear, I was to carry on towards the border. I would have to cross it on my own. In the darkness I reached out and squeezed her hand to let her know that I had understood.

At dawn I was woken by a vicious scratching, and I sat up

quickly, thinking someone was trying to get in. Then I realised it was coming from above me. Through the skylight's blurry plastic I saw arrowheads, delicate as pencil drawings. It was just birds' feet. Birds walking on the roof.

We left the caravan soon after, fells rising in blue-black curves above the mist. Later, the sun burned through. We drank from a stream that tasted metallic, as if we were sipping the water from a spoon. We walked south and then west, clouds tumbling in the sky, huge sweeps of land on every side. We saw no people, not even one. There was only the sound of our boots in the grass and, sometimes, the clatter of a pheasant's wings as, startled by our approach, it heaved itself into the air.

That night we curled up in a hut that smelled of sheep, the ground outside littered with shotgun cartridges and brittle clumps of fleece. The wind kept me awake, levering its way into every crack and crevice in the walls. In the morning we climbed down to flat land. Houses now, and villages, with youths standing around. They would be smoking or kicking a football about or trying to put each other in headlocks. Their eyes would flick in our direction as we passed, and I sensed the shape of their thoughts, dark and splintery. I had to work hard not to show any fear. The memory of those strangers stretched across the road still lingered. I noticed a boy leaning against a wall next to a newsagent's. He watched us go by, then slid a few words out of one side of his mouth, and the boys who were with him laughed, the noise so abrupt and harsh that two crows lifted from a nearby tree. No one actually confronted us, but that wasn't the point. It was the constant, unremitting threat of violence that I found wearing. It was the sense of apprehension, the dread.

In the early afternoon we stopped to rest. The road shadowed a railway cut, and we climbed over the wall and installed ourselves on the embankment, so as to be hidden from any passers-by. Odell unwrapped the cold meat and bread, leftovers from the day before. A passenger train rushed past below us as we ate. Odell eyed it thoughtfully. The sky had clouded over.

A chill wind bent the blades of grass beside me, and I huddled deeper into my creaky leather coat.

We were about to move on when a goods train rattled down the line towards us. Instead of the usual trucks, it was hauling several transporters, each of which had a tarpaulin lashed over its main frame. Odell began to slither down the embankment, signalling for me to follow her. When she reached the track she ran alongside one of the transporters. Catching hold of a stanchion, she swung herself up on to a metal footplate. I tossed her my bag, then hoisted myself on to the same section of the train. She was already loosening the ties on one corner of a tarpaulin. We ducked under the heavy plastic and found ourselves pressed up against a yellow sports car, one of three, all identical in make and colour. I tried the door on the driver's side, fully expecting it to be locked, but it opened with an expensive click. I hesitated for a second, then climbed inside. The smell of leather upholstery enfolded me – the smell of newness itself. Odell climbed in after me. Settling behind the steering-wheel, she pulled the door shut. The smooth swaying motion of the car, the darkness beyond the windows, the presence of a girl beside me – for a moment I was able to fool myself into thinking that it was my first night at the Bathysphere and nothing else had happened yet.

'I've got another story for you,' Odell said.

I turned to face her.

'Not so long ago,' she said, 'I was in love with someone . . .'

I smiled. It was a good beginning.

His name was Luke, and they had met when she was twenty. One Sunday evening she was waiting on the platform of a provincial railway station. She wanted to get back to the city, but there had been all kinds of delays and cancellations, and people were standing three or four deep by the time the train pulled in. Then she saw him, through one of the carriage windows. He was reading a book, his face lowered, his black hair falling on to his forehead. In that same moment she noticed that a window in his carriage had been left open. She tended not to use her gift for her own personal gain, not any more, but that evening she decided

343

to flout the rules for once. A damp flurry of wind took her over the heads of the other passengers, through the window and down into the seat directly opposite the dark-haired boy. When he looked up and saw her, his eyes widened and he breathed in sharply.

'What are you staring at?' she said. 'Do I remind you of someone?'

'No.' He seemed momentarily dazed by the speed and boldness of her questions. 'I didn't hear the door open.'

'Perhaps you were asleep.'

'Asleep? I don't think so.' He glanced at his book. 'I was reading.'

'Then perhaps you were in another world,' she said.

The train shook itself and then began to move. She stared out of the window, pretending to take an interest in the lights of unknown houses, distant towns.

'I'm sorry,' he said after a while. 'I didn't mean to be rude.'

What she had loved most of all about Luke was lying next to him while he was sleeping. He always looked so untroubled. She thought that if they slept in the same bed for long enough she would acquire that look of his. At the beginning she would stay awake for hours and try to draw the calmness out of him. She used to see it as a grey-blue vapour drifting eerily from his body into hers.

She had wanted to be with him for ever – in fact she'd been quite unable to imagine *not* being with him – but she had made a mistake: she told him what she could do. In bed one night, with all the lights out, she turned to him and said, 'You know when we first met, on that train . . .'

'I *knew* it,' Luke cried when she had finished. 'I knew there was *something*.'

Initially, he was seduced by the glamour of it. He saw a kind of peculiar, inverted celebrity, and that excited him. But he soon started to feel that their relationship had its roots in deception – *her* deception – and the subject would come up whenever they argued. The fact that she had fooled him. Made him look stupid.

'No, no, you don't understand,' she would cry. 'It was because

I loved you. And anyway, you almost guessed. Even then, at the beginning.'

She should never have told him. She should've been content simply to have profited from her gift. But she had been unsure of herself, perhaps. She had hoped to bind him to her still more closely. Once, many years ago, a great-aunt had given her some advice. *An air of mystery is just as valuable as wit or beauty. It keeps people interested – especially men.* And certainly, for the first few months, Luke had suspected there was a side to her that he hadn't understood, and he would worry at it almost pleasurably, as you might push your tongue against a loose tooth. When she told him the truth, however, it allowed him to think that the riddle had been solved. He had reached the end of her, and there was nothing more to discover. Far from binding him, the knowledge set him free. He could move on.

And another thing. Although she had sworn him to secrecy, he was always nearly giving the game away. He couldn't bear it that people didn't know about her. To start with, she thought it was because he was proud of her, but then she began to realise it was something far less healthy. He had sensed that people found the relationship odd, and that reflected badly on him. If they knew who she was, though, they'd get it. In other words, it wasn't that he wanted people to know she was different, or special, or extraordinary. No, in the end he was only concerned with his own image.

Odell sighed. 'I wasn't as beautiful as he was. People were always admiring him, and he'd pretend he hadn't noticed. I didn't mind that, really. I just wanted him to see the beauty in me. A beauty others didn't see. Maybe he couldn't, though. Or maybe it wasn't enough.'

I see it, I said inside my head.

The train had slowed, and I could feel every joint in its body as it picked its way cautiously through what felt like a maze of points. Odell sighed again. Opening her door, she said she was going to take a look outside.

When she returned, she told me we had reached a city. She thought it might be Ustion, but she couldn't be sure. In any case, it would probably be wise to leave now, before the transporters were either checked or unloaded.

Although the train was still moving, we had no trouble jumping down on to the tracks. The station loomed about half a mile ahead of us, a harsh recorded voice echoing from the cavernous interior. *Any luggage found unattended will be destroyed.* A mist had descended, and all the lights were ringed with gauzy haloes. Crouching low, I followed Odell across the rails, then we scaled a wall of dark bricks and dropped down into a side-street.

We weren't prepared for the sight that greeted us when we turned the corner. Men rampaged along the main road, red shirts worn outside their trousers, open cans of beer in their hands. Cars raced past, honking their horns. Some had pennants tied to their aerials, others had scarves trapped and flapping in their wound-up windows. Odell bought a paper from a news-stand. *The Ustion Gazette.* She had guessed right. As she took her change, she asked the vendor what was happening.

'Important game tonight,' he said.

We ducked into a doorway as a second group of men swayed towards us. They were singing strange savage songs that I'd never heard before. With their cropped hair and their hard, exultant faces, they seemed to have sealed themselves off from the rest of us. It was like the divided kingdom in miniature – the same tribalism, the same deep need to belong. If you supported a football team, you saw all other teams as forces to be challenged, ridiculed, defeated. You stuck together, no matter what. You dealt with everything life threw at you. The triumphs, the disasters. The thick and thin of it. *People have to have something they can identify with,* Miss Groves had told us once. *They have to feel they're part of something.* I watched as a man with a shaved head heaved a rubbish bin through a plate-glass window. His companions whooped and roared. They began to chant his name, breaking it into two raucous syllables. Then on they went towards the ground, which rose out of the terraced streets like some great cauldron, bubbling furiously with noise and light.

Given the conditions, Odell thought it best if we got off the streets. We found a hotel not far from the station and registered as Mr and Mrs Burfoot, a new name for me, and one that gave me an unexpected thrill. Later, we had dinner in a bar on the ground floor. We chose a table that had a view of the TV. The football was on. As we took our seats, the two teams walked out of the tunnel, flanked by police with riot shields and visors. Fights had already broken out on the terraces. The camera homed in as the crowd surged in two different directions at once, and I thought of how the sea looks when a wave rebounds from a breakwater and meets another wave head-on. We ordered steak pie and chips from the blackboard behind the bar, and I drank a pint of dark, flat beer, which was what the other men were drinking. Once the game began, I turned my back on Odell – a perfect example of choleric behaviour, I thought – and when we left more than an hour later I still hadn't so much as glanced at her. At the door a shrill whistling from the crowd had me looking over my shoulder. One of the home side's star players was being stretchered off the pitch with his hands covering his face. They showed a slow-motion replay of the foul. A defender from the opposing team hacked him to the ground and then stood back, arms raised in the air, palms outwards, as if innocent of any wrongdoing. They were like children, these footballers, with their transparent lying and their endless tantrums. Nothing was ever their fault. They wanted to get away with everything.

Once we were back in our room, Odell locked the door, then leaned against the wall with her hands behind her. I was reminded of Sonya for a moment – she often used to stand like that – but, at the same time, the comparison seemed obscure, even meaningless. I had loved Sonya, I really had, but she had become intangible to me, not quite real, as had almost every other aspect of the way I had lived before. When I considered my return to the Red Quarter, when I tried to imagine what that might entail, my mind closed down. The question Odell had asked me – *Do you want to get out of here or don't you?* – expressed it perfectly. Yes, I wanted to get out of the Yellow Quarter, of course I did, and yet, once that had been achieved, I couldn't actually visualise a life. If I thought about

347

the people I used to see on a regular basis – Vishram, Sonya, Kenneth Loames – they appeared as ephemeral and irrelevant as ghosts, whereas the ghosts themselves – Ob, Neg, Lum – had true substance and even – strange, this – a kind of nobility. If I survived, who would I be exactly? Which version of myself would I be left with? How would I fit in? Turning away from Odell, I walked to the window. A helicopter hovered in the middle distance, its searchlight aimed at the ground directly below it.

She came and stood beside me. 'It's only crowd control.'

Of course. The football would be over any minute. Even so, when the helicopter veered towards us, with its head lowered and its searchlight sweeping the streets and buildings, we both instinctively stepped back from the window. All of a sudden the angry stutter of its rotor blades was on top of us, the air itself vibrating. I shaded my eyes as blinding light flashed through the room. It was as though some supernatural force had just flown in one wall and out the other, as though we had been visited by a creature to whom concrete and plaster meant nothing. The helicopter moved on, heading westwards, restless, inquisitive.

'I didn't finish my story about Luke,' Odell said.

I drew the curtains, shutting out the night.

'You're not too tired?' she said.

I shook my head. We settled on the bed, Odell leaning against the pillows with her knees drawn up while I lay on my side, my cheek propped on one hand.

Luke had left her eighteen months ago, she said, and in all that time she had heard nothing from him. Then, in late November, the day after she saw me being arrested by the Blue Quarter police, she had gone home for a few hours. She lived in an old petrol station on the outskirts of Aquaville. The ground floor had been a working garage – it still smelled of diesel oil and spray-paint – but the upstairs was like a loft, with windows running along one side and a view over the fields.

She was just sorting through her mail when there was a knock on the door. It was Luke. His dark hair stuck up at all angles, and the whites of his eyes looked dingy, almost stained. He was in trouble, he said.

It took another hour and most of a bottle of wine for him to get to the point. His girlfriend was about to be transferred. He didn't want to lose her, though, so he had hidden her. When Odell reminded him of the penalties he would face if he was caught, he snapped at her. Yes, he knew about the penalties. He *knew*. Then he lowered his voice again. He was sorry. He was tired. He hadn't slept.

'You have to help me,' he said.

She couldn't, she told him. Didn't he have any idea who she worked for? It turned out that he didn't – so she'd kept something from him after all! – but once he got over the shock he tried to persuade her that it was perfect. They'd never suspect a person in her position. She shook her head. She couldn't risk it. When he made a half-hearted attempt to blackmail her, she lost her temper. He backed down.

'I don't know what to do,' he said after a while. 'I feel so hopeless.'

Outside, a bitter wind scoured the cracked concrete where the petrol pumps stood. Ice had formed on the puddles, as fragile and transparent as a layer of skin. She bled the radiators with a small grey key. They groaned and clanked a little, but the room didn't seem to get much warmer.

Later that night Luke asked if he could stay. When she hesitated, he told her not to worry. He'd be gone in the morning. It was strange how he could still wound her, how words like that made her heart hurt.

'Yes,' she said. 'All right.'

'Do you want me to sleep in the chair?' he said. 'I'll sleep in the chair, if you like.'

'You'll freeze,' she said.

He climbed beneath the blankets. His body smelled of nutmeg, the way it always used to. She knew she shouldn't have slept with him, but she did it anyway. She hadn't been doing it for him. She'd done it for herself.

No one ever bothers to imagine how alone other people are.

It was almost dawn before she noticed that the grey-blue vapour she'd once coveted had disappeared. Turning in the bed, she looked straight at him. She saw how the surface of his skin fluttered, and how he brushed constantly at phantoms with his hands. From his lips came whimpered protests and entreaties. He had become as phlegmatics were supposed to be – tremulous, inert – but unlike most of them he had nothing to fall back on.

In the early morning they stood near the car-wash, the big blue brushes foolish, incongruous, like someone's idea of a joke, and she knew this was the last time she would ever see him. The tears ran from her eyes. She had lost him, but that wasn't really why she was crying. She was grieving for all the things that don't come again. She was grieving because things end, and she wished they didn't have to.

He put a hand on her shoulder, then turned and walked across the buckled forecourt, his whole body hunched against the cold. Though her tears had given him a kind of strength, he looked unequal to his surroundings; he had the air of a man who was about to be crushed by the weight of his own existence. At that moment, miraculously, a bus appeared on the road. Luke broke into the semblance of a run, waving an arm, but the bus passed smoothly by, and it was then, as his arm dropped back, that she climbed the steps to her front door and went inside.

Odell was picking at the edge of the hotel blanket. In the distance a siren swooped, then hiccuped. 'What do you think?' she said.

I looked up at her. I didn't see it as a love story, despite the way it had begun. No, I saw it as more of a cautionary tale. The special substance that makes each one of us unique is finite, ethereal. It can be whittled away, almost without us knowing. It can be used up altogether. I had been so many different people during the past few weeks, and, in the end, I had been nobody at all. Odell knew that, and she was using stories from her life to try and bring me back. She wanted to return me to myself, but slowly, gently. In my own time.

'You think it's sad,' she said.

I nodded.

'Who for? For me?'

For him, I said inside my head.

'That's right,' she said quietly, looking out across the room. Later, as I drifted on the edge of sleep, I heard her speak again.

'Yes,' she said. 'That's what I think too.'

The sky was ash smeared on silver where the sun was coming up. The pavements and gutters glittered with crushed beer cans and broken glass. Sunday. The city had a stunned feel to it – the temporary numbness of a dead leg. I wondered idly who had won the game. I never did find out.

We left the hotel early, just after seven, the girl on reception smothering a yawn as she handed us a copy of the bill. Most people would stay in bed until mid-morning, Odell told me, sleeping off their hangovers. It was a good day to be travelling. We bought bacon sandwiches and cups of tea from a café near the station, then set off along a main road that led south. I kept my face twisted into a permanent scowl and chewed sullenly on a wad of gum. I was thinking of my brief stay in Athanor, and how my cuts and bruises had protected me. If I looked danger-ous enough, I'd be safe. That was the theory, anyway.

The bars were still open. Every once in a while, a drunk would stagger towards us, hands aloft and twitching in some mad semaphore, but we automatically crossed the road before any of them got close. Their curses reached us like the light from distant stars – faint messages from a world already super-seded, left behind. We no longer needed to look at each other, Odell and I. We had a kind of understanding now. I swept my eyes from side to side, constantly aware of my environment. At the same time I walked through it all as though none of it could touch me.

By dusk my lungs felt tight with the exhaust fumes I had been forced to breathe, and my feet ached from walking on nothing but paving-stones and tarmac for hour after hour, and I let out a sigh when Odell, who seemed tireless, finally announced that we'd be stopping for the night.

She had chosen a place called the Hot Hotel, the word *Hot* glowing on and off like brake lights in a traffic-jam. To reach reception, which was located one floor up, we had to walk down an alley that ran along one side of the building. We were given a room on the third floor, with a circular bed and an orange shag-pile carpet. It had the atmosphere of somewhere that was rented by the hour, and if I turned my head fast enough I seemed to glimpse the shady outlines of those who had preceded us. Access to the room was from an open-air walkway or corridor. I leaned on the parapet, looking out over an all-night service station and a supermarket car-park. Opposite the service station I could see a strip club called the Tinder Box. Sometimes I wanted to question the wisdom of Odell's decisions, but I wasn't sure I had the right. Maybe she had been drawn by the number of people around, which would lend us a certain anonymity. She had already saved me once, I thought. Probably I should have more faith in her.

In fact, she had saved me a second time that afternoon. We had been walking along a main road, its four lanes packed with cars. To our left, some fifty feet below us, lay a river, its waters viscous, thick as soup. At one point, Odell had spotted a public toilet. It was in a shopping centre on the other side of the road. She told me to wait. She'd only be a moment. No sooner had she disappeared than I sensed something close by, a kind of force or pressure. Half turning, I saw a boy's face on a level with my elbow, his eyes dark-brown and startled-looking, his teeth bared. Then my arm jerked backwards and the bag with my white clothes in it was gone. At the same time I felt hands reaching into all my pockets. I swung round. A dozen children swarmed on the pavement behind me, some as young as five or six. The boy who had snatched my bag was making off down a steep slope to the river. The others followed.

For a few seconds I saw the world as if through soundproof glass.

A concrete landscape. Sky creamy with pollution.

Then the sounds flowed back – the rush of traffic, the roar of yet another unknown city – and I was running towards the river.

At the water's edge the boys had already spread the contents of my bag out on the ground. Without thinking, I swooped down and took hold of the bag, together with my cloak, my long johns and my undershirt, then started up the slope again. The boys came after me, their voices shrill and jagged. Somehow I was aware of the smallness of the hands that pushed and pulled at me. Since I was clutching my possessions, though, I was powerless to defend myself. As I regained the pavement I saw Odell threading her way through the traffic towards me. She produced an aerosol and sprayed something into the faces of the two boys who were nearest. They doubled over, howling, hands pressed against their eyes. The other boys fell back. They watched us for a while from a distance, as though contemplating a second assault, and then turned reluctantly away. They would find richer pickings elsewhere, perhaps. Or less resistance. I began to tremble uncontrollably. 'You were lucky not to get hurt,' Odell told me. 'Those gangs of kids, they often carry knives – or guns.' She gave me a hard, steady look. 'Next time, let it go.' Later, she relaxed and smiled. 'Next time,' she said, 'I suppose I'll have to take you with me.'

Yes, I thought as I stood on the walkway, looking out over the car-park, I should probably have more faith in her.

We both had showers. Then, once we were dressed, Odell took me to the bar on the ground floor. It was still fairly early, and there was almost no one there, just an older couple on the dance floor at the back, shuffling beneath maroon and purple disco lights. While Odell ordered our drinks, I sat in a booth and let my eyes drift through the interior, trying to convey a sulky indifference to everything I saw. I stared at the couple, who seemed glued together. The woman had her eyes closed, and her head rolled on the man's shoulder as though attached to her body by a piece of string. Their dancing bore no relation to the music, which was upbeat, corny, before my time.

Odell came back with two double brandies. When I seemed surprised that she knew what I drank, she told me we'd had brandy on a train, in late November. Again I thought back, but no matter how often or how hard I tried, I could never match what she said with anything that I'd experienced.

She smiled. 'You'll just have to take my word for it.'

It was part of her gift, she told me. She knew how to make herself unmemorable. A skill she had developed over the years was to shake hands without leaving the slightest impression. As she offered her hand, she simultaneously withdrew from it, retreating into the most distant part of herself, both physically and mentally. She had done it to me on the train to Aquaville, she said, and at the conference as well, a couple of weeks before.

'You really don't remember, do you?' She shook her head and reached for her drink. 'I must be better than I thought.'

And she started telling me her story, which was also my story, of course. She had first met me, very briefly, at the cocktail party in the Concord Room – though she had used her gift to 'absent herself', as she put it. She'd been officially assigned to keep me under observation until I returned to the Red Quarter. Little did she know, at that point, how long the assignment was going to last! She had flown to Congreve, just as I had, her seat two rows in front of mine. She had watched the fireworks, and attended the banquet afterwards. When the bomb went off, she was in a club in the basement of the hotel, socialising with some other delegates. 'As I told you once before,' she said with a crafty grin. Anyway, they were all evacuated on the spot. Later, she slipped through a police cordon and found me on the fourteenth floor, walking back towards my room – walking in the wrong direction, in other words. It was enough to prompt her to call Adrian Croy, who immediately switched her role to that of 'shadow'. Though I'd hitched a number of lifts that night, she was able to keep track of me. She sat behind me as I ate breakfast in that out-of-the-way transport café. She followed me as I climbed up into the hills. She stood at my shoulder during the burning of the animals, an event that had given her bad dreams. Afterwards, I had vanished into the crowd, and she was still trying to locate me when the riot squad arrived. In the ensuing chaos she had lost her favourite piece of jewellery. A ring. By the time she secured her release, I was already making for the coast –

Odell was still talking, but I had stopped listening. I slipped a hand inside my shirt and felt for the ring I wore around my neck. *So you don't drift too far . . .* With an inscription like that, I should have guessed it would belong to a phlegmatic. Undoing the knot, I freed the ring and held it out to her. At first, in the dim light of the bar, she didn't seem to recognise it. Then, slowly, she reached out and took it from me. For a long time she said nothing, her head lowered, then she lifted her eyes to mine.

'That's a miracle,' she said.

I watched her slide the ring on to her finger.

'The strangest thing about it is,' she said, 'it proves I was telling you the truth.'

We had more drinks to celebrate the return of the ring, which to my mind now linked us inextricably, and it was while Odell was buying another round, our third or fourth, that I overheard a man at the bar ask if she would dance with him. Odell told him she was sorry, but she was with someone. He seemed to be friendly with the bartender, who was also the manager of the hotel, because they exchanged a few words and laughed, then the man came over to the booth where I was sitting. He wore black jeans and a leather belt with a metal vulture for a buckle. His boots were crocodile-skin, and their toes were so sharp that he could have dipped one of them in ink and written with it. I thought of the book Victor had made. What stories would these boots have told?

'You with her?'

He had lifted a hand, his thumb angled back over his shoulder, but I knew better than to look where he was pointing. I didn't meet his gaze either. Instead, I stared at his other hand, which hung against his hip, the fingers curling and uncurling as if they were trying to work themselves loose.

'You don't mind if I have a dance with her, do you?'

Though the disco was still going on, a silence had risen underneath it, which made the music seem strident and hollow. We were only seconds away from the type of situation Odell had warned me about. I put my glass down and stood up. The man stepped back. He was probably hoping he would have to defend himself. He probably wanted a fight even more than a dance. His flexing fingers would not be satisfied until that happened. But I just walked around him and moved towards the exit. I didn't touch him or brush against him, didn't even acknowledge his presence. He could have been a column or a pillar. I could have been walking in my sleep. As I pushed the door open, he started to say something, his voice pitched high in disbelief, but I let the door slam behind me, cutting off his sentence halfway through.

Outside, a drizzle was coming down. I hurried round the corner and along the alley to the hotel. Cars hissed by on the main road as if they were carrying snakes. When I reached our room I locked myself in, as Odell had told me to, then I sat on the edge of the bed, my eyes veering constantly towards the door. Its stillness seemed temporary, unsustainable. I kept expecting the flimsy wood to crash inwards and shower me with splinters, but I couldn't imagine who or what would be standing in the gap. Perhaps no one, nothing. An upright box of darkness. A piece of the night.

I sat there, motionless. The minutes passed.

Once, I lifted my wrist into the air in front of me to check the time, but the watch I was wearing had no hands.

In the end, I reached for the remote. Wrestling was on. Huge men with flaxen manes bounced off each other, their bodies the colour of roast chicken. I turned the sound down. Through the wall behind me came a series of breathy rhythmic cries. At first I thought it was the people next door having sex, but it went on far too long. Somebody must have tuned in to one of the many adult channels. The wrestlers with their roasted skin, the endless mechanical orgasms – I fell into a kind of trance. So much so that when I heard a voice whisper my name I almost leapt off the bed.

I opened the door and Odell slipped past me. By the time I had locked the door again, she was in the bathroom, running the tap. I heard her spit. Standing in the bathroom doorway, I watched her wash her face and hands.

'Don't ask,' she said.

There was something about her that I didn't understand. She

clearly thought of herself as strange-looking, if not actually ugly, and yet it was precisely that sense of aberrant uniqueness that drew your eye to her and held it there. I remembered what she had said about Luke, how his looks overshadowed hers. Her beauty might be reluctant or arcane, but I could see it none-theless. And another thing. In telling Luke what she could do, she believed she'd lost her air of mystery. Maybe for him. But true mystery could not be compromised, nor could it be dissipated quite so easily. It was as much a part of her as her freckles, or the fine lines below her eyes.

She walked out of the bathroom, the tips of her hair dark and wet. As she eased off her coat and let it slump to the floor, I took her in my arms. I felt her stiffen against me – she was thinking of pushing me away, perhaps – but then, in the next moment, all the tension left her and she relaxed.

You can't do everything, I said inside my head.

'What are you saying?' she said. 'Are you saying something?'

The warmth of her breath eased through my shirt. I became aware of the parts of her that I was touching – a shoulderblade, the small of her back. I could feel her spine under my right hand, the tip of my middle finger bearing the subtle imprint of a vertebra. I was getting an erection. I hadn't meant anything like that to happen. In the meantime she had attained a new stillness, which seemed alert somehow, as though her body were listening to mine. I kissed the top of her head, where her parting was, then I kissed the outer rim of her ear. I could smell the beer and smoke of the bar, and the smell of her clean skin underneath reminded me that when she was only a few hours old she had been held against the window of a houseboat so she could watch the snow come down. And now she did push me away.

'What are you doing?' she said.

I don't know, I said inside my head.

She sat on the bed. As she bent over to unlace her boots, her hair fell forwards into her eyes. I sat beside her, tucking the loose strands back behind her ears.

'Not you as well,' she said.

Yes, me, I said. *Me more than anyone.*

I leaned forwards to kiss her mouth, and she didn't move away. Her lips were cool, much cooler than the rest of her. I wondered if she had already withdrawn, if she had – what did she call it? – 'absented herself'.

'Somebody said once,' she murmured, 'somebody said my face looked like one of those road signs in the country that people have fired shotguns at . . .'

I stroked the face they'd said bad things about.

She lay on the counterpane, her arms thrown backwards, bracketing her head. I leaned down and pressed my lips to the milky insides of her wrists. She held herself quite still, her breathing shallow. I slowly unbuttoned her black cardigan. Underneath she was wearing a camouflage T-shirt. I untucked the T-shirt and pushed it up until I could see her stomach. I kissed the plump flesh around her belly button. A kind of vibration went through her, somewhere beneath the surface, deep down. Her heartbeat showed on the skin between her ribs, a shimmer on the drum of her body. I kissed her where the tremor was. I felt the beating of her heart against my mouth.

You're not like any sign I've ever seen.

Her hand appeared as a slow blur to my left and came to rest on the back of my neck. It was my turn to go still. I waited to see what she would do next.

At that moment footsteps sounded on the walkway outside. I was hoping they would go past – there were plenty of rooms beyond ours – but they stopped and somebody knocked twice, firmly. Odell's hand tightened in my hair. She wanted me not to move. The knocking came again, harder this time.

'Open up.'

We lay on the bed, our faces turned towards the door.

'I know you're in there.'

It was the manager's voice – the man who had served us in the bar downstairs. He rattled the door-knob, then swore under his breath. There was another silence, during which nothing happened. Finally his footsteps receded.

Odell levered herself upright. Without looking at me, she tucked her T-shirt back into her trousers, then bent quickly and did up the laces on her boots. She sat for a moment with both hands braced on her knees. She shook her head.

'We're going to have to leave,' she said.

She put her coat on. Picking up a heavy glass ashtray from the top of the TV, she went over to the door and listened, then she opened it and peered out. Bag in hand, I stood behind her. Though it had stopped raining, I could hear water everywhere, dripping and tapping. The cars parked near the supermarket glistened. Out of the air came the quaint, exotic scent of petrol.

I followed Odell along the walkway to the stairs. On the first floor we tiptoed past the door that led to reception. Then down another flight, to street-level. We paused in the shadows. There was nobody about. Odell placed the ashtray on the ground at the base of the wall, then darted across the alley and into the car-park where she crouched between two cars. I was only seconds behind her.

Halfway across the car-park, we looked back. The manager was standing at the foot of the stairs. His paunchy upper body faced out into the night, but his head was turned to one side, the nose lifted, predatory. As we watched, two men joined him. I would have been prepared to bet that one of them wore crocodile boots. Stooping, the manager picked up the ashtray. He seemed to examine it for a moment, his chin tucked into his open shirt-collar, then his arm swung sideways and the ashtray landed further up the alley, a dull ringing that sounded like a hammer being brought down on an anvil.

We moved towards the service station, keeping our heads below the car windows. Still doubled over, we skirted the forecourt, its pumps lit by a fierce mauve-white glare, and ended up against the side-wall of a bar. Half-smoked cigarettes, the smell of urine. A used syringe. Odell put a hand on my arm. Her gaze had fixed on the row of motorbikes that stood outside the bar. They looked oddly muscular, their bodies gleaming in the sultry light. She told me to stay put until she gave me a signal, but when the signal came I was to move fast. I leaned against the wall, my eyes on the hotel entrance. The men had vanished. There was only a yellow rectangle now, divided into horizontal segments by the stairs. How I wished we hadn't left that room on the third floor. I hadn't known what was going to happen next and, if I had interpreted Odell's behaviour correctly, nor had she, but the uncertainty had been fertile, exquisite – a kind of pleasure in itself. Who could say where it might have led? And then that knock on the door, that voice, and the whole situation had been instantly dismantled. I wasn't sure how something so unlikely, so delicate, could possibly occur again. I turned to see where Odell had gone. She was loitering beside a bike that had a naked woman painted on its petrol tank. The woman was on fire. Beneath the flames that licked at her thighs were the words *Burn Baby Burn*. Swinging a leg over the saddle, Odell reached sideways and down. I heard a sudden snarling, deep and guttural. Before I could work out how she had done it, she was motioning to me. I hurried over and fitted myself behind her.

The next thing I knew, we were on the main road, doing fifty, her hair whipping against my cheeks. I felt I was following her through a forest, branches springing at me from the darkness.

When I opened my mouth, it filled with wind.

We joined the motorway. The traffic thinned to nothing. It was late now, almost two in the morning. From time to time I glanced round to see whether anyone was coming after us – the men from the hotel, the bikers from the bar – but the road stayed empty. It all looked too close back there, somehow, as though everything we were running from was just over our shoulders.

Thirty miles from the capital, we took a slip-road up to a roundabout. As we crossed the bridge over the motorway, I saw a cluster of single headlights to the north. I removed one hand from Odell's waist and pointed.

She could have accelerated. By the time the bikes passed by, we would have been long gone. Instead, she braked and shifted into neutral. She switched off the lights, but left the engine turning over. When I thought about it later, I decided I would have done the same. It was something to do with trying to pinpoint the whereabouts of our pursuers. If it had been left to my imagination, I would have been unable to rid myself of the conviction that they could appear at any moment.

I could hear them now, their engines blending into one low growl. Would they be able to see us from down there? Would they even think to look up? Had it occurred to them that we might be watching? Apparently not. One by one, they flashed beneath the bridge. The bikes registered with brief but visceral force, like a series of punches. Then they were beyond us, heading south.

They might not have been after us at all, of course. They might have been another motorcycle gang entirely. I watched their tail-lights sink rapidly into the night – a handful of red berries dropped in dark water.

There was a click as Odell shifted into first. For the next hour she took less obvious roads and kept to the speed limit. I had my arms wrapped round her waist, and my upper body was moulded against her back. We both shook with cold. Parts of me felt as if they were plated with metal.

Finally, at half-past three, we rode into the city centre – Thermopolis at last – the shop windows all lit up but nobody around, the bike in low gear, its engine popping and crackling in the eerie, incandescent silence.

'I've got another story for you,' Odell said. 'It's the last one.'

We had checked into the Hyatt Regency, on a special weekend rate. Lying in bed with the curtains open, twenty-seven floors up, I could stare out into a forest of concrete, glass and steel. Office lights were left on throughout the night in what I imagined to be a deliberate configuration. Only people who worked in high finance would be able to decipher their true meaning. Odell lay beside me, fresh from the shower, a towel wrapped turban-style around her head. How would I survive without her stories? How would I survive without *her*?

An hour earlier she had joined me at the window. Between two towers we could just make out the river, identifiable only by the absence of illumination. Beyond it lay the murky, suicidal boroughs of Cledge. Given the east-facing aspect of our room, we hadn't been able to see the Red Quarter, but it was there, behind us, no more than a mile away. 'Not far now,' Odell had murmured. Though I knew what she was saying, I couldn't agree. The distance I had to cover seemed bigger than ever. Crossing a border illegally was daunting enough – I hadn't forgotten those Yellow Quarter guards – but what if I succeeded? What would happen then? When I whispered the word 'home' to myself, I felt panic, a swirl of vertigo.

Odell turned in the bed to look at me. 'This story starts really suddenly.'

All right, I said inside my head. *I'm ready.*

The man had hit her once, the bunched knuckles of his right hand solid as brass or stone; the curve of bone behind her ear was buzzing, numb. Now he was closing in on her again, his upper arms and shoulders looming. As he raised his fist to hit her for the second time, she rolled off the sofa on to the carpet. He swung and missed. Thrown off balance by the weight of his own wild punch, he stumbled into a lamp. The shade flew off horizontally, like a hat blown from a man's head in a gale. The lampstand tilted; the bare bulb shattered against the wall. She remembered watching wafers of glass float to the floor.

The darkness filled with short, crude words – what he thought she was, what he was going to do to her. The stench of his breath was everywhere, a dense haze of beer and whisky. All the air she was breathing was coming from inside him. She scrambled to her feet and moved away, hands on either side of her hips, palms facing backwards, feeling for the wall. She had been to the Yellow Quarter many times, and yet she always forgot the violence, how quickly it occurred. It was like blood in an artery. It was stored at the same high pressure. One nick, and out it burst.

He had something in his hand, she saw, a piece of flex wrenched from the video. The plug came hissing towards her like the blunt head of a snake. She twisted out of reach. The teeth gnawed on empty air and then drew back, preparing to strike again. If she had wanted to, she could have got away. There were things she could have done. But then she would have been showing her secret self to him, then he would have known – and too many of the wrong people knew already.

At last the wall gave behind her. She fled down the hall. The front door lay ahead of her, and she was round the edge of it like water round a rock. The stairwell hummed with low-voltage electricity. From somewhere came the smell of garlic being fried. She took the stairs two or three at a time, almost turning her ankle at the bottom of the first flight. She didn't remember climbing stairs on the way in. They must have used a lift. She heard him surge on to the landing, his voice ballooning in the dim air overhead. He was still listing all the things he would do to her. All the things he'd never do, more like. She couldn't believe that she had almost slept with him. That thought was astonishing to her now.

On reaching ground-level, she slowed to a walk. She was a stranger, an intruder; if unmasked, she would probably be lynched. She invented a role for herself. I've been out for the evening, she thought. I've had a good time, but it's late, and I'm looking forward to getting home. She nodded at the night porter in his office. He ignored her. She pressed the knob on the wall that released the front door and then slipped out into the street, absorbed at once into its humid smoky atmosphere. She glanced over her shoulder at the building she'd just left. The security light had clicked on, but there was no sign of the man whose name she had already forgotten. She doubted he would think of chasing after her. He would have realised by now that she was too fast for him. A man in his state only stood a chance in a small space.

She should never have agreed to go back to his flat. There she was, out on the town illegally, her first visit to choleric territory in months, and he had asked if he could buy her a drink, his brown hair pushed back to reveal a wide, clear forehead, his eyes blue as a jay's wing – classically, almost foolishly good-looking. He was drunk, of course, but who wasn't drunk in the Yellow Quarter on a Saturday night?

'Why do you want to buy me a drink?' she had said.

'Because you're different.'

'Different?'

'You're not like all the others. You're special.'

You got that right, she thought.

He bought her a drink that tasted of strawberries, a miniature paper umbrella leaning jauntily against the rim of the glass. She asked him what he did. He was a fire-safety officer, he told her. The previous year, he had been called to a train crash. She pretended to remember it. He talked about the bodies, and how they had melted, one into the other, making them impossible to identify. Then he bought her another strawberry drink with an umbrella in it.

She went back to his flat. In a large glass tank in the living-room, sinuous shapes glided this way and that, emitting tiny bolts of light.

'Electric eels,' he said, giving her an odd look. 'Imported from the Blue Quarter.'

She thought he'd seen through her, but he only wanted to impress.

Later, he made a lunge at her, his hand closing round one of her breasts. She tried to push him away, but he laughed and pulled her roughly towards him. She threw her drink in his face. That was when he hit her.

No, she should never have gone back with him. Some people would say she was perverse, or just plain idiotic, but she liked to think that she could get out of any corner, no matter how tight. She got too cocky, though. Thought she could handle anything. Sometimes she needed reminding.

On the pavement outside his building, she snapped her eyes from left to right, scanning her surroundings. The streets weren't safe, CCTV or no CCTV. No public spaces were. All the same, she stood still for a moment until the gaps between her heart-beats lengthened. The whisper of banknotes came to her, the chink and jangle of loose change. Shock waves from that fist of his. Or maybe it was the soundtrack of the Yellow Quarter, she thought. Listen hard enough and you could hear all the money being made. Listen hard and you could hear the wealth.

She started to walk again.

The border lay ahead of her, the high pale wall topped by rolls of glinting razor wire. She could see a watch-tower too. Squat body, spindly legs. It looked as though a spider had built a nest in the night sky. At the checkpoint itself, a bright-yellow barrier had been lowered, blocking her path. An armed guard stood suspended in the sentry hut's bright cylinder like something on display in a museum. He would only let her pass if she had documents. She had no documents, of course.

The next ninety seconds, from the guard's point of view:

Glancing up, he thought he saw a young woman walking towards him. When he stepped out of the hut, though, gun at the ready, the road was empty. He called up to the watch-tower. *See anything?* The answer came back. *Only the top of your fucking head. You're going bald, you know that?* The guard shrugged. But he still couldn't take his eyes off that stretch of road. He couldn't shake the feeling that someone was out there. Or had been.

Just as he was turning away, seeking the comfort of his newspaper and his mug of tea, a breeze pushed past him. The hair stirred on his forehead; even the stiff bristles of his moustache shifted a little. It was only air, a gust of wind, and yet it seemed personal. He felt that he'd been touched. He reached up and wiped his face, one quick downwards motion of his hand, then he stared out along the road again, but his gaze was unfocused now, without object. He remained in that position for some time, as though he believed that an explanation would eventually present itself.

The wind dropped. All was still.

Something altered at the very edge of his field of vision, something minute, almost imperceptible, but he had been trained to pay attention to such things. He looked over his shoulder, into the wide, bleak strip of no man's land. Beyond the concrete obstacles and areas of heavily mined ground, beyond the electric barrier that controlled admittance to the Red Quarter, he could just make out the figure of a woman walking away from him, erect, unhurried, oddly familiar . . .

He tried to shout 'Halt!' but the word came out husky, strangled, as if he had phlegm in his throat. The guard in the watch-tower peered down at him. *Did you say something?* He shook his head.

That woman, that was her. She had just crossed the border illegally. She had broken the only law that really mattered. Her name was Odell Burfoot, and she was a shadow. They told her there were others like her, but she'd never met one yet.

As I lay in the hotel bed, close to sleep, I finally realised what she was doing – what she'd been doing all along, in fact. She wasn't telling me stories to distract me (though, obviously, they performed that function too). No, every narrative had a specific purpose of its own. Some were supposed to create an atmosphere of serenity and trust. Others were intended to console, or to warn, or to encourage. Different situations demanded different narratives, and each one had its proper moment. A tale about a war would precede a war, for instance. A tale about a death would follow a funeral. But if you wanted something to happen, then you told a story in which that 'something' happened. Look at Odell's most recent offering. She had walked into the lion's den and then walked out again. The task that lay ahead of us might have its dangers, she was saying, but they were not insurmountable. We had to believe in ourselves without succumbing to complacency. We should be confident, but not reckless. A story of this type had a magical or spiritual dimension, as befitted the phlegmatic tradition out of which it came. It cast a spell over the people listening, enabling them to accomplish feats similar to those described. It also bestowed a blessing. In short, it acted as a catalyst, an inspiration, and a self-fulfilling prophecy.

The order in which she had told her stories seemed important too. The first had been set in the long-distant past. The second had approached the present, but in a roundabout, almost incidental manner, as though to diffuse anxiety. The third had closed in rapidly, both in space and time. Taken as a sequence, they led up to the task in hand, and I knew that everything I needed was contained within them, if only I looked carefully enough. Like any good story-teller, Odell had resisted the temptation to spell it all out for me. If knowledge was imparted in that way, it had no purchase. She had showed patience, insight. She had allowed me to see things for myself.

My name is Odell Burfoot, and I'm a shadow.

They tell me there are others like me, but I've never met one yet.

That evening we broke into a derelict house next to the border. We found a smashed window on the ground floor at the back and climbed through into the kitchen. Ivy had wrapped itself around the taps. Dead insects filled the grooves on the stainless-steel draining-board. Against the far wall stood a fridge with its door flung open, like a man selling watches from the inside of his coat. I followed Odell down a passage that led past two or three dim rooms, then opened out into a hallway with a chess-board tile floor. The house smelled dry and peppery – of plaster, cobwebs, dust. Through the clear glass fanlight came an alien glow, glittery as quartz, reminding me that a checkpoint lay just beyond the door.

We started up the stairs. On reaching the first floor, we entered a room whose three tall windows let in slanting rectangles of light. I moved over the bare boards and positioned myself to one side of a window. The concrete wall stood opposite the house, no more than a hundred feet away. Some Yellow Quarter guards huddled by the barrier. I saw one of them laugh, then wag a finger. His colleagues exchanged a knowing look. I was that close. Beyond them, further to the left, a viaduct of sooty brick angled across the street. Trains would once have passed this way, linking the northern suburbs of the old metropolis, but a section of the structure had been knocked down to accommodate the border, and the railway line now came to an abrupt halt in mid-air. Its one remaining arch, though monumental, served no purpose other than to frame a view of the deserted road that ran adjacent to the wall. I had forgotten how the city borders looked. They had an operating theatre's ruthless glare. They were bright, lonely places. Last places. I swallowed. Stepping back into the room, I opened my bag and pulled out my white clothes.

Once I was dressed, Odell gave me my final instructions. She would cross first, she said. I could watch, if I liked. See whether Croy's theory about her 'escaping notice' was right. When she was safely over the border, I should wait five or ten minutes, then I should follow. She would meet me on the other side.

I took her hand in both of mine and turned it over, as though I were thinking of telling her fortune. I stared down into her palm so hard that I felt I was falling.

'Goodbye,' she said. 'For now.'

She gently removed her hand from mine, then stepped away from me and left the room. I had to repress the urge to rush after her. Instead, I forced myself to face the window. A rancid stink lifted off the cloak. That part of me, at least, would be authentic. I gazed out over no man's land. Beyond the concrete walls and the electric fences, beyond the eerie lunar glare, and seeming insubstantial by comparison, if not actually unreal, were the sheer glass towers of downtown Pneuma.

The stairs let out a creak. It would be Odell, returning. There was something she'd forgotten to mention, perhaps. Or perhaps – and my heart leapt wildly, absurdly – she wanted to kiss me before we parted. I spun round. In the doorway stood a girl of five or six. She was wearing a white dress and satin ballet pumps, and from her shoulders rose a pair of iridescent wings on which the light from the border pooled and glistened. I thought for a moment that Odell's gift must have betrayed her, and that she had accidentally transformed herself into someone else, as people do in fairy tales.

'Are you dead?' the girl said.

I shook my head.

'You're not a ghost, are you?'

I shook my head again. This time I tried a smile.

'It's all right,' the girl said quickly. 'I'm not afraid of ghosts.' She let her eyes run over me – my face, my hair, my clothes. 'You *look* like a ghost.'

I knelt down in front of her. Taking one of her hands, I singled out the forefinger and placed it on the inside of my wrist, where my pulse was.

'You're real,' she said.

As real as you are, I said inside my head.

She gave me a look from close up, a look that was shiny, clean somehow, as if she had understood me perfectly, and I remembered what a friend had told me once, that it's the eyes of children that make you feel old.

The girl was reaching over her shoulders with both hands. 'These wings are hurting. Could you help me take them off?'

I began to undo the ribbons that held the wings in place.

She wrinkled her nose. 'You smell bad.'

I know, I said. *That's the whole idea.*

Another brief examination from those oddly knowing eyes.

I handed the wings to her. She solemnly surveyed the room, then bent down and leaned them against the wall next to the fireplace. Straightening up again, she looked at me across the point of one shoulder.

'I have to go now,' she said.

She turned, just as Odell had done, and vanished through the doorway. *Odell.* I hurried to the window, but there was no sign of her. Had she already gone across? I strained my eyes, trying to look beyond the floodlights. Nothing.

Panic scurried through me.

It was time.

I withdrew from the window, making for the stairs. In the hallway, I doubled back towards the kitchen. As I passed the open fridge, I saw a figure crouched inside, hands round his ankles, knees pushed up into the space below his chin. It was Brendan Burroughs.

'Take me with you,' he whispered.

I had to steel myself against his pleading. I had to pretend he wasn't there.

But whispers were still coming from the fridge. 'I can't stay here any longer. I'm going rotten.'

Leave me alone, I said inside my head.

I climbed out on to the patio. Stone steps led up into a tangle of undergrowth. If I looked round, I knew Brendan's mysteriously unlined face would be framed in the broken window, and I didn't even have a lighter on me any more.

I didn't look round.

Scaling a brick wall at the end of the garden, I dropped down on to the pavement and then started towards the border. I summoned the spirits of all those who had travelled with me. Their innocence, their singularity. Their freakishness. I repeated their names inside my head, over and over. If nothing else, I would remember what they used to sound like, how they moved about.

Neg, I said inside my head. *Lum. Neg. Ob.*

People running, falling. Burning.

I was still walking, but I had covered my face. My knees trembled, my ankles quaked. My joints appeared to have loosened, as if in readiness for a dismemberment. That little girl would be watching from a window, her gaze intent, dispassionate. *Are you dead?* I brought my hands down from my eyes. In front of me, no more than fifty yards away, stood the checkpoint with all its sinister and hostile apparatus. Though the three guards were silhouetted against the floodlights, I recognised the swagger, a casual brutality apparent in both their body language and their speech. I faltered. It was then that I noticed the piece of dog shit lying in the gutter. An idea came to me, and I experienced a burst of something like euphoria. What I was about to do would establish my authenticity beyond all doubt. It might even save me from harm. I pretended to notice the shit for the first time, taking an exaggerated step backwards, then bending low to study it more closely. I seemed to hear the guards draw breath. Now that I had their attention, I picked up the shit and examined it painstakingly from every angle, then I crushed it between my fingers and smeared it on to my cheeks and hair. That done, I began to move towards the checkpoint. The guards stepped away from me, waving their hands in front of their faces. Even the attack dog whined and shunted backwards. I just kept going, oblivious, serene. I might even have been smiling. As I passed the sentry hut I heard them talking.

'It's true what people say. They're just like animals – '

'They're worse than animals . . .'

370

While two of them debated the point, a third aimed a kick at me and sent me sprawling on the tarmac. The dog barked excitedly but stayed well back. All three guards were arguing now. It hadn't occurred to them to challenge me. In fact, they seemed eager to keep their distance. I'd made myself untouchable.

I picked myself up, walked on.

In no man's land the lights were so intense that I could see the veins beneath the surface of my skin. I felt transparent. At the same time four shadows splayed out on the ground around me, as if I were a flower with black petals. My face itched, and the stench that lifted off me was unbearable. At the risk of drawing attention to myself, I started walking faster. I wanted this part over with.

The Red Quarter guards were already waiting for me. As I approached I held my hands out, fingers spread. I was making noises that were intended to communicate distress.

One of the men took me by the arm. 'Who did this?' he said.

I stared at him, round-eyed, slack-jawed.

He pointed back towards the Yellow Quarter. 'Did they do this to you?'

My mouth still open, I nodded repeatedly, more than a dozen times.

The guard led me to a tap behind a prefabricated hut. He handed me a bar of carbolic soap and ran the tap for me. I gazed at the dark patch the water made as it splashed on to the concrete.

'You can wash here.' The guard mimed the act of washing for me.

I watched him carefully. Then, slowly, I put my hands under the tap and began to rub them together.

'And your face.' He patted his cheeks, his hair.

He went away, returning with a roll of paper towels, which he placed on the window-ledge above the tap. 'When you've washed it off,' he said, 'use the paper to dry yourself. Then go that way.' He pointed to the steel barrier behind me.

I nodded again, then pointed at the barrier, just as he had done.

The whole time I was washing off the muck and stink I was talking to myself inside my head. I don't know what I was saying. Anything that would keep me from thinking, I suppose. All I had to do was turn off the tap, dry my face and hands, and then start walking, and yet I found myself delaying the moment, as if I couldn't quite believe in the notion of safety or the possibility of home.

In the end the guard had to come over and switch off the tap himself. He stood in front of me, smiling and shaking his head. 'What are you trying to do? Flood the place?' He tore a few sheets of paper off the roll and gave them to me, then he put a hand on my back and steered me towards the barrier. 'Off you go now. Move along.'

As soon as I turned the first corner, I began to run as fast as the cloak and boots allowed. I was like something that had been wound up and then let loose, and I was laughing too. I could hear myself.

'Thomas?'

I slowed down, stopped, looked round. Odell walked up the pavement towards me. In the light of the street lamps her bracken-coloured hair looked darker, almost black.

'You took such a long time,' she said. 'I thought they'd got you.' She reached out to take my hand, but I stepped back so sharply that she almost overbalanced.

'No,' I said. 'Don't touch me.'

She listened carefully while I explained what I had done. She didn't seem shocked or disgusted. On the contrary. According to her, it had been an inspired piece of tactical thinking. I had given both sets of guards something to react to. I had used myself to create a diversion. I'd become my own decoy. She was so enthusiastic that I could imagine the idea featuring in the next edition of some underground manual for asylum-seekers. I apologised for having been abrupt with her. I had washed pretty thoroughly, I said, but I wasn't sure it had all come off. She moved closer, sniffing at my face and hair. I smelled of soap, she said. Border soap.

'There's something you haven't noticed,' I said.

She smiled. 'You're talking.'

'The strangest thing. It just started. When you walked towards

375

me.' I stared past her, down the street. Light and shadow on the paving-stones. Overhanging trees. 'Of course, I've been saying things all along,' I said. 'In my head, though.'

'I thought so.'

'You couldn't hear me, could you?'

'No. But sometimes I felt as if I understood you. And I talked to you before, on the train, so I knew what you sounded like.'

'I don't remember that.'

We looked into each other's eyes. The air between us appeared to shrink.

In a nearby house somebody was playing the piano, each note separate, perfectly rounded, yet fragile, like a raindrop on a leaf. Odell turned to one side, as though captivated by the music. As I stood there with her, listening, the smell of coffee came and went. Some dinner party drawing to a close. We had crossed into one of Pneuma's northern suburbs, an area called Gulliver.

'What happens now?' I said.

'I make sure you get home safely.'

'And that's all? That's it?'

She was looking at her feet. 'You live here,' she said quietly. 'I don't.'

'You could visit, though, couldn't you, from time to time? If you felt like it. You could cross the border illegally. Nobody would know.'

She kept her eyes on the ground.

'You told me you had to keep in practice,' I said.

I was back on the peaceful tree-lined streets I knew so well, where crime didn't exist and cheerfulness was second nature, but it seemed that things were being taken from me. I felt abandoned, deprived.

I felt bereft.

The direct route to my flat lay through the city's most famous park. We followed a footpath that ran down one side of the zoo, stopping to watch the wolves lope with almost liquid grace through their enclosure, then we cut diagonally across an open grassy area where football was often played on Sundays. We circled the dark glitter of the lake. To the south, beyond the boathouse, I could just make out a crescent of creamy neo-classical façades and, further west, the mosque's burnished dome. Though it was late now, after ten o'clock, the mildness of the night had tempted people outdoors. A man with a ponytail was trying to coax a squirrel on to a bench. Then an elderly woman walked past, holding a tennis racket. A black dog padded along beside her. She took a ball out of her pocket and hit it into the lake. The dog swam after it. Spring had come early, it seemed, with daffodils and primroses showing in the long grass beneath the trees, as pale and innumerable as stars.

'It's beautiful here,' Odell said.

I looked glumly around and murmured in agreement, but all I felt was a faint tingle of resentment. I had so many questions for her, so many important questions, and yet, burdened by the knowledge that she would soon be gone, I couldn't seem to give them voice. I fell into a kind of trance, paralysed by what I had not said and could not say.

As we neared my building, Odell went into a supermarket. From outside, I watched her moving up and down the aisles – her freckled face, her copper-tinted hair, her coat the colour of avocado skin. I tried to imagine that we didn't know each other, that we had never met. It was all too easy. But I had hoped it would be difficult, if not impossible. I'd wanted confirmation that my life was irrevocably bound up with hers.

When she walked out of the shop she grinned and handed me a plastic bag. Groceries, she said. I might find I was hungry when I got home, and there wouldn't be anything in my flat, not after all these months. Opening the bag, I peered down. The almost luminous glow of the oranges, the dull glint of the silver wrapping on the butter. The drops of condensation on the milk. Everything was mundane and practical, but at the same time improbable somehow, miraculous.

'That's the future,' I said. 'That's all I know.'

She watched me carefully with her head at an angle, as though

I were some kind of mechanism and she was trying to see how I worked. Her grin had faded. She trained a loose strand of hair behind her ear, then she pushed both hands into the pockets of her coat and looked across the street to where a theatre's glass doors had just been flung open and members of the audience were spilling out on to the pavement, their voices raised in exhilaration against the night.

We arrived at the cul-de-sac where I lived. I had already told her that she didn't need to see me to the door. Apart from anything else, there would be Loames to deal with – unless, of course, he'd been transferred during my absence. The fact that nothing could be relied upon was the one sure sign of a stable society, Vishram had told me once, and I had never been able to work out whether or not he was joking.

Odell scraped at the join between two paving-stones with the heel of her boot. 'I almost forgot,' she said. 'Did you see me cross the border?'

'No. I missed it.'

She tried to hide her disappointment, but didn't quite succeed. I could have mentioned the girl with the wings, I suppose. It might have made her feel better. In the end, though, I couldn't summon the energy. Or perhaps I wanted to punish her for leaving me.

'Maybe another time,' I said.

'Maybe.' She took a breath. 'I should be going.'

I reached up and touched her cheek. When I took my hand away I could still feel the heat of her skin on my fingertips. She turned and walked off down the hill, the gate-house of the old palace rising into the sky ahead of her.

When she was fifty yards from me, she appeared to hesitate. Swinging round, she lifted both her hands up to her mouth to make a megaphone.

'Watch this,' I heard her say.

For a moment she seemed to be turning away from me again, but turning at great speed, as if spun by an unseen force. Then she simply vanished. I thought I must have blinked. Or had she tricked me? I felt dull-witted, slow. I stared hard at the place where she'd been standing.

'Thomas?'

The voice came from behind me. I whirled round. Odell was leaning against a pillar box at the other end of the street with her arms folded, and even though she was some distance away I could see that she was smiling.

She cupped her hands around her mouth again. 'Believe me now?'

'Yes,' I shouted. 'I believe you.'

I kept my eyes fixed on her until she reached the top of the street. Once there, she turned the corner and disappeared from sight. Just like anybody else.

I had to ring the caretaker's bell half a dozen times before the shadowy figure of Kenneth Loames appeared in the lobby and the glass front door clicked open. I watched various reactions pass across his face – indignation, then distaste, and finally astonishment as he looked more closely and realised who it was.

'Mr Parry!'

'How are you, Mr Loames?' I said.

'Fine, sir,' he said. 'How about you?'

'I'm fine. Just tired, that's all.'

His eyes dropped to my cloak, then veered away again, lifting past my shoulder.

'I seem to have mislaid my keys,' I said. 'Sorry to disturb you like this. I know it's late.'

I waited while he went to fetch the spare set for me. I hadn't mislaid my keys at all, of course. I'd left them in that hotel in Congreve, along with most of my clothes and the final draft of my lecture. At that point I hadn't known whether I would have a use for them again – but here I was, four months later, with the pale-green carpet stretching before me and the marble-topped table standing over by the wall beneath the oval gilt-framed mirror. Nothing had changed. The lobby smelled as it had always smelled, of something sweet and baked. Like the inside of a cake tin.

When Loames returned with the keys, I thanked him and said goodnight, then I moved towards the lift and pressed the call button. Although I sensed him loitering behind me, I didn't look round. He would pretend to be doing his job – checking the post on the table, or straightening the mirror – but he would actually be staring at my filth-encrusted garments and my ill-fitting boots, his curiosity more rampant than ever and even harder to articulate. Only when the lift's cables looped down into the bottom of the shaft did I hear his front door softly close.

In my flat, all the lights were on. I stared at the switches, wondering if I could have forgotten to turn them off when I left for the conference. It would have been unlike me, certainly. And anyway, a light bulb couldn't last four months, could it? Perhaps Loames had let himself in while I was away. After all, there might have been meters to read, or a gas leak to take care of – though surely he would have mentioned it . . . Perhaps he'd just wanted to have a snoop around. I was standing in the hall, weighing the various possibilities, when a rapid but subtle movement registered to my immediate right, in the very corner of my eye. I turned slowly. The toe of a man's black shoe showed beyond the jamb on the right side of the living-room door. He was sitting in my favourite chair, it seemed, and if my reading of the movement I had caught a glimpse of was correct then he had just either crossed or re-crossed his legs. I walked towards the living-room. There in the armchair, and looking very much at home, was Ajit Vishram.

'You must be surprised to find me here,' he said.

But I wasn't, not really. My capacity for surprise had been exhausted long ago. Instead – for a few seconds, at least – I found I was able to treat Vishram not as my superior, or even as a work colleague, but as yet another stranger whose significance had still to be determined.

'I hope you'll forgive me for intruding like this,' he went on. 'I wanted to be the first to welcome you when you returned.' His right foot see-sawed in the air, suggesting that he was both intrigued and entertained by the unusual situation. Either that, or he was nervous. I couldn't imagine why Vishram might be nervous, though.

I stepped into the room, but chose not to take a seat. I instinctively felt that the act of sitting down would signal acquiescence on my part, if not actual complicity. Whatever we said to each other from now on, it was somehow already apparent to me that our relationship had altered for ever.

I moved towards the picture window that opened on to the terrace. My dim reflection, the darkness of the night beyond. The coolness of the glass. Like Loames, Vishram would be studying my clothes, but I couldn't imagine what he would be thinking. I had never been able to see into that intricate, shuttered mind of his.

'You must have been worried about me,' I said at last.

'Yes.' Vishram cleared his throat. 'We did have some moments of anxiety.'

I looked over my shoulder, waiting for him to go on.

'There were a number of occasions,' he said, 'when you eluded us.' He paused again. 'After the bomb, for instance.'

The clock on the nearby church struck midnight.

'You wouldn't believe how dangerous it is out there,' I said.

'That's why we had you followed.'

'How did you arrange that exactly? I'm curious.'

'I can't go into specifics, I'm afraid. Suffice to say that we have contacts.'

'Adrian Croy.'

Vishram smiled to himself, then he looked down and picked a piece of lint off the sleeve of his jacket. For the first time in my life I found myself wondering whether there might not be some higher authority – a committee made up of representatives from each of the four countries, for example, that would convene in secret and oversee the running of the divided kingdom. It would be a natural extension of the clandestine meetings that had resulted in the Rearrangement. A rainbow cabinet . . . It seemed logical – even necessary. Before I could take the thought any further, though, Vishram spoke again.

'Was she good?'

'Was who good?'

'Your shadow,' he said. 'Your guide.'

'She was very conscientious. I was impressed.' Then, keeping my voice impartial, I said, 'You must care about me a lot, to go to such lengths.'

'I would've thought that was obvious.'

'Because I'm an employee?'

Vishram appeared to hesitate. 'That would be one way of putting it.'

I studied him as he sat there in my favourite chair. He was wearing a typically elegant and yet understated suit. His feet were neat and slender in their highly polished shoes. He looked immaculate, omniscient.

'Did you know I was going to do something?' I said. 'Have you always known?'

'Not always.' Vishram let the words sink in for a moment. 'I didn't know *what* you were going to do, of course, or when you were going to do it. I suppose I expected something out of the ordinary, though.'

'Really?'

'Yes. I would have been disappointed otherwise.'

'But I broke the law.'

'Sometimes it's the only way.'

'I'm not sure I understand.'

'You've been to so many places. You've met the people who live there. You've learned about their difficulties, their dissatisfactions, and that knowledge is invaluable.' Vishram paused. 'I'm almost a little envious.'

'You could have sent me,' I said. 'Officially, I mean.'

'Not for more than a few days. And anyway, you wouldn't have seen half the things you've seen. You wouldn't have gone as far as you did.' He indicated my cloak and boots with one of his vague but graceful gestures.

'In a sense, then,' I said slowly, 'you've been using me.'

'You're forgetting something. It was your decision to go missing, and yours alone. We had no control over you, and we chose not to interfere. All we did was arrange for someone to keep an eye on you.'

Each time I tried to better him, each time I thought he might be about to yield, he took the force that lay behind my words and turned it back on me. It was as if he had studied an oral version of the martial arts. And yet I sensed a weakness in him somewhere, an uncertainty, which made me want to probe further.

'How did you explain my absence from the office?'

'You were ill,' Vishram said, 'in hospital.'

'No visitors?'

'You were quarantined.'

'What was wrong with me?'

'Something that was never properly identified. Something that resisted diagnosis.'

'A mystery condition.'

'Exactly.'

We exchanged a smile, our first of the evening.

Rising to his feet, Vishram announced that it was late and that he really ought to be going. He was sorry, he said, if it had upset me to find him in my flat.

'Have you eaten yet?' I said.

Both Vishram's eyebrows lifted. 'No.'

The wariness in his voice released a kind of adrenalin in me. I felt I had wrested the initiative from him at last.

'Why don't you stay?' I said. 'I'll cook.'

Without waiting for an answer, I went out to the hall and fetched the bag of groceries Odell had bought for me. Back in the kitchen, I reached for the frying pan and placed it on the stove. Dropping a wedge of butter into the pan, I lit the gas. I broke four eggs into a pudding basin, then beat milk into the eggs with a whisk, adding sea salt, black pepper, and a few brittle sprigs of parsley from the freezer. When the butter had melted, I tipped the beaten eggs into the pan where they sizzled loudly, as if in protest, and then began to spread.

The phone on my bedside table woke me at five-past nine the next morning. I let the machine take the call. Pulling on my dressing-gown, I opened the curtains. The city glittered beneath a sky of unadulterated blue, every roof and dome and spire clearly defined. From my bedroom window I couldn't see any checkpoints or watch-towers. They were lodged deep in the jumble of buildings that lay before me, as were the rolls of razor wire and the attack dogs with their sharpened ears. Standing on the sixth floor, looking south, it would have been easy to imagine that the borders didn't exist, and that the city was a single entity. An illusion, of course. A heresy as well. A crime.

I turned and went through to the kitchen. The frying pan was still soaking in the sink, traces of omelette welded to the rim. Vishram had offered to wash up before he left, but I had called him a taxi instead. I'd had enough of him by then. As I ran myself a glass of water, I remembered how I had brought him back to his moment of hesitancy, asking once again why he had gone to all the trouble of having me followed. I had been thinking he would tell me, with some small show of embarrassment, that it was because he had grown fond of me, because he enjoyed my company, because – who knows? – he had come to think of me as a kind of son. But that was not how he replied.

'I'd like you to take my place,' he said, 'at the Department.'

At last he had succeeded in surprising me.

'Are you retiring?' I said.

'There's some research I want to do. I might even return to academia.' He smiled downwards at his plate, as if the idea was both shameful and absurd.

'I'm not sure,' I said.

His face stiffened a little. My reaction had disappointed him. I ought to have been enthusiastic or grateful. I ought to have considered it an honour.

'I shouldn't have mentioned it,' he said in a quiet voice. 'It's probably too soon to be talking of such things.'

I nodded.

Later, I asked how his biography of the Prime Minister was going. He seemed to flinch slightly at the question. 'Fine,' he said. 'Yes. It's going very well.'

'I never told Sonya, I'm afraid. About the job.'

'That's all right.' He gave me another of his opaque looks. Soon afterwards his taxi arrived.

Still standing at the sink, I went back over the encounter. It had been awkward for any number of reasons, most of which were entirely predictable, but there had been an aspect to the awkwardness that I wouldn't have expected, and which seemed to have something to do with Vishram's state of mind. I could only think that he had problems of his own. The second hand ticked on the cooker's built-in clock. I drank half my water, then put it down. Whatever doubts or reservations I may have had about him, I couldn't help but be amused – and curiously touched – by the fact that he had been so intent on being the first person to greet me when I got home that he had somehow contrived to break into my flat.

I fell back on my usual routine that morning – laps in the swimming-pool downstairs, followed by a shower, then breakfast with the papers – but I had the constant, niggling sense that I was only pretending to be myself. At times I could even detect flaws in my own performance. I put the kettle on. I poured cereal into a bowl. The flakes tinkled against the china like tiny bits of metal. Everything felt familiar, and yet the notion of familiarity was, in itself, strange.

As I reached for my glass of orange juice, a fly landed on my newspaper. It wasn't a normal house fly. It was much smaller than that. In fact, if it had remained airborne, I'm not sure I would've noticed it at all. I leaned forwards to inspect the fly, but it chose that moment to rise unsteadily off the page. Seconds later, it alighted on the edge of my plate. This time I was able to crush it. There was no blood, just a minute dark stain on my fingertip. I lifted the finger to my nose. The dead fly smelled exactly like a Brazil nut. I wondered what kind of fly it was, and how many more of them there were. I'd ask my cleaning lady to look into it – if I still had a cleaning lady.

When I was dressed, I took the lift to the ground floor. The front doors of the building stood open to the street, and Loames stooped in the gap, polishing the curved brass handles. He had rolled his shirtsleeves back to the elbow, and his strong, unusually hairless forearms gleamed in the sunlight.

'Morning, Mr Loames.'

'Morning, sir.' He stepped aside to let me past.

Once on the pavement, though, I paused. 'Lovely day.'

He straightened up, his eyes on a smart middle-aged couple who were emerging from the hotel opposite. 'They say it's going to last all week.'

'That's good,' I said.

There had been no allusions to my sudden bizarre appearance the previous night. There had been no ambiguous glances either, no attempts at wit, just ordinary, solid words whose only concern was that life should go on as before, as always.

'I heard you were ill, sir,' Loames said after a while.

'Yes, I was.'

'Feeling better now, are you?'

'Much better, thanks.' Casting around for a change of subject, I remembered what had happened at breakfast. 'You know those flies you mentioned once?'

'Flies?'

'Back in October. You told me you had flies.'

Loames was nodding slowly now. 'Ah yes, I remember.'

'Were they small? Like this?' And I curled my forefinger against my thumb so tightly that only a pinpoint of daylight could squeeze through.

He studied the shape I'd made with my hand almost as if he were afraid of it. 'They were normal flies, sir,' he said. 'House flies.'

'I see.'

'I could call in the exterminators if you like – or I could do the job myself.' His head lunged heavily towards me, like a cow's.

'Don't worry,' I said. 'I'm sure it's nothing.'

I was supposed to have been ill, and appropriately enough, I found myself behaving like an invalid. I had the same dazed responses to the world, the same naive blend of gratitude and reverence. On leaving my flat the previous night, Vishram had told me that he didn't expect me back at work until the end of the month, which was a fortnight away. We would call it my convalescence, he added in a light but conspiratorial voice, then he invited me to dine with him at his house on Saturday – or perhaps I had other arrangements . . . *Other arrangements?* I had laughed at the idea. He must have been referring to Sonya, but I hadn't spoken to her. I couldn't, not just yet. I wouldn't have known what to say. I was like somebody who had jumped out of a plane. I had watched my parachute bloom in the vast, empty dome of sky above, and now I was drifting earthwards. A deep silence enveloped me. No doubt the ground would rush up to meet me soon enough, but in the meantime I wanted to keep everything the way it was – distant, abstract, peaceful.

I had left my flat with no clear purpose in mind, drawn out by the fine weather, but I soon realised I was following the same route Odell and I had taken the night before, only in reverse, of course, a route that now seemed thoroughly saturated with her presence. I lingered outside the supermarket where she had bought my groceries. Her image bent over the tilting shelves of oranges and pears. Further on, I turned down a street renowned for its jewellery, and I remembered how she had stopped once or twice to look in windows. I had ignored her and walked on. I regretted that now. I would like to have known what it was that had attracted her. That row of antique rings, perhaps – but which one in particular? I crossed another, larger thoroughfare, still heading north. Not long afterwards I entered the park.

I rounded the boating lake and arrived at the bench where the man with the ponytail had been sitting. In the daylight I could see that somebody had carved a heart into the wood. Close by, on the grass, a notice said NO BATHING FISHING OR DOGS ALLOWED IN THE WATER. I thought of the woman with the tennis racket – the plump sound of the ball landing on the surface of the lake, the black dog plunging after it – then I smiled and moved on. I passed the wolves asleep in their enclosure, and leaving by one of the park's north-eastern exits, found myself in Gulliver once more. The smallest details came back to me. The smell of coffee, the piano music. The tree where Odell and I had stood and talked.

At last, towards midday, I reached the checkpoint, its steel barrier lowered, two guards on duty in their scarlet helmets. At the rear of the guard-house I could see the place where I had washed. The tap was dripping. Tiny glass beads shattered on the concrete, one after another, without a sound. Otherwise everything was still. The shadow of the watch-tower lay across the road like something that had been run over. I stared out into no man's land, remembering the tension, the bright-white glare, the stench. It was hard to believe the memory was mine.

I had been standing there for several minutes when one of the guards walked up to me. He had a gaunt, clean-shaven face and clear grey eyes. I didn't recognise him from the night before. The shift must have changed.

'Just having a look, are we?' he said pleasantly.

I nodded. 'That's right.'

'Pretty quiet today.'

'Do you get much trouble?' I asked.

'Not much,' he said. 'It's not like twenty years ago. Things have settled down a lot since then.'

He thought for a while. I had the impression that he wanted to convey something of his life.

'Sometimes the Yellow Quarter guards do things,' he said.

'Like what?'

'Once, about eighteen months ago, they released some pea-cocks on to the area that's mined. We had to stand here and watch as the birds exploded, one by one.'

'That's barbaric,' I said.

The guard shrugged. I was stating the obvious.

'This section of the border's haunted,' he added a moment later.

'Not the peacocks?'

He smiled. 'No. There's a young woman. Mid-twenties. She's always walking away, into the darkness. You only ever see her from the back.'

'Have you seen her?'

'Me? No.' He paused. 'She must be someone who was killed here during the early days, I suppose.' He stared out into no man's land. 'Some say they can feel her sort of brushing past them. It gives them the creeps.' He grinned at me, rendering his scepticism apparent, then glanced at the guard-house. 'I should be getting back.'

'Nice talking to you,' I said.

That afternoon I sat in my living-room and tried to read a book, but I couldn't seem to concentrate. My eyes kept skidding across the lines of print. Eventually I put on a choral work that Victor had given me one Christmas, then I lay down on the sofa and closed my eyes. Though my mind seemed coated with a kind of scale, the residue of everything I had experienced, the singing had a cleansing effect, the voices overlapping and merging in such a way that the inside of my head became a smooth, shining space. How remarkable, I thought, that my early life had been inaccessible to me for so many years! But might that not reflect how happy I had been back then, how loved? Surely there had to be a correlation between the two. That total blankness stood for something, in other words, something immensely powerful, and it might prove a source of strength and comfort to me, if only I could learn to trust it . . .

The next thing I knew, the music had finished and the phone was ringing. I fumbled for the receiver, said hello.

'Thomas?'

I didn't recognise the voice. 'I'm sorry –'

'You haven't forgotten me already, have you?'

'Odell!' There was the most peculiar sensation inside my chest, as though my heart had just been dropped from a great height. 'I'm sorry,' I said. 'I was asleep.'

'It's me who should be sorry. I shouldn't be disturbing you like this, but I didn't know who else to call.'

'Why? What's happened?'

'Mr Croy,' she said. 'The man I work for. He's been arrested.' I began to say something, but she talked over me. 'If they've arrested him, then they'll probably want to arrest me too. I left my flat as soon as I heard. I haven't dared go back.'

'What will you do?'

'I don't know.'

'I just had an idea,' I said. 'You'll have to trust me, though.'

'Be quick. I haven't got much time.'

'Do you remember walking round a lake last night?'

'Of course.'

'We saw a woman hit a ball into the water. Her dog swam after it.'

'Yes, I remember.' Her voice had softened a little.

'There was a bench,' I said. 'Meet me there at seven o'clock. Will you be all right till then?'

'I think so. But what –'

'Don't ask me anything else. Just meet me there tonight. At seven.'

I put the phone down and then leaned back against the cushions. I wondered if Luke had betrayed Odell in order to save that girlfriend of his. Judging by what Odell had told me, it would have been in keeping with his character. Or perhaps, in the end, she had brought disaster on herself. She had broken the rules too many times, and Croy was guilty of having indulged her. Not that it mattered much. When we met that evening, I was going to suggest that she stayed with me for a few days. She could stay as long as she wanted.

Moments later, I seemed to wake up again, which puzzled me, since I wasn't aware of having gone back to sleep. Outside, the church clock chimed the half-hour, its notes trembling, forlorn. I remembered my appointment with Odell. Jumping to my feet, I hurried out to the kitchen. The oven said 5:32.

I returned to the living-room, switched on a lamp. Thinking back to the phone-call, it struck me how unlike herself Odell had sounded. It would be the shock. After all, her whole existence had been disrupted. Though I sympathised with her – I had a pretty clear idea of what she would be going through – I couldn't suppress a feeling of excitement. First Vishram's offer of a job, now Odell's predicament: both unexpected, to put it mildly, and yet the one dovetailed with the other in a way that was almost symbiotic. A future was beginning to open out before me, a future I could actually imagine. Odell would stay at my place. I would nurture her as she had nurtured me.

How beautifully things had turned around!

Night has fallen on the city like black snow.

I sit in the appointed place and wait for her. It doesn't matter if she's late. My patience knows no boundaries. In fact, I don't even think of it as patience; I have no anxiety, no sense of time.

While I was on the phone to her, I came up with a plan. I'm going to forge papers that will give her the right to stay in the Red Quarter. Then no one will be able to harm her. She'll be safe. That's why I've decided to take the job Vishram offered me. It will make things easier. No, it will make things *foolproof*.

To live with her, that's all that interests me. To live with her – and perhaps, after a while, to have a child. We would be undermining the system, of course – its ethos, its integrity . . . We'd be making a mockery of it. I don't care, though, not any more. I owe the system nothing.

Imagine what Victor would say if he were still alive!

I tilt my head back until it's on a level with the sky. Such clarity up there. The stars seem to echo the freckles on her face. *Like one of those road signs in the country.* I smile to myself and shake my head. In the faint stirring of the air I can feel her breath, her gift – her mystery.

The thought of her has me trembling, as if with cold.

I want to hear my name on her tongue. I want to feel her skin on mine, my body mingling illegally with hers. I want to learn her off by heart. *You're not going to forget me again, are you?*

I'll never turn my back on her. I promise.

The lake twitches below me, restless, like a dog dreaming. A broken branch floats on the water, its buds already open. In the east I hear the wind rise.

Now she'll come.

And I'm standing in the truck again, with strangers all around me and a light rain falling, and I can see my mother and father on the road, and I call out to them.

It's all right. I'm going to be all right.

ACKNOWLEDGEMENTS

I would like to thank the British Library, the late Fred Clements, the staff at the Darlington Railway Museum, the staff at the Dorchester Hotel, Di Harrison, the staff at Lanercost Priory, the staff at the Museum of Mining in Wakefield, the late Professor Fred Norbury, John and Maria Norbury, Dr Emilie Savage-Smith, Rupert and Sophie Scott, Stephanie Stannier, the staff at Stump Cross Caverns, Jyoti Tamana, the staff at the Tourist Information Centres in Darlington and Lewes, Gray Watson, the Wellcome Library for the History and Understanding of Medicine, and the Reverend John Wraithte. Particular thanks go to Dr Faye Getz for her help in guiding me through the intricacies of humoral theory.

I am indebted to Beatrice Monti della Corte for her kindness and inspiration at Santa Maddalena, where the process of editing *Divided Kingdom* began.

Finally, my immense gratitude goes to Liz Calder, Gary Fisketjon, Katharine Norbury, Alexandra Pringle, Peter Straus, Mary Tomlinson, and Binky Urban. All seven helped significantly, each in their own unique way. This book would not be what it is without their invaluable encouragement and their undoubted brilliance and skill.

The following books proved especially useful: *Freedom and Its Betrayal: Six Enemies of Human Liberty* by Isaiah Berlin (2002), *Galen on Bloodletting* by Peter Brain (1986), *The Druid Animal Oracle* by Philip and Stephanie Carr-Gomm (1996), *A Generation Divided: German Children and the Berlin Wall* by Thomas A. Davey (1987), *Ley Lines* by J. Havelock Fidler (1983), *Lee Kuan Yew's Singapore* by T. J. S. George (1973), *Medicine in the English Middle Ages* by Dr Faye Getz (1998), *Western Medical Thought from*

Antiquity to the Middle Ages edited by Mirko D. Grmek (1998), *Handbook of Psychological Assessment* by Gary Groth-Marnat (1997), *Secret Teaching of All Ages: An Encyclopedic Outline of Masonic, Cabbalistic, Hermetic and Rosicrucian Philosophy* by Manly P. Hall (1999), *Happiness through Tranquillity* by Richard Hibler (1984), *Nature of Man* by Hippocrates, translated by W. H. S. Jones (1931), *Saturn and Melancholy* by Raymond Klibansky (1964), *S,M,L,XL* by Rem Koolhaas and Bruce Mau (1995), *The Celtic Book of the Dead* by Caitlin Matthews (1992), *Narratives of Guilt and Compliance* by Barbara Muller (1999), *Paracelsus – An Introduction to Philosophical Medicine* by Walter Pagel (1958), *Iconology – A Collection of Emblematic Figures* by George Richardson (1778), *Medieval and Early Renaissance Medicine* by Nancy Siraisi (1990), *The Hippocratic Tradition* by W. D. Smith (1979), *Scientific Tourist through England* by Thomas Walford (1818), *The Optick Glass of Humours* by T. Walkington, Master of Artes (1631), *The Ley Hunter's Manual* by Alfred Watkins (1983), and *Amnesty International Report* (Nov/Dec 1978).

A NOTE ON THE TYPE

The text of this book is set in Linotype Janson. The original types were cut in about 1690 by Nicholas Kis, a Hungarian working in Amsterdam. The face was misnamed after Anton Janson, a Dutchman who worked at the Ehrhardt Foundry in Leipzig, where the original Kis types were kept in the early eighteenth century. Monotype Ehrhardt is based on Janson.

The original matrices survived in Germany and were acquired in 1919 by the Stempel Foundry. Hermann Zapf used these originals to redesign some of the weights and sizes for Stempel. This Linotype version was designed to follow the original types under the direction of C. H. Griffith.

Visit www.dividedkingdom.co.uk for an interview and video clip, the *Divided Kingdom* personality test, an interactive map, a readers' guide to the book and many other extra features.